Cowboy Be Mine

NEW YORK TIMES BESTSELLING AUTHOR

VICKI LEWIS THOMPSON

COWBOY BE MINE

MILLS & BOON®

First Published 2014
Second Australian Paperback Edition 2017
ISBN 978 1 489 24716 2

MIX
Paper from responsible sources
FSC® C001695
www.fsc.org

Published by
Harlequin Mills & Boon
Level 13
201 Elizabeth Street
SYDNEY NSW 2000
AUSTRALIA

Printed and bound in Australia by McPherson's Printing Group

CONTENTS

ABOUT THE AUTHOR

New York Times bestselling author Vicki Lewis Thompson's love affair with cowboys started with the Lone Ranger, continued through Maverick and took a turn south of the border with Zorro. She views cowboys as the Western version of knights in shining armour—rugged men who value honour, honesty and hard work. Fortunately for her, she lives in the Arizona desert, where broad-shouldered, lean-hipped cowboys abound. Blessed with such an abundance of inspiration, she only hopes that she can do them justice. Visit her website, www.vickilewisthompson.com.

Riding High

Dear Reader,

I support animal rescue organisations no matter what species they're rescuing. Although my favourite shelter these days is The Hermitage No-Kill Cat Shelter in Tucson, I've also volunteered at Best Friends Animal Sanctuary in Kanab, Utah, where they take in almost any creature, including potbellied pigs!

I had an up close and personal experience with these adorable creatures, and yes, one of them was named Harley. The real Harley is way better behaved than the fictional one I created for this story, but how else was I going to arrange that first kiss between Regan and Lily without a misbehaving pig? And you know there will be lots of kissing and...other stuff, because we're starting a whole new summer of the Sons of Chance!

I've had *such* fun with this series, and apparently, so have you, so here we go again! Take one equine veterinarian who craves order, and one genius-level woman determined to save every animal on the planet and let them do whatever they choose, and you have a beautiful mess. Throw in the Chance family, who can be helpful or meddlesome, depending on the circumstances, and you have *Riding High.* I can't wait for you to read it! You're gonna love those pigs.

Charitably yours,

Vicki

DEDICATION

To Mary Jo LaBeff, friend and colleague.
Your feature article about an equine rescue organisation near Tucson inspired me to write Lily's story. Thank you for that and dozens of great conversations about the writing life!

Prologue

June 10, 1990, Last Chance Ranch,
from the diary of Eleanor Chance

THANKS TO MY grandson Nicholas, we have another orphaned puppy ensconced in the boys' room upstairs. Nicky calls him Hercules, and he's supposed to stay in his box because he's not housetrained yet. The whining has stopped, so it's a safe bet the little bugger's in Nicky's bed. Mark my words, we'll be washing sheets in the morning.

I know it's foolish to imagine what profession a child will take up as an adult, but I'm convinced that Nicky is going to be a vet. Yes, I realize he's only eight and boys his age change their minds on a regular basis. One day they want to be a firefighter, and the next they'd rather drive an eighteen-wheeler, or maybe fly a jet.

Nicky's different. He brings home enough strays to start a shelter if we were so inclined. But that's not why I figure he'll end up running a veterinarian clinic when he grows up. Half the time the animals he rescues have some injury or other. This puppy has a torn ear and a limp, and instinctively, Nicky knows what to do. It's remarkable for a boy so young.

Henry Applegate, our large-animal vet from Jackson, makes regular visits to the Last Chance, and Nicky follows him around like a rock-star groupie. He watches every move that man makes and asks so many questions it's a wonder Henry doesn't complain. I guess he's flattered that Nicky idolizes him so.

Fortunately Jonathan and Sarah are encouraging this interest. Jonathan agrees that his middle son has a gift, and Jonathan's already hoping that Nicky will one day take over the medical care of the Last Chance horses. Personally, I'm glad there's at least one steady boy in the batch.

Jack, the oldest, has a wild streak and is guaranteed to turn his father's hair prematurely gray. Gabe, the youngest, is the most competitive kid I've ever known. Jonathan plans to enter him in cutting-horse competitions when he's old enough. Now that school's out for the summer, Gabe's driving us all crazy setting up contests of every kind. Yesterday it was rope climbing. Today it was an obstacle course. Thank God he doesn't expect me to participate! I could probably climb that rope and navigate the obstacle course, but I'd rather not find out I couldn't. Now that I'm almost eighty, I prefer to maintain my illusions.

Whoops, gotta go. Nicky's calling for us. He says Hercules peed in his bed. Now there's a shocker.

1

Present day. Shoshone, Wyoming

DEAR GOD IN HEAVEN. Regan O'Connelli, DVM, parked his truck outside the large double gate of Peaceful Kingdom Horse Sanctuary, nudged his Stetson back with his thumb and leaned his forearms against the steering wheel while he contemplated the sight before him. If his hippie parents ever ran an animal rescue operation, it would look like this.

Nick Chance, his brother-in-law and business partner, had mentioned that Lily King was slightly...different. Judging from the psychedelic colors she'd painted the ranch house, the barn and the outbuildings, *different* was an understatement. Even though he was wearing his Ray-Ban sunglasses, the neon green, pink, orange and turquoise hurt his eyes.

She had to be the one who'd chosen the color scheme. She'd taken over from an elderly couple two months ago, and prior to that, it had been too cold to paint. Maybe if she'd stuck with one color per building, the effect wouldn't have been so startling. But a pink barn with turquoise doors and trim was wrong on so many levels. It was a wonder the horses agreed to go inside.

Or maybe they'd refused. He counted at least twenty of them milling around the property, which was a dozen more than Nick had told him to expect. There was a corral—he could see it from here—but the gate was open—accidentally or on purpose? He had a feeling she'd meant to keep it open so the horses wouldn't feel constrained by any artificial boundaries. His parents would have done that sort of thing, too.

Regan wished Nick had given him a little more information before sending him off on this mission of mercy. All he knew was that Lily's parents were two of Nick's favorite high school teachers and their daughter had an extremely high IQ, although she'd never stuck with one major long enough to earn a degree when she attended Berkeley. She had, however, invented a video game that continued to pay royalties, and she'd wanted to do something charitable with the money.

Maybe Nick had been vague about Lily's free-spirited persona because he knew Regan's history. Regan and his seven siblings had lived a vagabond existence with their parents, traveling the country in a van painted the same colors Lily seemed to favor. Nick wouldn't want to make fun of Lily's setup and insult Regan's folks in the process.

Everybody at the Last Chance Ranch had come to love his unconventional parents, Bianca Spinelli and Seamus O'Connor. Regan loved them, too, even if they had saddled their kids with the surname of O'Connelli to avoid hyphenating O'Connor and Spinelli. They'd also given each child a gender-neutral first name to prevent stereotyping. Grade school had been hell, especially because the family had moved constantly and the name thing had to be explained every time they'd enrolled somewhere new.

Regan had forgiven his well-meaning parents long ago, but Lily's paint job brought up memories he'd rather forget. He had a job to do, though, and the color of the buildings had no bearing on that. Nick, who'd invited Regan into his vet practice six months ago, had volunteered out here for several years when the Turners had run the place. Nick had said he was grateful Lily had come along. Without her sudden decision to buy it, the sanctuary would have closed.

Regan agreed that Lily was performing a valuable service, so he was prepared to do his part. As he climbed out of his truck and closed the door, a second truck pulled up. He didn't recognize the middle-aged couple inside, but he instantly identified the crated animal in the back of the truck.

When the man left the driver's seat and started toward the tailgate, Regan walked over to find out what was going on. "Looks like you have a potbellied pig there."

"Yes, sir, I do." The man adjusted the fit of his ball cap. "If you wouldn't mind, I could use a hand carrying the crate. My wife helped me get Harley up there, but I think she did something to her back in the process. Harley's put on a lot of weight since we got him."

"They tend to do that." Regan made no move to help with the crate.

"We didn't figure on him getting this big. When he was little, we'd let him in the house, but now he's even too big for the patio. We like to barbecue outside in the summer, and with Harley's mud hole expanding by the day, it's impossible."

Regan's jaw tightened, although he knew this kind

of thing happened all the time. People saw a cuddly baby animal and took it home while conveniently forgetting that baby animals grow into adults. "Where are you taking him?"

The man looked at Regan as if doubting his intelligence. "Isn't that obvious?"

"Not to me. This is a horse sanctuary, and what you have there is a pig."

"True, but I know for a fact the lady running the place accepted a pig last week from a guy I work with. So if she took one pig, I imagine she can take another. I'll make a donation to the cause. If you'd grab one end of the crate, I'd be much obliged."

"Before we do that, let's make sure she'll take him." Regan didn't know a lot about animal rescue, but asking first seemed like common courtesy.

"She'll take him. My buddy said she's a softie."

Regan held on to his temper with difficulty. "She may be, but if there's a potbellied-pig rescue organization in the area, that would be a better place for Harley."

"Look, mister." The man's eyes narrowed. "This is the day I set aside for handling this problem. My wife and I managed to get the pig into the crate and into the truck, which wasn't easy. If you're not gonna help me with the crate, step aside and I'll do it myself, although God knows what that'll do to *my* back."

"Hey, guys, what's up?" On the far side of the gate stood a young woman of medium height with the kind of bright red hair that made people take a second look. It was so kinked it fanned out like a lion's mane. Unlocking the gate, she stepped out and refastened it. She wore a tie-dyed shirt knotted at her waist, faded jeans and scuffed boots.

Regan told himself to ignore the cuteness factor as

she walked toward them. Nick could have mentioned *that,* too. Or the fact that sunlight made her hair glow. Maybe happily married Nick didn't notice those things anymore. "Lily King?"

"That's me. I'll bet you're Regan, the vet who moved here from Virginia. Nick said you'd be coming today instead of him."

"Right." At her approach, his senses went on alert. She smelled great, like a fresh meadow, and as she drew nearer, he noticed the freckles scattered across her nose, as well as her intensely blue eyes fringed with pale lashes. No makeup to speak of. It should all add up to wholesome, but instead she looked sexy and approachable. Good thing he wasn't in the market right now. "Listen, this guy has a potbellied pig he wants to—"

"So I gathered." She glanced up at Regan, laughter in her gaze, as if they shared a secret.

Oh, yeah. Sexy lady. And he didn't think she was trying to be, either, which made her all the more interesting.

"And I could use a *hand* with the *crate,* people." The man had adopted a martyred tone.

"I'll help you." Lily started toward the tailgate.

"Hang on a minute." Without thinking, Regan grabbed her arm and felt her tense. He released her immediately, but not before feeling firm muscles under her sleeve. This was no delicate flower. He admired that. "Is there a potbellied-pig sanctuary where he could go, instead?"

"There is, but last I heard they're at capacity. I already have one pig, so—"

"Told you," the guy said to Regan, folding his arms and looking smug.

"So I think Wilbur would be happier if he had a friend," Lily said. "I'm willing to take this pig."

Regan accepted defeat. "In that case, I'll help carry him."

"Thanks." She gave him a brilliant smile. "I'll get the gate."

Moments later, the crate was inside the chain-link fence that surrounded the approximately five acres of her property and the couple had left without making the donation the husband had promised. Regan wasn't terribly surprised. "Where should we take him now?"

"I'll let him decide where he wants to go."

"Maybe that's not such a—" But she'd already unlatched the crate and Harley burst forth in an apparent frenzy of joy. The horses trotted out of his way, and he flushed several chickens, which rose up in a cloud of feathers and angry clucking.

Chickens?

Lily smiled as she watched the pig cavort. "See how happy he is?"

"You have chickens?"

She shrugged as she continued to follow Harley's progress with her gaze. "It's the new thing to get chickens and have fresh eggs every morning. Urban farming is very in. But when the thrill is gone, people don't want those chickens. I've had a few people ask, and I've got room, so why not? Oh, look. Here comes Wilbur to see his new friend."

Regan watched as a considerably smaller potbellied pig came around the end of the ranch house and approached Harley. "What if they fight?"

She laughed, and the warmth of that laugh said a lot about her. She was obviously an optimistic soul who believed everything would turn out well. "Then you and

I can wade in and separate them, I guess. But they're not going to fight. They like each other. See? Is that sweet or what?"

He had to admit the pigs seemed okay with each other, but it could have just as easily gone the other way. Then one of the horses, a sway-backed buckskin gelding, walked calmly past the pigs and began munching on what was left of a flower bed in front of the ranch house porch. "You let him do that?"

"If it makes him happy."

"Then I guess you don't care about having plants there."

She turned to face him. "I took over the sanctuary because I want to give these horses a home and a sense of self-worth. If they want to eat the flowers, so what? They've been arbitrarily yanked away from the life they used to know, so they deserve to be spoiled, right?"

"Philosophically, yes. Practically, no. These are two-thousand-pound animals, and they need to live by a set of rules. In fact, all domestic animals function better that way." Kids, too. He and his siblings had been given more freedom than they'd known what to do with. Somehow they'd avoided the serious consequences of that freedom, but he shuddered when he thought of how their lives might have turned out.

"I disagree." She said it cheerfully, though.

"Is that why you don't have the horses confined in the corral or the barn?" Or did the horses stage a rebellion when they caught a glimpse of that pink-and-turquoise monstrosity? The jury was still out on how well horses could see color. At the moment Regan wouldn't mind a little color blindness, himself.

"Exactly. I let them wander as they wish, and they all show up in the barn at mealtime. When it's cold, they tend to stay in there during the night, but they're welcome to go wherever they want on the property."

"Makes my work more complicated if I have to chase them down."

She nodded. "That's what Nick said. He'd rather have them all in one place when he comes out, and I meant to close them in the barn while they ate breakfast. But the sunrise was so beautiful that I got distracted. Before I realized it, they'd all eaten and headed out. Once they're loose, it's nearly impossible to get them in again until dinner. I should have arranged for you to come before mealtime, instead."

"Next time I'll do that." He sighed. "Guess I'd better get started."

"I'll help, but I wonder if…"

"If what?"

She hesitated, her expression earnest. "Would you consider, just this once, rescheduling for this evening?"

"Well, I—"

"Never mind. That's asking too much. You probably have a wife or a girlfriend who expects you for dinner."

"I don't, but that's not the issue."

"And there's the matter of making a second trip. I'll help you catch them and we'll get 'er done. I know I'm too lax with them, but I think about the fact that the poor things have never been in charge of their lives, and that's why I like to give them more control over their comings and goings. I promise next time I'll remember to keep them in the barn when you're due to arrive."

He gazed into her solemn blue eyes. Only a man of stone wouldn't warm to the compassion shining there, even when he knew she didn't have the faintest idea how to run this operation. "Have you spent much time around horses?"

"Not until I took over the sanctuary, which was a leap of faith. I wanted to come back home and do something good for the community, and this place really spoke to me. Now I'm around horses 24/7."

Déjà vu. Either of his parents could have delivered that kind of speech, except that none of their seat-of-the-pants decisions had involved horses.

"And you know what?" Her expression grew more animated. "They're such individuals! Buck, the one who likes to eat the flowers, is really stubborn, while Sally, that little bay mare over there, is shy. You have to coax her to be friends, but once she trusts you, she'll follow you around like a dog. I have to watch out she doesn't try to come in the house."

Oh, boy. So at least one of the horses had started crowding her, a typical power move. No doubt they all sensed that Lily wasn't the leader of the herd. She didn't understand that they'd take more and more liberties until some of them would become unmanageable and even dangerous, both to themselves and to her.

But she was genuinely fond of them after only two months, and he didn't want to mess with that. Homeless animals needed all the friends they could get, so he'd tread lightly. But she was going about this all wrong. If she didn't create some order and discipline soon, the situation could become unworkable.

Yeah, Nick could have been more forthcoming. Regan wondered why Nick hadn't put a stop to this laissez-faire attitude of hers. Regan planned to ask. In fact, he had a whole list of questions now that he'd been here.

Glancing around, he calculated how much time he'd need to rope each horse and do an exam. Even with her help, it would take too long, considering the other appointments he'd scheduled today. The horses might not be cooperative, either. Nick hadn't been to Peaceful Kingdom since early May, so no telling how they'd react to being examined after a month of doing as they pleased. "Maybe I should come back during their dinnertime, after all."

"That really would be better. Tell you what. If you'll do that, I'll feed you supper."

"That's really not necessary." He'd bet the keys to his truck that she was a vegetarian, maybe even vegan.

"I know, but it would make me feel better about inconveniencing you. Please say you'll stay for dinner."

"I wouldn't want to put you to any extra trouble on my account." Some people could make vegetables taste yummy and others couldn't. The minute he'd left home he'd reverted to being a carnivore, and so had his brothers and sisters. Even his parents weren't as strict these days, especially when they hung out at the Last Chance Ranch.

She grinned at him. "You think I'm going to serve you sprouts and tofu, don't you?"

Apparently she was good at reading expressions and had figured out why he was hesitating. "Are you?"

"Nope. I make a veggie lasagna that's out of this world. My parents love it, and they're dyed-in-the-wool carnivores."

"Real cheese?"

"Absolutely. I haven't hitched my wagon to the vegan concept yet. I still might some day, but I do love my cheese and ice cream."

She really was adorable. Had he been looking for adorable...but he wasn't. A mere six months ago he'd been kicked in the teeth, romantically speaking, and that had left a mark. "Then I accept. What time?"

"I feed the horses around five."

"I'll be here a little after five, then. It'll be much easier to examine them when they're each in a separate stall."

"Uh, they won't *all* be in separate stalls. About half won't, actually."

"Why not?"

"I have twelve stalls and twenty-one horses, so most of them double up."

Regan looked more closely at the pink-and-turquoise barn. Judging from the size of it, those twelve stalls wouldn't be oversized. "So you have a space problem?"

"I'm afraid I do." She gazed at him with those soulful blue eyes. "The thing is, I can't help but say yes."

That comment shouldn't have had a sexual connotation. But long after he'd driven away from the Peaceful Kingdom Horse Sanctuary, her words floated around in his traitorous brain.

She appeared to be a free spirit. That didn't necessarily mean she would embrace the concept of a no-strings affair, but it might. The thought created a pleasant ache in his groin. He hadn't felt that surge of desire in some time. Apparently he'd repressed it, because sure enough, thinking of sex brought up what had happened back in Virginia. Last Christmas Eve he'd found Drake Brewster, his best friend and business partner, in bed with Jeannette Trenton, his fiancée. That discovery had affected him more than anyone knew.

Jeannette had accused him of being cold-blooded because he'd refused to discuss it afterward. Instead, he'd handled the situation with surgical precision. Within a week he'd moved out of their shared condo, ended their engagement, sold his share of the veterinary practice to Brewster and relocated from Virginia to Jackson Hole, where Nick Chance had welcomed him into his practice.

The move had been a no-brainer. He couldn't continue to work with Brewster after what the guy had done, and the previous summer Nick had mentioned needing a partner in his clinic.

Even more compelling was the prospect of being surrounded by family while he put his life back together. Nearly twenty years ago his folks had spent several months in Jackson Hole. His older sister Morgan had loved the place so much she'd vowed to return. When she finally made good on that promise to herself, she'd met and married Gabe Chance. Thus had begun the growing connection between the Chance family and the O'Connelli brood.

Next, Regan's twin sister, Tyler, had married into the Chance extended family. She was happily hitched to Alex Keller, brother of Jack Chance's wife, Josie. And most recently, eighteen-year-old Cassidy, youngest of the O'Connelli siblings, had apprenticed as the ranch housekeeper.

Sarah, the Chance family matriarch, had insisted that Regan stay at the Last Chance until he'd decided whether to live in town or buy some acreage. Six months later he was still there soaking up the ambiance. He'd never lived in a place that felt more like home, and he craved that sense of permanence.

For half a year he'd managed to convince himself that he'd moved past that fateful Christmas Eve when two people he'd trusted had betrayed him. He hadn't dated, but that seemed natural under the circumstances. Lily was the first woman he'd met who interested him, which was ironic. All the evidence suggested her philosophy of life was exactly like his parents' and the complete opposite of his.

But did that matter? He wasn't ready for anything

serious. As for Lily, if she was the least bit like his parents, she'd grow bored with the horse sanctuary eventually and search for a new challenge somewhere else, so she wouldn't be around long.

But while she was, maybe they could hang out together. During their conversation she'd slipped in a comment about a potential wife or a girlfriend. Sometimes that meant a woman was trying to find out that information for her own reasons.

He'd know soon enough. She didn't strike him as a woman who was into mind games. No, she seemed forthright, playful and creative. Instead of wincing at her paint job, he should rejoice, because it told him that she enjoyed having fun. It had been so damned long since he'd had fun.

2

LILY STOOD BY the gate and waved as Regan drove away. She continued to watch until the plume of dust kicked up by his truck's tires disappeared. Long after he was gone, she stayed where she was, lost in thought. Regan O'Connelli was a pleasant surprise, even if he had informed her that she needed to change how she was running the sanctuary.

He'd meant it in a helpful way, though, and he might have a point. Nick had hinted at the same thing, but she'd been so convinced the horses deserved spoiling that she hadn't paid much attention. Besides, he was Nick, someone she'd known since she was a precocious whiz kid and he was one of her parents' favorite students in high school. He behaved toward her like the big brother she'd never had, and she expected him to dispense advice, most of which she would ignore.

In this case, maybe she shouldn't have ignored it. She was a little embarrassed by how quickly her situation was getting out of hand. Each day she worked to be more efficient, but then a new horse would arrive and she'd struggle to get all her chores done.

She probably shouldn't accept any more horses, but how could she turn them away if they had nowhere to go? She needed to find homes for some of them, but she hadn't figured out the adoption part of the plan. Come to think of it, the Turners hadn't mentioned it, either. They'd both been a little absent-minded during the transfer of ownership, and she hadn't thought to ask.

Regan might have some suggestions. She smiled to herself. The guy was hot. As she finally admitted that she'd noticed that, she laughed. His hotness was the real reason she was standing here dreamy-eyed over her new vet.

He was one juicy dude, in a Johnny Depp kind of way. That comparison couldn't be confirmed until she'd found out whether he had dark eyes, and he'd kept his bad-boy shades on the entire time, darn it. What a great idea, inviting him to dinner so he'd be around after the sun went down.

Maybe he'd kept the shades on because he had sensitive eyes, but she wondered if something else was going on with him. Sunglasses could also provide emotional protection. She'd always been super conscious of people's emotions, and after hanging out with rescue animals, she picked up on their moods, too. Understandably, many of the horses had trust issues, and she'd felt the same vibe coming from Regan.

Buck plodded over and nudged her from behind, so she turned to give the sway-backed horse some neck scratches. "I could be wrong, Buck, old boy, but I think that guy might need to be rescued as much as the rest of you around here."

The horse bobbed his head, and Lily smiled. "Thanks for validating my hypothesis." She patted his neck and reached for the cell phone in her back pocket. "Let's see if Dr. Chance agrees with me." She scrolled through her contacts and called Nick.

He answered on the second ring. "How'd it go with Regan?"

"Fine. You busy?" Holding the phone to her ear, she set off in search of the two pigs. They were probably okay, but she wanted to make sure.

"Yeah, I'm an extremely busy and important man, but for you, I'm willing to postpone my critical work for a few minutes."

"You are so full of it. I'm convinced you passed my mom's class purely on your ability to BS."

"I might've. But I aced your dad's science class with a minimum of BS. Just ask him."

"Don't have to. You two have a mutual admiration society going on." She located the pigs wallowing in the large mud pit she'd dug a few days ago for Wilbur. Harley was going to fit right in. "I like Regan a lot, although he's already telling me I'm doing this horse thing wrong."

"What does he think you're doing wrong?"

"Letting the horses roam the property, for starters."

"Well, Regan prefers more order than that, but those six horses are pretty old. I don't think it'll hurt to let them have some freedom in their golden years."

"I, um, have more than six, now. And they're not all in their golden years."

"Oh? How many do you have?"

"Twenty-one."

"Good golly, Miss Molly! What did you do, advertise?"

"Not exactly, but I've talked to people when I go into town. Oh, and I redesigned the website and made sure it came up on all the search engines. It's a kick-ass site, if I do say so."

"I'll bet."

"I guess the word got out that I was here and had room for more horses."

"I'm sure it did." Nick was quiet for a bit. "Lily, you don't have room in your current barn to keep twenty-one horses forever. You'll have to renovate that barn and add more stalls."

"What do you mean, *forever?* Won't people come and adopt some of them?"

"Not usually. You have a sanctuary, which means you take in animals that are too sick or old to be ridden anymore and you keep them until they die."

"Oh." How embarrassing. She hadn't understood the basic premise of the project she'd taken on. "What do you call a place where you adopt out some of the horses?"

"I'm not sure. Maybe an equine rescue facility. But not a sanctuary."

Lily swallowed. "Well, that's what I need this to be, then, an equine rescue facility, at least for the animals I've taken in since I arrived. They're not old and ready to die. People didn't want them, so I accepted them. I thought that was what I was supposed to do."

"It's okay. No harm done. But you can't ever adopt out those original six. They're there for the duration."

"I did figure that, but the barn holds twelve, and I thought it was a shame for the other stalls to go to waste." Still, she felt like an idiot.

"Don't worry. You can sort this out. What's your plan for the adoption process?"

"Um…I'm working on it." She hated to admit that no plan existed yet, but it couldn't be that hard. She'd had no trouble finding people who wanted to get rid of horses, so now she needed to find the other half, the ones who wanted horses. "I should also probably mention the chickens."

"What chickens?"

"Rescue chickens. I have nine of them."

"How the hell did that happen?"

"I said yes to one person, and before you know it, I had nine."

Nick sighed. "Do you know anything about chickens?"

"Enough to know I don't want a rooster!"

"That's a start." He didn't sound quite as confident now.

"I'm okay with the chickens, Nick. Mom and Dad had some a few years back, so they're helping me figure it out. I also have two potbellied pigs. You'd be amazed how much info Google can dig up on potbellied pigs."

"Good Lord. You know, Lily, you don't need to accept every animal that shows up at your gate."

"That's what I tell myself, but I worry what will happen to them if I don't."

He sighed. "Yeah, that's a problem when you get into the rescue business, but here's the deal. You have accepted twenty-one horses, nine chickens and two pigs. I'm sure they keep you busy."

"They do." She had almost no downtime these days. She hadn't played a video game in weeks, and her meditation practice was shot, but so far she'd kept up with the critters.

"Think about the animals you already have before you take in any more, okay? You owe those animals your best, and the larger your numbers, the less you'll be able to give them your best."

"I could hire help."

"You could, but you're still limited to the space you have. When winter comes, you'll want to keep the horses in the barn most of the time, and that barn's not big enough for twenty-one horses."

"I could add on or build another one, like you said."

"But where does it stop? Are you planning to buy more land and just keep building barns? How big an operation do you want?"

Lily took a deep breath. "I don't want a big operation. I love this property just the size it is. It suits me, and the idea of employees gives me hives. I'd have to fill out IRS stuff and get them health insurance and learn how to be the boss of them."

"If you don't want to expand, you know what you have to do."

"Right. Turn away any incoming horses until I adopt some out and make room." Her stomach hurt. How could she refuse to take a homeless animal? That would kill her.

"Good. And about letting them roam everywhere, you might want to—"

"I know. Regan pointed out that they won't be adoptable unless they have good manners, and some of the younger ones aren't all that well behaved. A couple of them act like they want to fight with each other. I probably need to stop letting them run loose."

"Yes, you do. They need to adapt to normal restrictions or nobody will want them. A well-trained horse is much easier to adopt out."

For the first time since she'd moved onto the property, she felt uncertain that she'd done the right thing. She should have asked more questions instead of blithely leaping into something because it had sounded cozy.

She'd liked the idea of doing something good for the planet. On the surface a horse sanctuary had seemed romantic and not particularly complicated. She'd loved the name of the place. Someone with the last name of King should have a kingdom, right?

If she'd understood that she was only supposed to take care of animals on their last legs, she might not have bought Peaceful Kingdom. Sure, somebody needed to do it, but she didn't have the temperament. She'd be bored out of her tree, which might have been why she'd encouraged the locals to bring in more horses and liven things up.

Now she had to whip these newly acquired equines into shape fast and find them good homes so she could keep taking in the needy ones that would be lining up outside her gate with woeful expressions in their beautiful big eyes. The word was spreading, and in tough economic times, many people couldn't afford to keep the horse they'd bought in a burst of optimism. That was the story most everyone had given her when they'd arrived at her gate.

Her next admission was so hard to make. "Nick, I don't know how to train a horse."

"That's no problem. You're a smart person. I'll talk to Regan and see if he can help you. I'll help you, too, when I can, but Regan has a little more free time than I do. He'll probably agree. He's a good guy."

She latched on to this new topic with relief. "Speaking of Regan, what's his deal, Nick?"

He hesitated. "What do you mean?"

"You don't have to tell me if you shouldn't, but I get the impression something bad happened to him recently. He seems…wounded."

"What made you think that?"

"He didn't take off his shades."

"He examined all the horses with his sunglasses on? That doesn't sound like Regan. He's usually super professional."

"He didn't examine the horses. He's coming back tonight when they're all in the barn." As she said it, she realized that expecting him to make a second trip really was ridiculous. Both Regan and Nick were right. She had too many horses and no control of them. That had to change.

"So what did he do while he was out there, if he didn't examine the horses?"

"Helped carry the pig crate in here, and then we talked for a little while. That's when he mentioned that I might be headed down the wrong road here at Peaceful Kingdom." She gazed at the porch rail Sally was currently chewing on. Then she walked over and gave the mare a swat on the rump. Sally barely flinched and kept chewing. "So am I right? Is Regan hiding behind those shades?"

"I never thought about it before. He does wear them a lot. Most of us are fine with using our hats to shade our eyes. Sunglasses just get in the way."

"He had the hat on, too. Double protection. I just thought, if he's going to be advising me, I should know if there are certain subjects to avoid. I don't want to stumble over a psychological land mine." That was absolutely true. Regan was beginning to look like her savior, and she didn't want to tick him off accidentally. She'd already created a problem for herself with the horses. She couldn't afford to make the situation worse by alienating someone who could help.

Nick was silent for a moment. "I suppose it might be

good for you to know. Everyone at the ranch does. But you can't tell him I told you."

"I won't."

"Okay, last Christmas Eve, he found his fiancée with his best friend."

Lily's chest tightened. "In bed?"

"Yeah."

"Damn." Now she wished she hadn't been right about Regan's vulnerability. "No wonder he's wearing shades. I would, too. I've never had a fiancé, but I can imagine that would feel pretty awful, especially if it was with your best friend."

"Don't let on that you know, although maybe it *is* better that you do know. We all feel protective of him. He'll be fine, but I don't think he's totally over it yet."

"How could he be? Poor thing. It's only been six months." That meant he was off-limits to her, though. She had no interest in being some gorgeous guy's rebound girl, even if she did want to soothe his wounded heart. She'd tried that once and it hadn't turned out well. The rebound girl served a purpose, she'd discovered, but once that purpose was gone, so was the guy, which left the girl feeling used. "Anyway, thanks for filling me in."

"You bet. Gotta go. He just walked into the office."

"Okay. 'Bye." She disconnected the call. What a shame about the fiancée and the best friend. Good to know, she supposed, and she owed Nick big-time for telling her. But her Johnny Depp fantasy had officially bitten the dust.

TECHNICALLY, REGAN SHOULD be frustrated as hell with the situation in Lily's pink-and-turquoise barn. The quarters were cramped and the horses tested him continually. He'd countered every attempt to gain control with a stern word and a flick of the lead rope. So far that had kept any misbehaving animals in line.

But he'd had to remain vigilant. He should hate being here in this chaotic environment, except that it also contained Lily, who watched his every move. She asked excellent questions and took detailed notes on her phone, which he found endearing.

Earlier today he'd talked with Nick, who'd clarified the sanctuary-versus-rescue mix-up. Regan hadn't been clear on the terms until then, either, but now he understood a little better how Lily had landed in this mess. Nick had wanted to know if Regan could spare some time to help her. Damn straight. Catching a glimpse of her bright hair and ready smile made his heart lift. He wouldn't mind coming out here on a regular basis. It would be no sacrifice at all.

At last they were done, and she turned to him. "Should I keep them inside tonight so they'll start getting used to the idea?"

"It's pretty crowded. How about if we split them up and lead a few into the corral, instead?"

"That's a good plan, except the gate's broken. Mr. Turner told me he'd meant to fix it, but his arthritis was so bad he never did."

"How broken is it?"

"It's coming off the hinges. I decided not to worry about the corral, so I don't know if it could be easily fixed or whether I need a whole new gate."

"Let's leave them in here for now and take a look."

She nodded. "Sounds like a plan."

As he walked with her toward the corral, he noticed that the orange-red glow of the sunset matched the color of her hair. Nice. But the setting sun also brought out the unusual colors of the ranch buildings, prompting him to ask the question that had been nagging him for hours. "Why did you paint the buildings such…unusual colors?" He was proud of himself for substituting *unusual* for *god-awful.*

"Several reasons. First of all, these colors make me happy. I also like doing the unexpected thing to keep me from being bored. Nobody in this area has a pink-and-turquoise barn or an orange-and-green ranch house."

"That would be true."

"Besides that, I wanted to make sure people could find the place, and you have to admit that the colors make it stand out."

"Also true."

"But you don't care for them."

He smiled to soften his response. "No, not really."

"I'm not surprised." She said it in a conversational tone, as if his answer hadn't fazed her in the least. Apparently she'd been expecting him to turn thumbs down.

Damn, now he wanted to know why. Did she think he was too boring to appreciate her creativity? Had he come across as someone with no imagination who always did what others expected? That was a stodgy image he wasn't crazy about, but it might be accurate.

In any case, he didn't have to worry about hurting her feelings. Obviously she didn't need his approval to feel good about her choice of paint, and she'd accepted his comment without taking it personally.

Her attitude made him look at the colors differently. Why shouldn't she be surrounded by colors that made her happy? It was her place, after all, and a little paint wasn't going to hurt anything. If it shook people out of a rut—stodgy people like him, for example—that could be a good thing. And she was right about making the place easy to find.

"I may have made the place too accessible, though." She paused and turned toward him. "The truth is, Regan, I blundered into this without the necessary skill set, and that's embarrassing. I don't have the foggiest idea what I'm doing, other than I want to help homeless horses."

"That's a good start." Her honesty touched him. "Don't be too hard on yourself. If everybody waited until they had the necessary skills before they started something, we'd still be living in caves."

"What a nice thing to say." Gratitude shone in her eyes. "Nick said he'd ask you about helping me. Did he?"

"Yeah."

"Will you? Do you have time?"

He didn't even have to think about it. "I'll make the time."

Her expression brightened. "Thank you, Regan."

As he gazed into her eyes, the pressure that had constricted his chest for months began to ease. Exercise hadn't eliminated it, and neither had booze. But granting one heartfelt request from Lily King made him feel lighter than air.

He should be thanking *her.* He wanted to stick around and see if she had any other miracle cures up her tie-dyed sleeve. An emotion washed through him, one he couldn't immediately identify. Then he figured it out. For the first time in ages, he was happy.

3

LONG BEFORE THE sun went down, Lily found out that Regan had brown eyes. He'd taken off both hat and sunglasses while he examined the horses. Whenever he'd glanced up to discuss something with her, she'd looked into the velvet depths of those brown eyes and wished like hell he hadn't been dumped so recently.

Later on, he'd delivered a line guaranteed to make a woman swoon—*I'll make the time.* He'd compounded the effect of that by demonstrating that he knew exactly how to fix her broken gate. A man with multiple skills—now that was sexy. She was handy with a paintbrush, but she hadn't taught herself to use the array of tools Mr. Turner had left her.

She would learn eventually, but watching Regan took away a big chunk of her incentive, especially after he rolled up his sleeves to reveal the play of muscles as he worked. She'd have no trouble being into Regan O'Connelli. As she held the gate steady while he reattached the hinges, she wondered what sort of idiot would cheat on a guy who seemed so special.

Then she chastised herself for making a snap judgment. She didn't know the whole story, only the version presented by Nick, who was clearly biased in Regan's favor. There might have been extenuating circumstances. If she kept her distance as she planned, she'd never know.

Maintaining that distance would be more of a challenge than she'd counted on, though. He was definitely a wounded man in need of comfort. She'd sensed it when they'd met, but at that point his shields had been firmly in place.

Apparently his thinking had changed in the intervening hours, because now he was lowering those shields. She heard it in his voice, as brisk efficiency was replaced with mellow goodwill. His body language was more open, too. No more crossed arms or clenched jaw when he talked with her.

But mostly she saw it in his eyes. They flashed with interest now instead of wariness. Fortunately she could resist those flashes of interest. What sucked her in were the brief moments when she glimpsed sadness and pain in those beautiful brown depths.

If a more powerful aphrodisiac existed, she didn't know what it was. Responding to it was a huge mistake, as she'd long ago discovered to her sorrow. But he was a gorgeous man with a broken heart, and what woman wouldn't yearn to help him heal?

This woman. Taking a deep breath, she tightened her resolve to keep Regan at arm's length. She'd learned her lesson, right?

"That should do it." He swung the gate back and forth a couple of times and made sure the latch fastened securely.

"Thank you." She gave him a smile and vowed to get comfortable with repair work. The less she needed from Regan, the easier it would be for her to resist temptation.

"Let's gather a few horses." He started back toward the barn.

She fell into step beside him. "I promise that's the only handyman chore I'll ask of you."

He shrugged. "It's no problem. I'm used to repairing things."

"Maybe so, but if I'm going to run this place, I should make friends with hand tools."

"I would agree with that. Shouldn't be too tough for you to learn. Nick said you were a smart cookie."

"He did?" That pleased her. "Just out of curiosity, what else did he tell you about me?"

"That you created a video game that's paying for all this." He swept an arm to encompass the property. "That's impressive."

"I guess. But I'm not sure it makes much of a contribution to the betterment of humanity."

"Why, is it violent?"

"God, no. I'm not into that kind of game. It's about elves and magic. There is a dragon, but he's more comic relief than scary. If you give him enough treats, which are increasingly hard to come by as the game goes on, he doesn't cause problems."

"Sounds like fun. Maybe we could play it some—" He was interrupted by the high-pitched scream of a horse followed by several loud thuds. "Shit." He took off at a run toward the barn.

Lily ran after him, her heart thumping. Two of the geldings, a big roan named Strawberry and a palomino named Rex, had never cared for each other. She'd put them in different stalls with horses they seemed to like, so it couldn't be them fighting, could it?

Regan beat her into the barn and grabbed a lead rope from a peg on the wall. He strode quickly to Rex's stall.

The palomino bared his teeth at a young gelding named Sandy who had never caused a single problem since he'd been brought in two weeks earlier. Sandy cowered against the far wall, eyes rolling with fright. At least he didn't seem to be bleeding anywhere.

"Hey!" Regan's voice rang out. Opening the stall door, he walked in, the tail end of the lead rope flicking back and forth in front of him. "Back off!" He edged into position and snapped the rope in front of Rex's face.

Lily held her breath. A rope didn't seem like much protection against a riled-up horse, but it was working some kind of magic on Rex. The palomino backed up a step, and then another.

Regan followed and kept that rope dancing in front of Rex's nose. Then, in one quick move, he clipped the front end of the rope to Rex's halter and pulled the horse's head down. "Enough of that, mister. We're going for a walk."

As Regan led Rex from the stall, Lily stood to one side and gave them room. "What can I do to help?"

"Latch the door after me, then walk ahead and open the corral. We'll put him in there to cool off."

"Right." She wanted to comfort Sandy, but that would have to be put on hold. After securing the stall door, she waited until Regan and Rex had left the barn before scooting around them and heading for the corral.

As she passed Regan, she heard him talking to Rex in a low, soothing voice. She didn't like to think about what would have happened if Regan hadn't been here. Of course, if he hadn't, the horses would have been free to leave the barn once they'd eaten, so this confrontation wouldn't have happened in the first place. Rex was used to eating and leaving for a far corner of the property. He usually took several horses with him.

This time he'd been kept inside while all twenty-one animals were examined, and then the humans had disappeared without letting him loose. Apparently that hadn't sat well with him.

After opening the gate, which moved smoothly on its hinges, Lily watched Regan approach with the horse. Rex ambled along as if he had nothing on his mind besides walking docilely toward the corral. He didn't crowd Regan the way Buck tended to crowd Lily, but he didn't hang back, either. Instead he behaved like the well-trained horse he might be if someone like Regan was in charge.

Speaking of the bodacious Dr. O'Connelli, he looked mighty fine coming toward her with that loose-hipped stride that emphasized the fit of his jeans. Each time he put a booted foot forward, the denim stretched across his thighs. She couldn't help but notice that. Any woman worth her salt would agree that he was one good-looking dude.

Fate wasn't being kind to her. She'd broken up with her steady boyfriend last fall. He hadn't approved of her plan to leave her job with a tech company in Silicon Valley and find a worthwhile charity to support in her hometown. Instead he'd been after her to create another moneymaking game and buy a Porsche or some other stupid luxury car.

She didn't miss Alfred, who'd turned out to have a completely different value system from hers. But she sure missed the sex. Until Regan had shown up outside her gate, she hadn't realized how much she missed it.

Unbeknownst to him, probably, he was a walking invitation to partake of those pleasures. Much as she strove to be nonjudgmental about his ex, the thought continued to surface—the woman was an idiot. Regan was brave, resourceful and breathtakingly handsome. Maybe he left dirty socks on the floor and the toilet seat up. Lily could forgive even those sins for a chance to jump his bones. His off-limits bones. Damn.

He continued to talk to Rex as he led the gelding into the corral. Then he removed the lead rope and gave Rex a slap on the rump. The palomino took off, and Regan came to stand beside her, coiling the lead rope. "We're going to have to watch that one."

"I can see that." Lily closed and latched the gate. "You scared me to death walking into the stall with only a rope."

"It usually works. I was ready to back out again if he'd turned on me. I'm no hero when it comes to dealing with a two-thousand-pound animal in a bad mood."

"Could've fooled me."

He gave her a lopsided grin. "Aw, shucks, ma'am. T'weren't nothin'."

Please don't be charming. She was having enough trouble keeping her libido in check. "Why does flicking a rope work?"

"Most horses hate having something flicked in their face, and the more you do it, the more they back away from it. It's a great way to get them to move without hurting them."

Lily thought of her futile attempt to coax Sally away from the porch railing this morning. "What if you don't have a rope handy? I can't picture myself carrying one around all the time."

"Ideally you would have a lead rope clipped to their halter when you're working with them."

"Okay, but what about the times I'm not working with them and they're..."

"Loose?"

She flushed. "I know. They shouldn't be loose, but there's no way I can adopt out six or seven horses in the next few days, and I don't like the idea of keeping them cooped up in the barn all the time. Even the corral is confining."

"You're right. You should only be using the corral for training. You could fence off a couple of acres so they have some room to run around, and then they won't be chewing on your house or pooping in your front yard."

She stared at him. "That's *brilliant.* Why didn't I think of that?"

"You didn't want to restrict their freedom."

She had said that, but coming from him, especially after the scare they'd just had, it sounded naive. "I've revised my opinion. But getting someone out here to construct the fence will take a while. What should I do in the meantime? Walk around carrying a rope?"

"You could carry a leather quirt and stick it in your back pocket."

"So I could hit them with it? I don't want to do that."

"Chances are you wouldn't have to touch them. You'd just wave it in their face like you would a rope."

"I'll think about it." She couldn't imagine walking around with a quirt stuck in her back pocket, either. She'd probably lose the darn thing. "Couldn't I just clap my hands and achieve the same thing?"

"Not really."

She sighed and glanced over at Rex, who was prancing around with his tail in the air, as if he owned that little circle. "Rex seems to like this setup just fine. He's king of the corral."

"So that's his name? I couldn't remember, but it fits him. He wants to rule any situation he's in, I'll bet. Did the people who brought him in say anything about his personality?"

Lily thought back to the young woman who'd left Rex at the sanctuary. "She said he was too much horse for her. She was small, so I thought that's what she meant. Rex came here shortly after I took over, so at first he only had the old horses to deal with."

"And he could boss them around."

"They didn't seem to mind. Strawberry, the big roan, was the first horse to challenge Rex, but after they did a little snorting and pawing, they stayed away from each other. I kept Rex in a stall by himself until recently. I thought he'd be okay with Sandy, who's not aggressive at all. And it worked out until tonight."

Regan nudged back the brim of his hat and glanced over at the barn. "I don't want to chance putting anyone else in the corral with Rex tonight. He might be fine, but he might not. I guess we have to turn them all loose again. It's what they're used to."

"And now I have a strategy to prevent Sally from trying to come in the house. I'll keep a rope handy."

"You know why she does that, right?"

"Sure. She thinks she's a dog. Or a person."

"No, she's trying to gain more control over you. Horses will push when they sense you're not in charge."

That made her laugh. "I think it's pretty obvious by now that I'm not in charge. Far from it, in fact."

"But you need to be," he said quietly.

"Boy, that sounded serious."

"It is serious. These are big animals, very strong animals. They're used to having a leader of the herd, and if you don't accept that role, one of them will take it. Rex may think he already has. Strawberry might decide to fight him for it. Losing control is dangerous to them and dangerous to you."

Her pulse rate picked up, and this time it had nothing to do with how beautiful his eyes were and how much she wanted to do him. "Regan, you're scaring me."

"Good. I mean to. You've been lucky so far. Most of the horses haven't been here very long, and at least six of them are too old to harm anyone. But you need to let them all know you're the boss, and very soon."

A shiver ran down her spine. "I don't have the skills to do that, yet. I'll need training as much as they do. And practice. I'll call somebody first thing in the morning about fencing in a couple of acres. Oh, wait, what's tomorrow?"

"Saturday."

She groaned. "Some fencing companies will be closed, and even if I find one that isn't, they probably won't be able to finish it up until the first part of next week."

"I could ask Nick if he could pull in a favor. The Chance name might help."

"Sure, okay." She combed her fingers through her hair while she thought through her options. "I'm not too proud to accept that. If you'll call him now, I'll let the horses out."

"Look, I'm sorry to be the bearer of bad news, but I'm worried about you."

"I know." She drew in a shaky breath. "I just never imagined that my good deed could turn into a life-threatening situation—for me or for the other horses. Call Nick. I'll be right back. Then we should feed the pigs and the chickens."

Turning, she walked toward the barn. Her rose-colored glasses were smashed to smithereens, and as she entered the overcrowded space, she could swear ominous music played in the background. The horses looked the same, though, and gazing into their liquid-brown eyes as she opened each stall door calmed her. She gave an extra pat to Sandy, who seemed to have recovered from his fright.

They all walked out of the barn in the same leisurely fashion they normally did. But she couldn't quite erase her mental image of Rex and Strawberry battling to the death for control of the herd. That wasn't going to happen, though. She had Regan on her side, and he knew his way around these animals, thank God.

At last she opened the stall where Sally stood with a chestnut gelding named Brown Sugar. The gelding meandered out, but Sally lingered as if hoping for a treat. That was Lily's fault. She'd often slipped the little mare pieces of carrot and apple.

"Sorry, girl. No treats on me, tonight." She stroked the horse's silky neck. "You aren't really trying to control me, are you? You just want to be good friends."

Sally butted her head against Lily's chest.

"See, that's what I thought. Come on. Everybody else has left the barn, so you might as well, too." She turned and started down the wooden aisle.

Sally followed, but she didn't stay slightly back the way Rex had when Regan had led him toward the corral. She came right up to Lily, her nose often bumping Lily's arm. Lily moved over, and Sally moved with her.

As an experiment, Lily kept moving to the right each time Sally crowded her. Pretty soon she was out of room. She turned to face the mare. "Are you *herding* me?"

Sally's big brown eyes gave nothing away.

But Lily had her answer. Sally was in charge, and

Lily wasn't. She had no rope or quirt, so she untied the tails of the shirt knotted at her waist and flapped those in front of the mare's face. "Back off, sweetheart!"

Sally's head jerked up and she took a couple of steps backward.

"Yep, that's what I'm talking about! Give me some room!" Lily flapped her shirt a few more times, and Sally retreated again. "Huh. Amazing."

She'd managed to intimidate Sally a little bit, but she had no illusions that she'd get the same respect from Rex or Strawberry. For that matter, most of the new arrivals might not pay any attention to her efforts. She had a lot to learn, and not much time to learn it. Knotting her shirt at her waist once again, she walked out of the barn into the soft twilight, followed at a respectful distance by Sally.

Regan, looking better with every minute that passed, came to meet her.

She was excited to share her small triumph with him. "Hey, you may not believe it, but I backed Sally off by undoing my shirt and flapping the ends in her face."

"Excellent!" He smiled. "Creative solution. Maybe you don't need a rope after all."

"Yeah, I do. I don't think my shirttails will make much of an impression on Rex."

"Maybe not. Anyway, I talked to Nick, and he'll do what he can, but summer is the worst time to get a crew ASAP. Busiest time of the year for fence companies because it's when they repair winter storm damage."

"Not surprising." But it wasn't the news she'd hoped to hear.

"He said he'd offer to send out some of the ranch hands, but there's a special riding event in Cheyenne this weekend, so he's short a few guys as it is. He can get right on it Monday morning, though."

"So I'm on my own with twenty-one horses who could decide to revolt at any moment."

"No, they won't." Concern shadowed his eyes. "I didn't mean to scare you *that* much. I just wanted to make a point."

"You made it, and I'm not sure how well I'm going to sleep tonight."

"You'll be fine. You can call me if there's a problem. I don't have any appointments tomorrow, so I can come out and check on you. I can do the same thing on Sunday."

"I have a better idea." It wasn't a wise idea, but desperate times called for desperate measures. "Don't take this the wrong way, but would you be willing to spend the weekend with me?"

4

REGAN GULPED. "EXCUSE ME?" His heart galloped out of control. Surely she hadn't suggested what he thought she had. He suddenly had trouble breathing.

Lily, she of the sunset-red hair and sky-blue eyes, seemed completely calm, though. "To be clear, that wasn't a proposition."

"Of course it wasn't. We barely know each other. I didn't think that at all." The hell he hadn't. Stupid of him, but he'd immediately created a cozy scenario for the two of them. Apparently his subconscious had been building a whole fantasy on her *I can't help saying yes* comment.

"The ranch house has a guest room. My mom insisted I should have one in case any of my friends from Berkeley show up. I realize this is a terrible imposition, but after Rex's little stunt, I'm worried about being alone here."

That was mostly his fault. "It's highly unlikely you'll have a problem." But what if she did? What if he drove away from here and something happened? What if she tried to break up a fight and got hurt in the process? He'd never forgive himself.

"I may be overreacting, but I've been jerked out of my blissful ignorance and there's no going back to it. I now understand the potential danger here. You know horses, and you're a vet who could deal with an injury if we were unlucky enough to have one. I'd consider it a huge favor if you'd do this."

He struggled to get his bearings. "Well, I—"

"This is spur of the moment, so if you're willing to stay, you might want to go home and get some things. Where are you living, by the way? I never thought to ask."

"At the Last Chance. Sarah gave me a room there in January, and I haven't decided whether to buy property, so I'm still at the ranch." He worked hard to seem as cool as she was about this discussion. She needed him to be there in case she had a problem with the horses. After the picture he'd painted, he couldn't blame her. Because he'd contributed to her nervousness, he should agree to her plan. It was the gentlemanly thing to do.

Unfortunately, the thought of spending the night in her house continued to suggest ungentlemanly ideas. That didn't mean he would act on them, though. He might have considered a relationship down the road, but getting sexually involved with her when they'd met only this morning would be insane. He'd never operated that way, and he wouldn't start now.

That didn't take into account how *she* operated, however. He considered the psychedelic colors of the buildings and her belief in letting all creatures run free. That could add up to a woman who didn't have rigid rules of behavior when it came to sex. But apparently he did. Could he change those rules given the right circumstances? Yes.

"I can feed the pigs and the chickens if you want to head back to the ranch and pick up a few things. That's if you're even willing to consider doing this."

"So it would ease your mind if I did?" Dumb question. He knew it would because she'd already said so. And he knew his answer was yes.

He was stalling because he hadn't decided whether to drive back to the ranch for a change of clothes and a shaving kit. That could be problematic if he ran into someone who asked questions. No one kept close track of him there, so if he didn't show up, they might assume he was out on a call that lasted into the night. That would be sort of true. He'd like to keep their arrangement on the down-low for now.

"It would greatly ease my mind." She looked up at him. "Please say you'll stay. I'm a decent hostess."

His breath caught. She was pleading with him to do this because she was frightened, not because she wanted him in her bed. Thoughts of sex were far from her mind, and they should be far from his, too. They would be. He'd stay for a couple of nights and guarantee her a peaceful weekend free of worries about her horses.

Maybe in a few weeks the situation would resolve itself and he could ask her out. But only a jerk would take advantage of a woman's fears—fears he'd helped foster. He was better than that.

"I'll stay," he said. "I don't need to go back to the ranch for anything. If you have a spare toothbrush, I can manage." And if he didn't go back to the ranch, he wouldn't be tempted to grab the box of condoms that he'd discovered in the upstairs bathroom. Even more reason to stay right here and be virtuous as hell.

"Thank you, Regan. You're a good guy."

He wasn't so sure about that, but he would do his damnedest to be a good guy for the next forty-eight hours. "Ready to feed the pigs and chickens?"

"Absolutely!" Her bright smile flashed.

Yeah, he could do this. The relief in her smile was all the reward he needed. If he hadn't believed every word of warning he'd spoken, he'd feel guilty about scaring her. But she needed to understand what she was up against. Chances were nothing would happen this weekend, but if it did, he'd be here to help.

Feeding the chickens, it turned out, was easy. He felt like Old MacDonald as he scattered seed over the ground. The pigs were a lot more work. First he and Lily had to chop up an ungodly amount of fresh vegetables. They stood side by side tossing cut-up veggies into two large bowls about the size needed for a batch of cookie dough. He'd never expected to have fun preparing a meal for pigs. Once again his happiness meter registered somewhere near the top of the scale.

He threw a handful of carrot chunks into the bowl. "I thought they ate kitchen scraps."

"Most people think so, but they won't get a balanced diet that way." Lily chopped with rhythmic precision as she talked. "I found all kinds of information online, and everyone says to feed vegetables loaded with vitamins if you want a happy, healthy pig. And you're not supposed to overfeed them or they'll get fat. Harley looks a little overweight to me. What do you think?"

"I didn't spend any time studying pigs, so I'm no expert." Regan started in on a head of cabbage. "But he's definitely chunkier than Wilbur."

"And from what I've researched, Wilbur's about right. I'll have to make sure Harley doesn't try to steal any of Wilbur's food."

Regan finished with the cabbage and moved on to a sack of potatoes. "What if someone wants to adopt these guys? How will you know they'll feed them right?"

"Excellent question. I've thought about it a lot today.

I've considered having the adopters sign an agreement that they'll follow the guidelines I give them and read the information on keeping pigs as pets. But what if they don't? How will I know?"

"You won't, which is why they might need to provide references."

"I think so, too. That's still no guarantee, because they can give me names of people who will say whatever they're supposed to, but it makes the process more complicated. People who want to adopt a pig on impulse won't want to go through all that."

Regan picked up a bunch of golden beets. "At least these are adult pigs, so nobody can kid themselves about the amount of room they'll need."

"I've toyed with the idea of a home visit before I let the pig go."

"It will take lots of extra time to do that."

"I know." Lily topped off her bowl with some bib lettuce. "But after you filled me in about Harley's deal, where his mud hole was competing for space with folks enjoying a backyard barbecue, I think viewing the future living space would be good. The requirements for the pig have to come first."

"Because pigs can't speak for themselves."

"Exactly!" She turned to beam at him. "Most of those who bring me horses, pigs or chickens are ready to dump an inconvenient nuisance. They've never thought about how they play havoc with the lives of creatures who can't speak for themselves. Or how they've contributed to the problem, which I've certainly been guilty of with the horses. I'm determined to fix that."

Regan laid down his knife and turned toward her. "I owe you an apology."

"For what?" She glanced up at him. "You've been nothing but helpful and kind."

"Not really. I've implied that you don't know what you're doing, but at your core, you know exactly what you're doing. You respect the rights of creatures who can't speak our language. They may have their own language, but they can't speak ours—and many of us marginalize them. You don't, and that's...that's wonderful." He had the strongest urge to kiss her, which would be so inappropriate. Coming on the heels of his little speech, it would seem opportunistic.

"Wow. Thank you." She seemed taken aback. "Lately I've been thinking I don't belong in this place."

"Don't ever think that." He'd watch how he worded his suggestions from now on, because he didn't want to discourage her from sticking it out. This morning he'd figured she might leave as soon as she grew bored, an assumption based on how his parents might react in this situation. But listening to her now, he wasn't sure about that.

"I can't help it, Regan. I wasn't qualified to take over, although I didn't have sense enough to know it at the time. But there was no one else, which helped me make up my mind. Now that I realize what I'm up against, I should probably advertise for someone more experienced to buy it and run it."

Damn. In trying to make a point, he'd been too hard on her. "I hope you don't do that. If I've made you insecure about being here, I'm deeply sorry. You may not understand the herd mentality of horses, but that can be learned. What you have, empathy for all animals, is far more important."

She swallowed. "That means a lot to me, Regan. I was feeling pretty much like a dweeb an hour ago, but... what you just said helps."

"I'm glad." He could drown in those blue eyes, and he dared not. She'd invited him here for the good of the horses and so she wouldn't make some terrible mistake that would cause them harm. The emotion he saw in her eyes was related to that, and not to a personal connection between them.

She gazed up at him, her expression soft. Yeah, he wanted to kiss her.

Then she broke eye contact, and the moment was gone. She cleared her throat. "Ready to feed Wilbur and Harley?"

Either he'd misinterpreted the way she'd been looking at him, or she didn't want to get romantically involved. Either way, he'd do well to cool his jets. He gestured toward the bowl he'd been filling. "Nothing else will fit in here, so I suppose the answer is yes."

"Then let's go."

Resolving to avoid any more dreamy-eyed moments, he walked with her out to the mud hole she'd dug behind the ranch house. Once again he marveled at how deep it was. She'd engaged in some serious digging because she'd wanted Wilbur to feel at home, and now Harley could enjoy the results of her labor, too.

Both pigs lay in happy abandon in the mud, but they perked up the minute Lily and Regan arrived with dinner. Regan set down Harley's bowl, careful to put it a distance away from Wilbur's. With squeals of delight, each pig waddled toward his respective dinner and buried his snout in the pile of veggies.

"They're cute." Regan surprised himself by saying that.

"I know. I've already bonded with Wilbur. I have about fifty pictures of him on my phone. I took some of Harley today. They both have the most adorable faces."

"I can't see much of their faces right now, but I like the way they wag their little tails when they're happy. I also expected it to smell bad out here, but it doesn't."

"I'm pretty fanatical about cleaning up after my animals. These pigs may wallow in the mud, but I don't want them to stink. That's gross."

Regan hadn't thought much about it before, but the stalls had been spotless, too. No wonder he'd felt muscles when he'd grabbed her arm. She must be shoveling a good part of the day. "Have you thought of hiring someone to help deal with cleanup?"

"Nick mentioned that, too. I kind of like not worrying about an employee. If push comes to shove, I might have to get someone, but I don't want to rush into it."

Regan nodded and turned his attention back to the pigs. "They sure are tearing into that food, especially Harley."

"From what I've read, they'll eat as much as you give them, and they'll allow themselves to get overweight. But in other ways they're very smart. Their IQ is—wait, I don't need to tell you. You're a vet. You probably know all that."

"I've heard they're intelligent, but that's about all I know. Aren't they smarter than most dogs?"

"They are, and I like that they have brains. I might have to keep these two instead of finding new homes for them."

Regan opened his mouth to say that more pigs would be coming because the word was out. She'd have to make sure she didn't bond with the next one, and the one after that, or she'd be overrun with pigs. Then he closed his mouth again.

If she wanted to keep twenty pigs, it wasn't the same as twenty horses. When the fence crew finally arrived, she could decide if she wanted an enclosure for her current potbellied friends and those who were sure to come later.

"You're worried that I'm going to load up on pigs the way I loaded up on horses and get myself into more trouble, aren't you?"

"Nope."

She laughed. "Liar."

"I do think you'll get more pigs, though. The guy who brought Harley heard about you from the people who had Wilbur. I don't know if there's a potbellied-pig hotline, but I wouldn't be surprised."

"I'm sure there is. I've thought about joining a potbellied-pig chat group, but I haven't had time. Maybe once I reduce the number of horses, I can hook up with other people who have pigs. These guys fascinate me. They're so different from your average domestic animal."

"That's for sure."

"Some people let them in the house, but I'm not ready to—whoops. There goes Harley after Wilbur's food." Lily hurried over and blocked Harley's progress. He let out an ear-splitting scream of frustration and plowed past her, knocking her smack-dab into the mud hole.

Without thinking twice, Regan waded in after her.

"Forget about me!" she wailed. "Pick up Wilbur's food bowl!"

"To hell with Wilbur's food bowl." He extended his hand. "Grab hold."

Harley had shoved Wilbur aside and was eagerly crunching on the remainder of the smaller pig's food. "I guess it's too late to get the food, anyway," she said. "He might try to bite you."

"*Might?* Did you hear him? I don't think there's any

doubt he'd bite me." Harley wasn't the least bit cute anymore, either. Lily, on the other hand, was very cute sitting in the mud, her face and clothes splattered with globs of the stuff. He had a sudden image of her as a teenager in an old T-shirt and jeans with the knees busted out. In fact, she didn't look much older than sixteen now.

But the water and mud had begun to soak through her shirt. Very soon she'd go from cute to voluptuous, and that wouldn't be a good thing for a guy trying to keep his mind off sex. He wiggled his fingers. "Come on. Let's get you outta there."

With a sigh of resignation, she reached for his hand. "I'm all muddy."

"Are you? I hadn't noticed."

"Smart-ass. The sad thing is, your boots and the bottom of your jeans are muddy, too."

"That's the breaks." She was slippery now, and he had trouble getting a grip on her. "Better give me both hands so I don't drop you back in the water."

He pulled, and she came out with a giant sucking sound, and way faster than he'd expected. Before he could adjust for her trajectory, she'd slammed into his chest. Good thing he'd dug in his heels before starting this maneuver or they would have both gone down. Instead they were plastered together like sheets of wet newspaper. He wrapped his arms around her to steady himself and discovered he was enjoying it far too much.

"Sorry. Didn't mean to do that." She tried to extricate herself.

Thrown off balance by her movements, he wobbled. "Careful. I don't have the best of footing. We're teetering."

She stood still. "Yeah, no point in making this any

worse than it already is." She lifted her chin and looked into his eyes. She must have seen something more than simple concern there, because her breath hitched. "How do you suggest we proceed?"

"With caution." His pulse rate skyrocketed. So she'd guessed that he wanted to kiss her, mud specks and all. If she didn't want him to, he'd see it in her expression—a slight frown, a subtle narrowing of her eyes.

But she wasn't doing either of those things. Instead her eyes widened and her pupils dilated. "I absolutely agree." She ran her tongue over her lips, not in a seductive way, but quickly, as if checking for mud in case he decided to follow through.

"About what?" He'd lost track of the conversation. All his attention was focused on her plump lips, which were shiny from her tongue.

"Caution. Proceeding with it."

"You want to proceed?"

"I do." Her eyes darkened to midnight blue and her gentle sigh was filled to the brim with surrender as her arms slid around his neck, depositing mud along the way.

As if he gave a damn. His body hummed with anticipation. "Me, too." Slowly he lowered his head and closed his eyes.

"Mistake, though."

He hovered near her mouth, hardly daring to breathe. Had she changed her mind at the last minute? "Why?"

"Tell you later." She brought his head down and made the connection.

And it was as electric as he'd imagined. His blood fizzed as it raced through his body and eventually settled in his groin. Her lips fit perfectly against his from the first moment of contact. It seemed his mouth had been created for kissing Lily, and vice versa.

He tried a different angle, just to test that theory. Still perfect, still high voltage. Since they were standing in water, it was a wonder they didn't short out. He couldn't speak for her, but he'd bet he was glowing. His skin was hot enough to send off sparks.

She moaned and pressed her body closer. She felt amazing in his arms—soft, wet and slippery. He'd never imagined doing it in the mud, but suddenly that seemed like the best idea in the world.

Then she snorted. Odd. Not the reaction he would have expected considering where this seemed to be heading.

He lifted his head and gazed into her flushed face. "Did you just laugh?"

She regarded him with passion-filled eyes. "That wasn't me."

"Then who—"

The snort came again as something bumped the back of his knees. A heavy splash sent water up the back of his legs.

She might not have been laughing before, but she was now. "Um, we have company."

Although it didn't matter which pig had interrupted the moment, Regan had his money on Harley. Whichever one had decided to take an after-dinner mud bath, they'd ruined what had been a very promising kiss. Well, except for Lily's comment that it was a mistake.

Regan had hoped to move right past that comment, but he had a feeling she'd want to explain it more fully now that they weren't in a lip-lock. He knew one thing for sure, though. He was no longer a fan of those pigs.

5

Lily and Regan took off their muddy boots on the stoop outside the back door, which led directly into the kitchen. Once they were both inside, she grabbed some paper towels so they could clean off their hands. "Stay there for a sec." She finished wiping her hands. "I'll be right back with a robe for you."

She left the kitchen, hurried away from him through the small dining room and down a short hallway to the master bedroom and bath. She didn't want to discuss their kiss until they'd dealt with the mud.

She needed to tell him why the kiss had been a mistake, and therein lay her dilemma. She'd promised Nick she wouldn't mention Regan's breakup. Yet the breakup was at the heart of why she and Regan shouldn't become involved.

A brief period of insanity in a mud hole didn't have to turn into a full-blown disaster if she played this right. She'd lost focus when she'd inadvertently ended up in his arms, but she could make that momentary slip right. To fix it permanently, though, she had to explain how she felt about catching a guy on the rebound. That meant unearthing the truth about his situation…somehow, without involving Nick in any way.

Snatching her white terry robe from the hook on the back of her bathroom door, she returned to the kitchen. "This won't fit very well," she said as she handed him the robe, "but at least it's not pink."

He took it gingerly, being careful not to let it brush up against his muddy clothes. "I'm afraid I'll bust out your shoulder seams."

"It's roomier than it looks. And it's all I have for you to wear while I wash and dry your stuff. Just try it. I think you'll be surprised."

The corner of his mouth quirked up. "This whole evening has been one big surprise. I can't wait to see what happens next."

She decided not to touch that line. "The guest room is through the living room and down the hall on your right. There's a bathroom down there, too, and it's stocked with towels and stuff."

"Because your mom insisted."

"Yep. Turns out you're my first guest."

"I'm honored." He gave her an assessing glance. "Listen, are we going to talk about…"

"Sure. Absolutely. But let's get cleaned up, first. The lasagna is almost done."

"I figured. It smells great."

"I'll meet you back here in a little while. You should find everything you need. My mom's thorough about such things."

He nodded. "I'll be fine. See you in a few." Dangling the robe several inches in front of his body, he left the kitchen.

She retreated to her own bathroom. Moments later she stood under a hot shower and evaluated her predicament. She'd brought it on herself, every bit of it. Her decision to buy Peaceful Kingdom had caused her to add more horses, two pigs and nine chickens. And she'd let them all roam at will. As if she hadn't created a big enough mess, she'd begged Regan to spend the next couple of nights in her house.

She'd had some room to maneuver…until she'd kissed him. She couldn't even claim that was his fault. He'd given her every opportunity to back out, but once she'd been chest to chest with all that glorious male beauty, she hadn't been able to resist him.

She could have stopped him at the very last minute, but what had she done? Pulled his head down and kissed the living daylights out of him, that's what. She was not what anyone would call a clutch player.

So now she had to clean up this fuster-cluck. Sending him home wasn't a solution, because sure as the world, she'd have an emergency and he'd end up back here, anyway. She was sitting on a keg of dynamite in more ways than one. Even her pigs weren't behaving themselves. Until she could get someone to build some sturdy fences, she needed Regan around.

That would work out just ducky if she could keep her hands to herself. He wasn't a Don Juan type who was plotting a seduction. If she set the boundaries, he'd abide by them. But she'd kissed him as if boundaries meant nothing. How to explain why she didn't want to continue with an activity she'd so obviously enjoyed?

Only one strategy occurred to her. If she could loosen his tongue so that he'd tell her about the breakup, she could explain why she chose to stay away from rebound relationships. She could say she'd sensed he might be hurting but hadn't wanted to pry. He might buy that.

It wasn't the greatest plan in the world, but she

couldn't think of anything better. She had both beer and wine chilling in the refrigerator. The trick would be getting him to drink it while she only sipped.

Her bathroom routine took longer than she would have liked, but she'd had to wash her hair, and that meant doing something with it afterward. Blowing it dry would take forever, so she gathered it into a loose, damp arrangement on top of her head.

Leaving makeup off was a no-brainer. She wasn't trying to be more alluring, for crying out loud. Some old underwear might keep her from getting frisky.

Oh, hell, whom was she kidding? She'd never been the type to fuss with her appearance. She was strictly WYSIWYG—What You See Is What You Get. But if she didn't look sexy, that might make a difference to Regan. She put on her most raggedy sweatpants and a faded sweatshirt from Berkeley.

One glance in the mirror convinced her she'd done an awesome job. Only a desperate man would want to hit that. Of course, if Regan had gone without for six months, he might be on the desperate side. That also should be a warning to stay clear. He might not be hot for her, specifically. Maybe any reasonably good-looking woman would do.

After shoving her feet into some ratty slippers that once had been blue but had faded to a mottled gray, she padded into the aromatic kitchen with her armload of muddy clothes. Regan was nowhere in sight, so she carried her bundle into the laundry room located right off the kitchen and loaded the filthy clothes and some soap into the washing machine. Technically they shouldn't all be washed together, but mud was a game changer, in her opinion. Once he arrived with his clothes, they'd do a load of mud laundry and call it good.

"Here's my stuff."

She turned, and much as she tried not to, she stared. No woman with a pulse would have done any different when faced with Regan O'Connelli in an undersize bathrobe. He stretched the shoulders of that white terry to the breaking point, and the lapels didn't quite meet, so a sliver of his chest, complete with enticing dark hair, peeked through the opening.

He'd belted the robe as tightly as possible. Because he had narrow hips, the overlap was more than adequate there. Good thing, if he'd included his briefs in that pile he'd brought her. Although, in the long run, whether he was covered up didn't matter much. She still knew he likely was naked under that robe. How had she failed to calculate the effect of that on her little plan?

She accepted the clothes and shoved them in the washer. If he had any loose change or important pieces of paper in his pockets, oh, well. She wasn't taking the time to check. Her primary goal was to get everything washed and back on his body. His muscled, golden-skinned, infinitely lickable body…

Dear Lord, she was done for. Turning away from the washer, she dusted her hands together. "There. That's done."

"Lily?"

"What?"

"You didn't turn it on."

No, I didn't, because I'm already turned on enough for both me and the washer to operate at top speed. "Thanks." She walked back and punched the button.

"You were right." He held out his arms. "This fits better than I thought it would."

"So it does." She spun on her heel, because if she

looked at him for even one second longer, she'd grab the sash of that robe and have her way with him. "Let's eat."

"Sounds good. I'm starving." He followed her into the kitchen.

She could swear, even though he was a good ten feet away from her, she heard every breath he took. She imagined what it would be like to run her fingers through his still-damp hair, to lay her palm against his chest and feel his heart pumping hot blood through his veins. Despite the spicy aroma of baked lasagna, she could smell the soap-fresh scent of his skin, and the underlying musk of virile, almost-naked male.

Her plan for resisting him seemed flimsy at best, but she'd stick to it as well as she could. "Which would you like with dinner, wine or beer?"

"With lasagna? Wine, I guess."

"Wine it is, then!" She knew she sounded deranged. Grabbing two wineglasses out of the cupboard, she took the Chardonnay out of the fridge.

"Let me open it." He walked over to the counter. "Got a corkscrew somewhere?"

"You bet. Second drawer from the left." She snatched up a couple of pot holders and made a beeline for the oven, which put some distance between her and Mr. Yum-Yum. If she'd had anything else to cover his body besides the terry robe, she'd be hauling it out now. There was the Hawaiian muumuu her mother had brought her from a trip to Maui a few years ago. Regan probably wouldn't go for that.

She pulled the lasagna pan out of the oven and managed to set it on top of the stove without dropping it. That was a little miracle in itself, considering how her hands were shaking.

"Wine?"

"Oh!" She turned to find him right next to her, a glass of Chardonnay extended. "Sure. Thanks." She accepted the glass and promptly gulped down a third of it before she remembered that hadn't been the strategy. But Regan O'Connelli was standing in her kitchen, naked except for a bathrobe that could come open *at any moment.* How could she be expected to keep her cool under those circumstances?

"Can I set the table?"

"Good idea." And it would get him out of the kitchen for a little while. "Utensils are in the first drawer from the left. You're a terrific guest. Somebody must have trained you well." No telling why she'd been compelled to say *that,* except that she tended to babble when she was nervous.

"My ex. I think she'd memorized the etiquette books."

Lily went completely still. Damn. A clue. Without getting him sloshed, she'd managed to extract a significant clue. But she had to handle the information with great delicacy. "You have an ex?" She hoped her nose wouldn't grow for that whopper.

"Doesn't everybody?"

Beep. Wrong answer. She closed her eyes in frustration. "I suppose so. I have an ex-boyfriend. What sort of ex do you have?" She crossed her fingers.

"Ex-fiancée."

"Ah. Recent?" She held her breath.

"Since last Christmas."

"Ouch. Tough time to break up."

He walked back, leaned in the archway separating the kitchen from the dining room and sipped his wine. "Is there ever a good time?"

"Guess not." Her heart ached for him. Nobody should

be betrayed at Christmas, when everyone else was laughing and partying and kissing under the mistletoe. But he hadn't said his ex had betrayed him, only that they'd broken up. Lily vowed to remember that she was supposed to know only what he'd told her and nothing more.

She had enough information to make her case against sleeping with a guy on the rebound. Once they got into a discussion about the kiss they'd shared while standing in the mud hole, she'd be ready with her argument. She'd apologize for surrendering to the moment.

Most women succumbed to a man's charms under a silver moon while surrounded by fragrant blossoms and serenaded by violins. She'd almost given it up in a mud puddle.

"How soon before we eat?"

She snapped out of her daydream. Men liked to eat. She'd been without a boyfriend since last fall, and she'd forgotten a few things about the male of the species. "Let's give it ten more minutes to cool and set. I'd suggest we have a seat in the living room, but I don't have any furniture in there yet."

"I noticed."

"I'll get some eventually. My parents gave me their old dining room table and chairs, but they're not ready to replace their living room stuff."

He gazed at her, a question in his eyes.

"You probably wonder why I don't just go out and get my own."

"It crossed my mind. You must care about this place, since you spent a lot of time painting the outside of all the buildings."

"Because painting is fun! I would have painted inside, too, but then more horses arrived, along with the chickens, and now the pigs, so I don't have time. And everyone knows you're supposed to paint before you bring in furniture." She tried not to stare at his legs, but the hem of the bathrobe reached only to his knees. Nice calves. Yeah, very nice.

"That's a good point. Painting should come first."

"But that's not the real reason. I can't get excited about furniture." But she was getting quite excited about watching the gentle rise and fall of his chest. Whenever he breathed in, the terry shifted to reveal more of that delicious territory. It would be so easy to walk over and slide her hands under the lapels…

"I thought women like shopping for furniture. In general, I mean."

Furniture. Right. She redirected her thoughts to the topic at hand. "It all looks the same to me—boring." Which certainly wasn't a word she'd use to describe Regan. His thighs were probably as impressive as his calves. "I'd be fine with those throw pillows you might have seen stacked in the corner, and maybe a beanbag chair. But my mom convinced me I need a couch. They'll be replacing theirs soon, and at that point my dad will bring me their old one."

"Is their couch boring?" Amusement lit his brown eyes.

Luckily her attention had been on his face at the time, so she caught that. "I'm afraid so, but then, what couch isn't? And it's not just the color, which in this case is beige. I realize you can find them in red, or purple, or paisley. I object to the basic shape—a big, bulky rectangle that takes up space and dominates the room. And is heavy. Omigod. A couch can weigh you down."

"I never thought of it that way." He sipped his wine and the bathrobe sleeve gaped open, exposing his entire forearm. His skin was tanned to a golden hue, probably a gift from his Italian ancestry.

She bet he tasted as good as he looked, but she continued the conversation as if she had no interest in licking him all over. "Couches aren't practical, either. Three people *could* sit there, but then they'd be like birds on a rail, or people waiting to have their group picture taken."

He laughed at that, and the terry lapels shifted again. *Mercy.* "No, really! In practice, only two people ever sit on a couch, even though it takes up so much floor space."

"Sometimes two people lie on a couch." Was that a challenging gleam in his eye?

"Yes, and it's crunched and crowded. A bed's better." She sucked in a breath. Where had that come from? Yikes!

"More wine?"

She glanced at the glass in her hand and discovered it was empty. Apparently she'd been chattering, ogling and drinking. The only thing she could say in her defense was that she hadn't been licking and kissing. Did she know how to draw a line in the sand or what?

Setting her glass firmly on the counter, she opened a cupboard. "I'm going to hold off on the wine for now. I'm sure the lasagna's ready. I'll dish up."

"I have an idea."

If he had one idea, she had twenty, and they all involved untying the sash of his robe. She pulled two plates out of the cupboard. "What's that?"

"Let's build a fire and sit on the floor in the living room. It's cool enough tonight for one, and I noticed you have wood."

"The Turners left me some, and I used some last

month. It was a cool May." His idea sounded different and fun. And potentially dangerous.

"So what do you say? We can sit on two of those floor pillows."

"I guess that would work."

"It'll work great." He drained his glass and left it on the counter. "I'll start the fire while you serve the lasagna."

He'd already started a fire, and she had no extinguisher handy. Eating picnic style on the floor could heat things up even more. The whole setup was becoming too cozy, and she wasn't helping. She gave herself a stern reminder about the speech she was going to deliver, even if she could have done that more effectively while sitting at the dining room table.

Too late to change her mind, though. The sound of crinkling newspaper and logs settling onto the grate indicated he was into his fire-building routine. "Is the flue open?" he called out.

"No, it isn't. Pull the lever toward you."

Metal creaked. "Got it. You know, I figured you for a picnic-on-the-floor kind of woman. I couldn't ever convince Jeannette to do this, but I thought for sure you'd be all over it."

So his ex's name was Jeannette. And she didn't go for picnics on the floor in front of the fireplace. Lily should ignore that thrown gauntlet. But being a normal woman, she wanted to prove that she was more accommodating than dumb old Jeannette, the idiot who had betrayed this beautiful man on Christmas Eve. The question remained, how accommodating did Lily plan to be?

6

REGAN WASN'T OBLIVIOUS to the effect he was having on Lily. He wasn't above using it to his advantage, either. He could hardly be blamed for wearing a bathrobe that was several sizes too small for him. His only other option was a towel, and that wouldn't have helped matters.

As they settled themselves on her colorful striped pillows and balanced their plates in their laps, he was careful to keep the bathrobe closed over his crotch. This game was all about teasing, anyway, not flashing the goods. Besides, nothing could happen between them without those little raincoats. He doubted she had a supply. The woman didn't even own a make-out couch.

She was a puzzle in so many ways. Even though she couldn't stop looking at him, he could tell that she was fighting her reaction tooth and nail. She'd kissed him with enthusiasm, but she'd cautioned him that it was a mistake. He needed to find out why she'd said that, and sitting casually in front of a fire seemed like a better venue for sharing confidences than perched at the formal-looking dining table.

She'd agreed to a second glass of wine, but she was

taking tiny sips instead of knocking it back the way she had her first glass. Her speech about furniture in general and couches in particular had been entertaining. Enlightening, too. She viewed a couch as a boring anchor, so maybe she was more like his parents than he wanted to believe. Maybe, despite her dedication to these animals, she'd grow tired of being in one place and take off. He might want to keep that in mind.

For sure Lily was nothing like Jeannette. Jeannette had been perfectly okay with owning an expensive and very boring couch. Now that he thought about it, that couch might have been a symbol for whatever had been missing in their relationship. He'd asked Jeannette to marry him because he'd cared for her. Now, though, he questioned whether they'd truly been in love.

She'd appealed to him because she was deeply rooted in her hometown and she had ambition. After growing up with his rootless and unfocused parents, he craved Jeannette's lifestyle and figured they'd be blissfully happy enjoying emotional and financial stability. And a boring couch.

They'd had all that, but not much in the way of wild passion. If he were honest, he'd admit that the life they'd created as an engaged couple hadn't been very stimulating. Getting married wouldn't have changed that dynamic. She might have been bored, too, although she'd never said so. That she had sex with his best friend might have been a small indication. Ha. No kidding.

One thing he could say after spending time with Lily King—he wasn't bored. She appeared to have as many facets as the crystals hanging in her living room windows. They were the only decorations she'd put up, and there was something soothing about her minimalist approach, especially with a cheerful blaze crackling in the fireplace.

Crystals always reminded him of his mother, who loved them. As he watched the crystals reflect the light from the fire, he felt a tug of nostalgia. And he was *never* nostalgic about his parents.

His vegetarian folks also would have praised Lily's lasagna. Regan glanced over at her. "You didn't exaggerate about your cooking skills." He pointed his fork at the generous helping on his plate. "This is terrific."

"Thank you. Listen, Regan, we need to talk about that kiss."

Good thing she hadn't said that when he was drinking wine. As it was, he nearly tipped the lasagna right off his plate. But he recovered quickly enough to keep it from falling into his lap, which would have been bad on many levels. The food was hot, his privates weren't well protected and this was his only outfit.

Putting the plate safely beside him, he cleared his throat and turned to her. "Okay. Let's talk."

"You don't have to stop eating."

"I think I do. This is important."

"All right then." She put down her plate, too. "The kiss was a mistake." She looked him in the eye, her expression resolute.

"How come?"

"You broke up with your fiancée six months ago, right?"

"Right."

"I'll take a wild guess that you haven't dated anyone since then."

"Nope, and that's why I felt completely free to kiss *you.* And from the way you kissed *me,* I'd say you're not dating anyone, either."

"I'm not, but that isn't the point I wanted to make. If you haven't dated since you ended your engagement, you're on target for a rebound relationship."

He blinked. Although he hadn't known what to expect from this discussion, that comment took him by surprise. "Who says?"

"It's common knowledge."

"What the hell? Is the entire population of the Jackson Hole area discussing my love life?"

"No, of course not. I didn't mean it that way. I'm just saying it's generally accepted that people suffering a breakup usually rebound to someone else for temporary comfort and a chance to get their groove back."

"Yeah, yeah, I know what you're talking about, but not everybody goes through that. And what's with me being *on target* for it? Is six months significant? Is there some timetable I don't know about?" And underneath that barrage of questions was guilt, because his thoughts this morning could easily be interpreted as a guy wanting to *get his groove back,* as she'd termed it.

"No timetable. But why haven't you dated since you broke up with Jeannette?"

"Didn't feel like it." He took a gulp of his wine. His mellow mood was disappearing fast.

"But now you do feel like it?"

"I did until this conversation started. Not sure that's still true."

"So you're not attracted to me anymore? Is that because I hit the nail on the head?"

He gazed at her, and his irritation faded. "You might have hit the nail a glancing blow."

She blew out a breath. "Thanks for admitting that."

"And for the record, I'm still attracted to you."

"Maybe because you're at the stage where you need someone and I'm handy."

"No. It's not like that." She was so much more than *handy.* Tendrils of her hair had escaped from the arrangement on top of her head, and they seemed to dance and glow whenever she moved. The freckles across the bridge of her nose beckoned to him, tempting him to kiss each and every one.

He anticipated his next move. The scent of her shampoo drifted across the space between them, drawing him closer. He longed to slide his hand up the curve of her neck, cradle her head and finally allow himself to taste her pink lips again. This time they would make that magical connection without benefit of mud or pesky pigs.

But for some reason, she was trying to give him the brush-off. He could feel it coming. But he couldn't let her think his interest was based on her being *handy.* "You're beautiful, Lily. Any man would feel lucky to be with you."

Her expression grew tender. "Not true, Regan. I don't have men beating a path to my door."

"You should."

"I understand why they don't. I'm different from most women. As you've noticed, I paint things wild colors. I mean *really* wild. I don't care about fancy clothes, or jewelry or makeup."

"You don't need those things."

"That's sweet of you to say, but I have a few other handicaps where men are concerned. I'm smart, although I've never understood why that makes men nervous. Nevertheless, it does. Earning piles of money doesn't interest me. The computer game seems to be bringing in a fair bit, but that wasn't my goal. I was just goofing around when I created it. Some guys, maybe most guys, would say I'm weird."

Her description of herself included many of the tendencies he'd worked hard to banish from his life—impulsive behavior, indifference to money, lack of defined career goals. The woman *was* on the flaky side, which should make him avoid her like the plague. Instead he wanted her so much he ached.

He decided against saying that. She was convinced that he wanted her only because they'd met when he was ready to get back in the game. "You mentioned an ex-boyfriend. What happened there?" If she could discuss his situation, then he should be able to ask about hers.

"Simple. He works for a computer-game company and he taught me how to create a game. So I did and sold it to his company. But then I lost interest."

Regan took note of that, but he wasn't ready to build a whole case on it. Making up a computer game would have been a one-shot deal for him, too. It was about electronics, not living creatures. "So then what?"

"He begged me to create more computer games and make a bunch of money. He started test-driving fancy cars and checking out coastline real estate. Then he offered to take over as my manager-slash-accountant because I obviously didn't want to deal with the financial side of my business, according to him. I didn't have a *business,* just one silly game."

"In other words, he wanted to use you to get rich."

"Pretty much. We had a big fight, and I threw him out of my funky little apartment in San Francisco."

"Which had no couch."

She pointed a finger at him. "Right. Anyway, we'd managed fine there for about a year until I sold the game and he started seeing dollar signs whenever he looked at me. Come to think of it, his affections increased in proportion to the size of my royalty checks."

"Bastard."

"He said I was wasting my talent. He even tried to make a case for a troubled world needing my happy games. That way he could pretend he was pressuring me for the good of humankind, when all he really cared about was the good of Alfred G. Dinwoody."

"That was his name? Alfred G. Dinwoody?"

"Yep. After my game became a hit, he insisted I start calling him A.G. instead of Al. He said it sounded cooler."

"And I thought I had it rough being stuck with O'Connelli."

"Are you kidding? Your name is fantastic! I've been dying to ask you where it came from."

So he told her, and naturally she loved the concept. She'd get along with his parents like peanut butter and jelly. His explanation led to more questions, and eventually she wormed the whole story of his vagabond childhood out of him.

Sometime during the telling, she suggested they eat their dinner before it got stone-cold. That made sense, so they picked up their plates and dug in while they continued to talk and drink more wine. He refreshed the fire, and she left with their empty plates while promising to bring back a package of sandwich cookies for dessert.

She didn't fancy them up by putting them on a plate, either. She arrived in the living room with the open package and handed it to him. "Be warned that I twist them apart and lick out the filling. If that grosses you out, too bad."

He reached inside for a cookie. “I’m used to it. Half my family eats them that way.” He gave her the bag.

“The O’Connor half or the Spinelli half?” She pulled out a cookie and set the bag between them.

“Some of each.” He bit into his cookie. The taste rocketed him right back to his childhood. Jeannette wouldn’t have dreamed of serving packaged sandwich cookies for dessert, let alone right out of the bag.

“I figure you took after your mom’s side. Do any of your brothers and sisters look Irish?”

“They do. In fact, two of my sisters have red hair like my dad’s, but it’s not the same shade as yours.”

Lily groaned. “I’m not surprised. Nobody has hair the shade of mine. It’s the bane of my existence.” She twisted her cookie apart.

“You’re kidding, right?” This time he took out two cookies.

“Why would I be kidding? It’s a shocking color that goes with almost nothing, and it’s so curly it’s impossible to style. Most of the time my head looks like a giant orange chrysanthemum.” She proceeded to lick the frosting from her cookie.

Watching her clean the last bit of vanilla from the chocolate didn’t gross him out, but it might turn him on if he paid too much attention. He’d recently been in intimate contact with that tongue of hers and wouldn’t mind repeating the experience. But she seemed to think he wanted to kiss her only because he was ready to start kissing girls again and she was available.

His attraction to her didn’t feel like that, but he was unsure of his position and didn’t want to argue the point. That meant no kissing would happen anytime soon, no matter how her cookie-eating affected him. So he focused on the burning logs, instead, and continued the conversation. "I happen to like your hair."

"You're just saying that to be nice, but thanks, anyway."

He finished chewing and swallowed. "No, I mean it." He looked at her so she'd know he was serious. She'd already twisted another cookie apart but wasn't into the licking routine yet. "You said that the wild colors on the house and barn make you happy. When I look at your hair, especially in the sunlight, it makes me happy."

"Really?" She smiled. "That might be the best compliment a guy has ever given me. Thank you." She lifted the frosted half of the cookie to her mouth.

That was his cue to turn away.

"You *are* grossed out! I can tell!"

"Nope." He bit down hard on his latest cookie and stared into the flames while he chewed.

"Yes, you are, or you wouldn't have turned your head like that. You turned it really quick, too. I know avoidance when I see it."

He swallowed and reached into the bag without looking at her. "I'm just enjoying the fire." That wasn't working, either, because the flames were systematically licking the wood. He'd never considered fireplace logs to be phallic symbols, but they were tonight.

"Sorry, I don't believe you. If it bothers you that much, I'll eat this one the normal way. I'm putting the top back on, so you can relax."

He glanced at her. "I really don't care how you eat that cookie."

"Oh, you care, all right. It surprises me, because after the way you waded into the mud, I didn't peg you as a finicky person."

"I'm not." He hesitated, torn between admitting the real problem or letting her think he was squeamish.

Finally his ego won out. "Watching you lick the frosting is...erotic."

Her eyes widened. "Oh."

"Happy, now?"

"No, I'm not happy. I apologize. I had no idea."

"We might as well get this out in the open. I'm sexually attracted to you, Lily. You seem convinced it's only a rebound situation, which means my reaction would be the same with any good-looking woman and isn't specific to you. Do I have that right?"

"Um, I guess so." Color rose in her cheeks, making her freckles stand out. "When you explain it like that, it sounds kind of insulting."

"It insults both of us."

"I suppose it does. Sorry about that."

"Apology accepted. But I assume that the possibility of me being on the rebound is why you think kissing me was a mistake."

She nodded.

"But when you kissed me, I hadn't told you about breaking up with Jeannette. Yet you said then it was a mistake and you'd explain later."

Her color heightened further and she glanced away. "I...sensed that you had some...secret anguish."

"Oh?" That sounded like bull to him. "Are you psychic?"

"A little, maybe. I pick up on things. Besides that, you kept your sunglasses on the whole time we talked this morning."

"The sun was very bright." But he had to admit he'd taken to wearing those shades more often following that last miserable Christmas, so she could have a point. He'd think about that one. "Okay, let's say that was a clue that I had a...how did you put it? Secret anguish?"

"I said that, yes." She looked uncomfortable as hell.

"What made you jump to the conclusion that it was connected to my love life?"

"Well, it was!"

"Yes, but you didn't know that until after we kissed. A *secret anguish* could apply to all kinds of things. It didn't have to be about romance gone wrong. Something's not adding up."

She swallowed. "You're right. And I can't tell you what it is."

"Why not?"

"I just can't." She grabbed the bag of cookies and pushed herself to her feet. "I need to put our clothes in the dryer."

He got up. "I'll help."

"No, don't. I'll handle it." She glanced at the fireplace. "The fire's going out."

"Want me to build it back up again?" He doubted it.

"No." She avoided looking at him. "I think it's time to call it a night, don't you?"

"Apparently so. But I can load the dishwasher while you're dealing with the clothes."

She finally met his gaze. "The dishes are taken care of. I put everything in before I brought out the cookies. If you'll bank the fire and put the pillows back, I'd appreciate it. Good night, Regan. Sleep well."

"I doubt I will." He looked into her blue eyes. She might say she didn't want to get involved with him, but her eyes told a different story. Desire flickered there, waiting for him to fan the flames.

"Why?"

"Damn it, you know why." His control threatened to snap.

"I don't. I—"

"Because I'll be thinking about doing this." With a growl of frustration, he reached for her, cookie bag and all. He had one brief glimpse of her startled expression before he kissed her for all he was worth.

And she kissed him back. God, did she ever. Open-mouthed and frantic, she burst into flames as he'd known she would. Wiggling closer, she pressed her sweet body against his in a move guaranteed to send him into orbit.

He moaned and shoved both hands under her sweat-shirt, desperate to touch her silky skin. She answered by dropping the cookies and sliding her palms under the bathrobe's lapels. Eager hands. She touched him as if she couldn't get enough. The rapid stroke of her palms against his skin drove him wild. *This. Yes, this!* His cock thrust against the terry cloth, and he wanted her with an intensity that made him dizzy.

Abruptly she twisted out of his arms. Breathing hard, she spun away from him.

"Lily…" He heard the plea in his voice. Couldn't help it.

"I don't want this."

"Yes, you do."

"Okay, I do." She gulped for air. "But it's a bad idea."

"I don't get it. That kiss was *hot.* And I've seen the way you look at me. Before dinner, while we were standing in the kitchen, I half expected you to jump my bones."

When she faced him again, her cheeks were bright pink. "I'm…I'm sorry about that. The robe is revealing."

"Something I couldn't do much about."

"I know. I apologize for ogling."

"Don't apologize! I was flattered, but I'm confused as hell. What's going on?"

She straightened her shoulders. "Let me explain. I was involved with a guy on the rebound a couple of years ago. My friends warned me not to get too attached, but I did." She took another unsteady breath. "I won't pretend that we were soul mates or anything, but I didn't expect him to take off the minute he was over his breakup."

"But…he did." He could see where this was going. He would pay for another guy's callous behavior.

"Yes, he was gone like a shot and immediately hooked up with another woman. None of that was pleasant. My friends were right. He used me to feel better about himself, and once his ego was repaired, he dropped me for someone else. Maybe I was a reminder of that bad period. Whatever. The girl who comes after a breakup usually doesn't make the cut."

"I don't know the statistics on that, but the guy was a jerk." That made two users she'd been involved with recently.

"He was, but from what I hear, the pattern is fairly predictable, so that's why I have a rule. No rebound relationships."

"I understand why you would make that rule." He ran his fingers through his hair and dragged in some air while he tried to think this through. Something didn't add up. He gazed at her in confusion. "How do you know my ego needs repairing? All I said was that I broke up with my fiancée. As it happens, it was my decision to leave. For all you know, my ego's in fine shape."

"Then why haven't you dated before now?"

He didn't have a good answer for that, so he countered with a question of his own. "Have you dated since you broke up with your boyfriend?"

"No, but that's different."

"How?"

Her blush deepened. "Good night, Regan. I'll put your dry clothes in your bathroom. See you in the morning."

He thought about pushing the issue. She'd already proved she was a softie, as the guy had said this morning. When someone needed her, she couldn't say no. But taking advantage of her generous heart would be a lousy thing to do. It wasn't how he rolled.

They still hadn't finished their discussion, though. Why had she assumed that his ego had been bruised by his fiancée? He was missing some key fact.

Well, he had time to sort it out and examine his own motivation for wanting her. She deserved more than a rebound guy, and if that was truly his deal, then he should admit it and move on. If not, then he would convince her that this attraction was real and exceedingly specific to her, Lily King of the wild red hair and blue, blue eyes.

She'd asked him to stay through the weekend. In the next couple of days, he'd figure everything out. He wasn't about to give up on her yet.

7

Ironically, Lily had asked Regan to stay for the weekend so she wouldn't be awake all night worrying about the animals. Instead worry about Regan and the potential of causing a problem between him and Nick kept her awake. Well, that and sexual frustration. Her resolve to stay out of the rebound trap was being seriously tested, and she was kept awake for longer than she'd like to admit.

She woke up earlier than usual, too, but that was fine because she wanted a head start on Regan. Putting on a clean pair of jeans and another of her favorite tie-dyed shirts, she pushed her feet into the boots she'd wiped off before going to bed. Then she brushed her teeth and wrestled with her hair until she had it secured with a clip at the back of her neck. The soft glow of dawn had just begun as she headed for the kitchen.

It was empty, as she'd expected it would be, which gave her time to brew the coffee, feed the horses and chickens, and maybe even chop veggies for the pigs before he woke up. The more she could accomplish, the less they'd end up doing together.

If it weren't so early, she'd call Nick Chance and confess that she'd made a mess of things. But he wouldn't appreciate being roused from sleep on a Saturday morning so that she could unburden herself. Basically she wanted his permission to tell Regan what she knew about the breakup.

As she plugged in the coffeepot, she wondered if she could find a way to take all the blame for Nick spilling the beans. She could say she pestered him until he accidentally said something that had allowed her to guess what had happened. Under the circumstances, Regan might not care if she knew, anyway. They'd moved past the acquaintance stage, so it might be fine with him that she knew.

On the other hand, Lily wasn't keen on telling Nick about the mud incident, which had led to the kiss encounter and prompted yet another kiss later on. Nick didn't need to know any of that, or that Regan had ended up wearing her bathrobe for the evening meal. She tried not to think about that too much, either. The mental image of Regan in the bathrobe still got her hot.

She probably should move past her fears about the animals rebelling and find a gracious way to let him leave today. She had no idea how to bring that up after begging him to stay, though. Besides, asking him to go implied that she was more afraid of an ill-advised relationship with him than she was worried about the animals running amok.

That didn't say much for her self-control or her priorities, now, did it? She'd have to think this over while she fed the horses. Tucking her phone in her hip pocket, she started to unlock the back door and realized it wasn't locked in the first place. Either she'd forgotten last night or Regan had beaten her to the punch, after all.

She had her answer as soon as she stepped out onto

the stoop and glanced to her left, toward the corral. Regan, dressed in the dry clothes she'd left in his bathroom and wearing his hat, was working with Rex. He'd clipped a lead rope to the palomino's halter, and from the look of things, he was teaching the horse to back up on command. When Rex failed to obey, Regan waved the rope in his face until he followed the command.

Horse and man put on an interesting show, and she wasn't the only one captivated by it. Several other horses had gathered around the corral in apparent fascination. Lily couldn't resist taking out her phone and snapping a few pictures. School was in session and the pupils were in attendance, and the rising sun gave her just enough light to capture it.

She'd be crazy to send this guy away. He was exactly the person she needed to keep order in a potentially chaotic environment. Her personal issues with him faded in importance next to the benefit he'd provide to the animals in her care. So that was that. If he was willing, and she hoped to God he was, she wanted him to stay.

That decided, she watched a little longer because she didn't know how often she'd be in a position to study Regan unobserved. He and the flashy palomino made quite a pair. Regan's broad shoulders and slim hips seemed specifically suited to his jeans, boots and Western shirt. He looked great, but it was his confident movements as he worked with Rex that stirred her. Competence in any man was sexy. In someone who looked like Regan, it took her breath away.

She started to slip her phone into her hip pocket and paused. One more picture, a close-up this time. Zooming in on Regan, she waited until she had him in profile. Damn, but he was gorgeous. Just as she clicked the picture, he turned his head and looked straight at her. Busted.

Or maybe not. From this distance he might not have been able to tell that she was taking pictures with her phone, but he certainly knew she'd been standing on the stoop watching him. She'd have to own up to that.

With a deep breath, she started toward the corral. Regan adjusted the tilt of his Stetson before leading Rex to the gate. When the horse started to crowd him, he turned and gave a quiet command. Rex stepped back.

"Awesome," Lily called out. "Looks like he's learning some manners. I hope the rest of them were paying attention."

"I think they're here because they're hoping I'll feed them. I didn't want to do that without asking, but I figured you wouldn't mind if I spent some time with Rex." He opened the gate and led the big horse through it.

"Not at all, but don't you want to leave him in there? I can feed him in the corral."

"He's had enough of a time-out. Horses really don't like to be isolated from the herd for very long. And I think Rex considers himself the leader of this one. He can't very well lead from inside the corral."

Lily fell into step beside Regan. "What if he starts acting up again?"

"We'll keep an eye on him, but let's feed the way you normally do and see how he reacts. He might be a perfect gentleman, at least for the time it takes everyone to have breakfast."

"Sounds good." She glanced over her shoulder and discovered the rest of the horses falling in line behind Rex in Pied Piper style. "Thank you for coming out early to work with him."

"Couldn't sleep."

"Sorry."

"It's my own damn fault. You made it clear when you asked me to stay that this was a platonic arrangement."

"But then I kissed you."

"I prefer to think we kissed each other. And then I kissed you again."

Lily sighed. "And I kissed you back. My bad."

"No way was it bad." His voice caressed her nerve endings. "It was good. Very good."

Heat shot through her veins. Somehow she managed to keep walking, but her brain was filled with X-rated images.

Regan cleared his throat. "I've been doing some thinking while I was not sleeping."

"If you want to leave, I understand, although I hope you don't. I haven't made this an easy situation for you."

"You don't want me to leave?"

She looked at him. "No."

"That's a relief. All my thinking would have gone to waste if you'd decided to kick me out."

"I wouldn't do that. I wondered if you should stay or not, but then I saw you working with Rex and all the others standing around watching. Our issues aside, you're exactly who these animals need, and that's what's important."

"Thanks." He led Rex inside the barn. "Let's put him in a stall with a mare this time. He might like that better."

"Sally?"

"Maybe a younger mare. Let him dream of the days when he was a stallion."

Lily chuckled. "Okay. Gretchen, then. I'll go get her and we'll stick them both in the third stall on the left."

"I really do think he'll be fine, but let's close all the

stall doors once they're situated so we can keep track of who's where."

"Gotcha." She started sorting horses, and when all were securely in a stall, she and Regan distributed flakes of hay. Rex seemed perfectly content to share a stall with Gretchen, and Lily made a mental note for the future.

She and Regan kept busy until all the horses were happily munching their breakfast. Leaving the stall doors closed meant hanging around until they were finished. She wandered up and down the wooden aisle. All seemed to be well, and a peaceful feeling settled over her. Having a buddy to help her monitor the horses was something she hadn't considered before, but it certainly lowered her stress level. She might want to take on an employee, after all.

"Have a seat," Regan said, gesturing to a straw bale at the end of the aisle, "and I'll tell you my brilliant idea."

"Okay." She sat down.

He settled next to her, but not too close. He had room to swivel a bit and look at her more directly. She did the same. Now their knees almost touched.

He nudged his hat back with his thumb. "First point—you need to set up an adoption fair. Advertise it, offer refreshments, get a bunch of people out here to look at the horses and maybe take one home."

She fought panic. "That sounds like a huge project."

"Not so huge if we get some help."

He'd said *we,* which calmed her a little. "Like who?"

"The Chance family. They put on events like that all the time to showcase their Paints. My twin sister, Tyler, is an event planner, and I guarantee she'd help.

Nick would, of course, but I'll bet a few others would pitch in. What do you think?"

She listened to the horses munching, all twenty-one of them. Intimidating as an adoption fair sounded to her, if the Chance family would help, she'd do it. "That's a great idea, Regan. Thank you for suggesting it."

"Good. We can call the ranch today and see if anyone's available to discuss the details. If they are, we'll drive over and see what weekend they have free. We need to start planning and advertising now."

"But we're not ready to set a date! Rex is the only horse you've worked with, and you didn't spend much time with him. How can we set up an adoption fair when so much needs to be done with the horses?"

His gaze was steady and his voice calm. "Setting a date will give us a goal. We can concentrate on the most adoptable horses first and work with them for as long as we have."

"Okay." She pressed a hand to her chest. "But this is making me nervous. I don't know how to train a horse yet, and I'm sure I won't be as effective as you are at first. Plus I don't have a lot of extra time, as I've explained. I don't know when—"

He put a hand on her knee and gave it a gentle squeeze. "I can do most of it. We'll be fine."

"But you have a full-time job."

"True." He took a long breath. "So I'd have to train your horses during my time off, which would be evenings and weekends, or whenever I don't have an appointment scheduled. Logistically, that could be accomplished more easily if I move in here until the fair."

She gulped. On the surface, the plan was perfect. She needed help, and he was obviously good at handling horses. As a single guy with no ties, no lease and no mortgage, he was free to switch his place of lodging from the ranch to her rescue facility.

"So, Lily, what do you think?"

"I would pay you, of course."

"No, you wouldn't. You're running a charitable organization and I'm volunteering my time. If you started paying me, I'd be an employee, and I don't care for that dynamic."

"Why?"

He fixed her with a penetrating stare. "I think you know."

"The whole attraction thing."

"Right. Suppose you started paying me, and then we became involved. I'm not saying we will, but it could happen. That would be awkward."

"It would be better if we didn't get involved, but I suppose, if we're living under the same roof..." The thought made her nerves hum in anticipation.

"I won't push, Lily. I promise you that. I decided last night that wouldn't be right. You're susceptible to me, but you don't want to be."

"For good reason."

"I get that. But I've given the rebound concept a lot of thought, and while I can see why you'd think that was my motivation, it isn't. Or it isn't now." He hesitated. "It might have been yesterday, before I spent more time with you."

She blinked. "That's honest."

"I'm being as honest as I possibly can. I don't want to be like those other two guys, the ones who were only using you. I like to think I'm not like that. I like to think I see you as a person and not as a means to an end."

How she wanted to believe him.

"I know this might be difficult for you to accept after

dealing with two greedy losers in a row, but I'm risking as much as you are with this arrangement."

"You are? Why?"

"I don't want you to take this the wrong way and become even more convinced that I'm on the rebound after all, but the truth is..." He paused. "I, uh, found Jeannette in bed with my...my best friend. On Christmas Eve."

"Oh...that's terrible!" She hadn't been prepared for him to confess that, and she was a beat too slow in her shocked response.

His eyes narrowed. "You already knew that."

She was afraid the truth was there in her eyes, no matter what she said. But she didn't have to confirm it by opening her mouth.

"Nick told you, didn't he?"

"It's not his fault! I wormed the information out of him! I thought you had—"

"A secret anguish. I remember."

"Please don't be upset with him, Regan. He's very protective of you and wishes you the best. I've known Nick ever since I was in junior high, and—"

"He mentioned something about that."

"We're good friends. I told him that if you and I would be working together, I didn't want to walk into a minefield without realizing it. I can be very convincing when I'm after something."

He gave her a lopsided smile. "I can imagine."

"Nick wanted us to get along, so he very reluctantly gave me the basic information. I can't emphasize enough how reluctant he was. He thinks the world of you. You're family. He didn't reveal any more than you just said. He gave me no particulars, I promise!"

"He'd have a tough time doing that when he doesn't

know the particulars. Nobody does except me, Jeannette and Drake. And it'll stay that way."

"Which it should." She saw the raw pain in his eyes and longed to reach out to him, but he might think she did it out of pity.

"This explains a lot, though. You had the info on me before you asked me to spend the weekend, right?"

"Right."

"So at that point you decided I had to be on the rebound and you wanted nothing to do with that kind of deal."

"Exactly."

"But, inconveniently for you, I flip your switches."

She sighed. "You do."

"That makes two of us with that problem. But considering where we're both coming from, it could turn into a disaster. I wasn't willing to admit that before, but it's possible one or both of us could get hurt."

She allowed herself to look into his eyes again and sink into the warm chocolate depths. "True."

"I wasn't just dumped. I was betrayed, which is a whole other kind of hell. In the wee hours this morning I faced the fact that I'm at least as nervous about getting into a relationship as you are."

"Are you saying we both have something to lose?"

He nodded. "I think so, yes."

"That does shine a different light on things."

"It does." He held her gaze for a moment. "The horses are getting restless. We need to let them out."

"Sure." She stood. "So we'll keep things platonic between us?"

"I didn't say that." He got to his feet, too.

"What are you saying, then?"

"We should think it through as best we can and be honest with ourselves and each other. No secrets."

"Regan, please don't call Nick and chew him out. Put the blame for the security leak on me."

"Don't worry. I won't call him. I've only known you for twenty-four hours, and I can already see how you'd maneuver Nick into giving up information. I'm sure he thought it was the right thing to do. Obviously I was ready to tell you, anyway. No harm done."

She let out her breath. "I'm glad. I was a little worried that you'd be upset with him."

"No. From now on, though, this is between you and me. Nick doesn't need to know what's going on with us."

"You thought I'd tell him?"

"You said you were really good friends."

"Not *that* good."

Regan smiled. "Happy to hear it. Although I warn you, once our living arrangement becomes public, some people will make assumptions."

"They can assume all they want. That doesn't mean they'll be right."

"It doesn't mean they'll be wrong, either." He gave her a long look. "When I see you standing in the light pouring in through the door, your hair so bright and your eyes so soft…" His voice grew rough with emotion. "I ache for you, Lily King."

She watched in stunned silence as he turned and ambled down the row of stalls, unlatching doors as he went. No man had ever said anything remotely like that to her before, with such intensity. She might not be psychic, but she had a premonition that from this moment on, her life would never be the same.

8

FROM THE WAY the rest of the morning went, Regan concluded that he'd changed the game with that statement. The tension level between them had zipped from yellow to orange and was edging into the red zone. But he'd promised to be straight with Lily from now on. No secrets. So when he'd felt his heart shift as he'd seen her standing in a sunbeam, he'd told her the absolute truth. At that moment, he'd wanted her more than his next breath.

After that, she'd treated him with wary respect, as if he might lose control at any moment. He wouldn't, of course. But as they drove over to the Last Chance after all the chores were done, he noticed a flicker of excitement in her eyes whenever she glanced at him.

The night before when he'd been forced to wear her robe, she'd looked at him with pure lust. He'd enjoyed that, even if he'd felt a little like a Chippendales stripper. Early this morning she'd taken pictures of him with her cell phone and he'd sensed the same motivation: she was admiring the packaging, not the man inside. He wouldn't knock that because it was damned flattering, but a steady diet of it would be like eating only dessert all the time. After a while, he'd crave something more substantial.

Now, after his confession in the barn this morning, he was getting the substance he wanted. Besides the current of electricity that constantly arced between them, she was taking the time to really look at him, as if trying to see more than the obvious. He'd risked being more intense, and she seemed fascinated by that. He'd also made himself vulnerable, which was a little scary.

How strange to think that yesterday he'd been imagining them simply having a little fun together. No big deal. A few laughs. Some great sex. Parting as friends when it was over. But from what he knew of himself and what she'd told him about her background, neither of them were good at that kind of no-strings affair. They'd be kidding themselves if they tried it.

So if they became involved with each other—and on some level they already were involved—they'd both be all in. Maybe it would last two weeks, and maybe it would last much longer than that. He wasn't predicting the outcome, only the emotional investment from the beginning. They wouldn't be able to help themselves.

He pictured them standing at the top of a cliff hand in hand as they prepared to dive into a deep pool. Every time he thought about holding her in his arms again, adrenaline rushed through him. The tension here in the small confines of his truck's cab told him the moment would come sooner rather than later.

As he pulled into the circular gravel drive in front of the Last Chance's main house, he wondered if any of the people they were about to see would pick up on that tension. Judging from what he'd observed about Sarah Chance, she would. The matriarch of the family didn't miss much when it came to those she cared about. Luckily for Regan, she cared about him. He'd always be grateful for that.

Sarah made him feel at home in this massive two-story log house, but the structure itself seemed to welcome him each time he pulled up in front. The wide center section flanked by two wings jutting out at a forty-five-degree angle reminded him of arms spread in an embrace. A covered porch lined with rocking chairs ran the length of the house and symbolized hospitality. Now that summer had arrived, evenings found the chairs occupied by any of the Chance clan who happened to drop by.

He stopped the truck and shut down the engine before turning to Lily. "How long since you've been here?"

"Oh, gosh, quite a while. I've been so busy with Peaceful Kingdom that I haven't been over since I moved back here. My parents were invited to Nick's high school graduation party, and they brought me along, but we're talking almost fifteen years ago. After that…let me think. I kept in touch with Nick off and on through email. When Jonathan Chance died in that roll-over, I was at Berkeley. My parents went to the funeral, but I couldn't come home for it. I would have missed too many classes and my parents advised me not to come." She paused. "I should have, anyway."

"I'm sure everyone understood."

"Of course they did. The Chances aren't petty about things like that, but I still wish I'd made the effort. I've run into various family members in town since I've been back, and they're always nice to me."

"Have you met Pete, Sarah's new husband?"

"I have." She smiled. "They were eating lunch at the diner one day when I was there. Seems like a terrific guy, and I love the idea of the camp for disadvantaged boys that he and Sarah run every summer."

"Uh-oh. I just remembered something. That camp starts next Sunday."

"It does? Well, I guess it would. I tend to lose track of time, especially lately."

"I forgot about it until now, too, but that means we might only have next Saturday as an option for the adoption fair."

"Yikes." She blew out a breath. "That's too soon."

"Maybe not. If we concentrate on training five or six horses and get those adopted, we'll significantly reduce the overcrowding. By then you'll have the fence built. You'd be in much better shape."

"I don't know. A week..." Uncertainty shadowed her blue eyes.

"We can do it. I have several gaps in my appointment schedule next week. I won't fill them."

"No! You'll lose money!"

He shrugged. "I'll make it up later. No big deal."

"I should pay you, then."

"We've been over that. No dice. I'm not hurting for money, so let's not talk about it anymore, okay? I want to do this. It's important to me, too, now."

"Okay." She hesitated. "But do you really think we can be ready in a week?"

"Yeah, I do." Unfastening his seat belt, he leaned toward her and gave her a quick kiss. "Have faith." The kiss had been a last-minute decision, and he needed every ounce of willpower he possessed to end it immediately and open the driver's-side door.

But he'd wanted to try a small laser strike and see what happened. Apparently his strategy had the desired effect. By the time he rounded the front of the truck and opened her door, which took several seconds, she was still seated and she seemed a little dazed.

"Ready to go in?"

"Sure." She swallowed hard and started down.

He offered her a hand, which she accepted without comment. He released his hold the moment she had both feet on the gravel drive.

"That was sneaky, Regan." She glanced up at him.

"Meaning you didn't like it?"

"Oh, I liked it. But I wasn't expecting it."

That made him smile. "Aren't you the woman who told me she likes the unexpected? The one who doesn't want to be bored?"

Her expression was priceless. He'd turned her words back on her, and apparently she wasn't used to that. She couldn't seem to decide whether to challenge his statement or laugh. In the end, she laughed. "Touché."

"Just so you know, I've wanted to do that ever since you showed up at the corral this morning, but I couldn't find the right moment."

"You've wanted to kiss me all that time?"

"Not a full-out kiss, because we had stuff to do, but something quick and to the point, just to let you know I'm thinking about it."

"By *it,* are you referring to kissing…or something else?"

"Kissing."

She looked skeptical.

"That's all, I swear. If I allowed myself to think of *something else,* the drive over here would have been painful."

Her eyebrows lifted. "My, you are being honest, aren't you?"

"That's my goal. Come on." He tilted his head toward the steps leading up to the front porch. "Let's go see if the Chance contingent has next weekend available for our adoption fair. But first I need to warn you about something."

"What's that?"

"They have a couch in the living room. Don't read too much into that. They're still very interesting people."

She rolled her eyes. "This is going to turn into a thing, isn't it?"

"Yeah." He grinned at her and felt that flash of happiness he was beginning to associate with Lily. "Our first inside joke."

SARAH, HER SILVER hair styled in its usual sleek bob, met Lily and Regan at the door. She was dressed casually in jeans and a denim shirt, but Sarah could make any outfit look elegant. As she greeted them, Lily remembered why she admired this woman so much. Sarah behaved as if she'd been gifted with two of the most anticipated guests in the world, A-listers who had graced her with their presence.

When Sarah was glad to see someone, she pulled out all the stops. Rumor had it that when she wasn't glad to see someone, her reception could turn a sunny day into an ice storm. She never lost her poise, but she could freeze people in their tracks. Lily planned to stay in Sarah's good graces.

"I'm so happy about you buying Peaceful Kingdom, Lily." Sarah took her by the arm. "You were the perfect person to do it. We're all gathered in the kitchen gobbling up the last of Mary Lou's coffee cake, but she saved two big pieces for you and Regan."

"Mary Lou's still your cook?" Lily remembered her

from the graduation party fifteen years ago. The feisty woman had taken Lily aside and told her not to settle for some guy who wanted to keep her barefoot and pregnant. It was good advice, and Lily had never forgotten it.

"She's still our cook," Sarah said. "I don't know what we'd do without her. She's married now, you know."

"Mary Lou? She's the one who urged me not to get married."

"And she was against it for years." Sarah chuckled as she guided Lily through the living room, which had, as Regan had mentioned, a leather couch, not to mention some heavy-looking leather armchairs. "But we have a ranch hand named Watkins who'd had his eye on her ever since he came to work for us. He's wooed her off and on, and finally, two summers ago, he convinced her to marry him."

"I'm astounded. I thought she'd never tie the knot." Lily had a brief glimpse of the large rock fireplace that anchored the living area, and she decided that a room like that needed a weighty couch and several sturdy armchairs. The high beamed ceilings, the winding wooden staircase that led to the second floor, and the immense wagon-wheel chandelier all seemed to demand substantial furniture. Lily's modest living room did not. Case closed.

"They seem pretty happy." Sarah led Regan and Lily down a long hallway lined with family pictures. "They ran off and got married on a cruise ship, so they've been threatening to renew their vows with a ceremony here at the ranch. We have a busy summer coming up, but if they really want to, I'll make it work."

Lily didn't doubt Sarah's abilities, which gave her hope that an adoption fair really could take place at Peaceful Kingdom, even within the short time frame.

Usually she went with the flow and didn't worry too much about how everything turned out. But she felt more responsibility for the animals than she had for any project she'd taken on in the past. She needed more clarification. "You must be getting ready for the boys to arrive."

"We are, but we've been doing this for several years, now. We're not as panicked about having those nine kids here as we were the first couple of times. And Regan, I have to say that your little sister Cassidy is the most energetic young woman I've ever met. She'll have no trouble keeping up with those boys. I just worry that they'll disturb you, even if your room is in the other wing. They can be loud."

"I'm sure I'll be fine," Regan said.

Lily pressed her lips together to keep from smiling. She didn't think Regan wanted to move in with her specifically to avoid living on the same floor with nine adolescent boys, but that had to be a bonus. She wondered when he planned to let Sarah know he was changing his place of residence. Maybe not right now, when several family members were gathered, including his twin sister, Tyler. Lily appreciated him holding off.

When they entered a large dining room with several round tables for eight, Lily was disoriented. "I don't remember this part at all."

"It hadn't been built when Nick graduated from high school, and I think that was the last time you were here," Sarah said.

"Wow, you have a good memory. I had to stop and go back over some dates before I could be sure about that, but I think you're right. It's been almost fifteen years."

"Jonathan and I designed this room because we had a habit of gathering all the ranch hands for lunch as a way to keep in touch on a regular basis. As we hired more hands over the years, they didn't fit in the old dining room anymore. We added this one, turned the old space into a family dining area and enlarged the kitchen and Mary Lou's living quarters."

Lily glanced around and pictured the tables filled with cowboys joking with each other while they tucked into Mary Lou's excellent meals. Although Lily would never want a big operation like this, she appreciated the ranch's contribution to the community. It employed a lot of people and was famous for taking in both animals and people who needed another shot at straightening out their lives.

Thinking about that, Lily had an epiphany. Her urge to take over Peaceful Kingdom had its roots here at the Last Chance. As a thirteen-year-old she'd been dazzled by the Chance mystique. But until now, she hadn't made the connection between the ranch's reputation for helping others and her current decision to save Peaceful Kingdom.

She decided against mentioning that now, when she was about to ask a favor. It might not come across as sincerely as she meant it. She knew now, though, that without being exposed to the Last Chance, she wouldn't have been motivated to buy Peaceful Kingdom. She wouldn't have met Regan, either.

She didn't want to put too much weight on this budding relationship, but several of her friends at Berkeley would be raving about karma at this point. She wasn't ready to do that, but Regan's intensity this morning in the barn made her wonder what kind of cosmic energy they were stirring up.

Whatever was going on, she experienced the world more vividly as a result. The stealth kiss from Regan lingered on her mouth and continued to send little shock waves through her system. Her energy level was unusually high even though she hadn't slept much, and she couldn't blame caffeine because she'd had only one cup of coffee this morning. She also kept involuntarily glancing at Regan as if needing to make that visual connection on a regular basis. Weird. That was a new habit she needed to break now that they would be in a room full of people.

As it turned out, the kitchen was extremely crowded. Sarah waved Lily to a vacant chair at the oval table before sitting down herself, but Regan remained standing, as did all the other men.

Fortunately Lily knew most of those gathered there. She immediately recognized dark-haired, dark-eyed Jack Chance, and Lily had met his blonde wife, Josie, one night when Josie happened to be checking on things at the Spirits and Spurs, the tavern she owned in Shoshone. Josie's brother Alex stood behind the chair of his wife, Tyler, the event planner.

Lily noticed the strong resemblance between Regan and his twin, and she saw a look pass between them after Lily had been introduced. Tyler's expression said clearly *we need to talk.* Regan merely smiled.

Until this moment, Lily hadn't met Nick's wife, Dominique, although she'd seen pictures. Dominique was even more beautiful in person. With her short hair and big eyes, she reminded Lily of a young Audrey Hepburn. No wonder Nick had fallen for her.

Morgan, Gabe Chance's obviously pregnant wife and one of Regan's redheaded sisters, greeted Lily with enthusiasm. "Yay, another redhead in the group! That makes four of us if I count Sara Bianca, which I most certainly do."

“Speaking of my favorite niece,” Regan said, “where did you stash her?”

“Cassidy’s watching her and the other kids so we can have a little peace and quiet while we talk about this adoption fair,” Josie said. “So ignore whatever you hear from upstairs, because we all plan to.”

“Everybody have coffee?” Mary Lou Simms, a little grayer than Lily remembered but just as perky, appeared with a carafe in hand. “Hey, I know you! You’re the little King girl, all grown up. Nobody told me it was you. I just heard the name Lily, but I didn’t put two and two together.”

“You remember me?” Lily was flattered.

“’Course I do. You were smart as a whip.” She laughed. “’Spose you still are. With all that brainpower, I hoped you wouldn’t get married too soon and stunt your potential. You didn’t, did you?”

“Nope.” Lily held up her left hand. “No ring. But I see you’re wearing one.”

“I am.” Mary Lou’s cheeks turned pink. “That old coot wore me down. And I have to say, I’m not quite as opposed to matrimony as I used to be. It has a few benefits.”

Jack Chance put his arm around her. “Good thing you said that, Mary Lou, considering that every person in this room with the exception of Regan and Lily are hitched. Voicing the opposite opinion might affect your popularity.”

“Nah.” Sarah’s husband, Pete, a lanky man in his sixties, pushed away from where he’d been leaning against the kitchen counter. “Mary Lou can voice any opinion she wants as long as she keeps making that coffee cake. Is there any left?”

"Two pieces," Mary Lou said. "And they're reserved for our guests."

"Oh, that's okay," Lily said. "Someone else can have mine."

Jack's eyebrows lifted. "Careful what you say, there, Lily King. Turning down a piece of Mary Lou's coffee cake is loaded with implications. Implications you may not have taken into consideration before you made that rash statement."

"He's right." Nick winked at her. "You're in danger of insulting the cook."

"Oh, I didn't mean to—"

"And, besides that," Nick continued, "everybody for miles around knows this is the best coffee cake in Wyoming, so if you won't at least try it, we'll all doubt your intelligence."

"Okay, then, I—"

"Furthermore—" Nick held up a third finger "—if you don't eat your cake, you'll cause a brawl in this kitchen when we all get to fighting over your share. I know you don't want any of that to happen, so you'd best eat up and be quiet."

"I'll just do that, then." She smiled at everyone and picked up her fork. The cake was incredible, so she didn't have to fake her moan of pleasure, but after that first bite she spent a solid minute praising the taste and texture, until Nick made a slicing motion across his throat and she went back to eating.

"You'll have to get used to this kind of thing," Morgan said. "I'd like to tell you that they're not always like this, but they are. You should have seen them on skis last winter. Not a one of them would agree to wear regular ski clothes. Instead they showed up for the bunny slope in jeans, sheepskin jackets and Stetsons."

"We were stylin'," Gabe said.

His wife glanced at him. "You were ridiculous."

"We were not. C'mon, guys, back me up on this one. We made a statement on the slopes, did we not?"

A chorus of agreement was followed by protests from the wives, and no telling how long the argument would have continued if Jack hadn't banged a spoon against his coffee mug. "As I recall, we gathered here to discuss Lily's adoption fair. Shall we proceed?"

"Yeah," Mary Lou said. "And you were worried about your kids making too much noise. But for the record, my Watkins was the only smart guy who wore ski pants on the bunny slope."

That started it up again. Lily thought they were hysterical. She'd known the adoption fair was necessary, but she hadn't known it would be fun. She glanced at Regan and grinned. Being connected to the Chance family was a good thing. She just hadn't realized how good.

Then she thought of something else. She'd been warmly welcomed into this group because she was with Regan. If things worked out between them, the door to the Last Chance would always be open to her. But if the relationship went downhill, then all that lovely friendliness could disappear.

As Jack might explain it, becoming involved with Regan was filled with implications, implications she might not have considered before she rashly kissed the guy. She'd been able to take back her rejection of the coffee cake, but she couldn't take back those kisses. Nor did she want to. In fact, she hoped there would be more to come. She'd take Regan's kisses over coffee cake any day.

9

PROUD OF HIMSELF for coming up with the adoption fair plan and suggesting the Chance family as a resource, Regan watched as the event took shape. His twin sister really knew her stuff when it came to planning shindigs like this. He loved seeing Tyler in action, her Italian heritage coming out in elaborate hand gestures as she described her vision of the fair.

Lily caught her excitement and was soon leaping in with ideas of her own. She'd create a website, a Facebook page and the graphics for a flier. Regan stood by the counter eating his coffee cake while he watched them interact, Tyler's dark head leaning toward Lily's fiery red one. Yep, this had been a great idea, if he did say so himself.

Alex made an excellent counterpart to Tyler. He volunteered to help with local publicity and organize music if they decided to have any. These days Alex handled marketing for the Last Chance, but he used to be a DJ, which meant Alex and Tyler were the couple you wanted for a successful event.

Josie offered to put up Lily's fliers around town, including at the Spirits and Spurs. Morgan had connections in the business community, too, because she was a successful real estate broker, and Dominique said she'd push the adoption fair in her photography studio and give away portraits of any horse that was adopted. Pete's experience with charity events would be valuable, too.

"I think they have it together." Jack walked over to the counter and refilled his coffee mug. "Let's talk about the horses."

"Yeah, we need to do that." Regan finished the last of his coffee cake. "We only have a week."

Jack beckoned to Nick and Gabe. "We need a confab over here. That bunch at the table will bring in the folks. That puts us in charge of the horses."

Nick topped off his coffee and turned back to Regan. "So six out of the twenty-one aren't going anywhere. That leaves fifteen that could potentially be adopted."

"Right."

Gabe nodded. "That's doable, I think. We'd have time to showcase each horse during an all-day event. You have a corral, right?"

"Yes."

"We can give each horse fifteen or twenty minutes in that corral. Three an hour works out to five hours. We can take turns so each of us gets a break and a chance to talk to anybody who's interested."

"They aren't all ready for their spotlight," Regan said. "These aren't your expertly trained Paints, Gabe. They're a little rough around the edges."

"So what kind of behaviors are we dealing with?" Jack cradled his mug in both hands. "Have you had a chance to evaluate them?"

"To some extent. Several have bad habits. They're not well mannered on the lead, or they've tried to crowd me in the stall. A couple are biters."

Jack nodded. “I figured as much. People say they don’t have the money to keep a horse, but sometimes it’s more that the horse has developed bad habits and they don’t know how to correct them.” He looked at Regan. “You don’t want to adopt out any horses that misbehave. Either they’ll come back, or they’ll be mistreated or passed on to some other unsuspecting person. Bad for the horse.”

“I know.”

“And Lily doesn’t know how to retrain them yet,” Nick added. “She admitted that when I talked to her on Friday. Oh, and by the way, Regan, a fence crew will be out there Monday morning to build her a paddock.”

“Excellent. Thanks, Nick.”

“I convinced them she doesn’t have the time to wait for them to work up a detailed estimate, so they’ll just give her a ballpark figure before they start. If she okays that, they’ll get to it immediately.”

Regan nodded. “Good. I’m sure Lily will be thrilled. The fact is, we can’t have an adoption fair without a paddock. Penning the horses up in the barn for the day isn’t a good idea.”

“I’m still working on the issue of how we’ll get them trained,” Gabe said. “I could spare some time at night, but that means leaving Morgan to deal with the kids, and she gets tired now that she’s PG again. Besides, I like being there for those rug rats.”

“I’m in the same boat with little Archie,” Jack said. “And Josie’s been shorthanded at the bar recently, so she needs me to be at home when she has to go into town.”

“I probably can help some,” Nick said. “But I’m coaching Lester’s Little League team, so that takes up three nights next week. Luckily his Saturday game is at night, so it won’t conflict with the fair.”

"Even if it did, the game's more important." Regan had become fond of Lester, a small but spunky fifteen-year-old who'd been in the first batch of campers a couple of years ago. Dominique and Nick had fallen in love with Lester, and when they'd discovered he was in a dicey foster-care situation, they'd adopted him. "If you wanted to come out and train some night when he doesn't have a game, you could bring him along."

"That's an idea. And you know what? We don't have to showcase all fifteen on Saturday. This will be an ongoing process, so we should plan to do another fair later on, maybe in the early fall."

"I agree," Regan said. "If we can adopt out six or seven, that would be huge." He glanced at Jack and Gabe. "I don't want either of you to worry about anything except coming out on Saturday. Your kids are young. You have to be away from them most of the day. You don't need to be sacrificing your evenings. I can handle the training."

Jack set his empty mug on the counter. "I'm sure you can, especially if you only concentrate on six or seven horses. But it'd be a lot more convenient if Peaceful Kingdom was located on this side of town instead of in the other direction. You're going to be doing a lot of driving."

"Not necessarily." Regan hesitated. He didn't want to make Lily uncomfortable by discussing their new living arrangements while she was in the room, but she seemed to be absorbed in her conversation with the publicity team. "I don't want you guys to read anything into this, but I've decided to stay in Lily's guest room for the time being."

"Yeah?" Nick kept his expression carefully neutral. "Does she know about this decision?"

"She does. We had a little incident yesterday where one of the geldings went after another one, and it scared her. She doesn't have the background to deal with that kind of thing, so she asked if I'd hang around this weekend. If I'm going to work with the horses in my spare time this coming week, it seems logical for me to stay on."

"Yes, it certainly does." Jack nodded and ducked his head to take a sip of his coffee.

"Absolutely." Gabe stroked his mustache, which allowed him to cover his mouth except for the corners, which were twitching. "Brilliant idea."

Jack spit his coffee back into his mug and his shoulders shook. When he looked up, his eyes brimmed with laughter. "Sorry, buddy, but your story has so many holes in it, Mary Lou could use it to strain her spaghetti. We all know why you're staying out there. The animals will benefit, but there's a lot more going on than training a few horses."

Nick grinned. "When Jack's right, he's right. Fortunately, Lily thinks you're pretty cute, too. I could tell that from the way she talked about you."

Heat rose from Regan's collar. "Is that so?"

"Yeah." Nick regarded him with amusement. "In fact, I called this one last night." He glanced over at Jack. "Didn't I, bro?"

"You did. While we were sitting on the porch drinking beer and speculating on where, oh, where Regan O'Connelli might be, since he hadn't been seen after heading out to Peaceful Kingdom around dinnertime."

"I'm sorry I missed that conversation," Gabe said. "Morgan and I took the kids to a movie in Jackson last night so I wasn't porch-sittin' like these railbirds. But I didn't miss the way you two were shooting sparks when you walked into the kitchen."

"Yeah, Tyler noticed it, too," Nick said. "I saw that look she gave you. She's gonna want to make sure you don't hook up with another loser like Jeannette. Fortunately I can vouch for Lily. She's a good kid."

"You need your eyesight checked, Nicky," Gabe said. "She's not a kid anymore, if you get my meaning."

Regan pointed a finger at Gabe. "And you can just keep your eyes to yourself, mister."

"Classic." Jack smiled and shook his head. "Possessive and protective already. This will be fun to watch."

"Keep it down, okay?" Regan quickly glanced over at the table, but Lily and the rest of them seemed oblivious to the discussion going on over by the coffeepot. "I don't want to embarrass her."

"Neither do we," said Nick. "Don't worry. We won't make a big deal out of it. But don't you need to pack a few things before you drive back?"

"As a matter of fact, I do." He thought about the box of condoms. And clothes, of course. But the condoms topped his mental list.

"Go ahead and handle that now," Jack said. "I'll explain to Mom later that you won't be sleeping here for the foreseeable future. We'll keep it on the down-low. Get your stuff and put it out in the truck. We can say you went upstairs to see Sarah Bianca."

"Which you should, anyway," Gabe said. "SB will be devastated if she finds out you've been here and she didn't get a hug."

"Good point. I'll make it fast."

Jack checked the situation at the table. "Take your time. They're into it, now. We'll need to break it up soon, though, or they'll be renting a jumping castle and a cotton-candy machine."

"Be back shortly. Oh, and Nick, will you be sure and tell Lily about the paddock? She'll want to thank you for setting it up."

"I'll tell her. Go take care of business, Romeo."

"Right." Regan turned to leave but glanced over at Lily one last time.

As if they'd choreographed it, Lily looked up and met his gaze. The moment was short and packed with meaning. When she turned her attention back to the notes she was taking on her phone, the corners of her mouth tipped up in a secret smile.

He had the distinct feeling that she knew he was sneaking out to pack his clothes. Unless she was psychic, though, she couldn't know what else he was going after. Then again, she'd claimed to be a bit psychic.

She confirmed that she knew he'd packed a suitcase as they pulled away from the ranch house about thirty minutes later. "That was slick, Sherlock."

"What?"

"Do you, or do you not, have a suitcase full of your stuff in the back of this truck?"

"I do."

"I figured that's what you were up to when you sidled out of the kitchen. What excuse did you give the Chance brothers so you could execute that maneuver?"

"Didn't need an excuse. Jack suggested I slide out and take care of that while nobody was looking."

"He didn't! Are you saying they know you'll be staying with me at least until Saturday?"

From the corner of his eye, Regan noticed that her cheeks were very pink. "I had to tell them, Lily. They were twisting themselves into pretzels trying to figure out how we'd get these horses in shape, but the obvious answer was for me to move in and have regular access to them so I can make the best use of my free time."

"So they think this is strictly a business arrangement?"

"Well…no. They don't think that."

Lily groaned. "I'm afraid to ask what they think it is. But I guess it couldn't be avoided. This is exactly what you warned me about."

"It's not surprising." He gave her a quick smile. "You're a caring, beautiful woman, and I'm a man with a…" He started laughing and couldn't finish.

"What?"

"A secret anguish." And he laughed some more.

She whacked him on the arm, but she was laughing, too. "I'll never live that down, will I?"

"I kind of like it. It gives me a certain Phantom of the Opera appeal."

"It used to, before you started making fun of my tenderhearted description." She folded her arms and did her best to look stern and disapproving. "See if I worry about your secret anguish anymore. Or, to be more direct, O'Connelli, *bite me.*"

He laughed so hard he almost ran them off the road. Fortunately they were still on the dirt stretch leading to the main highway into Shoshone and nobody else was coming from the other direction. "You are such a redhead. But I grew up with redheaded sisters. You can't scare me."

"You sure?"

His laughter faded. "No. You scare the hell out of me."

"I know."

"How do you know?"

Her voice grew quiet. "Because you scare the hell out of me, and I recognize the look of panic that sometimes flashes in your eyes."

"Yeah." He sighed. "I'm sure it does."

"I like you, Regan. I like you a lot."

"Ditto." He took a deep breath. "Want to know how I picture us?"

"Probably not, but now that you've asked me, of course I'll die of curiosity if you don't tell me."

"Is that a yes or a no?"

"Yes! How do you picture us?"

Now that he was about to tell her, he decided it was sort of stupid. Ridiculously romantic. Dopey, even. He shouldn't have brought it up.

"Come on, Regan. You have to tell me now."

"You'll laugh."

"No, I won't. I promise. You're not thinking of us as Romeo and Juliet, are you? Or Anthony and Cleopatra? I don't want to be a tragic couple."

"We're not. At least I hope not. But I see us as two cliff divers standing at the top of a cliff, about to dive into a deep pool. Or maybe it's a volcano, like in that old Tom Hanks movie."

"I remember that movie. He held hands with Meg Ryan before they jumped. Are we holding hands in your mental picture?"

"Yeah." Sheesh. Good thing nobody else was around to hear this sentimental claptrap. He'd be drummed out of the manly man corps.

She was quiet after that, and he had to look over to make sure she wasn't biting her lip to keep from laughing at him and his sappy image.

She wasn't laughing. Instead she gazed at him with

a soft light in her eyes. "I think that's a lovely image," she murmured.

"You do?" He waited for her to start giggling. When she didn't, he returned his attention to the road, relief easing the tightness in his chest. Guilt followed. She was a nicer person than he was. "I shouldn't have teased you about the secret anguish thing."

"I deserved it. That was way too dramatic. A cringe-worthy description."

"And cliff diving isn't?"

"No, it's sweet and brave." She paused. "And I like that we're holding hands."

The warm feeling that he'd now recognized as happiness spread through him. "Me, too." Without taking his eyes from the road, he reached for her hand. She met him halfway and laced her fingers through his. They rode in silence, hands clasped, all the way back.

10

Lily thought about Regan's cliff-diving metaphor on the drive home. He hadn't said they were jumping off a cliff together into the unknown. He'd said they were diving into a deep pool. It still sounded a little scary, but they had a destination, and it involved going beneath the surface of things.

If she couldn't trust a man like Regan not to treat her as if she was disposable, then she couldn't trust anyone. She'd known from the moment she agreed to have him stay the rest of the week that she wouldn't be able to resist him for seven solid days. As they pulled up in front of the locked sanctuary gate, she realized she couldn't resist him for another seven minutes.

She'd been the one to toss up objections with all her talk about rebound relationships, so she had to be the one to remove those objections. Yes, they had a lot to do in the next few days, but the world wouldn't come to an end if they started a little bit later.

"The house and barn are still in one piece." Regan flashed her a smile as he squeezed her hand and released it. "Can't say that for the flower garden, but that was a foregone conclusion."

As she absorbed the beauty of that smile, her breath caught. She'd been drawn to him because he was gorgeous, but behind that million-dollar smile was a depth of character that she'd only begun to appreciate. She vowed to use these seven days to find out what made Regan O'Connelli so amazing.

"Lily? Are you going to let us in?"

"Uh, sure." She scrambled out of the truck and opened the gate. Standing guard, she waited until Regan had driven through before locking up again. Once the critters were all penned in, she wouldn't have to continue this little routine. But for now, because of the locked gate, no one could come to her door unannounced. Considering what she had planned for the next hour, that was a good thing.

"Are you okay?" Regan climbed out of the truck, which had been fitted with a camper shell to protect his medical supplies.

"I'm fine." And soon she'd be mighty fine. So would he, if she had anything to say about it.

"I know we didn't talk much the last few miles of the drive." He opened the tailgate and pulled out a small duffle bag. Closing the tailgate again with a clang, he turned to her. "Is something bothering you?"

"Yes, as a matter of fact, there is." She was glad he'd traded in his sunglasses for his Stetson. Looking into his eyes had become one of her favorite pastimes.

His gaze darkened with concern. "Is there anything I can do to help?"

"Yes." She kept her expression neutral, but inside she was a bottle of champagne about to pop its cork.

"What? Tell me and I'll do my best to fix whatever's wrong."

What a caring man he was. How had she ever thought

he'd end up hurting her? "Let's go inside before we get into it."

"Yeah, sure." He followed her up the steps and across the small front porch with the chewed-up railing. "I'll replace that railing once the paddock is finished and Sally can't get to it anymore."

"Or I could ask the fence company to replace it. You may be too busy."

"I'll be busy, but not *that* busy. I can replace a railing. It won't take long."

"You may be busier than you think." She opened the front door and started toward her bedroom. "Come in here a minute." She used the kind of matter-of-fact tone that would suggest more home maintenance issues. But she quivered in anticipation. "I have a problem in this room."

"If it's a plumbing issue, I may need help. I'm good with the carpentry stuff and a few minor plumbing repairs, but I won't guarantee I can handle the big jobs." He set his duffle on the living room floor before continuing to follow her.

"It's not the plumbing." She turned back toward him and gestured toward his duffle. "You might want to bring that with you."

"It's only my clothes. I don't have any tools in there or…anything…" He stood in the middle of the living room and stared at her as comprehension dawned. "Lily?"

"Does your duffle have anything in it besides clothes?"

His breathing changed. "A few other things. Shaving gear, a toothbrush." He shrugged, but his gaze never left hers. "The usual. Was there something in particular you wanted to know about?"

"There is." She swallowed. "You might not have brought it. If you didn't, then I guess my…problem will have to wait." Her heart beat so fast she grew dizzy.

Heat flared in his dark eyes. "I think I might have what I need to fix your problem."

"Good." She struggled to breathe. "Then would you please come in and evaluate the situation?" She turned and walked on shaky legs through the doorway into her bedroom. Sunlight streamed in through the set of double-hung windows on the west wall. This wouldn't be a scene enacted in the dark, with shadows to hide in. But with Regan, she didn't need shadows. Taking the clasp from her hair, she tossed it on the bedside table. Then she turned and watched him walk into the room.

He paused just inside the door and the duffle slipped from his fingers, hitting the floor with a soft thud. "The sun…" He cleared his throat. "The sun is all around you. Just like this morning…in the barn."

"I'll never forget the way you looked at me, Regan. And what you said."

His voice dropped to a low, urgent murmur. "I still ache for you, Lily."

"I'm counting on that." She untied the tails of her shirt and slowly began unbuttoning it with trembling fingers. "Because I ache for you, too." Sliding her shirt off, she let it fall noiselessly to the floor. "Are you ready to take that dive?"

"God, yes." He closed the distance in two long strides and cupped her face in both hands. For a long moment he gazed into her eyes as his thumbs lightly caressed her cheeks. The air seemed to crackle between them. "Thank you for trusting me enough to be here."

She flattened her palms against the solid wall of his

chest and absorbed the warmth. "Your heart's beating fast."

His mouth tilted in a soft smile. "And I'm not even kissing you yet."

"I noticed that. Are you planning to get around to it?"

"Oh, yeah. But I have a feeling that once I start kissing you, all hell is going to break loose. It sure did last time." He combed his fingers gently through her hair. "You're potent."

"Backatcha."

He sucked in a breath and his attention dropped to her mouth. "Oh, Lily. This is going to be wild."

"Good."

His fingers tightened on her scalp as his gaze met hers. The fire in his eyes burned with enough heat to melt the clothes off her body. "See how you are?" His voice roughened. "No wonder I'm half-crazy with wanting you, Lily King. But that's why I thought that maybe, before we got into it, I should apologize in advance if I…forget myself and become a little…out of control."

A tsunami of lust slammed into her. "Now, Regan. Kiss me *now*."

With a groan, he captured her mouth with such urgency that she clutched his shirt in both hands. Her world began to tilt. Oh, yes. Oh, *yes*. His tongue, deep and questing, his lips demanding all she had to give, his fingers pressed against her jaw, coaxing her to open to him—she surrendered to it all with reckless abandon.

His mouth found the pulse at her throat and nipped the soft skin there, sending a jolt of desire straight to her core. She grew moist and pliable, eager to offer herself to him in every way a woman could offer herself to a man.

And he took, continuing down the slope of her breast.

Somehow her bra had been eliminated, but she couldn't remember how or when. Bending her backward over his arm, he teased her aroused nipple with his lips and tongue. She arched shamelessly into his caress and held his head there, right *there.* His cheeks hollowed as he rhythmically sucked, and each firm tug heightened the pressure coiling within her.

When she thought she would surely come apart in his arms, he eased his mouth from her breast and began a new journey. Holding her steady with hands bracketing her hips, he crouched down as he trailed kisses from the underside of her breast to the fastening of her jeans.

"Undo this." His hot breath wafted against her skin as his tongue dipped into her navel and he kneaded her backside with supple fingers.

She barely managed the job. Her hands shook as she fumbled with the metal button.

"Hurry." He nibbled and licked her fingers as she worked.

His questing mouth gave her a vivid preview of what he intended once her jeans were undone, and her hands trembled even more. "You're…you're not helping."

"I'm an impatient man." He thrust his tongue into the crevice between each of her fingers.

Her womb clenched in response. Finally she worked the button free and reached for the zipper.

"Never mind." He nudged her out of the way with his chin and caught the tab between his teeth.

Continuing his sensuous massage through the soft denim of her jeans, he drew the zipper down. The ragged sound of their breathing mingled with the rasp of interlocking metal giving way. Anticipation pounded through her veins and threatened to shove her over the edge before he even touched her.

The zipper reached the end of its track. Deft hands slipped inside the waistband of both jeans and panties and eased them over her hips and down to her knees.

She quivered, and a soft moan slipped unbidden from her lips.

His voice was tight with restraint. "You might want to hold on, pretty lady." As he gripped her from behind, his fingers gently coaxed her forward. Then he leaned in and touched her throbbing pulse point with the tip of his tongue. "So beautiful." He made a slow circle, and another.

She cried out and clutched his head in both hands as a spasm shook her and her knees nearly buckled.

Tightening his grip, he began a steady, relentless assault. The liquid sound of his talented mouth caressing her, whether the pace was slow and languid or rapid and urgent, never stopped. She began to pant as heat sluiced through her veins and gathered, heavy with promise, at the quivering juncture of her thighs.

Then he shifted his angle and delved deeper, tasting her so intimately that she gasped. His boldness should have shocked her, but she was too far gone, too immersed in the whirlpool of pleasure he'd created. She wanted what he was giving her—all of it.

As her climax bore down on her, she dug her fingertips into his scalp and arched her hips, shamelessly inviting him to take everything he wanted. He ramped up the pressure one more notch, and she came, and came hard, in a spiraling surge that lifted her to her toes and wrenched a long, keening cry from her throat.

And still he didn't stop. Burrowing deep, he brought her upward again, until her breathless cries filled the room and she lost track of whether she was standing or falling. Then strong arms swept her up and laid her, quivering and moaning, on the bed.

He kissed her mouth, her closed eyelids, her cheeks and her hair as he crooned soft words of praise. Yet he was the one who deserved praise. She would give it, too, if she ever recovered, if her vocal cords ever began functioning again and her lungs could drag in enough air.

For now, all she wanted was to lie here with her eyes closed and savor the wonder of an orgasm to end all orgasms. And she thought she'd understood what sexual pleasure was all about. Not even.

At some point he stopped kissing her and the next thing she felt was her boots coming off. She thought that was funny, because she'd forgotten she was still wearing them. But she didn't have the energy to laugh. Once the boots had hit the floor, he pulled off her jeans and panties.

Then she heard nothing but silence. Wondering if he'd left the room, she opened her eyes to discover him gazing at her. She didn't mind. After what they'd just shared she could hardly play the modesty card.

Besides, judging from his expression, he was mighty happy with what he saw. He looked—there was no other word for it, although thinking it made her blush—awestruck. She'd never experienced that before. It felt kind of nice, but strange, really strange.

He swallowed. "You're so beautiful, Lily."

Now she really was blushing. Letting him stare at her as if she had an amazing body was one thing, but hearing him say it out loud was going a little far. "Thanks, but you don't have to say that just because we—"

"It has nothing to do with that. Yeah, I wanted to get you naked for my own selfish reasons, but I hadn't counted on how seeing you that way would affect me. I was too busy a while ago to pay attention, but believe me, I'll pay attention from now on. You're magnificent."

"Magnificent? No." She rolled to her side and propped her head on her hand. "I'm reasonably good-looking." She swept a hand down her body. "Except for all the freckles."

"Are you kidding me? Your freckles are the best part of you." He grinned. "Well, okay, maybe not the *best* part."

"You're referring to my brain, of course."

He continued to smile as he unbuttoned his shirt. "Of course."

"I always wanted to be that tanned girl you see in bathing-suit commercials, but I don't tan. Mostly I look as if someone sprinkled me with nutmeg."

"Or cinnamon." He unsnapped the cuffs of his shirt, took it off and tossed it on the old rocker she had sitting in a corner of the room. "I like nutmeg and cinnamon."

Talk about spicy. The guy could fill out a white cotton T-shirt. A few minutes ago she'd thought her sexual urges were tamed for now, but watching him undress taught her that wasn't exactly true.

"Nutmeg and cinnamon remind me of pumpkin pie. You know, your hair is sort of pumpkin colored, so it all fits." He reached behind his back and grabbed the neck of his T-shirt to pull it over his head.

"FYI, most girls don't like to think their hair is the color of a pumpkin, even if it is."

"Uh-oh. Did I lose points?" His voice was muffled as his head disappeared temporarily inside the T-shirt.

By the time he'd pulled it off and tossed it on the rocker with the other one, she'd dismissed the pumpkin-colored-hair remark. Regan O'Connelli stood before her, a tousle-haired, shirtless cowboy fantasy if she'd ever seen one. She gazed upon the bounty he presented so casually, as if the sight of him half-naked wouldn't set her heart to thumping.

"No, you didn't lose points." She couldn't stop staring. Women bought calendars with photos of guys like this, men with broad shoulders, powerful pecs, washboard abs and a sprinkling of dark hair as a final touch. But Regan was no two-dimensional pinup. He was the real deal—irreverent enough to make her laugh, sexy enough to send her libido into overdrive and sentimental enough to hold images of emotional cliff diving close to his heart.

"I'm glad." He sat on the rocker and pulled off a boot. "I'd hate to lose points at a critical time like this." His muscles bunched as he took off the second boot.

"I wouldn't worry about it." She considered going over to help him with the rest of the process, because she desperately wanted to touch him. At last she'd be allowed, probably even encouraged, to smooth her hands over the sculpted planes of his body.

But if she stayed where she was, she could watch him take off the rest of his clothes, which would give her a visual that she'd cherish forever. It wasn't every day that a girl had such a fine specimen of manhood undressing in her bedroom.

After pulling off his socks, he stood and walked barefoot over to the duffle he'd left by the door. Unzipping it, he reached inside, took out a box and held it up. "Could this be the item you were asking about earlier?"

"Uh-huh." Seeing the box in his hand and knowing he'd soon be using its contents brought her right back to the trembling anticipation she'd felt when he'd first walked into her bedroom.

"Didn't know if I'd need these." Opening the box, he held her gaze as he walked over to the bed.

"Really? You couldn't tell I was folding like a cheap card table?"

His smile flickered. "I thought maybe you were, but sometimes when you desperately want something, you imagine what isn't there."

"It was there." A tremor of desire ran through her, making her hot and shaky. She lay back on the bed and drew in a deep breath. "Still is."

His hungry gaze swept over her, lingering on her tight nipples and flushed skin. "I can see that." He took out a packet and laid it on the bedside table. "You can open that if you feel like it."

"Not quite yet, cowboy. Not until I've had my hands…and my mouth…all over you."

That got the reaction she was hoping for. He peeled off his jeans and briefs in no time.

Her eyes widened as she beheld the gift she was about to receive. Regan O'Connelli had been blessed. And so had she, because for a solid week, that spectacular equipment would be hers to command. She couldn't get much luckier than that.

11

REGAN WAS A huge fan of making love in broad daylight, but he'd never found a woman who agreed with him. Until now. Lily hadn't suggested pulling the curtains or lowering the blinds. Instead her blue eyes sparkled as she demanded that he stretch out on her blue flowered quilt, smack in the middle of a patch of sunlight.

He didn't much care if he was illuminated, but when she straddled his thighs and sat there surveying the territory, those same sunbeams played with her curly red hair. He would still want her if she cut it all off, but he hoped she wouldn't do that, because that hair symbolized her in a way he might never be able to explain. Maybe it was the shockingly bright color, or the riotous curls, or her decision to keep it long so it fanned out around her shoulders in such dramatic fashion.

The sunlight also lovingly showcased her breasts. They weren't large, but they were sweetly curved, tipped with rosy nipples and dusted with nutmeg and cinnamon freckles. Eventually he'd kiss every single freckle on her pale skin. But now she proclaimed it was her turn to kiss him, and he wasn't about to deny her that.

When she leaned forward, her stomach bumped his erect cock. She settled lower, brushing against it as if she had no idea what she was doing. Slowly she stretched down far enough to nibble on his mouth as her body swayed over his. Her tight nipples tickled his pecs, along with locks of hair that tumbled over her shoulders and onto his chest. And always, always, her flat stomach slid against his throbbing erection.

Each time her flushed skin came in contact with the head of his penis, the sensation was that of warm silk caressing that increasingly sensitive spot. He stroked her smooth back and squeezed her firm backside. Seeking to even the odds, he allowed his fingers to stray, seeking that moist cleft he'd so recently tasted.

"No." She nipped gently at his bottom lip. "Not allowed."

"I think you like it." The deeper he probed, the wetter she became.

Her breathing hitched. "Stop. I want to concentrate on you."

He loved knowing he could affect her that way. He kept stroking. "Don't mind me. Just keep doing whatever you're doing, and I'll keep doing whatever I… Ouch! That's my earlobe!"

"And those are my teeth."

"Sharp little dudes."

"I'll make it better." She sucked on the spot she'd bitten.

"Mmm." He hadn't known his earlobe was an erogenous zone. Maybe with Lily every inch of his body was an erogenous zone.

Her breath warmed his ear. "Move your hands away from my happy place, cowboy. It's my turn. I promise you'll be glad you gave me one."

That sounded promising, so he slipped his hands free and stroked his damp fingers up and down the backs of her thighs. "Can I do this? I love touching you, Lily. Your skin feels…almost as if it's humming."

"I know." She licked a path down the side of his neck. "And it's your fault, too. It's like I stuck my finger in a light socket. But I'm going to make you come, and then you'll be in the same shape as me."

He groaned as she continued to tease him. He didn't want to come yet. She could play around if she wanted to, but he wanted the joy of sinking into her and creating that ultimate connection. That was important to him.

But he was in danger of forgetting what was important as the underside of his cock grew slick with the moisture that gathered on the tip in response to her casual, seemingly accidental, touch. It was no accident, he was sure, and his balls drew up, aching with anticipation. At last she began nibbling lower, trailing kisses along his collarbone and gently biting his nipples.

He hadn't known that would make his bad boy twitch, but it did. Maybe whatever she did with her mouth would have that effect, but he was yearning for one certain caress. He hoped that was part of her plan, but if she didn't go that route, he might spontaneously erupt just thinking about her hot mouth taking him throat-deep.

No, no spontaneous eruptions. He clenched his jaw and stopped stroking her satiny back because he felt the need to grab a handful of her comforter in each fist. She made agonizingly slow progress down past his ribcage to his abs. His cock waited, rigid but under control, until she followed his example and dipped her tongue into his navel. *Damn.* His penis jerked. His body trembled, and by some miracle he didn't come.

He almost told her to stop right there and get the condom, but he wanted… Oh, he really hoped that she'd… Ah… Her mouth closed over his much-teased cock and slid down, down, down, until the vibrating tip touched the back of her throat. His heart beat like a wild thing, and breathing became his second most difficult task—not coming being the first. But this was what he'd been waiting for, what he didn't want to miss if he could hold out. If he could stand the pressure when she… began to suck.

His eyes rolled back in his head. He wasn't sure if it was her technique—wonderful!—or his supersensitized cock, but this felt like the best he'd ever had. He was tempted to let her finish it. So tempted. His body clamored for release. But then he wouldn't know how it felt to be joined with her in that most basic way. He couldn't explain why it was so important to him. It just was.

Putting a stop to the joy she was bringing him was easier said than done. He made several attempts, but then she'd use her tongue a certain way, or scrape her bottom teeth gently along the lateral ridge, and he'd be lost again.

Finally he gripped her head with firm purpose and lifted her away. "No more." His voice sounded like a rusty hinge.

"Is something wrong?"

"No." He gulped in air. "It's so right it's scary. But I want… Please get a condom. Please."

Her voice was gentle. "Sure."

As if she understood. He'd believe it. They had so much to learn about each other, but in this it was as if they'd always been linked. Crazy thinking. But he couldn't say it wasn't true.

She put on the condom, which was a good thing because he might have fumbled the job. He was still lying there panting and holding on to her quilt for dear life. But when she'd finished, calmness settled over him.

She would have straddled him, but he stopped her. "Lie back, sweet Lily. It's my turn again."

Maybe she saw the sense of purpose in his eyes, because she stretched out beside him. When he rose over her, she welcomed him into the haven of her arms and the shelter of her body with a knowing smile.

He found his way with unerring precision. Gazing into the twilight blue of eyes glazed with passion, he drove home. He watched the spark ignite in her and fed that flame with steady, sure strokes. He didn't speak. Neither did she. Their bodies said all that needed to be said.

Her breathing quickened and her lips parted. "Yes," she murmured.

"Yes," he echoed as he felt her body rise under him. He pumped faster and she tightened around his cock. "Yes, Lily."

"Yes!" She arched in his arms, and he loosened the iron grip that had kept him in control. One more thrust, two, and he surged into her with a bellow of satisfaction that mingled with her cries of release. Burying his cock deep in her body, he shuddered in the aftermath of a climax that felt absolutely, completely right.

So much in his life had gone wrong, but in this golden moment, with the sun warming his shoulders, he was happy. Perhaps a man couldn't ask more than that.

LILY BLAMED LACK of sleep the night before, but somehow she and Regan ended up wrapped in each other's arms and oblivious to the rest of the world for the rest of the afternoon. The sun was low in the sky when she woke up to a crunching noise just outside the bedroom window.

Regan obviously didn't hear anything. He held her close, his breathing shallow, his eyes closed. Slowly she extricated herself from his embrace and eased out of the bed without waking him. Poor guy was dead to the world.

It didn't take her long to figure out where the strange sound was coming from. Sally peered through the window for a moment before resuming her snack, which was the bedroom windowsill. That was new. Until now, the horse had eaten only the porch railing.

Lily glanced back at her queen-size bed, where Regan slept on. He probably needed the rest. For all she knew, he hadn't had a decent night's sleep for six months. Stress could do that to a person. But after the stress-relieving afternoon they'd shared, he might sleep for twelve hours.

Locating her go-to sweatpants and a sweatshirt, she decided to put on her socks and boots, because she'd learned the hard way that it wasn't smart to deal with a horse either barefoot or in flip-flops. The first time she'd been stepped on while wearing flip-flops, she'd been lucky and hadn't broken any toes. She wasn't willing to trust her luck that way again.

But what to do about Sally? Lily admitted that Sally destroying the house and Buck obliterating the garden had gotten old. The paddock was an excellent idea, and she was embarrassed that she hadn't thought of it before. The horses would still have a measure of freedom, but they wouldn't have access to the entire property. Horses shouldn't be allowed to chew on the house. They could munch on wild grass instead of whatever had struggled to grow in the flower bed.

Lily let herself out of the house as quietly as possible before crossing the porch and walking down the steps. She had to avoid two piles of horse manure on her way around to the bedroom window where Sally was helping herself to the windowsill. Normally Lily would've been on poop patrol with the little tractor parked behind the barn, but today she'd been otherwise occupied. Mmm, had she ever.

It occurred to her that normal people didn't live this way, with animals free to destroy property and leave their little offerings where someone might step in them. She might have come to that conclusion eventually, but maybe not before some disaster that was bigger than a chewed-up building. Thank heaven for Regan O'Connelli, although if Nick had come out here on Friday he probably would have advised her to change her ways.

But Nick didn't have time to help out regularly at Peaceful Kingdom. Besides his work at the clinic, he had a wife and a fifteen-year-old who desperately needed him to provide fatherly guidance. Nick would have advised her to hire some employees, which she might do, anyway, but Regan had been available to move in and prop up this teetering operation immediately.

When she thought about how she'd resisted her attraction to him because she'd worried about a rebound relationship, she had to shake her head. If she did turn out to be a rebound for Regan, so what? He wasn't the kind to use her and dump her, and he was offering to help her turn this dicey situation into a workable rescue operation. If she could help him through this difficult time in his life, then she would, without selfishly worrying about whether she'd get hurt in the process.

Rounding the corner of the house, she approached Sally, who glanced at her with disinterest before resuming her meal. The mare had probably chosen this end of the house because the pig wallow was on the other end. In general, the horses had avoided the pigs, and vice versa.

The pig wallow should be moved, too, now that Lily thought about it. She'd dug it there so Wilbur would be close to the shelter of the house and she could keep an eye on him. But a sturdy pen a distance away with added protection from the elements made more sense. And the pigs, much as she hated to say it, would have to be in separate pens at mealtime. She'd caved and given Harley more food this morning, which was the only reason he hadn't gone after Wilbur's dish.

With a sigh, she walked over and caught hold of Sally's halter. "I'm dealing with a steep learning curve, Sally, old girl. Good thing a knight in shining armor showed up. Come on, now, come away from the windowsill." She gave the halter a gentle tug.

The mare stopped chewing on the wood.

"Excellent. Now let's go back to the barn, okay?" She tugged again.

Sally planted her feet and gave Lily a look that plainly said *Make me.*

"Oh, for heaven's sake. Let's go." Lily pulled with more force.

Sally jerked her head up so quickly that she dislodged Lily's grip. When Lily made a grab for the halter, Sally tossed her head and backed up with a snort.

"Okay, you're away from the windowsill. That's a start." She thought of trying to move the horse with the flapping technique, but of course her sweatshirt didn't have tails. Besides, backing Sally all the way to the barn didn't seem like the way to go.

As Lily stood with her hands on her hips and tried to figure out a feasible plan, the mare walked back over to the windowsill and took another bite.

"Damn it, Sally!" Lily made another grab for her halter, and Sally moved deftly out of the way. Then she stood there, tail swishing and brown eyes placid. She seemed to be waiting patiently for Lily's next move in the chess game they were playing.

"Got a problem?"

She turned as Regan, shirtless and sexy, approached. In her frustration with Sally, she'd forgotten that she might be disturbing him. "I didn't mean to wake you."

"No big deal. Need some help with that animal?" He'd pulled on his jeans and boots and come to her rescue, but clearly a shirt would have taken more time than he'd wanted to spend.

Considering the potent image he presented in that outfit and how it immediately affected her with a case of raging lust, she forgave him his cocky grin. "She's determined to chew on the windowsill. I guess it tastes better than the porch railing. She's being stubborn about going back to the barn."

He paused about ten feet away and folded his arms across that beautiful bare chest. "I can see that."

"Do you think you could catch her and take her back to her stall? I'm not having much luck, and I don't want her to destroy any more of this windowsill."

"I could, but it would be better if you did it."

"So far she's defied me. If she had hands instead of hooves, I think she would have flipped me off."

He nodded. "She does have that look in her eye. How

about this? Instead of going over and trying to grab her halter like you've been doing, you—"

"You were watching the whole thing from the window, weren't you?"

"Yeah. I heard her chewing and wondered what you'd do about it. When I realized she wasn't going to mind you, I decided to come out. We don't want to let her think she's the boss of you."

"Even if she is."

"She won't be for long. How about if you walk over there slowly, arms at your sides, and talk to her in a nice, calm voice as you approach? She might stay right there."

"It's worth a shot." Although at first she'd been relieved that he might handle the problem, she recognized this was better. She needed to learn how to control the horses, and he was conveniently here to teach her.

Turning back to Sally, she opened the conversation and began walking. "Hey, girl, you really don't want to chew on that windowsill, even if I did use environmentally safe paint on it. You have green flecks in your teeth, and I have to say, that's not a good look, especially at your age."

Behind her, she heard Regan's soft chuckle. "That's good. Make sure you're completely nonthreatening in your body language."

She did a body check and relaxed her shoulders. "Sally, babe, let me also appeal to your generous nature. If you keep chewing up my house, I'll be out some money for repairs. If you stop the chewing, I'll have extra money to spend on some nice perks around here. What would make you smile? Ribbons in your mane? A little bling on your halter?"

"She's listening," Regan said. "See how her ears are pitched forward?"

"Yep. I'm almost there. Now what?"

"Walk past her head, turn slowly toward her and casually stroke her neck. And keep talking. As you talk, work your way up her neck, scratch around her ears and stroke her muzzle, but act like you have no desire to grab the halter. And keep—"

"I know. Keep talking."

"Right. Your goal is to eventually take hold of the halter without making any sudden movements. Once you have it, cluck your tongue and start walking. Make sure your mind-set is that she'll follow. Assume she'll come with you, and don't jerk or tug."

"This feels like Jedi Knight training." She walked past Sally's head and slowly turned toward the horse.

"It's not so different from that. There's a lot of mental stuff going on when you work with horses. They pick up on your moods and your body language so well that you'd swear they can read your mind. If you're feeling uncertain, they won't want to do a single thing you ask. So think success."

"Okay." She continued to talk to Sally while visualizing that this interaction would go smoothly. She began stroking the mare's neck and eventually worked her way to Sally's muzzle. She could do this. Sally would obey her. When Lily thought she'd loved on the horse enough, she took hold of the halter, clucked her tongue and started walking toward the barn.

Sally followed.

Lily wanted to shout and punch her fist in the air, but that would be counterproductive. She settled for smiling at Regan in triumph.

He answered with a wide grin and gave her a thumbs-up. Then he ambled over and joined her as they headed to the barn. "Well done."

"You're a good teacher."

"I learned from the best. Ever hear of a horse trainer named Buck Brannaman?"

"Nope."

"He's the original horse whisperer, and I attended a clinic he gave back in Virginia. I haven't mastered all his techniques by any means, but he helped me tune in to the horse psyche, and that makes me a better vet. And in some ways, maybe a better man."

She eyed him. "For the record, I'm sure you were already a darned good man."

"Thanks, but there's always room for improvement."

She took a deep breath. "In my case, too. I realized when I walked out to confront Sally, that I don't give a damn if this turns into a rebound relationship. That was a selfish concern and I'm over it. The animals are lucky to have you here, and so am I. You're welcome for as long as you want to stay."

He walked quietly beside her, not saying anything. When he finally spoke, his voice was rough with emotion. "Thank you, Lily. That…that means more to me than you can ever know."

Maybe so, but she had an idea why her words had that effect. Perhaps he didn't realize it himself, but like the animals in her care, he desperately needed someone to want him again.

12

After polishing off the roasted portobello-mushroom sandwich Lily fixed him for lunch, Regan decided eating vegetarian meals for a week wouldn't be bad at all. Turning into a carnivore after he'd left home twelve years ago might have been more of an act of rebellion than a dietary preference. It hadn't hurt that he'd been starving to death, though. Between the trip out to the Last Chance and all the fun they'd had in bed, they'd blown right past the normal lunch hour.

But now that one hunger was satisfied, the other one was making itself known. He and Lily had eaten their mushroom sandwiches at the formal dining table because she didn't have anywhere else to eat—other than the throw cushions from the night before. She'd taken the end seat and he'd grabbed the one on her right.

He'd also wolfed down his meal like a man who hadn't eaten in a week. Sex usually had that effect on him, which was why he often raided the refrigerator afterward. This time he'd been too worn out, but in a really good way, to do that.

They'd spent the meal discussing a training schedule, which was supposed to begin in fifteen or twenty minutes. If they kept to that schedule, they should be able to work with two different horses this afternoon before it was time to feed the animals. As Regan observed Lily finishing her sandwich, he had some very unworthy thoughts that involved deviating from the plan.

She swallowed her last bite and caught him watching her. "What? Did you want the last bit of mine? Are you still hungry?"

He laughed. "At the risk of sounding like a cliché, the answer is yes, I'm still hungry, but not for food."

"Oh." Her gaze locked with his. "I see."

"But we have a hell of a lot to accomplish, so…"

"True." She gave him a once-over. "But now I'm thinking about having sex with you instead."

"You weren't before?"

"Sure I was. But knowing you've been thinking about it, too, is a whole other thing, if you know what I mean."

His cock twitched. "I most certainly do." She was still wearing those easy-access sweatpants.

"It would help if you'd go put on your shirt while I clear the table. Sitting here with you half-naked is bound to get a girl all juiced up."

"Nice to know I'm appreciated." His cock began to swell.

"Oh, you definitely are, but we need to get going." She stood. "So put on your shirt before I forget myself and grab you."

"Okay." But he smiled as he walked into the master bedroom. She couldn't go around delivering lines like that and expect him to be a good boy and do as he was told. Comments like hers inspired him to be a very bad boy, indeed.

But he could be bad and still hold to the schedule.

She might not believe that, so he'd have to prove it to her. The benefits to that were many, including setting the stage for more such encounters. They'd both be able to concentrate on work much better if they took occasional breaks to release some tension.

He returned wearing a shirt just as she'd finished wiping down the table with a damp dishrag. He pointed to a place in the middle of the table. "Missed a spot."

"Are you sure? We sat at the end. We didn't even use that part of the table."

"Yeah, right there." He moved a chair aside to give her access.

She came over and peered at the area he'd indicated. "Maybe there is something left over from another meal. Oh, and FYI, buttoning your shirt would be a good thing, too. You still look like a *Playgirl* centerfold."

"Think so, huh?"

"I'll bet you're doing it on purpose to get me hot." Leaning over the table, she scrubbed at the nearly invisible spot he'd pointed out.

He coughed to cover a moan. "Is it working?" He unbuttoned his jeans.

"I'll never tell."

"Let's see." Stepping closer, he caught her around the waist.

"Hey!"

He slid his free hand neatly under the waistband of both her sweats and panties.

Her breath caught. "I thought we agreed to… Regan…"

"What, Lily?" Pulling her against the erection straining the zipper of his jeans, he thrust his fingers deep. She was slick and hot. Ready.

"Work."

"We will." He breathed in the scent of her hair and the musk of her arousal. "This won't take long."

"That's what you think." She gulped for air as he continued to probe her heat. "Once you get me back in that bedroom, we'll be in there for—"

"We're not going back to the bedroom."

"Then where are we going?"

"Right here. If we stay out of the bedroom, we'll be fine." He stroked faster. "Come for me, pretty lady."

"You're…crazy." She braced her hands on the table and widened her stance. "But that feels so…good."

"Thought you'd like it." Closing his eyes against the intense pressure in his groin, he pumped rapidly until she began to whimper and tighten around his fingers. "Let go," he murmured.

"I… Yes, there. *There!*" Gasping, she came, massaging his fingers with each contraction.

Gritting his teeth against the demands of his own body, he stayed with her until her tremors subsided. Then he slowly withdrew.

Hands still braced on the table, her face hidden by her curtain of red hair, she took a shaky breath. "Great for me. Not so great for you."

"It will be. Stay right there." Quickly unzipping and shoving his jeans and briefs down, he rolled on one of the two condoms he'd stuffed in his pocket when he went after the shirt. From now on, he planned to have one with him at all times.

Then he drew her sweats and panties down, exposing her creamy backside, which was also dusted with cinnamon and nutmeg. He longed to kiss her there, but this episode wasn't about leisurely kisses. There would be other times. Many other times.

She sucked in a breath. "Regan?"

"Lean over," he murmured. "Arch your back and raise your hips." He nearly came when she did as he asked, resting her upper body on the table and presenting him with an exotic view of his destination—pink, glistening and blatantly inviting him inside.

He certainly planned to accept that invitation, but the angle was different and he didn't want to hurt her. Breathing hard from the effort to maintain control, he grasped her hips, eased partway in and paused.

She moaned softly.

"Did I hurt you?"

"*No.* I want more."

He gave her that and fought to hold back his climax. Sweat beaded on his chest.

"More. I want it all, mister."

He sank in up to the hilt and groaned at the pure pleasure of it. He swallowed. "Still okay?"

"This is *amazing.*"

She sounded surprised. Hadn't she ever tried it this way before? "But surely you've—"

"He...he wasn't built like you. So it was...anticlimactic."

Regan smiled. All righty, then. His ego had been stroked, but not his impatient cock. It wanted to move. "Tell me if this is okay." He drew back and slid forward again.

"Outstanding. More of that."

"How about this?" He initiated a steady rhythm.

"Oh, *yeah.*"

"Faster?"

"Oh, please, yes."

As he picked up the pace, she began to pant and

urge him on. He didn't need much urging. His thighs slapped against hers in a frantic tempo amplified by bare walls and floors.

"I'm coming! Oh, Regan, I'm coming!"

Her wild cries and the undulation of her hot channel hurled him over the edge. He surged into her with a bellow of surrender. Locked tight against her firm bottom, he shuddered and moaned as his cock kept pumping. It was the most intense orgasm of his life.

Neither of them moved. He knew he should. He'd planned for this to be short and sweet. Timewise it might qualify as short, but no way had it been sweet. Sweet was lollipops and roses, unicorns and rainbows, kittens and puppies. This coupling had been black velvet, bloodred wine and the low wail of a saxophone. This was sex in its most earthy, sensual, primitive form. And he wanted more of it.

While she remained stretched out against the smooth tabletop, she drew in a shaky breath. "Wow. Way to sabotage a work schedule."

He smiled. "Couldn't help it." Then the smile became a chuckle, and the chuckle morphed into a belly laugh.

"That feels very strange, Regan, since you're still… you know…connected to me. It's sort of vibrator-ish."

He laughed harder. "Is it turning you on?"

"It might if I hadn't just had a peak orgasmic experience, but my private parts are currently in a state of shock and awe."

He couldn't seem to stop laughing. She had a way with words, this girl genius. He supposed that went with the high IQ. "Want me to disconnect so you can recover?"

"I may never recover my dignity. Dear Lord. Bent

over a dining room table and taken from behind. What next?"

"Is that a question or a challenge?"

"I'll let you decide. But you probably should let me get up before I dislocate something."

"Okay." Reluctantly he started easing away from paradise.

"Wait."

He paused.

"Promise me something first."

"Good timing. I'm in the mood to promise you anything."

"This one's easy. Don't look."

"At what?"

"Me! Bent over the table in this unflattering position!"

"I find it extremely flattering."

"Maybe before, when you were filled with lust, but I doubt you will now. So promise me you'll close your eyes, turn around and head for the bathroom. Okay?"

He hesitated. "That's a lot to ask of a guy who's all about visual stimulation."

"You don't need any more of that. We have work to do. Promise you'll close your eyes?"

"Sure. I'll close my eyes." He hadn't said when.

"Good. By the time you get back, I'll be presentable."

"All right." He reluctantly backed away. But he sure as hell looked his fill before he left. He could talk until he was blue in the face and never convince her that men enjoyed different visuals from women.

Oh, yeah. He wasn't about to miss that. Surely there wasn't a prettier sight than her freckled bottom, so rosy from the incredible sex they'd just enjoyed. Below that, peeking out seductively, were the moist pink folds of her sex, still swollen with arousal. Any man would remember that sight for the rest of his life. And he was no exception.

LILY SUSPECTED REGAN hadn't honored her request not to look. Her first clue was his soft hum of appreciation after he'd slid out of her. Her second clue was his heartfelt sigh as he walked away. Her third clue was when he started whistling in the bathroom.

He was one happy guy, and come to think of it, she was one happy woman. Too bad he'd shot the timetable all to hell. But once she'd peeled herself off the table, pulled up her pants and walked slightly bowlegged into the kitchen, she was astounded to discover that they weren't so far off schedule, after all. Who would have thought you could pack so much pleasure into so little time?

And oh, the pleasure. She'd never considered herself a hedonist, but a man like Regan could make her reconsider her position. That cowboy knew how to ride. In any position.

Even better, he had the equipment to take that ride to the next level. She'd never been so thoroughly massaged, inside and out. She'd told him that she couldn't be aroused again so soon after such an all-encompassing episode. Apparently that wasn't true, because as she stood in the kitchen, she wanted him again.

Speak of the devil. In he walked, looking fresh as a daisy with his shirt buttoned and tucked into his jeans. No one would ever know what he'd recently been doing at the dining table. "Ready to do some horse training?"

But anybody who looked at her would guess she'd been had, thoroughly and with gusto. She gazed at him.

"You know how women are always saying that guys have it easy when it comes to peeing in the woods?"

"Do they say that?"

"Trust me, they do. Because it's true, if you think about it."

"I suppose it's true. But how does this apply to our current situation? If you're proposing a hike in the woods, or a campout, I don't think that's in the cards. We have too many responsibilities."

He was cute. She had to give him that. "I was merely making the point that men also have it easier when they have sex. Everything's sort of contained in one place, and once they zip up again, they're golden. Women, on the other hand, tend to feel sort of squishy and in need of a hot shower afterward."

His dark gaze was gentle. "By all means take a hot shower, Lily. Meet me down at the corral whenever you're ready."

"I didn't want to wuss out on you."

He smiled. "You aren't wussing. I'm the one who convinced you we had time for sex, remember? You wanted to get right to work."

"And boy, did I hold on to my resolve. Did you notice how tough I was? You really had to labor at changing my mind about having sex. It took at least five seconds."

He closed the gap between them and combed her hair back from her face. "I love that about you. You want me and you don't care if I know it."

"I used to care. At first I did everything I could to hide my reaction to you."

"But the important thing is that you don't hide anything from me now."

"No, I depend on your chivalrous nature not to look

at things I'd rather you didn't see." She batted her eyelashes at him, daring him to confess.

"I looked."

"Hell, I know you did! I could tell! I hate thinking that you'll carry that picture around in your head for God knows how long."

"I'll remember it forever."

She groaned. "Great. Etched in Regan O'Connelli's brain forever—Lily King's freckled fanny and her recently enjoyed feminine parts. Lovely."

"They were. Both enjoyed and lovely." He stroked her scalp with his fingertips. "If I let myself dwell on the image too long, I'll drag you into the bedroom, after all."

She tamped down her immediate response to that. If she let him know that she still wanted him, too, they would never get to the training. "We have to exercise some control."

He gazed into her eyes. "I know that. I'm not losing sight of what we have to accomplish for the sake of those horses out there."

"Good. Neither am I."

"So we'll go work for a few hours. But eventually we'll have to give up, because the corral isn't lighted."

"Should I consider that?"

"Not at this point. Installing lighting would be a major disruption. The lines should be underground, so you'd have all kinds of equipment in here. I doubt a construction crew would be able to finish the project in time to do us any good."

"So when it's dark, we're done?"

He smiled. "With the horse training, yes. I'll bet we can find some other projects to occupy our time."

"I don't know what's left on the list. Oral sex, check. Missionary position, check. Doggy style, check."

Heat flickered in his dark eyes. "I'm sure we can come up with a few other variations. You're the brainy one. Set your mind to it."

"Not a good idea. I can't be thinking about sex with you and learning to train horses at the same time. In case you haven't noticed, we're not too good at multitasking."

"Then we'll have to explore the options together, won't we?" His gaze dropped to her mouth. "We'll have several hours to do that tonight. I'm sure we can think of some way to entertain ourselves."

"You're a naughty boy, Regan O'Connelli. You know perfectly well I won't be able to forget about sex now. If I'm not effective with the horses, it's your fault."

"You'll be effective with the horses." He dropped a quick kiss on her lips. "Compartmentalize. Horses for the next two hours. Sex after that. Now go take your shower, and think of me while hot water is streaming over your amazing, responsive body. Imagine my hands rubbing your—"

"Stop it!" Laughing, she pushed him away. "Go out to the barn, and *don't* think of me in the shower. It could be dangerous."

"You've got that right." He winked at her. "Don't do anything in that shower that I wouldn't do." Plucking his hat from the counter, he settled it on his head before sauntering out the back door.

Lily found the willpower not to call him back by reminding herself how much the horses needed his help. Yes, she also had to learn how to work with them, but this week the burden of the training would fall on him because he was more experienced and therefore more efficient. If she didn't make it out to the corral for another fifteen minutes, the world wouldn't come to an end.

Normally fifteen minutes was more than enough time for her to take a hot shower. But Regan had awakened a more sensual Lily, a Lily who might just decide to grab a little personal enjoyment while she was in the shower. He'd warned her not to do anything he wouldn't do, which left lots of room to maneuver.

13

REGAN HAD PLENTY of practice at compartmentalizing. He'd used the technique to wall off thoughts about Jeannette while he'd taken the necessary steps to leave Virginia and relocate in Wyoming. But that wall was developing some serious cracks.

As he walked to the barn to pick up a lead rope, Lily was on his mind for obvious reasons, but Jeannette was there, too. After such explosive sex with Lily, he had to face the truth. He and Jeannette had never had that kind of chemistry. Sure, they'd enjoyed the experience. He had some good memories of sex with her. But none of them compared with today's total sensual immersion.

He thought back over the last couple of months he'd spent with his ex-fiancée and reluctantly admitted he'd let their sex life grow stale. He'd planned to spice things up after discovering that he wouldn't be spending Christmas Eve delivering a valuable foal, after all, but that had been an afterthought. Too little, too late. Jeannette very well could have felt neglected and unappreciated. He hadn't wanted to accept any blame for what had happened, but he might want to rethink that position.

He began to remember little things—the sexy nightgown that he'd barely noticed because he'd been exhausted from an all-night vigil with a sick thoroughbred. The candlelight dinner he'd missed when a high-earning stud ate some moldy grain and almost died.

Jeannette had assured him she understood, and he'd believed her. After all, she'd been raised in the world of thoroughbred racing and he'd become the vet of choice for her parents' stable as well as others in their exclusive circle.

But he should have found a way to make it up to her for those little disappointments. He could have been much better at letting her know that he cared. He *had* cared, but in a low-key, comfortable, take-her-for-granted kind of way. Ugh. No wonder she'd been tempted by Drake.

That didn't excuse Drake, though. Regan wasn't cutting that guy any slack. He'd moved in on his best friend's fiancée, and a friend just didn't do that. They'd all known each other since freshman year in college, for God's sake. He and Drake had decided within weeks of meeting in a biology class that someday they'd open a clinic together in Virginia and specialize in thoroughbreds.

Drake had introduced Regan to Jeannette that first semester, too, and the three of them had been inseparable. If she'd cheated with someone else, *anyone* else, Regan wouldn't have reacted with such fury. He'd thought he could trust the guy with his life, but he hadn't even been able to trust him with the woman Regan had planned to marry.

A horse nickered, pulling him out of his dark thoughts. He found himself standing in the barn, fists clenched and jaw tight, wondering what he'd come down there for. Oh, yeah. A lead rope so he could catch himself a horse to train. Might as well grab two ropes and get both horses in the corral at once.

The barn was empty except for Sally, who was the one who'd called to him from her stall at the far end. She probably hoped he'd let her out so she could continue snacking on Lily's house. "Sorry, old girl. You're in a time-out for now."

A rope looped over each shoulder, he headed out of the barn into the sunlight. His shades were clipped to the visor in his truck, and he'd decided to leave them there. Lily thought they were a sign of his secret anguish, so he'd be damned if he'd keep wearing them when she was around.

He didn't want to, anyway. They interfered with his full appreciation of Lily walking through sunbeams, her hair glowing like fire. Damn, wasn't that poetic? She had that effect on him, inspiring him to think in ways that were totally new to him. He'd never had thoughts like that about Jeannette, and he realized now that a guy should be entranced by the woman he intended to spend his life with.

Bottom line, he hadn't loved Jeannette the way he should have, considering the big step they'd been about to take. He hoped she'd find someone who would love her like that. It felt good to wish her well. Thanks to Lily, he could finally do that.

As he walked the property, he evaluated which two horses should come back to the corral with him. Then he noticed Rex standing on a small rise, head up, mane and tail fluttering in the breeze. Okay, that one. He was one of the troublemakers, which meant he might require more effort, but he would show well in the corral. Getting him adopted would eliminate one of Lily's biggest headaches.

Instead of approaching the big palomino, Regan relaxed his posture and waited to see if Rex would come to him. They'd established a tentative bond yesterday. Regan visualized the horse walking right up to him.

Rex looked over at Regan and tossed his head. Then he posed. Regan couldn't describe it any other way, and it made him chuckle. Rex stood with his chest out and his head high, as if to showcase how truly magnificent he was. Regan wasn't sure how long this demonstration might last, so he tried a low whistle, just to see if Rex might have been trained to respond to that.

Rex whinnied exactly as a movie horse might have been taught to do, and walked straight over to Regan. Then he began nosing Regan's pockets for a snack.

"Sorry, no treats." Regan clipped the lead rope on the palomino's halter and started walking back to the corral. Maybe he'd pick up another horse along the way. "Something tells me that whoever brought you in wasn't your first owner. You've been spoiled by more than one person, haven't you, Rex?"

The horse snorted.

"Yeah, thought so." Regan glanced back over his shoulder, and sure enough, several horses had fallen into line behind Rex. Regan would have his pick of another animal to train.

By the time Lily arrived at the corral, Regan was making good progress with Rex. A big bay named Molasses was tied outside the corral waiting his turn. The rest of the horses had drifted away, apparently bored by the proceedings.

Regan spared a quick glance at Lily, who'd left her hair loose around her shoulders. He'd like to believe that was for his benefit. She'd also added a Western hat, which was wise considering her fair skin. She looked darned cute in it, too. After allowing himself one potent image of her red hair spread out on a white pillowcase, he shut down that avenue of thought and concentrated on Rex.

"What can I do?"

"How about untying Molasses and leading him around a bit? See how he does on the lead, unless you already know."

"I don't. Because I never cared where they wandered, I had no reason to put a lead rope on any of them."

"Then finding out how he leads would be a good thing. Holler if you need any help." He figured it would be a good exercise for Lily, too. "By the way, have you ridden any of them?"

"Nope."

"I never thought to ask—do you ride?"

She shrugged. "I rode my friends' horses every so often when I was a kid, but I wouldn't say I'm really confident. That's probably why I didn't think to ride any of these guys, especially being out here alone."

"That's okay, but we should know whether they can be ridden before we adopt them out. Did the people who dropped them off mention whether they were good saddle horses or not?"

"Uh, no. I'm embarrassed about how little information I asked for. I need some sort of intake form, I guess."

She should have created such a form early on, but that was water under the bridge. "Don't worry about it. You have a couple of saddles in the barn we can use. After I've worked with Rex and Molasses for a while, we can saddle them up and take them out."

"You mean go riding?"

"Sure." He had a sudden thought. "Unless you're too tender."

She laughed. "Not yet. But if I'm going to be riding horses this week, then maybe we should refrain from—"

"Sorry. Not acceptable. I'll ride the horses."

That made her laugh even more. "My, my. I can tell where your priorities are."

"As if you had any doubt."

"Let's see how it goes. Maybe I can do both. As for this afternoon, I'd love to take a ride with you, assuming neither of these boys is a bucking bronco."

"I'll make sure of that before I let you get on one."

"I'd appreciate that. Okay, I'm off for a walk with Molasses. I won't go far, in case I need your help."

"Good idea." He hoped she'd get along fine with Molasses, so he wouldn't be required to come to her rescue. That would bode well for both woman and horse. But he was a typical guy, after all, and he'd discovered that being a woman's white knight was pretty damned cool.

LILY DIDN'T HAVE a single problem with Molasses. She couldn't decide if he walked quietly behind her at a respectful distance because he was well trained, or if he was responding to her more assertive attitude. She followed the tips Regan had taught her earlier that day with Sally and simply assumed Molasses would do what was expected of him.

Fortunately for both of them, he did. When Molasses had his turn in the corral with Regan, he was a model horse, so maybe his behavior had nothing to do with her new attitude.

"I have a feeling we'll be able to take that ride,"

Regan said as he came through the gate leading Molasses. “I had no trouble with this boy.”

“Me, either.” Lily untied Rex and walked beside Regan as they all headed toward the barn. “I guess that’s because he’s just a good horse.”

“Not necessarily. It might be that he recognizes you mean business.”

“I really have changed my attitude. Sally chewing on the windowsill was the last straw.”

“That bothered you more than the porch railing?”

“You betcha it did! Replacing and repainting that railing would have been work, but doable. Replacing a windowsill, especially for an older, double-hung window like that one, would have been a pain in the neck.”

“Yep.” He glanced over at her and smiled. “I’m glad you saw the light.”

“I did. I’m a changed woman.”

“Hey, let’s not get carried away. I like you fine the way you are.”

“I was too permissive. I can’t be that way anymore.”

“With the *animals.* But I love it when you’re permissive with me.”

Her body began to hum. “Way to sidetrack me, O’Connelli. I was completely focused on this horse-training exercise until you said *that.*”

“You were? Honestly?”

“Mostly. A girl has to sneak a peek now and then.”

“So does a guy. Especially when he’s training a mellow horse like Molasses.”

“Mmm.” She began replaying their bedroom and dining activities, and her panties were suddenly no longer so dry. “Out of curiosity, how long a ride were you planning on?”

"Long enough to take us out to the back of your property."

"Okay. That's not very far."

"Just far enough."

"I suppose you don't need a cross-country trek to find out if they'll behave themselves with a person on their back."

"No, I don't. And there's a nice tree out there."

She couldn't imagine what the tree had to do with the riding test. "Are you into trees?"

"Sure."

"So do you want me to ride Molasses, since he seems like such an easy horse?"

"I'll probably have you ride Rex. I'm more confident of his behavior now that we've worked together twice. But let's see how they react to being saddled before we decide."

Lily stepped back and let Regan saddle both horses, in case either of them kicked up a fuss. They didn't, but she knew Regan was visualizing that they'd stand there without protest, so that's what they did. She was becoming a fan of assumed consent.

"I'll mount Rex first," Regan said. "If he reacts okay to that, you can get on him."

"I'm hoping I'll remember how to do this."

"I'm sure you will." Regan tightened the cinch on Rex's saddle. He talked to the palomino in that same low, calming voice that seemed so effective. Then he rubbed the horse's shoulder and scratched under his mane before leaning against the saddle for a couple of seconds.

Finally he swung up into the saddle. Rex turned to look at who was on his back. "Just me," Regan said. As if satisfied with that, Rex faced forward again.

"So far, so good." Lily was trying not to think sexy thoughts, but Regan looked mighty fine sitting on a flashy horse. When he'd swung into the saddle with that easy confidence of his, her heart rate had sped up.

Regan dismounted. "He'll be okay. Let me test Molasses before you climb aboard Rex, though."

"Okay." She stood back as he repeated the routine with the bay gelding. Turned out he looked equally good there. Regan was impressive no matter what he was doing, but when he mounted a horse—oh, baby. That ramped up his sexiness quotient by about a thousand percent.

"Molasses is fine, too." He swung down again. "Go on and get up on Rex so I can adjust your stirrups."

She climbed up on the horse and tested the stirrups. Definitely too long. She sat astride the saddle breathing in the scent of warm leather and warm man as Regan worked on the stirrups, his face inches from her thigh. "I'm having improper thoughts," she murmured.

"Good. So am I." He moved back. "Try those out."

She stood in the stirrups. "Perfect."

He glanced up at her. "Yes, ma'am, you are."

Her breath caught at the warmth in his eyes. Desire was there, but something more, something tender and sweet. "I'm far from perfect."

"Not too far." He gave her a crooked grin. "At least that's my totally unbiased opinion." He squeezed her thigh. "Visualize this horse doing everything you ask him to."

"I will." She wondered if the technique would work on Regan. Then again, she really didn't need it. Judging from the way he'd just looked at her, he'd gladly do everything she asked him to, especially when they were both naked.

Now there was an arousing thought, as if she needed one. As they walked the horses away from the barn, she discovered that riding as an adult was a far more sensual experience than she remembered from when she was a kid. Or maybe she wouldn't have noticed the erotic nature of sitting astride a powerful animal if she hadn't recently had amazing sex with the man riding along next to her.

He turned his head and caught her staring at him. "You doing okay, pretty lady?"

"Fine."

"Be sure and tell me if anything is making you uncomfortable."

She watched as his hips moved in rhythm with the bay gelding. Meanwhile she dealt with the soft friction provided by a denim seam as it rocked against the leather saddle. By the end of this outing, she would be more than ready for a different kind of ride. "Define *uncomfortable.*"

"Painful."

"Then I'm good." She faced forward, because she simply couldn't continue to look at him without wanting to have him six ways to Sunday.

"I think we have a couple of trained saddle horses here. I can tell that to people with confidence on Saturday. They're also good-looking, which never hurts. Somebody will see that showy palomino and fall in love, I'll bet. Molasses isn't as eye-catching, but he has good lines."

"You aren't worried about Rex's aggressive behavior yesterday?"

"We need to ask a lot of questions about the home he'll be going to. He'll want to be the herd leader, and he requires his own stall. But if they understand that and they're firm with him, I think it'll work out."

"I hope so." The conversation distracted her a little, but her gaze kept wandering to his tight buns cupped lovingly by the saddle. When her lust threatened to get the best of her, she faced forward again. Sure enough, they were headed for that tree he seemed so crazy about. "If someone adopted Rex, it would ease my mind about fights breaking out."

"That's my thought. We'll concentrate on him. But I plan to train Strawberry, next. If both of them left, you'd be much better off."

"I would." As they drew closer to the tree, she noticed that it had a little patch of grass under it. The horses must have been grazing there in the shade, because it looked as if someone had mowed it. "Nice little spot there."

"It is. Nicer than I expected, even. How about stopping for a minute? We can find out how the horses behave if we tie them to that low branch on the far side."

"Fine with me." She was ready to take a break from constant stimulation to her private parts augmented by the hot cowboy riding almost within touching distance.

Regan swung down from his horse. "Beautiful view from out here. I love the way the shadows fall on the Tetons this time of day."

"Do you miss Virginia?" It was as much as she dared ask. Of course he had some bad memories connected to the place, but he'd lived there for several years, both when he attended college and after he opened a clinic with his friend Drake. Wyoming's rugged terrain was nothing like the manicured pastures and wooded hills of Virginia.

"No, I don't." He walked Molasses over to the low

branch on the far side of the tree. "Getting accepted into the University of Virginia gave me an ego boost, and I made some…some good friends there. I stayed for the people more than the landscape, although it's pretty."

She heard the catch in his voice and knew he had to be thinking of the two people who'd betrayed him. "I'm sorry it didn't work out for you there." She walked Rex over to where Molasses was tied and secured her horse's reins to the same branch.

"I'm not. Not anymore." The emotion edging his words made his meaning clear.

As she met his gaze and saw the frank appreciation there, her chest grew tight. If she was his rebound girl, apparently she'd succeeded in mending his broken heart. She told herself not to worry that this was the beginning of the end. Just because she'd had a rotten experience once before—when the guy had recovered from a breakup and then left her—didn't mean it would happen again.

"Let's go sit on the grass for a minute." He held out his hand.

She took it, and her heart squeezed. They were holding hands, just like in his vision of cliff diving. She could fall for this man. She might already be falling. If that was a mistake, she didn't know how to undo it.

He led her over to the little patch of grass before releasing her hand. "Pick your spot."

She chose one dappled with shade and sat down cross-legged. Taking off her hat, she finger-combed her hair and lifted it off the back of her neck. He remained standing, and she looked up at him. From this angle, she had a fine view of his excellent and talented package. She'd take that view over the Tetons any day. "Aren't you going to sit down?"

"Yeah. I just like watching you." Pushing back his hat with his thumb, he settled down facing her so their knees bumped. "And I like touching you and kissing you and feeling you come when I'm deep inside you."

She quivered as heat surged through her. "How you talk, cowboy."

"I like it when you blush." His smile crinkled the corners of his eyes. "It makes your freckles stand out."

"You're about to make me vain about those freckles."

"You should be." Reaching over, he threaded his fingers through her hair. "I just want you to know that you're an amazing woman." He rubbed a strand of her hair between his fingers. "Until I met you… Correction, until you invited me into your bedroom to handle your problem—"

"Cheesy, wasn't it?"

"Nope. Fun. Like you." He held her gaze. "I had no idea what I was missing, Lily. I never dreamed I could want a woman this much. I lived in a colorless world with no real passion. You inspire me to be different."

She wanted him so much she could barely breathe. "You inspire me, too."

"When I suggested riding out here, I was thinking we could have some outdoor sex, since we hadn't done that yet."

"Oh." Surprisingly, she hadn't considered that, but now that he'd told her, she began to ache in predictable places. She hoped he hadn't given up on the idea.

"I pictured it as another quick romp to tide us over until after we'd fed the animals and had more time to ourselves."

"Sounds good to me."

"Now that we're here, it doesn't sound so good to me."

"It doesn't?" She certainly hadn't expected to hear

that. Canceling her ticket on the orgasm train wouldn't be easy. Maybe she should just tackle him. "Why not?"

"Because I don't want it to be quick. I want it to be slow and sweet."

"Oh!" Apparently they were back in business. Goody.

"I want you stretched out naked in this fragrant grass while I kiss every freckle on your silky skin. Then I want to slide into you, over and over, and tell you how beautiful you are while I make you come."

"Oh." If he kept talking like that, she might spontaneously combust without benefit of penis.

"What I want, Lily King, is to make love to you."

"Ohhhh." For the second time in two days, she nearly swooned.

14

REGAN HAD CHOSEN his words carefully when he'd announced that he wanted to make love to Lily. Earlier today they'd had sex, and maybe they'd just have sex again in the future. But this time was about gratitude. Six months ago he hadn't felt particularly fortunate. Today he'd realized he was the luckiest guy in the world.

Lily had shown him that. He wanted to show her what she meant to him, and for that, they needed to make love. He didn't confuse it with being *in* love. They hadn't known each other long enough for that to happen. But that didn't mean they couldn't *make* love. Besides, who knew? Maybe one day soon they would discover that they'd fallen, and fallen hard.

They undressed each other with care, taking time to lay their clothes in a neat pile. They took even more time to kiss and nuzzle each other along the way. When Lily finally lay back on the cool grass, Regan's cock felt as if it was made of tempered steel. He'd clenched his jaw as he'd rolled on the condom. If he wasn't careful, he could come just by looking at her lying there.

Yet he wanted to look at her and burn her image into his memory. So he knelt beside her, rigid cock notwithstanding, and memorized the picture she made. Green was definitely her color. The soft grass set her off like a jewel nestled in velvet, highlighting her fiery hair and pale skin dusted with cinnamon and nutmeg.

A breeze ruffled the leaves over her head, and shadows danced over her body. She seemed one with nature, a sensual female aroused and ready to be taken by a lustful male. And he was that male…for now.

An emotion stirred deep in his chest, an unfamiliar one. It felt…ancient. It had no place here, and he shoved it away, but still he heard it whisper. *Mine.*

Reaching up, she stroked his cheek. "Such a fierce expression you have."

"Do I?" He met her clear-eyed gaze. He must have been carried away by the setting. "I was concentrating while I counted all your freckles. I don't want to miss any of them when I start the kissing part."

She smiled. "We'll be here all night."

"Maybe." Leaning down, he kissed a sweet little freckle on her breast. "One." Then another. "Two."

She laughed as he kept kissing and counting, but then he paused and drew a nipple into his mouth. She didn't laugh then. She moaned and held his head to her breast, her fingertips pressing into his scalp.

Her urgency fed into that ancient voice telling him to claim her. No, he would not. But he abandoned freckle-counting for the more primitive pleasures of nibbling and licking her breasts while he caressed her damp thighs and sought out the slick heat waiting for him.

She moaned again and arched upward, inviting him deeper. Capturing her mouth to muffle her cries, he stroked her until she came, bathing his fingers in her juices. As she lay panting beside him, he trailed his hand up her flushed body and anointed her lips. Then he leaned over and kissed her.

The heady taste sipped from her mouth made him a little crazy. He wanted, *needed* more. Kissing his way back along the damp trail he'd made with his fingers, he moved between her thighs. The scent of crushed grass and fragrant earth mingled with the aroma of sex as he settled his mouth against her heat.

With the first lap of his tongue she sighed and opened wider, offering herself so completely that his breath caught. *Mine.* He feasted until her whimpering cries told him she was close.

Sliding slowly up her restless body, he effortlessly buried his cock in her drenched channel. He felt the quiver, knew she was almost there. "Wait," he murmured. "Wait for me."

She gulped. "Okay."

When he was locked in tight, he braced himself on his forearms and gazed down at her.

She looked right back at him, her eyes dark with passion, her red hair spread out over the grass like tongues of flame.

He was stunned by the force of his desire for her. "It's never been like this for me."

"Me, either."

That helped, knowing she'd been blindsided, too. "I don't know what's going to happen."

She smiled at that. "I do. We're both going to come."

"Yeah." He appreciated any attempt to lighten the mood, because wow, this was intense. "And we can't be loud and scare the horses."

"I know." She stroked his back and pressed her fingers into his backside. "Ready for some cliff diving?"

"Yes." And he began to thrust, holding her gaze as

the rhythm escalated, watching her eyes. He saw arousal there, but he also saw wonder, and maybe just a touch of fear. His expression probably told the same story.

Faster, now…almost there…

She gasped. "Now."

"Yes…" He gulped for air. "Jump." He kissed her and swallowed her cries as her climax rolled over his cock. Then he broke away to drag in a breath, clenched his jaw and came in a furious rush that left him reeling. He felt the shock of it from his scalp to his toes.

Breathing hard, he closed his eyes and somehow managed not to fall on her. When at last he felt recovered enough to open them, he discovered that she'd closed hers, too. She appeared suddenly more vulnerable lying there in the grass, her cheeks blushing from a recent climax and her mouth red from his kisses. As if waiting for this moment, the ancient whisper sounded again. *Mine.*

But she wasn't his or any man's. She was her own person, and yet…if she was into this as much as he was, she was trusting him not to hurt her as that other bastard had. She'd said she didn't care if this was a rebound relationship, but he wasn't sure he believed that.

God, he hoped he hadn't used her to get over Jeannette. A rush of protectiveness made him vow that he wouldn't let anyone hurt her. And that included him.

IN THE NEXT few days, Lily worked harder and enjoyed more great sex than she'd ever had in her entire life. She also couldn't remember being happier. She and Regan were creating a practical rescue operation at Peaceful Kingdom, and that was extremely satisfying. And bonus, so was the sex.

Somehow they managed to get the work done and

still have time to fool around. Often they had to get creative, such as when they made quiet but highly orgasmic love on a hay bale while the horses ate breakfast. They'd done that twice.

Lily found herself walking around with a song in her heart and a smile on her face. She'd always been a cheerful person, but these days it seemed as if nothing would get her down. She was in high spirits when Nick and Lester showed up late Thursday afternoon to help work with the horses.

Having someone around felt a little strange after all the private time she'd had with Regan. But on Friday night everyone would descend to help set up, so in effect, the isolation she and Regan had enjoyed was nearly over. Lester, it turned out, had a special affinity with horses and planned to be a trainer some day. So Regan invited him out to the newly constructed pasture to help pick out two animals they'd train until the corral became too dark. That left Nick and Lily free to lean on the corral and discuss the progress that had been made so far.

"Everything's in place," Nick said. "Your fliers have been distributed. Some basic food's been ordered, which Mary Lou will be in charge of on Saturday. Dominique will be here to take pictures, and we managed to nix the jumping castle and the cotton candy machine."

"I'm just as glad. I know Tyler was worried about entertaining the kids, but I'm afraid a jumping castle would involve a lot of noise that might bother the horses."

"She was going to set it up quite a ways from the corral, but still, I agree. It's expensive and potentially disruptive. Tyler's hired someone who does face painting, and she's organized an activity table for the kids with coloring and a few simple crafts."

"Did she decide to have a band?" Lily had been a little worried about that possibility.

"After much discussion, not doing it."

"That's a relief. I know some barns have music piped in, but since I don't do that, I'm afraid a band might be another distraction. Regan and I have enough on our hands getting the horses ready for all that activity without adding a potential hazard."

"Which brings me to another point. You two have done a terrific job this week. The porch railing's fixed, the flower beds are replanted and the new sign is gorgeous."

"Thanks." Lily beamed at the compliment. The sign read Peaceful Kingdom Equine Rescue, and it had turned out beautifully. "I was lucky to find somebody local who could create that sign on short notice. Regan and I have worked hard."

"I can tell. And hanging out with him must suit you," Nick said. "I've never seen you looking so…settled."

That startled her. "What do you mean by *settled?*"

"Don't take this wrong, but I've always viewed you as a tropical bird about to take flight."

"And now I look like what? A roosting chicken?"

Nick laughed. "I was thinking more like a turtle dove."

"Wait a minute." She panicked at the idea that her feelings for Regan were that obvious. "Don't go making any assumptions."

"What assumptions? You two like each other and you're both single. I'm happy for you."

"You haven't said anything like that to Regan, I hope." She would die of mortification if he had.

"No, I haven't, so don't get your undies in a bunch. He's been tearing in and out of the office all week like a madman so he can take care of his clients and help you out here. We've barely said two words to each other."

"That's a relief."

"But when I have seen him, he always had a smile on his face. I can't say that's been the case prior to his moving in here. So I figure you've been good for him, too."

"I hope so, but please don't jump to conclusions." She broke out in a cold sweat at the thought of Nick pushing Regan into an admission of his feelings for her one way or the other. Neither of them had taken that step, and maybe they never would.

"Okay, but tomorrow night you'll have a whole mob of people who are liable to jump to conclusions. You might want to decide how to handle that."

That was a scary thought. She sent him a pleading glance. "Could you caution everyone not to ask any leading questions? We're at an uncertain stage right now, and I don't want him to feel pressured."

"I can say something, but there's no way I can control that bunch. Regan knows what they're like. Have a talk with him. Come up with your standard responses."

"Okay, I will." She cleared her throat. "I can't deny that Regan and I are having a little fun, but I think it would be foolish of me or anyone to take his interest too seriously. He just broke up with his fiancée. He's not ready for another relationship."

"Could've fooled me." Nick adjusted the fit of his Stetson. "If anything, he looks happier than you do."

"Well, sure, he looks *happy.* That doesn't mean he's in *love* or anything." That last part had been harder to say than she'd expected.

Nick stared at the Tetons as the afternoon shadows gathered in the canyons. "Mighty pretty view."

"It is." She figured he was buying time as he decided how to approach an obviously delicate subject.

"Look, God knows I'm no expert on this subject, but I think both of you are heading into that kind of emotional territory, at least a little bit. And if you want my advice—"

"Not really."

"You'll keep an open mind," he continued, ignoring her protest.

"Nick, six months isn't long enough. Most people need a year to get over a thing like that."

"Maybe most people do, but don't assume he's most people and don't assume he's not ready. Everybody heals at a different rate. My guess is that Regan's more resilient than most because of his parents."

"His *parents?*" That shocked her.

"That's what I said. Got a banana in your ear?"

"I heard you fine, but judging from what he's told me, he doesn't agree with their lifestyle or their parenting skills."

"He might not, but I've had a few years to observe the O'Connelli crew, and while Seamus and Bianca might have been too permissive, their kids never doubted they were loved. They all have an unshakable belief in their own worth."

Lily thought about Regan's quiet confidence, especially when he was working with the horses. "You may have a point."

"I generally do."

She looked sideways at him and couldn't help laughing at his cocky grin. "I'll bet Dominique has to use a wide-angle lens to get you and your ego into the same frame."

He chuckled. "I'll tell her you said that. She'll love

it. She wanted to come over to see you tonight, but she's mounting a new show at the gallery, and that's sucking up all her spare time. Plus, as she pointed out, she's not a horse trainer."

"Neither am I."

"According to Regan, you're better than you think you are, which doesn't surprise me. You have a lot of empathy. I'm glad to see you getting into this. I think it suits you better than whatever IT gigs you had in Silicon Valley. Every time I talked to your folks you'd switched jobs."

"Because I'd get bored."

"Maybe that's because you're more into living creatures than electronic gizmos."

"You think so?" No one had ever said that to her before. "You don't feel like I'm wasting my intelligence on this project?"

"How could you be? In order to make a success of this venture, you'll have to learn to think like a horse, run a business and attract both donors and potential adopters. Isn't that enough of a challenge for you?"

"When you put it that way, yes."

"Who said you were wasting your intelligence?"

She thought back to a phone call she'd had yesterday, one she hadn't mentioned to Regan. "A computer game company in Palo Alto wants me to work for them. I told them I don't want to leave this place, and they said that while I might be able to telecommute from here, they generally discourage it. They've found that having everyone on site interacting with other designers contributes to more innovation."

"Are you considering it?"

"No, of course not." She watched Regan walking back with Lester, small for his age but incredibly likable. Each of them led a horse and both animals looked docile as could be. "Certainly not now, anyway."

Nick took a deep breath and blew it out. "Lily, you're not going to break that guy's heart, are you?"

"No." Longing tugged at her, as it always did when she looked at Regan. "But I'm still not entirely convinced he won't break mine."

15

REGAN WAS GRATEFUL for the Chance clan pitching in. Without them there would be no adoption fair, and Lily desperately needed to find good homes for at least six of the horses under her care. But their Peaceful Kingdom had been invaded late Friday afternoon by a Chance contingent ready to set up for the fair, and Regan knew he wouldn't get to be alone with Lily until late tonight. By then they'd both be too exhausted to make love.

On top of that, they'd agreed to be careful how they interacted with each other to keep gossip to a minimum. She'd told him about Nick's suggestion that they come up with a standard response to any questions. It was *We're just good friends.* Regan didn't think anyone would believe that BS, but he said it, anyway, because apparently that's what Lily wanted.

He was a little irritated that she didn't want to go public with their relationship. What was wrong with letting close friends and family know they were involved? They suspected it, anyway, so why be coy? But Lily insisted on a party line, so he was doing as she asked, because in the end, he'd do just about anything that woman asked.

They'd been on a deadline situation this past week, but once they got successfully past the adoption fair, he needed to have a heart-to-heart with her. Technically he'd have no more excuse to live in her house. Oh, yeah, and that was the other thing. He'd had to move all his stuff to the guest room and pretend he was sleeping there. Lame.

Anyway, he'd go along until after the fair, and then he'd flat out ask her how she felt about him. Would she still want him around when she no longer needed him to help her with the animals? Now that she had a paddock, a chicken coop and a pigpen, she could handle her menagerie a lot easier. Once a few horses went out the door, it would be a piece of cake for a woman of her abilities.

So then what? They each needed to lay their cards on the table. He wanted to stay. He thought they had something going and he wanted to find out where it would take them. She might feel differently. Thinking about having that talk made him nervous as hell, but it had to be done.

Right now, though, he didn't have much time to contemplate the next step in their relationship. He was too busy helping set up bleachers next to the corral, a canopy for Mary Lou's refreshment stand and another canopy for the kids' activity center. Jack, Nick and Gabe were in the barn grooming the horses so they'd shine like new pennies. Although they'd settled on showcasing only ten of the twenty-one, Jack had insisted that every horse look tip-top to enhance the image of the place. He had a point.

Regan was so busy moving from one job to the next that it was a wonder he even heard his phone. But when he did, he considered not answering. He knew that ring.

He'd assigned it to the caller several years ago and had never bothered to change it or delete the number from his contacts.

He couldn't just let it go to voice mail. At the last minute, he punched the button and walked over to a darkened spot in the yard, away from all the action. "What?"

"Hey, Regan." Drake's voice sounded strained. "I wasn't sure you'd pick up."

"I almost didn't."

Drake didn't respond at first. "I get that," he said at last. "The thing is, I'm here."

"Here?" Regan's grip tightened on the phone and he glanced toward the gate as if expecting Drake to come walking through it. "What do you mean, *here?*"

"In Jackson Hole. Not too far from that little town you always talked about, Shoshone."

"What the hell are you doing in Jackson Hole?"

"Two things. I needed some time to think, and I needed to see you."

"Can't imagine why you need to see me." The anger he thought he'd tucked away came boiling to the surface. "We have nothing to discuss."

"You said that six months ago, too. You may have nothing to say to me, but I have plenty to say to you. I'd like that opportunity, Regan. For old time's sake."

"Old time's sake?" He realized he'd gotten loud, and he walked farther into the shadows and lowered his voice. His heart was pounding like a snare drum. "I can't believe you can say such a thing. Old time's sake? You don't give a shit about old times, Drake. Don't pretend like you do."

More silence, followed by a sigh. "Okay, forget about that. Don't agree to talk with me because of our former friendship. I suppose that's not important. Something else is, though. You're still furious with me. I can hear it in your voice."

"What if I am? That's my business."

"True. But this situation isn't good for either of us. We're both festering, Regan. You're a doctor. You know wounds like this have to be lanced. Let's get together and take care of that. If we end up beating each other to a bloody pulp, so be it. At least we'll get it out, drain off the bad stuff."

While a part of him longed to get into a fistfight with Drake, he'd have to actually be in the same room with the guy to make that happen. He had no wish to do that. "Sorry. You've caught me at a bad time. I'm too busy to play your silly reindeer games."

"That's good, at least. It's good to be busy."

"Yes, it is. Now, if you'll excuse me, I have to get back to what I was doing."

"Yeah, okay. But if you change your mind, I'm going to be here for a couple of months."

"A couple of *months?*" In spite of not wanting to prolong the conversation, Regan couldn't resist asking about that. "It's the middle of the damned thoroughbred racing season! How can you afford to be out here instead of back at the clinic? Or even more to the point, how can you leave your parents and their cronies in the lurch like that?"

"I have someone covering for me. If he gets overwhelmed, there are plenty of vets in the area who will be glad to have the business."

Regan wasn't sure he'd heard right. "You don't care if your parents are pissed? You don't care if your business goes down the tubes because you needed a long vacation?" That wasn't the Drake Brewster he knew.

"No, I don't. Those things aren't a priority right now. I have two goals—getting my head out of my ass and talking things out with you. Since the first one will probably take at least two months, I thought I'd make a start on achieving the second one."

"Good luck with that. I have no interest in seeing you."

"Just think about it. I know you, Regan, and you *will* think about it. The cabin where I'm staying is just outside the boundaries of the Last Chance Ranch."

"How the hell did you know to go there?"

"That's where you had me forward your mail, Regan. The cabin's owner said the Chance family knows where the place is, so they can direct you if you decide to pay me a visit."

"I won't."

"Your choice."

"You bet it is. Goodbye, Drake." He disconnected the call and stood in the darkness, adrenaline pumping through his system. Damn Drake Brewster to hell and back. Regan began to pace in a tight circle, keeping to the shadows.

This *sucked.* Right when he was starting to mellow out and enjoy life again, specifically life with Lily King, and forget about that nasty chapter in his past, here was Drake to remind him of it. Worse yet, the guy intended to stay in that little cabin for two friggin' *months.*

Sure as anything, Regan would run into him at the Shoshone Diner, or at the ice-cream parlor, or...wait. The most likely place would be Spirits and Spurs. Shit! Now Regan wouldn't be able to go in for a beer without worrying about Brewster riding a bar stool and polluting the atmosphere by his very presence.

Regan wanted him gone, but it was a free country.

He couldn't make Drake leave. His only recourse was to convince him, one way or another. And that meant going over to that blasted cabin. Damn it!

"Regan?"

He turned, and there stood Lily looking worried. No wonder; he'd been pacing and muttering to himself like a crazy man. "What?"

"I came to ask you something, but…you're obviously upset. What's wrong?"

"I…" He took off his hat and scrubbed his fingers through his hair. His head hurt. His whole body hurt. He crammed his hat back on. "Never mind. It'll take too long to explain." With a supreme effort, he dredged up a smile. None of this was Lily's fault. "What's the question?"

She hesitated. "Is this problem something I need to know about?"

"Eventually. Not right this minute. What's up?"

"Dominique's offered to make up a poster showing each horse, just the face, and their name underneath. She can do it tonight, no problem. But should we include the lifers on there? And if so, how should we label them?"

"Not *lifers*." That made him smile for real. This past week he and Lily had started calling the permanent six by that nickname. "Sounds like we're running a prison. How about calling them permanent residents and the others temporary guests?"

"That works. I'll let her know." She paused. "Sure you can't tell me what's got you so upset?"

"Drake called." Just saying those words made it more real. His chest felt as if someone had wrapped a steel band around it and pulled it tight.

Her eyes widened. "Why?"

"He's here in Jackson Hole. Staying in a little cabin near the Last Chance boundary for two months. He wants to talk."

"Wow." She regarded him silently for a few minutes, her eyes full of compassion. "Well…maybe that's good."

"Good? How can that be good? I came here to get away from the bastard!"

"I know, but…if you could clear the air…"

He stared at her in disbelief. Apparently she hadn't been paying attention. "Sure, why not? Then everything will be fine. We can sit around a campfire, tell jokes and sing 'Kumbaya.'"

"I'm not saying it will be easy, but if he's holding out the olive branch, don't you have an obligation to take it after all you meant to each other?"

"No! I don't have a single obligation when it comes to Drake Brewster!"

She didn't respond to that, but he could tell from her expression that she didn't agree with him. She thought he should make nice with his former best friend, mend the fences and forge a new relationship. Bull. Her advice sounded familiar, though. His parents had counseled him to do the exact same thing the last time he'd talked to them.

"I'm not going to engage in some damned sensitivity session with Drake so that he can feel better about himself, Lily. I have no *obligation* to ease his guilty conscience. He did what he did, and now he can suffer the consequences. End of story."

She seemed about to say something, but then she didn't. "Okay, fine. I'll go tell Dominique how to label the horses." She walked away, clearly disappointed in his reaction.

He wasn't too happy with hers, either, but he shouldn't

be surprised. She was the softie, the one who couldn't help but say yes, the one who hadn't been firm with the horses because she hadn't wanted to damage their fragile egos. Naturally she'd want him to smooth things over with Drake. He wasn't about to do that. Not even for her.

THE CHANCE FOLKS left around midnight. Earlier tonight Lily had looked forward to them leaving so she could spend some quality time with Regan. Now the issue of Drake hung between them. She could sweep it under the rug and pretend it didn't matter while they frolicked in her bed, but that wasn't her style.

If she'd been in this relationship only for the sex, she might have considered ignoring Regan's attitude toward Drake. But wonderful as the sex had been all week, the friendship they'd created was even more important to her. And friends didn't let friends go off the rails, at least not without making some attempt to help.

They stood together on the porch waving as the last of the Chance trucks pulled away. Lily felt good about the preparations. The horses were better disciplined, and Peaceful Kingdom looked like an organized rescue operation instead of the helter-skelter project it had been a week ago.

She turned to Regan. "Thank you for all you've done. The adoption fair is going to be awesome."

"It should run smoothly." There was a reserved note in his voice that hadn't been there a few hours ago.

She hated that, but judging from his cautious mood, she couldn't have coaxed him into mindless sex even if she'd thought it was a good idea. They'd become so close in the past week, but they didn't have a firm foundation that would allow them to postpone an important discussion while they blew off steam. The discussion had to come first.

Earlier this evening she'd put on a fleece hoodie to ward off the chill of an early June night. Regan was wearing a denim jacket for the same reason. She decided to take advantage of that and suggest they stay out here and talk. For one thing, the porch was about the only place they hadn't made love. It could be their neutral zone.

"How about sitting on the steps here for a little while before we go in?" She visualized a positive response, the way he'd taught her to do with the horses. She'd discovered sometimes it worked with people, too.

He blew out a breath. "That's probably a good idea. I want to explain a few things."

"Good." She sat down on the top step. "I'm all ears."

He sat next to her but not close enough to touch. That in itself was telling. Usually when they were alone, he couldn't get close enough. "I told you nobody knew the details of that Christmas Eve but the three people involved. I want you to know them, so you'll understand."

"Okay."

Resting his elbows on his knees, he laced his fingers together. She wanted him to reach out and take her hand, but he didn't choose to do that. "Let me give you some quick background. Drake was the first friend I made my freshman year at UV. We did everything together. He introduced me to Jeannette, and then the three of us hung out a lot, sometimes adding whatever girl Drake was dating at the time. He never stayed with any very long."

"Could he have been secretly in love with Jeannette?"

"No."

"You're sure?"

"Yep. And before you ask, she wasn't secretly in love with him, either. We were together a *lot.* I would have picked up on it."

"Guess so." Lily wasn't totally convinced, but she let it go. This wasn't about what she thought.

"After graduation, Drake and I went into practice together. His parents own racehorses and so do many of their friends, including Jeannette's folks. With contacts like that, we couldn't help but succeed. To no one's surprise, Jeannette and I got engaged."

"Right."

Regan cleared his throat and stared into the darkness. "As I said the other day, I've thought about that engagement a lot lately, and I'll admit I wasn't the most attentive guy. I let work interfere too much. In fact, I'd expected to spend that Christmas Eve delivering a foal, but it turned out to be false labor. So I got to go home to Jeannette. Instead of calling to say I was on my way, I decided to surprise her."

Lily's stomach lurched. Poor Regan.

"When I saw Drake's SUV sitting in front of our town house, I figured he'd pulled his usual trick of shopping on Christmas Eve. He's famous for that. I thought he was delivering our last-minute gift."

She put her hand on his arm because she had to touch him. His muscles stiffened, but she kept her hand there. "I'm sorry. So, so sorry."

"I walked in, thinking they'd be in the living room, or maybe back in the kitchen, because Jeannette had promised to make cinnamon rolls for Christmas morning. Then I heard her upstairs. She was...moaning with obvious pleasure."

Lily sucked in a breath and laid her head on his arm. "Horrible."

"They said it was the first time they'd had sex, and the thing is, I believe that's true. But once was all it took for me to realize that I never wanted to see Drake Brewster again."

She squeezed his arm and gazed at his profile, which looked as if it had been carved in granite. "I don't blame you."

His shoulders relaxed a little. "Thank you. I figured if I told you the whole story, you'd understand."

"I do. Oh, Regan, I do. But…"

"But?" He looked squarely at her. "Surely after hearing my side of the story, you're not going to tell me I should meet with him."

"Not for his sake."

"Damn straight! Then why go?"

"For your sake, so you can put this behind you."

"I *have* put it behind me!"

"No, you haven't. If you had, then you wouldn't care if Drake showed up here. But he did, and you're beside yourself. You need to go see him, Regan, and make peace with the situation."

His jaw worked as he stared straight ahead. "You'll be happy to know that I do have to go see him. But I'm only doing it because it's how I'll get him to leave. I won't be going to make peace with the situation. I'll be going to get his ass out of my town." Standing, he walked into the house.

She didn't have to ask if he was moving his things back into her bedroom. She knew the answer. Clutching her stomach, she leaned over and rested her forehead on her knees. The pain of letting herself fall for Regan O'Connelli was about to start.

16

REGAN COUNTED the adoption fair a modest success. They'd adopted out only five horses when he would have preferred six or seven, but two of the five had been Rex and Strawberry. Molasses had also found a good home. That left sixteen horses for twelve stalls, but with the paddock available and the two most assertive geldings gone, it was workable.

He and Nick had finished dismantling the bleachers and strapped them onto the flatbed provided by the Chances. Regan took off his gloves and held out his hand. "Couldn't have done this without you, buddy. You and the rest of the family."

"Glad to. It's a great cause and I want Lily to succeed at this."

"Yeah, me, too." Thoughts of Lily were extremely painful at the moment, but he didn't want Nick to know that. Working with her all day and exchanging only clipped words had been horrible. The past few hours ranked as some of the worst of his life.

"So you think you'll be staying on here? Not that we don't love having you at the ranch, but those boys arrive tomorrow, and the second floor won't exactly be a quiet haven anymore."

Regan had no idea what he was doing at this point. "I have to talk to Lily," he said. "She might be ready to kick me out." He made it sound like a joke.

"I sincerely doubt that." Nick had a speculative gleam in his eyes, though, as if he was catching something bubbling under the surface. "Whatever you decide is fine. Just warning you about those boys."

"Thanks. I'm sure I could handle a few adolescent boys." His problem was one thirty-year-old man who was currently living way too close to the Last Chance for Regan's comfort. "I, uh, need to ask you about something."

"Sure."

"I hear there's a log-cabin rental just outside your fence line."

"Matter of fact, there is. We became better acquainted with that place a couple of winters ago when one of our hands chased a runaway horse over in that direction. He had to take refuge there. Do you want to rent it? I can put you in touch with the owner."

"No. I just need directions."

"Okay. Do you mind if I ask why?"

He hesitated. If he couldn't convince Drake to leave, word would get out sooner or later. The guy was bound to come into town. "Drake Brewster, my… former business partner, is staying there. He wants to see me."

Nick stroked his chin. "I see. I'm not sure it's safe to let you go over there by yourself, cowboy. I'd hate for you to get arrested for assault."

"Don't think it hasn't crossed my mind, but he's not worth it. He's here because he wants to salve his guilty conscience. If I can convince him he's wasting his time, I'm hoping he'll pack up and leave."

"And if he doesn't?"

Anger tightened Regan's gut. "I'll think of something else."

"Let me know what happens. Jack is friends with the owner of the cabin. If we put our heads together, we might come up with a way to get the guy evicted."

Regan smiled for the first time today. "Thanks. I always like a backup plan."

"Or, if the eviction idea isn't possible because of legal issues, Jack can send a work detail to that area with a few chain saws. They don't have to cut anything down, but they could make a hell of a noise. We could set up some battery-operated lights and start work around two in the morning."

"I like it." Regan chuckled. "Only thing is, if you drive a rat away from one hidey-hole, he's liable to take up residence somewhere else."

"Not in our town, he won't. Had I known about this cabin-rental deal, his sorry ass wouldn't be plunked down there, either. At the very least he'd be staying in Jackson, or even farther away in Cheyenne."

"I appreciate that sentiment more than I can say." Regan considered asking Nick to voice his sentiments to Lily, but then Nick would know things weren't great between them, and Regan wasn't ready to let that be public knowledge…yet.

"Want me to go with you?"

"No, but thanks for the offer. It means a lot."

"Just don't do anything stupid and slug him. Or if you do, make it look like an accident."

Regan was still laughing about that when the last of the Chance vehicles left Peaceful Kingdom. He wouldn't mind telling Lily how Nick had responded to the news of Drake's sudden appearance. But that wouldn't be very mature of him, and besides, he didn't want to stir up trouble between those two friends over something that was his job to handle.

Lily had gone into the house to put away the bowls they'd used at the kids' craft table, and he considered whether it was time to lock the front gate. Then he noticed a truck and horse trailer coming down the road. All five horses had been picked up, but he hadn't kept track of everything going on. Maybe a sixth horse had been adopted and he hadn't heard about it. That would be great.

He headed over to find out, but the driver climbed out of the cab and made for the porch before he could get there. The guy knocked on the door and Lily let him in. Although Regan was curious, he knew that she didn't need him to come barging in as if he didn't think she could handle the situation.

Instead, he headed to the barn, where he knew there were chores waiting. Feeding time was coming up, and plenty of people had been in and out of the barn today. A few things would likely be out of place. Stall doors that should be open might be closed. Little stuff, but it could make feeding take longer.

Nick's support with the Drake issue had improved his mood considerably. He shouldn't be too hard on Lily for thinking the way she did. That was her nature, and her generosity of spirit was something he appreciated about her. He'd benefited from that every time they'd made love.

Sleeping down the hall the night before had been a miserable experience he didn't want to repeat. So maybe they could agree to disagree about Drake and move on.

Regan planned to pay Drake a visit tomorrow and talk him into leaving. The jerk had ruined one relationship for Regan, and damned if he was going to ruin another one by hanging around and providing a bone of contention between Regan and Lily.

Regan had just coiled a rope and hung it up when Lily came through the barn door leading a horse Regan had never seen before. He nudged back his hat in surprise. "Hello. Who's this?"

She stood holding the horse, which had a sorry-looking mane and tail and a dull, butterscotch-and-white coat. "His name is Taffy." She sounded defensive.

Regan had a sinking sensation that Lily had just accepted another horse mere hours after they'd cleared out five. They'd agreed that she wouldn't take in any more horses until she had an empty stall. "So what's Taffy doing here?"

She met his gaze, and defiance flashed in her blue eyes. "He has nowhere else to go."

He didn't doubt the guy who'd brought Taffy had said that. Whether it was true or not, Lily had clearly decided she was the only thing standing between Taffy and some horrible fate. He understood the impulse. But she had to get over it if she ever expected to make Peaceful Kingdom work the way it should.

Taking a deep breath, he chose his words carefully. "Is the owner still here?"

"No. And he lives in Montana, so if you're thinking he'll come back for Taffy, he won't."

"He brought this horse from *Montana?*"

"Yes."

Regan groaned. "Lily, your reputation for taking in horses is spreading fast. Out of the state, even. You can't keep doing this."

She swallowed. “I know. But I can’t help it. So I have a big favor to ask of you. A huge favor. Would you live here until I can find a buyer to take over?”

“You mean live here with you? I’m already doing that.”

She shook her head. “Not live here with me. I can’t run this place. I might as well admit it and give up.” Her voice trembled. “I realized when I was walking over here with Taffy that I’ve failed. I can’t say no.”

“You *can.* I know you can! Don’t leave, Lily. These animals need you.” *I need you.*

“And I’m going to let them down by taking in more! You can see that, right? This horse came all the way from Montana, and I took him.”

“Because you weren’t mentally prepared to say no. Think about all the other visualization techniques we’ve worked on together. You have to visualize the animals you have, and the space they need, and picture yourself saying no for the benefit of those already in your care.”

She shook her head. “This isn’t what I’m good at, Regan. I need to go back to Silicon Valley and design computer games.”

“Don’t say that.” He felt sick to his stomach.

“I am saying it. Now if you’ll excuse me, I’ll take Taffy down to his stall. I’m putting him in with Sandy.”

Stepping aside, he let her go by. He couldn’t allow this terrible thing to happen, but he didn’t know how to stop it. She didn’t believe she could train herself to say no.

Once again, Lily spent the night alone in her bed. She and Regan had worked side by side handling the chores without talking. They both knew the routine and didn’t need to talk, but the silence was nonetheless excruciating. Now they seemed to have nothing to say to each other.

How quickly everything had fallen apart. But the seeds of the destruction had been there all along. She couldn't be happy with a man who insisted on keeping his anger walled up inside and wouldn't take a golden opportunity to deal with the issue. His stubborn attitude regarding Drake could turn into a deal breaker for her.

Yet she'd been hopeful that he might change his mind and talk with his former friend. Maybe he just needed time to work up to it. But time had run out for her and Regan, because when faced with her first test of her new resolve to turn away a needy animal, she'd failed. She didn't belong here.

After tossing and turning all night, she managed to oversleep for the first time since she'd moved in. That just proved that she wasn't up to the job. Leaping out of bed, she threw on her clothes and barreled into the kitchen. The smell of coffee should have alerted her to the fact Regan was up, but she'd been too distracted to notice.

The coffeepot was turned off, but a thermos carafe that she kept handy for keeping her coffee warm was sitting on the counter next to a note.

Lily—
The critters are fed. I have an errand to run. See you in a few hours.
Regan

She tried to imagine what errand he'd have on a Sunday that would take a few hours, and then she remembered Drake. Regan had gone to see his former best friend to get him to leave Jackson Hole. Now that was depressing. She'd wanted them to talk, but not so they could widen the gulf between them.

Pouring herself a cup of coffee, she walked through the empty living room and down the hall past Regan's bedroom. She glanced in, and saw that he'd made his bed. It was a small thing, but it touched her that he was considerate enough to leave the room looking neat.

The third bedroom served as what she laughingly called an office. It contained her computer, a table and chair, and some cheap shelves for her books. When she moved out of this house, she'd be able to pack everything in half a day or less, which was typical for her.

While she waited for the computer to boot up, she thought about the email she was about to send expressing interest in the game-designing job. And she'd confirm that yes, she'd be willing to move back to Silicon Valley and work at the company's headquarters. She imagined the thrill of trading ideas with fellow gaming nerds. The game she'd written had been a solo effort with some consultation from Al, but it might be fun to brainstorm with others while she created more games.

It pretty much had to be fun because that was the option open to her. She sent the email and decided not to think about it any more today. Her next step involved contacting Morgan Chance, who was a real estate broker.

Yeah, well, she could do that later on. No rush. The process of selling this place would take a while. She was fairly sure Regan would agree to stay on until Morgan found a buyer. He'd handle Peaceful Kingdom so much better than she had. Maybe he'd consider buying it himself. That would be perfect.

Okay, maybe not perfect. Perfection was eluding her every time she reached for it. Fitting, then. It would be fitting if Regan bought this place. Whoever bought it would have to be tougher than she was. Maybe she should leave the person a list of other horse rescue organizations within driving distance.

An online search turned up a few, so she printed out a list. The new owner would have options to give anyone who came to the front gate. That would help ease the pain. She wasn't sure why she'd never thought of it. She'd been too busy getting ready for the adoption fair and making love to Regan, apparently.

Hunger finally drove her back to the kitchen. On her way through the living room, she looked out the front window and saw a truck pull up to the gate, which Regan would have locked behind him. Sure enough, the truck was hauling a horse trailer. She sincerely doubted the trailer was empty.

A stocky man got out of the driver's side and rattled the gate to see if it was locked. What if it hadn't been? Would he have driven in, unloaded his horse and left? Lily had experienced that once, and she'd felt sorry for a horse that had been unceremoniously dumped.

Something occurred to her that never had before. People were arriving without calling first. Her number was online, so they wouldn't have to go to a whole lot of trouble to get it. That would be the respectful way to handle the situation. So far, no one had done that. They'd simply shown up without checking to see if she had space.

As she thought about that, the Irish temper she'd inherited along with her red hair flared and began a slow burn. People had been taking advantage of her good nature. By allowing them to take advantage, she was imposing restrictions on the sweet animals she'd already accepted. She didn't have an animal problem.

She had a people problem. She couldn't control how others behaved, but she could control her reaction to their behavior.

Returning to her office, she snatched up the list she'd printed and marched back through the living room and out the front door. The man was dressed like an average cowboy, but Lily had a high opinion of that label and she refused to assign it to this guy. He wanted to dump a horse without asking first. He was no cowboy.

She walked over to the gate. "Can I help you?"

"Yeah, I was told I could leave this horse with you. I wasn't sure how to get in. Good thing you came out."

"Who told you that you could leave a horse here?"

He waved a hand. "I dunno. Some guy I met in a coffee shop in Jackson. So, can you open the gate? I don't have a lot of time."

"Sorry, but I'm not opening the gate." She could hardly believe those words had come out of her mouth, but she was in a mood.

"How am I gonna get this horse inside?"

"You're not. I'm at capacity and can't accept any more horses."

"He's a good horse."

She steeled herself against thinking about the animal in the trailer. "I'm sure he is. But because I'm full, I can't take him." She rolled the list up and handed it over the gate. "You'll find several other options there."

He made an impatient noise low in his throat. "I don't want to go chasing all over the countryside."

She spared one moment of anguish for the horse stuck with such a subpar human being. But as Regan had suggested, she thought of the animals she already had in her care. They didn't deserve to be crowded because some idiot like this man showed up with another horse.

"So you really won't take him?" The guy seemed very disgusted.

"No." She stood there a moment and savored the sound of that word. "No, I won't." Then she turned and started back to the house.

But instead of going there, she found herself walking around the building and out to the new paddock. She counted, and all seventeen were there, including Taffy. Regan must have herded them in after he'd fed them breakfast.

She'd watched him do it several times before. Grabbing a fistful of mane, he'd vault onto whichever horse was handy. Then he'd ride bareback and use a coiled rope to direct the herd into the enclosure. He'd been poetry in motion. Suddenly she missed him with a deep, visceral ache. She wanted him to come home. She wanted to tell him that against all odds, she'd learned how to say no.

17

Regan parked in front of the little log cabin. He'd had to take a dirt road to get there, but the place sat all by itself in a clearing, so it had been simple to locate. Across the road ran a fence that marked the edge of Last Chance property. This rental was as close to the ranch as anyone could get without actually setting foot on it.

At least Drake had been smart enough to know he wouldn't be welcome at the Last Chance. Sarah welcomed nearly everyone who came to her door, but once Drake had introduced himself, he would have been sent on his way with a regal lift of Sarah's chin. Regan almost wished he had tried it, just so he could have experienced the Sarah Chance freeze-out.

Regan hadn't called ahead, either. Surprising Drake had a certain poetic justice to it after the way he'd startled the guy six months ago on Christmas Eve. Belatedly Regan wondered if Drake would have a woman with him. It was Sunday morning, and Drake could easily have gone into town last night in search of female companionship. What Drake sought, he usually found.

To hell with it. If he'd brought a woman home, so what? She might want to know what kind of man she was dealing with, so Regan would be doing her a favor by barging in on their cozy setup. He banged on the front door.

A moment later it opened to reveal a man Regan barely recognized. Drake had always leaned toward the preppie look—clean-shaven, neat salon haircut, crisp white shirts and tailored slacks. This Drake had several days' growth of beard and was in desperate need of a good haircut. He wore a faded UV sweatshirt and jeans that had seen better days.

Drake blinked. Then his signature feature, green eyes that were once filled with mischief and laughter, widened. "You came." Gone was the cocky attitude. Well, mostly. He looked almost, but not quite, humble. "Thank you. Come in."

"Don't thank me yet, Brewster." Regan walked past him into the open floor plan that combined a kitchen with a living room. The kitchen looked relatively neat, but the living room was strewn with books and magazines. A half-full mug of coffee sat on an end table.

Checking over the reading material, Regan noticed quite a bit of motivational stuff, the kind of thing his parents loved. He even spotted *Happiness Is a Choice* by Bethany Grace. He'd met Bethany on several occasions. She and her husband, Nash Bledsoe, lived on a small ranch down the road from the Last Chance.

Regan would share none of that with Drake, however. Drake needed reasons to leave, not reasons to stick around and meet one of his favorite authors. Regan was prepared to give him those reasons to leave, preferably without bloodshed.

"I appreciate you coming so quickly." Drake moved some magazines off the couch. "Have a seat."

"I'll stand. The reason I came quickly is because I want you the hell out of my town."

"Sorry." Drake sank into an easy chair. "Not leaving. Not yet, anyway. It took me a week of hiking and hanging out in this cabin to work up the courage to call you. But I'm slowly figuring things out. I was right to come. Being here is exactly what I need."

"Yeah, well that's what it's always been about, isn't it? What *you* need. Let me tell you something, buddy." Regan pointed a finger at him. "Six months ago you broke up my engagement. Now, just by your presence, you're causing a problem with the new lady in my life. I'm not letting you screw with me twice in less than a year."

"Somebody new?" Drake's eyebrows rose. "That's terrific."

"It was, until you showed up. Now you've become an issue between us, and I won't have it." He hadn't thought he wanted to be here, but saying that to Drake's face felt damned good. Drake didn't have to know that Regan's relationship with Lily was shaky for any other reason but his presence.

"How can I be a problem? I don't even know her."

"And you won't, if I have anything to say about it. I can't trust you around my girlfriends, remember?"

Drake's expression grew bleak. "Oh, I remember, all right. It was the low point of my life."

"It was no walk in the park for me, either, asshole."

"I'm sure it wasn't." Drake gazed at him. "I'll never be able to make it up to you, either."

"You've got that right."

Drake swept an arm around the room. "As you can see, I've done some reading in the past week."

"Yeah. So what?"

"I'm serving as my own therapist, which is always dicey, but near as I can tell, I was jealous and couldn't admit it to myself. So I acted like an idiot."

"Jealous? You wanted Jeannette?" He remembered what Lily had asked. Maybe he had missed the obvious, after all.

"No, I didn't want Jeannette. I wanted something you had. I wanted your…your self-confidence."

"My *what?*"

"Don't pretend you don't know what I'm talking about. You've always had that basic knowledge of who you are and what you want. You went to that Buck Brannaman clinic and you got it instantly, whereas I just faked it. You're ten times the vet I am." He held Regan's gaze. "I've been pea-green with envy since day one, O'Connelli."

Regan stared at him in stunned silence. If he'd had a million years to analyze the situation, he never would have come up with that.

"You want some coffee?"

"Yeah. Guess so." He walked over to the couch and sat down. Moments later, Drake handed him a mug of hot coffee, and he took it with a nod of thanks.

He used the familiarity of sipping coffee to buy himself some time and gather his thoughts. At last he had something of a handle on what Drake had confessed, but he was confused. "What you're saying makes no sense. You were the one with all the important connections. I was the poor kid on a scholarship. You belonged in that world. Your parents guaranteed our clinic would be a huge success. You had everything. I was riding on your coattails the whole time."

"Nope. Not true. I had the connections, but you had the grades. I had the trust-fund money, but you had the difficult-to-define qualities of a great vet. I needed you. If I'd tried to go it alone, I would have failed. I don't have the genius for the profession that you do. For your information, I got somebody else to fill your spot, but they don't have your skill. The clinic's about to go under."

Regan frowned. "I'm sorry." Surprisingly, he was. He'd put a lot of himself into building that practice, and he hated to think of it dying.

"It shouldn't survive. I'm not cut out for the profession. I'm a huge disappointment to my parents, but they've always suspected you were propping me up. Two weeks ago I told them why you left. I'll be surprised if they don't disinherit me." He shrugged. "And amazingly, I don't give a shit."

"What are you going to do?"

"That's what I'm here to find out. Until now, other people have told me what I'm supposed to want. I need to figure out what I actually want." He glanced at Regan. "But that's not why I asked you to come and see me. I crapped all over your relationship with Jeannette. I know sorry doesn't cut it, but short of giving you a kidney, I don't know what else I can do but say that I'm deeply sorry. That's not how you treat a friend."

Regan grinned, which shocked the hell out of both of them, judging from Drake's expression. "A kidney? You'd give me a kidney?"

And just like that, the tension eased. The old familiar spark was back in Drake's eyes. "You might not want it, dude. I boozed it up pretty good in college. But if you need one, I'm there for you."

"I'll keep that in mind. You never know."

"So what about this new lady? What's she like?"

"Terrific, but there are problems." Regan thought

one might be solved, but she might require evidence. Maybe if she was blown away by his renewed friendship with Drake, she'd listen to his ideas about learning to say no. "Would you like to meet her?"

Drake froze. "That would be okay with you?"

"Sure." Regan gave him the evil eye. "But if I ever think, for one second, that you would—"

"God, no. I've worked too hard to fix this mess." He rubbed his chin. "Guess I should shave first, huh?"

"I should probably present you like this, just to guarantee she won't take a shine to you, but as a measure of my faith in your trustworthiness, yeah, why don't you shave?"

BY LATE MORNING, Lily still hadn't contacted Morgan about listing the property. She kept finding other things to do. She made a sign, which she'd have laminated before she left, but she hung it on the front gate for now because a sign was definitely called for. If it looked like rain, she'd bring it in. It read: "Sorry, but our barn is at capacity. Please take a flier for other options."

To go along with the sign, she planned to install an information tube at the gate and keep it stocked with copies of the list she'd made up earlier this morning. She'd posted a prominent notice on the website requiring a phone call in advance of bringing a horse to Peaceful Kingdom. But because of her previous lax policy, people still might drive up to the gate unannounced and expect to drop off a horse. She didn't want a future owner to have to deal with that.

On impulse, she spent some time out in the paddock, loving on the horses, and some more time with Wilbur and Harley, and even a few minutes talking to the chickens. She'd miss all those critters. And not just a little bit, either. She'd miss them as if she'd suddenly developed a hole in her heart. Somewhere during her tour of the place, she began to reconsider her decision to leave.

After all, she'd turned away a horse. She'd come up with a list of alternative rescue operations, she'd posted a notice on the website and she'd made a sign to hang on the gate. The fence company had set up physical boundaries that made her life easier. But she'd needed some mental boundaries, and now she had them.

At last she stood in front of her green-and-orange house and admired the flowers blooming their little hearts out. Someone new might repaint, and that didn't sit well with her. They might forget to water the flowers. They might not love potbellied pigs.

Spreading her arms wide, she twirled around. "I'm staying!" she shouted at the top of her lungs. "You hear me, horses, pigs and chickens? I'm staying!"

About that time Regan's truck pulled up to the gate, and her bubble of happy optimism burst. She didn't want to hear how he'd chewed out his best friend and ordered him to leave Jackson Hole. She loved Regan, but if he insisted on clutching that anger to his heart, then… Her breath caught. She *loved* him? Well, of course she did. That's why she was so upset with him for the way he was handling his problem with Drake.

She waited as he unlocked the gate, got back in his truck and drove into the yard. Wait a minute. Someone was in the passenger seat. Her heart began pounding. If that man was who she thought he was, then maybe all was not lost.

The guy got out. His coffee-colored hair was on the longish side, but after years at Berkeley, she was used to that look. He was wearing a ratty old college sweatshirt and scruffy jeans with sneakers. That also reminded her of Berkeley. He had on shades that looked remarkably like the ones Regan used to wear. Maybe he needed protection, too.

Regan walked toward her, his smile hopeful. "Lily, I'd like you to meet Drake Brewster."

Her chest tightened. Regan had done it. He'd accepted his best friend's apology, and then he'd brought him home to her as a peace offering.

Turning to the man who had betrayed Regan, she wondered how much courage he'd required to come here and ask for forgiveness. Quite a bit, probably. She held out her hand. "I'm happy to meet you, Drake Brewster."

"Same here, ma'am." He took off his shades to reveal startling green eyes. "Regan's told me a lot about you." His accent made him sound like a plantation owner from *Gone with the Wind.*

"Oh? Like what?"

"That you're brilliant, and generous, and beautiful. Just between you and me, I think the guy's in love with you."

"Hey!" Regan frowned at Drake, but his mouth twitched at the corners, as if he might be holding back laughter. "Don't go poking your nose in my business."

Drake shrugged. "Just makin' an observation."

"Well, go observe somewhere else, okay? Take a stroll around the property or something. I need to talk to Lily privately."

Drake placed a hand on his chest in exaggerated shock. "Lord, boy! Are you telling me to get lost when I just got here? Where I come from, that's not how we treat our guests. No, sir."

"Okay, then go in the house and make yourself some coffee. Have a beer. Have a mint julep. Sheesh. I'd forgotten you were such a pain in the ass."

"Okay. I'll leave. But don't louse this up. She's obviously a find. Close the deal, boy, or mark my words, you'll regret it for the rest of your life."

Lily watched them with wonder and a bubbling kind of joy. Men didn't joke around like that unless they were close. As for the topic of conversation, that sent excitement skittering through her.

"Advice appreciated. Now git."

With a martyred sigh, Drake trudged off toward the house.

Regan turned back to Lily, his expression tender. Nudging back his hat, he closed the distance between them. "I saw the sign on the gate."

"I put that up after I turned away a horse."

His eyebrows lifted. "You did what?"

"I figured that whoever took over didn't need yet another horse to deal with. Besides, the guy had some nerve, just driving up to my gate without calling ahead. But FYI, you can't take over, because I'm staying."

"Is that so?" His mouth twitched again, as if he was having trouble holding back a grin. "Does that mean you don't need me anymore?"

"Oh, I need you." That came across with a little more emotion than she'd intended, but her feelings were running high at the moment.

He drew her into his arms. "Good, because I need you. And an FYI for you, Brewster totally jumped the gun, but he was right. I'm madly in love with you."

Joy thrummed through her as she looped her arms around his neck. "How convenient. I just discovered that I'm madly in love with you, too."

He pulled her in tight. "So what are we going to do about that?"

"Nothing right now. We have a guest."

"So we do. Damn. I brought him as Exhibit A, but I forgot about the fact that he'd stick around."

The screen door opened. "Have you proposed yet, genius?"

"Go back in the house, Brewster!"

"Better get on with it." The door banged shut.

Regan looked into her eyes. "He ruined the suspense."

"I don't care." If he weren't holding on to her, she might lift up into the sky like a helium balloon. She was just that happy.

"Will you marry me, Lily King?"

"Yes. Yes, I will."

The screen door creaked open again. "How about now? Have you accomplished what you came to do?"

Regan sighed. "I have one more important thing to take care of. I'm going to kiss this woman until her eyes roll back in her head. You might want to give us some privacy for that."

"Nothing doing. I'm going to watch."

"Suit yourself." Regan lowered his mouth to hers.

At first she felt a little embarrassed that Drake was standing on the porch taking it all in, but then she forgot about him. She forgot about everything but the explosive pleasure of kissing Regan O'Connelli. And if anyone were to ask, she'd happily confirm that her eyes really did roll back in her head.

* * * * *

Riding Hard

Dear Reader,

When the editors and I first settled on this title, I wasn't sure that it fit the story. I've changed my mind. Drake Brewster might be my most troubled hero so far. He's loaded down with guilt, and he's very hard on himself.

Ah, but he's a charmer, with his Rhett Butler accent and his bad-boy appeal. Those very charms are what got him into hot water, and now he's working to regain the trust of his best friend, Regan. While doing that, he meets Tracy Gibbons, bartender and temporary house sitter for Regan and Regan's fiancée. Tracy is not a Drake Brewster fan.

I'll admit right up front that the folks at the Last Chance Ranch are not enamoured of the guy, either. He wronged one of their own, and they're not inclined to be friendly under those circumstances. But you have to hand it to Drake. He sticks it out because that's the only way he'll be able to respect himself as a man.

Welcome to midsummer in Wyoming! The weather is gorgeous, and so is Drake Brewster. Tracy thinks she can resist him, but let me tell you, I couldn't. Come along on another Sons of Chance adventure and see if *you* can resist this Southern scoundrel! Betcha can't!

Scandalously yours,

Vicki

DEDICATION

To everyone who has ever made a mistake and wronged a friend. It's tough to go through life and not do that at least once, so I figure this dedication applies to all of us. Let's forgive ourselves and each other for being human. Oh, and to my dad, from whom I took Psych 101. It was an eye-opener.

Prologue

July 20, 1990

ARCHIE CHANCE WISHED he could be anywhere but here, sitting on a barstool at the Spirits and Spurs. Or, if he had to be here, he wished he hadn't invited his son Jonathan to have a beer with him while the women went shopping at the Shoshone General Store.

The bar was mostly empty, which allowed Archie to hear two strangers at a table about ten feet behind them. Jonathan's tight expression indicated that he could hear it, too. One of the men was reminiscing about a one-night stand he'd enjoyed in Shoshone many years ago with a woman named Diana, a woman who sounded a hell of a lot like Jonathan's ex-wife.

Archie pushed away his half-empty beer glass. "Let's shove off."

Jonathan shook his head. "Not yet."

"Look, does it really matter what—"

"Yes."

Archie understood. In Jonathan's shoes, he would have wanted to know, too. Diana had abandoned Jonathan and their young son, Jack, ten years ago and had severed all ties with the family. Archie wouldn't be surprised if she'd also had affairs during their unhappy marriage.

Archie had heard enough. Way too much, in fact. The woman named Diana had mentioned being married to a surly cowboy whose family owned a big spread outside of town.

Archie sipped his beer and stared straight ahead, because he didn't know what else to do. After what seemed like years, the two men left.

When Jonathan finally spoke, his voice was husky. "I was, you know."

Archie turned, not sure what his son was admitting to. "You were what?"

"Surly."

"Well, you had good reason to be, damn it. She was a difficult woman. Probably still is." Archie wasn't supposed to overreact to things and get his blood pressure up, but he couldn't help it.

"She was unhappy. I had no patience with her."

"Because you didn't love her." *None of us did.*

"I..." Jonathan picked up his glass, then put it back down. "No, I didn't love her. I realize that now, because of Sarah. I'm still not very patient, but when she reminds me of that, I don't get mad. I try harder. I'm lucky to have her, and I don't want to mess up a good thing."

Archie's eyes grew moist. He'd developed an embarrassing tendency to get choked up over his family lately. Nelsie assured him that grandpas were allowed, but he thought it was unmanly. He cleared his throat. "You're lucky to have each other."

Jonathan glanced at him. "Just like you and Mom. I always wanted what you two have, and now, I have it."

"Yep." Aw, hell, now he was tearing up again thinking about Nelsie, the love of his life. He took a long swallow of his beer and hoped his son didn't think he was turning into a sentimental old fool. Once he had himself under control, he looked over at Jonathan. "Hey, how about another beer? We can toast the ladies."

That boy's smile always could light up a room. "Great idea, Dad."

In nothing flat, Archie went from wanting to get the hell out of the bar to wanting to stay forever. Funny how a situation that started out as a disaster could end up turning into something pretty damned wonderful, after all.

1

Present Day

DRAKE BREWSTER WAS used to women liking him, but Tracy Gibbons, the beautiful bartender at Spirits and Spurs, clearly didn't. Oh, she was polite enough when she served him a beer, but her smile was mostly fake, as if she was forcing herself because he was a customer. He even knew why she didn't like him, but that didn't help much. When he thought about her reasons, he had to agree they were legitimate.

In point of fact, he wasn't particularly popular with anyone in Shoshone, Wyoming. He was the guy who'd had sex with his best friend's fiancée six months ago. On Christmas Eve. Apparently word had gotten out, and now everyone avoided him like a skunk at a Fourth of July picnic.

That very same best friend, Regan O'Connelli, happened to be quite popular in this neighborhood. Well connected, too. After severing his business relationship with Drake back in Virginia, as well he should have, he'd gone into partnership with Shoshone veterinarian Nick Chance. It had been a logical move since one of

Regan's sisters had married Nick's brother Gabe, and another had married Nick's brother-in-law Alex. Getting hooked into the Chance family opened all kinds of doors around here, apparently.

Getting crossways with the Chances, though, slammed those doors shut in a man's face. Regan, who swore he'd forgiven Drake for the fiasco with Jeannette on that fateful Christmas Eve, said Drake should give people time. They'd come around.

Three weeks into his stay, Drake wasn't so sure. The deep freeze was still on, except for Regan and his new fiancée, Lily King. Drake gave Lily much of the credit for Regan's willingness to forgive and forget. She was a softhearted woman.

In fact, her soft heart had nearly been her downfall when she'd bought Peaceful Kingdom, a horse-rescue operation outside of town, and had accepted every unwanted animal dumped at her feet. Besides the horses, she'd taken in two potbellied pigs and several chickens. Regan had saved her from herself, and in the process, they'd fallen in love. She encouraged Drake to visit as often as he could, but he didn't want to wear out his welcome. Couples in love needed alone time.

That should have fit right in with his plans. Before leaving Virginia, he'd put his vet practice in the hands of a colleague and hadn't specified when he'd be back. Then he'd rented an isolated cabin just outside the boundary of the Last Chance Ranch so that he could make amends with Regan and take a few weeks to reevaluate his life.

He'd imagined long solo hikes and intense periods of soul-searching would help him figure out how he'd veered so off track that he'd gone to bed with his best friend's girl. His life couldn't be working if he could do something that disloyal, and he'd hoped for some insights.

Surprisingly, his jealousy of Regan's self-confidence had been one of his issues. Realizing he'd set out to sabotage his friend's sense of self-worth was an ugly truth he'd had trouble facing. But he had faced it, and consequently he and Regan were okay.

His period of self-examination had yielded another nugget of wisdom. He wasn't into long solo hikes and intense periods of soul-searching. He was a sociable type, a Southerner who loved to talk, and he craved the company of others. But except for Regan and Lily, nobody within a thirty-mile radius craved *his* company, and that sucked.

Yet here he was, anyway, sitting on a barstool at the Spirits and Spurs during happy hour trying not to look as lonely as he felt. A few people had said hello, but then they'd gone back to talking to whomever they'd come with. Nobody seemed interested in a prolonged encounter with the guy who'd wronged Regan O'Connelli.

Tracy made a circuit of the bar area, her dark hair shining, her red lipstick glossy and inviting. She glanced at his nearly empty glass. "Another round?"

Drake considered giving up and going back to the cabin but couldn't make himself do it. "Sure. Thanks."

"Coming up." That fake smile flashed again.

He watched her walk away. She had the perfect figure for jeans, and he'd noticed other guys checking out her ass. But someone with his hound-dog reputation couldn't be caught doing it, so instead he studied her hair. It was up in some arrangement that kept it out of the way, but he pictured how it would look loose. It might reach halfway down her back, at least, and sway as she moved. Nice.

He didn't want her to see him staring like some wet-behind-the-ears doofus, so he grabbed the menu out of its holder. Then he proceeded to scan the offerings as if fascinated by what he'd found, although he knew them by heart.

"Here you go."

He glanced up, as if he hadn't noticed her coming toward him. "Thank you, ma'am." The beer foam was perfectly symmetrical. He raised the glass and admired it. "Very pretty." He meant the compliment for her, but he could always claim he'd been talking about the head on his beer.

"Thanks." She didn't quite roll her eyes, but she looked as if she wanted to. She gestured toward the menu. "Would you like something to eat?"

He wasn't hungry, but picking up a menu was a classic signal and there wasn't much in the refrigerator at the cabin. "I would, indeed. What do you recommend?"

She paused, confusion shadowing her brown eyes. "Don't you want your usual burger and fries?"

"I find myself wantin' something different." That she'd noticed his ordering pattern meant nothing, of course. Any good server would do that. But it pleased him, anyway.

"Well, then…you might try the barbecued-pork sandwich. Lots of people like that."

"Do you like it?"

She hesitated, as if not wanting to give him personal information. "I'm partial to the burgers here," she said at last.

"So am I. I'll stick with my usual, after all."

"Okay. I'll put in the order." She started to turn away.

"Tracy?"

When she looked back at him, her expression was guarded. "What?"

He tried to remember if he'd ever used her name, although he'd known it for days. Maybe not. Southerners tended to use *ma'am* most of the time. He took a deep breath, finally ready to tackle this situation head-on. "I've been coming in here quite a bit lately."

"Yes, you have." She didn't seem particularly happy about it, either.

"And you're always polite to me."

"I certainly hope so. If I'm not nice to the customers, I would probably get fired."

"I appreciate that, but I'll bet there are some customers you look forward to serving and some you don't."

Her gaze became shuttered. "I'm grateful for any and all customers who come through the door. Without customers, Spirits and Spurs wouldn't be in business."

"Nice speech. I admire your dedication. But the fact remains that you don't like me."

She opened her mouth as if to reply. Then she closed it again.

"Don't worry. I'm not going to complain to anyone about it." He sighed. "Hell, you're in the majority around here when it comes to holdin' a bad opinion of me. But nobody will say it to my face. They're unfailingly polite and then they act like I have a contagious disease."

"I'm Regan's friend." Her gaze turned very cold. "I'm also friends with his sisters. If you think my attitude is chilly, you should try having a conversation with Morgan, Tyler or Cassidy."

"Yeah, I figured that wouldn't work out, so I haven't tried."

"I know everything's supposed to be hunky-dory between you and Regan. Lily told me all is well, but she's the kind of person who would make excuses for a serial killer."

"A serial killer? Isn't that a bit harsh?"

"I know you haven't actually killed anyone, but you betrayed your *best friend.*" Anger kindled in her brown eyes. "If you ask me, Regan's letting you off *way* too easy." Then she blushed and glanced away. "Sorry. I get a little worked up when I talk about this. It's really none of my business."

He thought she was mighty pretty when she was worked up, but he wisely didn't say so. "I get the impression that it's everybody's business around here."

She didn't deny it, probably because she couldn't. When she looked at him again, her gaze was disconcertingly direct. "Why stay, then? You patched things up with Regan, so why not go back to Virginia where… where you're from."

Where you belong. Although she didn't say the words, they hung in the air. Except he didn't belong in Virginia anymore. He couldn't explain why, but the thought of returning to his old life made him shudder. Whoever he'd been back there wasn't the man he wanted to be here and now. The location might have nothing to do with it, but he wasn't going to take the chance that he'd fall into his old patterns.

He shrugged. "I must be a glutton for punishment."

Something shifted in her expression. It became more open, and unless he was mistaken, she seemed genuinely interested in him for the first time ever. "I see."

"What do you see?"

"That you're doing some kind of penance."

"I wouldn't put it that way." The assessment made him uncomfortable. He wasn't a masochist or a martyr.

"You just called yourself a glutton for punishment."

"That's an expression, something folks say. It doesn't mean that I—"

"Hey, Drake!"

Intensely grateful for the interruption, he swiveled to face Regan, who came toward him looking like the seasoned cowboy he'd become, complete with boots, worn jeans and a ten-gallon hat. Drake had bought some boots and a couple of pairs of jeans that still looked new. He was holding off buying a hat. He couldn't say why.

He held out a hand to Regan. "Hey, buddy! What's up?"

"Not much." Regan shook hands, but the dark eyes he'd inherited from his Italian mother moved quickly from Drake to Tracy. "Am I interrupting?"

"Nope!" Tracy waved her order pad. "I have to put in Drake's food order and check on my other customers. Can I bring you something?"

"I'll take a draft when you have a minute. I actually came in to see you, but I wanted to ask Drake a favor, too, so this is perfect."

"All righty, then. I'll be back." She hurried toward the kitchen.

Regan slid onto a barstool on Drake's right. "*Did* I interrupt something? You both looked mighty serious."

"Not really. I made a dumb remark and she picked up on it."

"What'd you say?"

"She wondered why I'm stayin' here when nobody likes me, and I—"

"Hang on." Regan shoved back the brim of his Stetson. "She actually said that nobody likes you? That doesn't sound like Tracy."

"Actually I'm the one who said that, but she didn't

disagree with me. You have to admit I'm not the toast of Shoshone, Wyoming."

"Maybe not yet."

"Maybe not ever. You have loyal friends who don't forgive easily. I understand that. Tracy asked a logical question, and I gave her a flip answer."

"Like what?"

"I said maybe I was a glutton for punishment."

"Oh, boy." Regan chuckled. "I'll bet that got her attention."

"It did, but why are you so sure it would?"

"She's studying to be a psychologist, but don't mention that I told you."

"Why? What's the big secret?"

"It's not actually a secret. As you've discovered, gossip is a favorite pastime in this little town."

Drake pretended to be shocked. "Really?"

"Yeah, yeah. Anyway, people kind of know because she keeps her books behind the bar and studies when it's not busy in here. But she's not ready to announce it to the world. I think she's worried that she doesn't have the intellectual chops to pull it off."

"You're kidding." Drake thought of her efficiency and the intelligence shining in those brown eyes. "She's smart as a whip. Anyone can see that."

"Yeah, but nobody in her family has ever set foot on a college campus. She's only taken online classes so far, and she probably doesn't want to make a big deal out of this and then fail."

"She won't fail."

Regan smiled. "Spoken like a man who always knew he'd end up with a degree and a profession. She doesn't have that kind of background, and she has doubts."

"Well, she shouldn't, but I see your point." He

paused. "Wait, are you saying she was trying to psychoanalyze me? That's all I need."

"At least it would be free."

Drake skewered his friend with a look and discovered Regan was working hard not to laugh. "It's not funny, damn it. I might need a shrink, but I sure as hell don't need a shrink in training. I'm messed up enough without accidentally gettin' the wrong advice."

"I wouldn't discount Tracy's insights. She's spent a lot of hours behind this bar, and she has a knack for reading people. She can't officially hang out a shingle until she graduates and gets licensed, but she has excellent instincts."

"Mmm." Drake didn't like this discussion any more than the one he'd been having with Tracy. He took another swig of beer.

"Look, you told me you wanted to get your head on straight while you're here. You could do worse than talk things over with Tracy."

"I beg to differ." Drake sighed. "Besides, aren't psychologists supposed to be nonjudgmental?"

"Yeah, I suppose so."

"Then Tracy didn't get the memo. She believes what I did was heinous and she's not cuttin' me any slack. I hardly think she's the person to help me."

"Okay, maybe not. I'm not sure why, but I know infidelity is a hot button for her."

Drake winced as he always did when that word came up. He'd willingly participated in an act of infidelity. Even though liquor had been involved, which created some sort of lame excuse, the sharpness of what he'd done couldn't be filed down, and it still cut deep.

"So I guess it's not such a good idea," Regan said. "Forget I mentioned it."

"I surely will. Besides, there's another factor that makes the idea a nonstarter."

"What?"

"I think she's hot."

"Oh." Regan's glance slid past Drake and focused on a spot over his shoulder. "Here she comes. I'd advise you to keep that information to yourself."

"Don't worry. I'm not about to make myself vulnerable to a woman who thinks I'm pond scum."

"She doesn't think that."

"I'll guarantee she does." Drake swiveled his stool back around and smiled at Tracy.

Her mouth responded with an obligatory upward tilt, but the rest of her face was devoid of emotion. Then she looked at Regan, and everything changed. "Here's your beer and some peanuts in case you get the munchies." She'd never offered Drake peanuts.

"Thanks." Regan pushed the bowl toward Drake. "Want some?"

"Don't mind if I do." He'd show Tracy that he wasn't too proud to eat Regan's free peanuts.

Tracy lingered in front of Regan. "Can I get you anything else?"

"Nope, this is great. But I have a big favor to ask."

"What's that?"

"Nick's going to a conference in Washington, D.C. next week and he's taking Dominique because she's never been to the Capitol. At the last minute he asked if Lily and I wanted to come along. The women can pal around and sightsee while we're in meetings. I wondered if you'd be willing to house-sit again while we're gone."

"Of course! I'll have to make sure my hours here will

mesh with feeding the critters, but that shouldn't be a problem. I can trade off with somebody if necessary."

Drake was flabbergasted. And more than a little hurt. A couple of weeks ago Regan and Lily had taken a two-day vacation and had asked Tracy to house-sit. When Drake found out, he'd told them to ask him next time.

He was a vet, for crying out loud, so he could easily deal with the animals. He also had zip going on. Instead Regan had asked a busy person who already had a full-time job and was studying to become a psychologist.

"Great!" Regan gave Tracy a big old smile. "Same deal as before. Don't accept any new animals."

"I won't."

"And because we'll be gone for so long, I've arranged for a vet in Jackson to take the routine calls at the office and help you out if you need it. But I'm hoping Drake will consider stepping in if there's an emergency." He glanced over at Drake. "Would you be able to do that, just until the guy from Jackson can get down here?"

"Uh, sure. Be glad to." He could have handled everything, if Regan had bothered to ask.

"Thanks. I really appreciate it. I keep most of my supplies in my truck, and it'll be parked beside the house. Tracy, if you have any problems at all, call Drake. He's an excellent vet."

Drake had been so busy having his feelings hurt that he hadn't seen that coming. Tracy hadn't either, judging from the way her eyes widened and her mouth dropped open.

"You'll need my number, then." He enjoyed saying it, even if she didn't enjoy hearing it.

"Uh, yeah, I guess I will. But I'm sure nothing will happen."

"Probably not, but just in case, you'd better take it. Call or text anytime."

"Right." She scribbled the number he gave her on her order pad.

"Then we're all set." Regan beamed at them. "We might stay a couple of extra days, if that's okay with you two."

You two. Drake was amused by the way Regan had neatly linked them up. Tracy probably hated it. "I'm fine with y'all staying longer," he said. "How about you, Tracy?"

"Uh, sure. Just let me know in advance so I can adjust my hours. Listen, I'd better get back to my customers. Drake's burger and fries should be up by now, too." She quickly made her escape.

Drake wasn't ready to let the issue go. "I could have handled all of it," he said in a low voice. "I believe I told you that the last time you asked her."

"I know, and I was keeping you in reserve if she had other plans. But she said yes, probably because she needs the money for school. I figured she did."

"Oh, you're paying her." Drake felt better. "I didn't realize that."

"We're absolutely paying her. We paid her last time, too. There's a lot of work involved. I wouldn't expect anyone to do it for free."

"I would've."

"And that's one of the reasons I didn't want to ask you. I knew you wouldn't take any money for it, and Tracy will." Regan studied him. "You do realize that I'm not mad at you anymore, right?"

"Yeah, I do." His chuckle sounded hollow. "Sadly, I'm still riddled with guilt."

"Well, hell, dude. Get over it." Regan tossed a peanut in his mouth.

"Believe me, I'm trying. Taking care of your place for free while y'all are gone would've helped, but I get why you asked Tracy. I wouldn't want to deprive her of a chance to earn extra money."

"And I hoped you'd be her backup if she has any issues. Legally I can't pay you since you're not licensed in Wyoming, but I know you don't care about the money."

"Nope. Don't worry about anything. I'll keep an eye on the medical side of things, but you do realize Tracy hates the thought of having to call on me."

"She won't hate it if one of the horses gets sick. Everything went fine last time, but we were only a couple of hours away if she'd needed us. Frankly, I wouldn't have agreed to a cross-country trip if I couldn't count on you in the event of a problem."

"I'll surely do that. But now I wish I hadn't told you that I think she's hot."

"Why?"

Drake looked away. "Because I don't want you to think I'll take this as a golden opportunity."

"Good God. You are not only riddled with guilt, you're drowning in it. You and Tracy are consenting adults. I like you both. What happens between you has nothing to do with me unless you scare the horses."

Drake glanced over to find Regan grinning. "I promise not to do that."

"Then everything else is up for grabs."

Drake didn't think so. Tracy had a poor opinion of him, and it would take a miracle to change her mind.

2

As the noonday sun beat down on her, Tracy stared at the pregnant Appaloosa that the sad-looking cowboy had insisted on unloading despite Tracy's protests. She was a striking mare with a Dalmatian-like coat. Her mane and tail mixed strands of black and white into a soft gray. Tracy instantly wanted to take in this lovely creature.

But her instructions from Regan and Lily had been crystal clear. Just like the first time she house-sat for them, she wasn't supposed to accept any animals while they were gone. "I'm sorry." She kept her tone friendly but firm. "I'm not authorized to admit any animals this week. Perhaps you'd like to come back at the end of the month when the owners are here."

"Can't wait that long, ma'am. I can't feed her no more. I've run through the money I got from selling my stud and I can't find work." The man could have been anywhere from thirty to fifty years old, but he'd obviously lived a hard life judging from his weathered skin and resigned expression.

"I wish I could help, but—"

"I came *this close* to selling Dottie to a guy in Jackson, but he wouldn't have treated her right. I'm beggin' you to take her."

"If she's valuable, and I can see that she probably is, surely you can find someone you trust who would buy her."

"No time. Got an eviction notice for the place I rent yesterday. I'm out of feed for Dottie and out of options. I heard about this rescue operation and figured it was my last hope to put her somewheres she'd be looked after."

Tracy heard the desperation in his voice. This wasn't some jerk who'd grown tired of his responsibility. The man genuinely loved his mare and was terrified something bad would happen to her because he'd lost the ability to provide for her.

Last time Tracy had taken care of Peaceful Kingdom, all twelve of the barn's stalls had been occupied. But Regan and Lily had worked hard to adopt out the young and healthy horses. Six of the residents were so old and feeble they'd live at Peaceful Kingdom forever. Two others needed to learn some manners before they'd be ready to go. Four stalls stood empty.

It wasn't her place to fill even one of them. She'd be acting against orders if she did. But this situation tugged at her heart. She met the cowboy's gaze and made her decision. "I'll take her."

His shoulders dropped and his eyes grew suspiciously moist. "Thank you, ma'am. Thank you."

His gruff tone choked her up a little, too. "Let me get the form for you to fill out." She hurried back to the house and returned in a flash with a clipboard, an intake form and a pen before doubts could change her mind. She held them out to him. "We need some information for our records." Regan and Lily would understand. They had to.

If possible, he looked even more miserable. “Sorry, ma’am. I can’t.”

For a split second she thought he was refusing to fill out the form, but then she realized he was illiterate on top of his other problems. “No worries. I’ll do it. Just tell me what to write.”

The man’s name was Jerry Rankin. He’d bought Dottie as a foal ten years ago, when times were good for him. Once Tracy started asking questions, Jerry offered all sorts of details that weren’t on the form.

When he’d been blessed with steady work, he’d bought an Appaloosa stallion with plans to start a breeding operation. His wife had handled the paperwork, and all had gone well. They’d bred the horses and sold three foals. But then his wife had died after an illness that ate up their savings, and he’d lost his job.

When Tracy finished filling out the form, she glanced up. “Can you sign your name?”

“My wife taught me that much.” He took the clipboard and pen and painstakingly wrote his name in awkward block letters.

“Thank you, Mr. Rankin.”

“Jerry’s good enough.”

“Jerry, then.”

“I surely do appreciate this.” He handed over the lead rope, but the mare stayed right by his side. Then he dug in the pocket of his worn jeans. “I ain’t got nothin’ but change, but I’ll give you what I—”

“No, no. That’s okay. You keep it.” She felt like offering him money, instead. “I don’t know if you’ve checked into this, but the county has programs if you find yourself…a little short.”

He nodded. “I know. I might consider that.” He returned the coins to his pocket. "Much obliged to you for taking Dottie. That's a load off my mind."

"You're welcome."

"She's a good horse."

"I'm sure she is."

He stroked the Appaloosa's nose. "You be a good girl for the lady, you hear?"

The mare turned her head and nudged his chest.

"I know. I'll miss you, too. It's for the best."

Tracy swallowed a lump in her throat. "Mr. Rankin… Jerry, she'll be right here. If things should start looking up for you, you can come and get her."

He touched the brim of his battered cowboy hat. "That's right nice of you, ma'am." His voice grew husky. "I'll…I'll keep it in mind." He stroked Dottie's nose once more and started for his truck.

"We'll take good care of her," Tracy called after him.

He didn't respond other than to give a brief nod.

The mare turned her head to gaze after him. Then she nickered.

Tracy feared she might start bawling. Apparently she wasn't cut out for this kind of work. She hoped that dealing with people problems turned out to be less emotionally difficult than dealing with animal problems. Otherwise she wouldn't be a very effective psychologist.

Dottie nickered again as the truck and trailer pulled through the gate.

"Come on, girl." Tracy rubbed the mare's silky neck. "Time for a cozy stall and some oats. I'll bet you haven't had any of those in a while." She exerted firm pressure on the lead rope and Dottie followed her obediently to the barn, proving that she was, as Jerry had said, a good horse. Tracy settled her into an empty stall at the far end of the barn and gave her the promised bucket of oats. The mare ate them greedily.

"Okay, this was a good decision…I guess." Tracy leaned on the stall door and watched the mare. She was a good-looking horse, the color of rich cream with a rump speckled in black.

"The thing is, Dottie, I know nothing about prenatal care, and I'll bet you could use a few vitamins and minerals." Gazing at the horse's extended belly, she realized she didn't know how far along the mare was. It hadn't been on the form, but she should have thought to ask, anyway.

She considered her options. She could call the vet in Jackson, who would charge a pretty penny to evaluate the mare and prescribe vitamins. She'd been instructed not to accept any animals, so adding an expensive vet visit seemed wrong when she could get the same services for free. All she had to do was call Drake Brewster.

Yeah, right. So easy. Just call up Mr. Gorgeous-But-Untrustworthy and ask him to give his professional opinion on the pregnant mare she'd just taken in against Regan and Lily's specific instructions. She wondered if Drake would mention that she'd overstepped. Probably not, considering his history. Talk about overstepping. He'd written the book on it.

Still, she knew Regan and Lily would want her to call Drake instead of the vet in Jackson. No question about that. If she phoned Drake, he'd come right over. The guy didn't seem to have a full schedule. And he'd be very nice. Charming, even. Of course he was charming or he wouldn't have been able to talk Regan's fiancée into going to bed with him.

At least, Tracy assumed that's how it had gone. She

couldn't imagine a woman cheating on Regan unless she'd had too much to drink and had been wooed by a master of seduction like Drake Brewster. Tracy was outraged by what he'd done. She was disapproving, scandalized and…so embarrassing to admit, titillated.

Face it, the man was breathtaking. She'd heard his disreputable story before he'd ever walked into Spirits and Spurs. Everybody in town had, and they were all ready to give Drake the cold shoulder and condemn Regan's fiancée in absentia. But when Drake finally did come into the bar, Tracy forgave Regan's fiancée immediately.

Not many women would be able to resist a full-court press by someone who looked like *that.* Those sleepy green eyes and a smile full of equal parts mischief and sin would make short work of any girl's virtuous resolve. Pair those attributes with broad shoulders, slim hips and coffee-colored hair with a slight tendency to curl, and you had the promise of intense pleasure wrapped up in one yummy serving of manhood.

She certainly didn't *want* to be attracted to him. God, no! Too bad. She was, anyway. Her line of defense had been a cool, distant manner. Apparently it had worked, because he thought she didn't like him. Actually, he was right about that. She didn't like him, or more precisely, she didn't like the kind of person who would betray his best friend.

Yet whenever Drake came within five feet of her, she tingled. At the three-foot mark, she burned. She'd made sure he never got any closer than that, because she didn't want to find out what would happen. She was afraid she'd turn into a hypocrite.

So calling him about the mare presented a problem. She'd have to keep her distance when he showed up.

No one would ever need to know about her inconvenient case of lust. She'd taken in the pregnant mare, and consequently she had to do the next logical thing and summon Drake.

Pulling her phone from her pocket, she located his number. Her pulse accelerated at the thought of talking to him. That was the other thing about Drake. He had a voice like aged bourbon, complete with the soft drawl of a man born and raised in Virginia. It was a bedroom voice if she'd ever heard one. He sounded like effing Rhett Butler.

He answered quickly. "Hey there, Miss Tracy. Problems?"

She hadn't counted on the effect of his voice murmuring in her ear, and she felt chills down her spine. She brought the phone to waist level and punched the speaker button. "Not a problem, exactly. I took in a pregnant mare today."

"You're kidding."

"I couldn't turn her away. The guy is down to his last dime, but he refused to sell her to someone he thought might mistreat her. He chose to bring her here instead of taking the money, which he obviously needs. He's being evicted and he has no job."

"Did you give him a job?"

His compassionate suggestion impressed her. "No, but that's a fabulous idea. Obviously I can't hire him, but Regan and Lily might. That's assuming we can find him again. We have no permanent address or phone number. Just a name."

"In a place where everybody seems to know everybody, that should be enough. How far along is the mare?"

"I didn't think to ask. But I assume she needs special care, and I didn't want to bring the vet down from Jackson and incur extra expense." She paused to see if he'd volunteer his services.

"She might be fine for a week or so."

Damn him, he was going to make her ask. "She might, but I would feel terrible if she or the foal had issues because I didn't give her what she needs. Besides, it would be nice to know her approximate due date."

"True, but Regan can figure that out when he gets home."

Tracy's frustration grew. "What if she's ready to pop?"

His laugh was like warm maple syrup. "Is that your roundabout way of inviting me over to take a look?"

"I'd appreciate it if you'd come and examine her." She injected as much formality into the statement as she could muster.

"I'll be right there."

Her stupid adrenaline level spiked. "Thank you. Bye." She disconnected quickly. Brisk and efficient. That was the key. Somehow she'd continue to strike that note.

Now that he was on his way, she was suddenly concerned about how she looked. She'd showered this morning, but she hadn't bothered with makeup and her hair was pulled back in a simple ponytail. Whenever Drake had seen her at Spirits and Spurs she'd been wearing makeup and a cute hair arrangement. To her secret shame, she'd spent more time on her appearance since he'd started coming into the bar.

How sick was that? She didn't really want to attract his attention. Well, apparently she did, and now he'd arrive and discover what she looked like au naturel. That was a good thing. No matter how much she longed to race into the house and slap on some lipstick, she would *not*.

Instead she picked up a brush and went to work on Dottie's speckled coat. To Jerry Rankin's credit, Dottie didn't look as if she needed to be brushed, but Tracy did it, anyway. Then she combed out the black-and-white mane and tail, all the while talking to the mare and telling her what a beautiful baby she would have.

Dottie stood quietly and seemed to enjoy the attention, but she'd maneuvered herself so that she could look out the stall door as if watching for Jerry to return. At one point she moved her head to gaze at Tracy as if trying to decide why this strange person had replaced her old buddy.

"He would have kept you if he could," Tracy said. "Bringing you here was an act of love. He didn't want you to fall into bad hands, or to suffer because he wasn't able to take care of you properly."

The explanation seemed to help. Dottie heaved a big horsey sigh and lowered her head to nibble on the straw scattered at her feet.

Tracy wondered if the mare was still hungry. After all, she was eating for two. What Tracy knew about such things would fit inside a bottle cap. She really did need Drake's advice.

As if her thoughts had conjured him up, she heard him enter the barn, his boot heels clicking on the wooden floor. She hurried over to the stall door and glanced quickly down the aisle. Sunlight streamed into the barn, outlining his manly physique in gold. He'd taken to wearing Western clothes recently, and they suited him. Boy, did they ever suit him.

She needed to gather her wits, so she didn't call out to him. Hoping he hadn't noticed her, she went back to brushing Dottie. For someone who had vowed to remain cool and distant, she sure had a lot of heat pouring through her veins. She drew in a deep breath and let it out slowly.

"Tracy? Are you in here?" His rich voice echoed in the rafters.

"Down here, last stall on the left." Damn, but her hands were shaking. This was not good.

"Thanks. I tried the house, but you didn't answer the door." His footsteps came closer. "My eyes aren't quite adjusted to the light."

She glanced up, and there he was, six-foot-something of testosterone-fueled male. His Western shirt emphasized the breadth of his shoulders. He wasn't wearing a cowboy hat, and she didn't think she'd ever seen him wearing one. She wondered about that. Most cowboy wannabes couldn't wait to show up in a hat.

When he opened the stall door, she realized her mistake. Jumpiness aside, she should have walked out to meet him. Then she could have let him go in the stall alone. Instead he was about to come in with her.

Unless she engineered a little do-si-do with him and then made her escape looking like a frightened rabbit, she was stuck here. Her three-foot limit was about to be violated, and she didn't know what to do about it.

He caught sight of the mare and let out a low whistle. "She's a beauty."

"I know." Her plan of maintaining a formal distance crumbled. She'd been through an emotional experience and she needed to talk about Jerry and his willingness to sacrifice for Dottie. "I'll bet he could have sold her, but he couldn't find the right buyer in time. I was touched by the fact he was choosy when he couldn't afford to be."

"Yeah, that's damned noble." He entered the stall and smiled at her. "For the record, I'm glad you followed your instincts and took her. Those instructions didn't anticipate a mare like this showing up."

Five feet, still just the tingle. "I'm sure she was the one bright spot in the guy's life. I hope Regan and Lily are ready to take on some help and that we can find him again if they are."

"I'd say there's an excellent chance that will work out."

"Then I'll think positive, too." *Three feet, starting to burn.*

"What's her name?"

"Dottie." She sounded breathless, but maybe he'd think she had allergies. She backed up a foot and hoped the move wasn't too obvious.

Drake laughed. "Appropriate. Hi, Dottie." He held out a hand, palm up. She saw he was holding a peeled baby carrot.

The mare snuffled against his open palm and took the carrot. She crunched it between her strong teeth as Drake ran his hands over her neck, her shoulders and her distended belly.

God help her, Tracy followed the path of that gentle stroking. After all the promises to herself that she'd ignore his considerable sex appeal, she couldn't help imagining how those hands would feel caressing a woman. No, not just *a* woman. Her.

She wanted to feel the magic of those hands. And they would be magic. Watching him with the horse was evidence of that. She longed to experience that lazy, sensual touch….

No, she didn't! What was wrong with her? She was falling under his spell. He probably didn't even realize he was casting one. Sensuality was instinctive with him, it seemed. He was surrounded by an invisible magnetic field, and just like that, she'd been drawn back into the three-foot zone.

"A more thorough exam would tell us for sure." Drake continued to stroke the horse. Typical female, Dottie was eating it up. "But from a preliminary evaluation, I'd say she's less than a month from delivering." He glanced over his shoulder at Tracy. "You weren't far off. She's almost ready to pop."

"Good grief." She placed a hand over her racing heart, which now had two reasons to be out of control—lust and terror. "I don't want that happening on my watch."

"You probably won't have to deal with it." His voice was soothing.

She wondered if veterinarians cultivated a bedside manner. If so, Drake had a hell of a good one. "But I might have to deal with it, right?"

"Mothers about to give birth are always unpredictable. But don't worry. I can drive out here at a moment's notice. If she goes into labor, you won't have to handle it alone."

"Good." The rush of gratitude, mixed with the sensual feelings he inspired, became a potent combination. She struggled to remember why she didn't like this man. Oh, yes. He'd betrayed his best friend. No matter how welcome his presence was at the moment, he'd chosen to trade years of friendship for immediate pleasure.

"She'll need some prenatal supplements."

Tracy fought to concentrate on what he was saying instead of imagining him naked in her bed. "Supplements. Right."

"I'll order them from a company I have an account

with. My professional discount will keep the cost down."

"Good. Thank you. I honestly didn't consider all the ramifications of this. Assuming her foal is okay, and I hope to heck it is, I've actually accepted two horses."

"True." He lightly scratched Dottie's neck, and her eyelids drifted down in obvious ecstasy. Lucky horse. "But I don't think you have to worry about Regan and Lily. They'll support what you've done."

"I hope so." But she wasn't terribly worried about Regan and Lily. They were animal lovers and would understand. The foal might even be fun for them.

But she was extremely worried about the inevitable contact with Drake and her increasingly intense reaction to his proximity. She had strong principles. Surely a sweet-talking Southerner wouldn't cause her to abandon those principles. *Surely not.*

3

DRAKE WAS PROUD of himself. He'd examined the mare and interacted with Tracy as if he had no interest in her whatsoever. Then he'd left after promising to order the supplements online the minute he got back to his cabin and his computer.

Driving home, he congratulated himself on being a perfect gentleman the whole time. Not once had he given in to the temptation to flirt with her. For him that was a major victory. Regan clearly thought that he would hit on Tracy if given the chance, and he was determined to prove that he could resist that urge.

It hadn't been easy. Before today, they'd always been separated by a massive wooden bar and surrounded by other people. This had been a far more intimate encounter, and she'd looked quite accessible in her T-shirt and jeans, no makeup, and her hair held by a little elastic thing that could be pulled off in no time.

At the bar he'd experienced a jolt of desire whenever he looked at her lipstick-covered mouth. She liked to wear red, and those lips had beckoned him, even when he'd known her smile meant nothing. Logically he shouldn't have been even more turned on by the soft pink of her bare mouth, but he had been. Seeing her like that made him think of how she'd look first thing in the morning. He yearned for the privilege of waking up next to Tracy Gibbons.

He yearned for what would precede that moment, too. He was a fair judge of women. Make that an *excellent* judge of women. Tracy had a lot of passion buried in her.

And here was the kicker. She was as hot for him as he was for her. During his visits to the Spirits and Spurs, she'd fooled him with her remote attitude and obvious disapproval. He thought she still disapproved of him. But underneath, lust burned.

He'd felt that energy the second he'd walked into the stall. He'd heard it in the pattern of her breathing. A week ago he would have attributed the undercurrent of tension to anger. Today, in the quiet confines of Dottie's stall, he'd recognized it for what it was—suppressed desire. She wanted him, and she was fighting it for all she was worth.

The man he used to be would have capitalized on the situation. He could have made love to her today. She was ripe for it. One touch would have tipped the balance in his favor, and the sex would have been glorious. She would have temporarily reveled in the unexpected encounter, the thrill of tasting forbidden fruit.

But afterward…ah, that was the problem. She would be ashamed of herself for surrendering to urges that violated her principles. Pleasure would quickly become tainted. And then, if the sex had been so good that she *still* wanted him, despite everything, she'd begin to hate herself and him. He knew all about that downward spiral. He'd put Jeannette through it. He'd put himself through it.

As he pulled up in front of the little cabin he temporarily called home, he vowed that he would not subject Tracy to the same fate as Jeannette. If that meant they'd never explore the possibilities presented by their strong chemistry…oh, well.

He'd been celibate for months, and he was almost getting used to it. He and Jeannette had tried to create a relationship after Regan had left, tried to convince each other that their betrayal of Regan had been motivated by a grand passion they couldn't deny. The fantasy hadn't held up for very long, and since breaking off with Jeannette, he hadn't felt like getting involved with anyone.

Parking his dusty black SUV, he went inside the cabin and turned on his laptop. He ordered the supplements to be shipped to the rescue facility and texted instructions to Tracy's cell so she'd know how and when to administer them. And that, he thought, should be the end of that.

He could have done more. A rectal and vaginal exam would have been normal procedure, but the mare appeared healthy and Regan would be back in charge in a week. Drake had enjoyed the chance to be a vet again, even briefly, and that surprised him. Lately he'd wondered if he needed to change careers as well as his place of residence, but maybe not.

Considering the delicate situation with Tracy, though, he would perform only basic care unless a problem cropped up. Tracy was a smart lady. If she needed help, she'd call. If she didn't, then they could avoid contact with each other, contact that might lead to actions they'd both regret.

As he decided whether to go on a hike or read a book, neither of which appealed to him, someone knocked on his front door. Although he was glad for an interruption in what promised to be a boring afternoon, he couldn't imagine who had come to visit. No one sought him out besides Regan, and he was in Washington.

Drake opened the door and discovered Josie Chance there. He tried not to look as astonished as he felt. Thanks to Regan making a few introductions after he and Drake had rescued their friendship, Drake recognized the attractive woman wearing her long blond hair in a braid down her back.

A few years ago she'd married Jack Chance, the oldest of the Chance brothers and their avowed leader. But that wasn't the most significant fact about Josie Chance. She happened to own the Spirits and Spurs, which made her Tracy's boss. Drake suspected that Tracy was the reason behind Josie's visit.

Josie didn't disappoint him. "This isn't exactly a social call, Drake. I'm here to talk about Tracy."

"Be glad to." He wasn't, but he'd been raised to say the polite thing. "Come on in."

She walked through the door and glanced around the small space furnished with a sturdy sofa and chair covered in green plaid. "Very nice."

"Yes, ma'am." He wasn't sure what she meant, but agreeing with her seemed like a good strategy.

She gave him a small, almost reluctant smile. "I wasn't sure if you'd be a typical bachelor living in chaos."

"Because that's what scoundrels do?"

Her smile widened. "Often, yes."

"I did live in chaos for a little while, but when the maid didn't show up I decided I might as well keep it clean myself before I started losing things in the mess I'd made. Please, have a seat. I can brew some coffee, and I also have iced tea in the refrigerator."

"Sweet tea?"

"No, ma'am. I know it's not very Southern of me, but I like mine plain."

"I'll have some, then. Thank you." She sat in the easy chair. "Tracy would kill me if she knew I'd come over here."

Drake took a couple of tall glasses out of the cupboard and filled them with ice. "I won't tell her, but good luck keeping a secret around here."

"You're right, but I'm going to attempt it. Jack's the only one who knows I rode over, because I needed someone who could watch little Archie without throwing a hissy-fit about me coming. Three of my potential babysitters are Regan's sisters, and they would *not* approve."

"I'm sure." He poured tea in both glasses. "Wait a minute. You *rode* over here from the Last Chance?"

"It's closer to go cross-country, and doing that made it less likely I'd be seen. My horse is out back, tied to a tree."

"I'll be damned." He walked over and handed her one of the glasses before sitting on the sofa with his own drink. "You've infiltrated enemy territory."

"Something like that." She took a swallow of her tea. "This is excellent. Thanks."

"It's one of the few things I know how to make." He settled back, his glass balanced on one knee. "So you're here on a secret mission to make sure the big bad wolf doesn't have designs on the fair maiden Tracy?"

"That about sums it up." She studied him. "You're charming. I assumed you would be."

"Back in Virginia, it's the law. Anyone who fails the Southern-charm test is shipped up north."

"Oh, boy." Josie sipped her tea. "This could be trickier than I thought."

"It won't be tricky." Drake met her gaze. "I've already thought this through. I'll admit that I find Tracy very attractive, but I—"

"I *knew* it. Unfortunately, she's fascinated with you, too. You should hear the way she carries on about your dastardly behavior, to the point where I finally realized she was into you."

If having that confirmed thrilled him, he didn't want to let on. "But she doesn't want to be."

"Exactly. Do you know why?"

"Sure. Like everyone else around here, she doesn't like what I did to Regan." He took a long pull on his iced tea and concentrated on the cool liquid running down his throat. God, but he was sick of this topic. Maybe someday in the distant future his indiscretions wouldn't be the main thing folks wanted to talk to him about.

"It goes deeper than that, and I decided it might help if you understood a little more about her."

Now this he did want to hear. "Shoot."

"Her father was a married man who claimed he was single and that he'd had a vasectomy."

"Oh." At one time Drake would have offered a comment on that kind of behavior, but he no longer felt qualified to pass judgment.

"That's why infidelity is such a complicated issue for Tracy. She hates it, but without it she wouldn't exist. Her dad sent a few checks, but by then he was back with his wife. When the checks stopped coming, Tracy's mom didn't go after the bastard because she's not well educated and didn't think she could get anywhere, legally."

"Is Tracy's mother still around?"

"She eventually married some old cowboy from

Idaho and she lives over there, now. But Tracy's roots are here, so she stayed. Most of us feel as if we helped raise her."

Drake nodded. "She probably feels that way, too." Setting his tea on the coffee table in front of him, he leaned back and blew out a breath. "I'm glad you told me all that, although I'd already decided after going over there today that I'd—"

"Going over there?" Josie straightened. "Was there a problem with the animals?"

"Not exactly." He gave her a brief rundown on what had happened with the pregnant Appaloosa.

"Okay. That's not so terrible. Regan and Lily will have a good time with a foal running around, and maybe they'll decide to hire this Rankin fellow. If not, Jack might have a spot for him at the Last Chance."

"His mare's in decent shape, so he's probably good with horses, but that's all I can vouch for."

"Jack can ask around about him. I just hope the mare will wait until Regan and Lily get back before she delivers."

"Me, too." He planned to be strong in the face of temptation, but he'd rather not be tempted by Tracy at all.

"You were saying something about a decision after going over there today. I didn't let you finish."

Drake wasn't sure he wanted to finish. They'd finally left the topic he was so sick of, and that was a relief. But he supposed he might as well say his piece. "I plan to keep my distance from Tracy. I already have one woman on my conscience who got involved with me against her better judgment. I don't need to make it two."

"You're talking about Regan's ex-fiancée."

"Yes, ma'am."

"For what it's worth, I don't believe in laying all the blame on you, but people are probably doing that because you're here. You're the sacrificial goat, the one who showed up to take the flak. I happen to think that half the responsibility is hers."

"I can't say that's true." Drake had gone over the night's events a million times, and he always saw himself as the one who could have stopped it. Should have stopped it.

"Noble of you. Egotistical, too, I might add."

He blinked. "Excuse me?"

"Do you really consider yourself so irresistible that a woman loses her ability to think for herself when you display your manly charms?"

He stared at her, and after the shock wore off, he started to laugh. Then he laughed until his sides hurt. Finally, he wiped his eyes and cleared his throat. "Thanks for that. You've lightened my load quite a bit."

She regarded him with amusement. "I wasn't prepared to like you very much, Drake. It's disconcerting to find out that I like you a lot."

"Good. I like you, too."

"The problem is, I'm not even supposed to be here, so I can't go around telling people that you're actually a pretty nice guy if they'd only get to know you."

He shrugged. "That's okay. Regan keeps telling me to give everyone time."

"Yeah, well, there are a few around here who are world-champion grudge holders, so don't expect a miracle. But now that you mention it, that's something I've been very curious about. What are your plans? Are you staying? Are you going back to Virginia? Regan's always been vague about your next move."

"That's because I'm vague about it. I don't want my

old life back, but I'm not sure what my new life should look like, or where it will take place. I'm at a crossroads."

She studied him quietly for a moment. "There's this spot out on the ranch, a big flat piece of granite laced with quartz that's sacred to the Shoshone Indians, although they really don't go out there anymore. Some say that if you're having trouble deciding what to do, standing out on that rock helps."

"What do you think?"

"I've never personally used that rock to make a decision, but some of my loved ones have. It couldn't hurt."

"Oh, yes, ma'am, it could. I've heard that in the Wild West trespassers get shot at, especially if they're considered villainous cads, which I am."

Josie grinned. "I wish you and Jack could spend some time together without starting a family feud. I think you'd get along. Anyway, let me give you my cell number. If you decide to head out there, call me and I'll make sure the coast is clear."

"It's a deal."

When they were finished with their tea, they went out back to fetch Josie's horse.

Drake walked outside with her. "It was mighty kind of you to come by," he said.

"I mostly did it for Tracy." She untied her horse, a large bay, and put on the hat she'd hung from the saddle horn. "I hoped to appeal to your better instincts."

"You did, although I was already headed in that direction."

She mounted up and gazed down at him. "That's good to hear, Drake. I wish you well."

"Sounds as if I have one more friend around here."

"You do, but if you mess with Tracy, I'll quickly become Enemy Number One."

"I understand."

"Call if you want a spiritual boost from the sacred rock."

"I will."

With a wave, she guided her horse to the front of the cabin and rode off. Drake followed and watched her dismount to lower the rail on the wooden fence marking the edge of Last Chance property. Then she led her horse across, replaced the rail and climbed back into the saddle before cantering across the meadow.

It struck him that although he'd devoted his life to horses, he hadn't ridden much. His parents owned thoroughbreds destined for the track, and so did all his clients. He'd passed the weight limit for being a jockey when he was twelve, and besides, he'd never aspired to that career.

As a kid, he'd been given one of the thoroughbreds that balked at the starting gate. He'd ridden Black Velvet for a few years, but then school and girls had claimed most of his attention. His riding had become sporadic and mostly confined to summer vacations.

He couldn't remember the last time he'd ridden. He knew everything about the animal—skeletal structure, muscles, tendons, circulatory system…the list went on. But somewhere along the way he'd lost track of the riding part.

Back in Virginia he rented a town house. It had never really occurred to him to buy horse property. He could guess why. He had no desire to own a stable of racehorses, and that was the only model he'd known.

But there were other models. The Last Chance was one of them. Regan and Lily's equine-rescue facility was another. He'd allowed his view to become very narrow, but a relationship with horses didn't have to involve running them around a track or even caring for their medical needs.

He wouldn't mind taking a ride now, but he couldn't go over to the rescue facility and borrow a horse, and he wouldn't be welcome at the Last Chance, either. He could try to find a riding stable in the area, but he probably was too spoiled to be satisfied with most stable ponies.

Still, he'd had another epiphany. Whatever his future held, he wanted it to involve riding horses. Good thing he'd made some wise investments, because horse property didn't come cheap no matter where he ended up. He had a rough idea what his parents' farm was worth, and the amount was staggering.

Eventually he chose a hike over spending the rest of the day in the cabin reading. He took an easy trail, one he could manage in hiking sandals and shorts. The afternoon was warm, so he wore a sleeveless T-shirt. Exercise was a great stress reliever and helped keep his mind off Tracy and his pesky libido. He pocketed his phone out of habit, and he was on the trail headed home when her call came.

"Dottie is leaking," she said.

"Leaking what?" His heart pounded. He didn't want anything leaking. He didn't want anything going wrong with the mare—for several reasons.

"I think it's milk, or something like milk. What does that mean?"

"It means I need to come over and check her out. Unlock Regan's truck. I've been hiking, so I'm hot and sweaty. You'll have to take me the way I am."

"Don't worry about that." She sounded frightened. "Just get here."

"I will, and don't be scared. Everything will be fine." He didn't know that for sure, but it was a good thing to say when people were upset.

Although he didn't shower, he pulled on jeans, boots and a long-sleeved Western shirt before hopping in the SUV. Shorts and hiking sandals weren't the most practical thing to have on if he ended up delivering a foal. As he drove back to the rescue facility, he concentrated on his reasons for being there. This was all about the horse and her foal. Taking her in had been an act of mercy that could end up with everyone feeling warm and fuzzy, unless something went wrong.

If she was lactating, that was a sign that she was closer to giving birth than he'd thought. But the colostrum she'd produce at first was critical to the health of the foal and should be collected. Lactating early could also be a sign of serious trouble that could lead to fatalities, both the mare's and the foal's. He didn't plan to let tragedy occur.

Tracy was standing in the yard, arms wrapped around her torso, when he drove through the gate she'd obviously left open for him. As he turned off the engine and climbed out, she hurried over, all hesitation swept away by panic. He was tempted to gather her in his arms to comfort her, but that wasn't a good idea, and it wasn't what she needed from him right now.

"It's not just the leaking," she said. "It's her whole behavior. She's pacing the stall. Sometimes she lies down, but then she gets up again. I drove Regan's truck down to the barn so you'll have whatever you need close by."

"Thanks. Good idea. Let's go see what our girl is up to." He walked fast, Tracy skipping to keep up with him.

Before this, she'd always maintained a certain physical distance between them, but that didn't seem important to her anymore.

"Maybe I shouldn't have taken her, but I don't know what Jerry would have done if I hadn't. If she needs veterinary care, he wouldn't have been able to afford that, either. I'm so glad you're here, Drake."

His heart stuttered. He hadn't realized how much he'd longed for someone—*anyone*—to say that to him. After being persona non grata for so long, those words sounded damned good.

She rattled on, obviously needing to vent. "I did some research online and found out she should have a bigger stall, but the stalls are all the same size. Do you think she'll be okay in there? The way she's been pacing, I thought maybe she needed more room, but I don't know what we can do about that."

"The one she's in will be fine. All the stalls in this barn are a generous size." He was touched by her anxiety. At Spirits and Spurs she was in complete control as she dispensed food and drink with flair. But now she was in unfamiliar territory. Fortunately it was familiar to him.

The July sun was drifting slowly toward the horizon, but it wouldn't be dark for another couple of hours. The barn faced east and west, and she'd opened the back doors to let in the afternoon light. Drake was happy to have the sun. A crisis always loomed larger in the dark.

Sure enough, Dottie was pacing restlessly in her stall and ignoring her flake of hay while the other horses munched their dinner contentedly. Drake talked calmly to her as he entered and kept talking as he ran his hands over her warm coat. Gradually he made his way to her udder and swiped a finger over the liquid oozing from her teat. Apparently he'd misjudged how soon she'd deliver.

Tracy hovered at his elbow, her breathing shallow. "Well?"

He turned to look at her. Her face was pale with fright, and this close, he noticed little flecks of gold in her dark eyes. "The discharge is colostrum, which is extremely important for her foal's immune system. It's good that you noticed. I'll get what I need from Regan's truck so we can collect and freeze it until she goes into labor. Then we can bottle feed it to her foal in the first twelve hours."

Her eyes widened. "When do you think she'll go into labor?"

"Could be anytime, and I can teach you how to—"

"Did you say *anytime?*"

"Yes, but I can't say for sure exactly when. Could be tonight, could be tomorrow, could be two days from now. In the meantime, you can—"

"Look, I hate to ask this of you, but I'm scared to death. I won't have the faintest idea what to do if she goes into labor, and I could freak. I'm freaked now, in fact. She's not safe with me."

He had to admit she looked petrified, but he could talk her down. She could do this. "She's perfectly safe with you, Tracy. I'm not far away, and all you have to do is call me. I'll be here before you know it."

She shook her head. "Not good enough. I can feed the animals, clean up after them and love on them, but I'm not fit to be a first responder when a mare delivers a foal. Besides, I have to work my shifts at the Spirits and Spurs, and Dottie would be alone for hours. That could be a problem, right?"

He'd forgotten about that. "Do you have to work tonight?"

"No, but I have to go in at eleven tomorrow morning. What if she waits to go into labor until then?"

"You can call me." But he was less sure that everything would work out easily. Dottie had changed the game considerably in the past couple of hours.

"Drake, if you leave, I'll spend the night camped out next to her stall worried sick with my phone right next to me."

He believed her. "Then *I'll* camp out beside her stall tonight. I'm sure there are some old blankets in the house I can use to make a bedroll."

"You don't have to go *that* far. Lily has a spare room. You could sleep in there, maybe set your phone to wake you up every few hours to check on her and collect that stuff the foal will need."

"Colostrum."

"Right. Colostrum."

He hesitated. Sleeping in the barn was one thing. Sleeping in the house with Tracy was a whole other deal. "That's okay. The barn's fine."

"No, no, just because I said I would sleep there if you left doesn't mean you should put yourself through that. You're a pro. You'll know whether it's safe to grab a few winks, and you'd be better off in a real bed."

"Yeah, but—"

"I'll bet you don't want to stay in the house because you think I don't like you."

"You don't like me." *But once your panic wears off, you'll be attracted to me, whether you want to be or not.*

"I don't like what you did to Regan, and I don't blame you for not wanting to hang around someone who's said some hurtful things, but I'm desperate. Please stay. And take the guest room."

He took a deep breath. "Okay." Once the crisis was over, they'd both be like dry kindling ready to ignite. He'd have to get the hell out of there before one of them lit the fire.

4

ON SOME LEVEL, Tracy knew she was taking a huge chance by having Drake close by, but she simply couldn't handle this alone. She walked out to the truck with him. "Since you're staying, I'll share the money Regan and Lily pay me for house-sitting."

"I wouldn't consider it." He opened the back end of the truck. "You need that money for school."

"I do, but if you're doing part of my job here, then it's only fair that…wait a minute. How did you know I'm going to school?"

He gave her a deer-in-the-lights look followed by an expression that clearly said *oh, shit.* He tried to pass it off with a shrug. "That's the way it is around here with secrets. Word gets out."

"Sure it does, but not to you. You don't talk to anybody except Regan and Lily. At least not about anything significant. One of them told you, didn't they?"

"Regan told me and then asked me not to mention it, which I just did. Blame it on my big mouth instead of Regan blabbing. He was trying to respect your privacy, but he thought I might want to know."

"Why?"

"He thought..." A dull red colored his throat and moved up to his cheeks. "Never mind. It's not important." He leaned into the truck and began sorting through Regan's supplies.

"Okay." She was ready to let the subject drop, at least for now. Apparently her previous high anxiety had blocked her sexual awareness of Drake, because as it fell, her heat level rose. And here she was, within the three-foot limit, which hadn't been a problem when she was hyperventilating over the possibility she'd have to deliver a foal.

Now it was a problem, especially with him leaning over like that, which showcased his tight buns. She backed away from the truck. "I need to feed the pigs and chickens. When I discovered Dottie leaking, I lost track of everything else."

"Sure. Go ahead." Rustling noises indicated he was still gathering supplies. He didn't turn around. "I'll take care of things here."

Then she realized something else. She should offer to feed *him*—another sticky wicket because logically they'd have to eat the meal together. He might have to spend considerable time within her three-foot limit. Maybe they could sit at opposite ends of Lily and Regan's dining table as if they were a couple living in a manor house with servants.

Then there was the menu. She doubted it would suit him, but she had to give it a shot. She'd talked him into occupying the premises, and the guy needed nourishment. A small town like Shoshone didn't have a pizza parlor that delivered.

She screwed up her courage. "After I feed the pigs and chickens, I'll warm up some dinner for us."

He turned around, a box in one hand. "That would be great." He gave her a quick smile.

The effect was potent. She backed up another step. "I should warn you that Lily's a vegetarian and Regan's reverted to vegetarianism, too."

"I know. I've been over for dinner a few times."

"Right. I guess you would have." So maybe this food situation would work out okay, after all. "Anyway, she was nice enough to prepare and freeze some food for me. I've thawed a container of lentil soup for tonight. There's plenty for both of us, and she also made corn bread."

"I'm good with that."

She detected a distinct lack of enthusiasm, but she wasn't surprised. Not a lot of guys became excited over lentil soup. "There's also a huge chocolate cake."

"*Now* we're talkin'!"

She couldn't help laughing. "Do you want dessert first?"

"No, I do not. I'm not five. I'll eat my lentil soup like a good boy."

"All right." She did her best not to be charmed, but it was cute the way he drew out the word *five.*

"Besides, it's got to be better than the frozen dinners I've cooked for myself whenever I didn't come into town for a meal."

She had a sudden image of Drake alone in the small cabin eating a microwaved meal by himself and felt a twinge of sympathy. She had so many friends, while he… No, she would *not* feel sorry for him. He could always go back to Virginia and resume his old life. For whatever reason, he'd chosen to stay here and be lonely.

"I've had Lily's lentil soup," she said. "It's good. Come on up to the house when you're finished here."

She turned and walked away. All the way to the house she lectured herself about not letting down her guard.

She knew all about the big flaw in Drake's character. That should have been enough to keep her far, far away from him. Her mother had been seduced by a charmer like Drake, but her mother hadn't had Tracy's advantage of knowing she was dealing with a cheating bastard.

Yes, he was coming to her aid at the moment, and she was thrilled about that. But she couldn't let gratitude and her natural susceptibility override her good judgment. Somehow she had to strike a balance between being properly appreciative and throwing herself into his arms in a fit of lust. She wondered if simple friendship was an option. That might be the safe middle ground, assuming she could pull it off.

Drake had betrayed his best friend, someone Tracy greatly admired. As she stood in the kitchen chopping veggies for the potbellied pigs, she faced a truth she'd been unwilling to admit until now. Drake was also extremely likable. Her choices would be so much easier if he could behave like an arrogant jerk. Then she'd have no trouble separating the guys in the white hats from the ones in the black hats.

She finished filling the bowls for Wilbur and Harley and carried them out to their pens. At one time the two pigs had been free to roam the yard, but the bigger one, Harley, had bullied Wilbur into giving up his food. Now they each had a separate pen for mealtimes, although both had a gate out to a common yard and mud hole they could enjoy together when they weren't eating.

Tracy set a bowl in each pen and then quickly closed them in their respective homes. "That's the answer." She leaned against the fence and watched the pigs eat. "I should be friendly, because after all, the guy is doing me a big-ass favor. But I need to set boundaries, just like you have these fences between you."

Having Drake sleep in the spare room would be no problem if they established some house rules. She couldn't appear inhospitable, because after all, she'd invited him to stay. Perhaps she'd even begged him. Her memory wasn't clear on that point because she'd been distraught at the time.

But now that he'd agreed, they needed to establish a routine that would minimize…temptation. No, she couldn't phrase it like that. The word *temptation* shouldn't come up. They would strive to minimize…unanticipated encounters. That sounded stuffy. She'd have to find a better description, but that's what she meant.

For example, he should keep his shirt on at all times. If he was in the habit of wandering into the kitchen for a midnight snack, he couldn't do that in his pajama bottoms. He had to put on… Uh-oh. He didn't *have* pajama bottoms.

She hadn't thought this through. She'd pleaded with him to stay, but he hadn't come prepared with extra clothes or toiletries. He certainly hadn't come with pajamas, either tops or bottoms. Besides, he wouldn't want to sleep in them, anyway, if he planned to check on Dottie periodically.

She *really* hadn't thought about how this would work. But now she could see it all playing out in living color. He'd sleep in his briefs, unless he chose to sleep naked. When he got up to check on the mare, he'd put on the basics—jeans, socks, boots. It was mid-July. Bothering with a shirt under the circumstances would be plain silly.

Well, then, she'd stay in her room. That would solve the problem. No, it wouldn't. She definitely wanted to be in on the action when Dottie gave birth. She couldn't picture herself cowering in her room like some nervous virgin because Drake was shirtless while he delivered a foal. That would be stupid.

"Still feeding the pigs?" The man in question walked toward her with a loose-hipped stride and a casual smile. He was sexy as hell.

"I'm just finishing up." He'd look amazing without his shirt. Tracy had no doubt about that. If only he could have a potbelly like the pigs, but then he wouldn't have been able to seduce Regan's fiancée, which was the crux of the problem.

She had no idea how she'd handle the temptation of a bare-chested Drake, especially in the likely event that Dottie delivered her foal in the middle of the night. Tracy vaguely remembered discussions among the cowboys at Spirits and Spurs that mares often gave birth at night.

"I didn't realize you'd be so fast." She pushed away from the fence as he moved past the five-foot mark and the tingle of awareness began traveling through her body.

"Dottie's colostrum production is still fairly minimal, which is good. The less she produces before giving birth, the better."

Three feet. Her skin began to warm. "I haven't started on dinner." She gestured toward the pigs. "I like to wait until they're done so I can let them back into their communal area. They love being together, except I can't allow it when they eat."

"Yeah, Lily explained that to me." Drake stood next to her and peered down at the two pigs. "Harley seems a little skinnier, though, so I guess the new program is working."

"It's working." And her libido was working, too. Overtime, in fact. Her hormones were racing around like a championship Roller Derby team.

He'd come here straight from hiking, something she remembered now. If the deodorant commercials were correct, his manly sweat should offend her. But something primitive was going on, because she longed to bury her nose in his shirt and take a big sniff of that heady scent. And then she'd…

"Look at that pig eat!" Drake sounded amused. "He's practically licking the bowl."

"Yeah. He's insatiable." Whoops. Not the best choice of words under the circumstances.

Drake's low chuckle held an undercurrent of awareness. "Hey, Harley, are you gonna let the lady talk about you like that?"

"Well, he is." As if she had no sense of self-preservation, she looked into Drake's laughing eyes. Oh, Lord. She glanced away, but not quickly enough to mute the effect. Every secret, private place in her body responded. "I can let them loose now." Her voice had a huskiness that she was very afraid he'd notice.

"You're sure that's a good idea? Lily used to let them roam the property, but from what I hear, that didn't work out well."

"I mean let them into their community area. They'll still be fenced in."

"Oh, right. Yeah, that's better."

As she walked over and opened the gates so they could both scurry into the communal pen, she told herself that she and Drake were having a conversation about the pigs. But if they had been, he should have been watching them. Instead his attention remained firmly on her, his gaze assessing.

After she let the pigs into their shared enclosure, she faced him. "I desperately need you to stay here tonight, and maybe for the next several nights."

He remained watchful. "I know, and I've agreed to do that. It makes sense."

"But asking you to stay doesn't mean that I—"

"Of course not." Pain was reflected ever so briefly in his expression. "I've been waiting for you to warn me off. Why would you get involved with a man you don't like very much?" Bitterness laced his comment.

In a flash of insight, she knew that he'd picked up on her unbidden reaction to him. Knowing she wanted him even though she didn't approve of him was…insulting? Degrading? Maybe both. "Drake, I—"

"No worries." His jaw tightened. "I wouldn't dream of causing you to do something you don't want to do. Women tend to have a certain response to me. Always have, ever since I was a teenager. Mostly it's fun for both parties, but in this case…"

She'd hurt his feelings. There was no way around it. "I'm sorry."

"Just for the record, I don't make a habit of moving in on another man's territory." He massaged the back of his neck and glanced away. "I've only done it once, and if I could take it back, I would." Then he sighed and looked over at her. "I've never said that to anybody. It sounds like doing it once is no big deal when I know it is. I just wish… Damn it, I wish that one stupid mistake wasn't the only thing you saw when you looked at me."

At that moment, it wasn't the only thing she saw. She saw a man who, for whatever reason, had betrayed himself as well as his best friend. She believed him when he claimed never to have cheated before or since. But why had it happened at all? She thought the answer would be complicated, and unraveling complicated motivations was her passion.

He gave her a crooked smile. "You have that look on your face again."

"What look?"

"The same one you got back at the Spirits and Spurs when I said I must be a glutton for punishment. I told Regan about your reaction, and that's when he mentioned your field of study."

"Huh." She wasn't sure which surprised her more—that he'd been paying such close attention to her expressions or that he and Regan had been discussing her that night and she'd had no idea. Apparently she'd been so wrapped up in being cool that she'd missed some things.

"I figure, when you look like that, you're fixin' to psychoanalyze me."

"And you wouldn't like that."

"Not much, mostly because you've already decided I'm a bad character. I don't think your evaluation would be unbiased."

She flushed at that truth. "You're right. It's a failing of mine. Being judgmental is a no-no for a psychologist, and I *am* judgmental. I'll have to give that up if I expect to be an effective therapist."

"Then why not start with me?"

"I thought you didn't want me to work with you."

"I don't if you consider me lower than whale poop."

"I don't consider you lower than whale poop." That was hard to say without laughing. "Whale poop is at the bottom of the ocean. That's as low as anybody can go, and I don't consider you that bad."

"Okay, then where would you rank me? How about lower than a snake's belly?"

She couldn't hold back a grin. "Stop it. You're being ridiculous."

"No, I'm not. I'm trying to get a bead on just how bad your bad opinion of me is."

"No, you're trying to charm me."

His expression was priceless, exactly like a kid caught with his hand in the cookie jar. "Busted." He gazed at her. "Was it working?"

"You know it was. It's what you do best. That's why I'm so leery of you."

"Leery? You mean like afraid?"

She thought about that. "Maybe."

"Why would you be afraid of me?" He spread his arms wide. "I'm completely harmless." Then he sniffed and made a face. "However, I stink to high heaven. I could use a shower before we sit down to eat. I can't stand myself, so I can only imagine what I'm puttin' you through. If you want to be judgmental about that, I wouldn't blame you a bit."

Smiling, she shook her head. "You just can't help it, can you?"

"Help what?"

"Never mind. Let's go back to the house so I can fix us some dinner and you can shower." She started walking in that direction, but her thoughts remained with their conversation. If she understood him correctly, he was offering himself as a guinea pig, but only if she could stop judging him long enough to help him work through some issues.

He fell into step beside her. "Obviously I didn't bring any spare clothes."

"I thought of that." She didn't want him to know how long she'd obsessed about it. "How close are you to Regan's size?"

"Pretty close, if you're willing to raid his underwear drawer and maybe snag me a shirt or two. The jeans will be okay for another day or so."

"I'll see what I can find and leave them in your room."

"That would be great. While you're at it, maybe if you nose around you'll come up with a spare razor, and maybe even a new toothbrush and toothpaste. Regan typically has backup stuff like that. He likes being organized."

"I'll look. Under the circumstances, I'm sure he wouldn't care if I raid his bathroom supplies."

"If you'd rather not, I could make a quick run home. Maybe that would be better."

"No." Just the thought of him leaving caused panic to well up again. Her sense of security depended on him being right here. "Please don't."

"Okay, okay. I won't leave until Dottie drops her foal."

"Thank you." Her panic disappeared immediately. But now that they'd mentioned Dottie, she wanted to reassure herself that the mare was okay. "Let's check on her before we go in."

He nodded and switched direction. "Okay, assuming you can stand being around me for another ten minutes. If you want to let me do it while you head for the house, I won't be offended."

"I'll come with you." She adjusted her path, too. "It's good practice for me."

"Practice?"

"For learning to be less judgmental."

"Ah." He laughed and glanced over at her. "How about it, Tracy? Any chance your practice could extend beyond putting up with my stench?"

"Such as what?" She had a pretty good idea what he was talking about, but she wanted to be sure.

"Would you be willing to practice accepting my considerable failings, too?"

She met his gaze. "I guess it's worth a shot."

"Good deal." He flashed his superwattage smile.

He might think he'd convinced her just now. In reality, he'd had her at whale poop.

5

DOTTIE HAD TEMPORARILY stopped leaking colostrum, so in short order Drake was back in the house and standing under a hot shower. He soaped up, grateful for the opportunity to get clean again. Tracy had found him a razor and a toothbrush. She'd even discovered an unused deodorant stick and a new tube of toothpaste that happened to be his brand. He'd replace all the items once this gig was over.

God, he hoped he knew what he was doing by agreeing to let Tracy muck around in his psyche. But he'd learned that solitary self-exploration didn't work for him, and he couldn't hang out in the little cabin forever waiting for enlightenment to arrive. He wanted a plan, but so far nothing had occurred to him.

As he'd predicted, his parents were royally pissed that he'd left in the middle of racing season. The guy who'd taken over his practice was quickly winning everyone's confidence, which irritated his parents even more. They'd shoveled clients his way for years, and now some other vet was reaping the rewards.

Drake didn't care. He might continue to be a vet, but not in the world of thoroughbred racing. He hoped his temporary replacement would be interested in buying him out, which would probably be the last straw for his folks. Oh, well. He'd tried it their way and had ended up so confused and miserable that he'd thought boinking his best friend's fiancée was a good idea.

Talking it out with Tracy would be a relief, providing she could give up her tendency to judge him. She'd admitted that was a problem area for her, so their cooperative effort might turn out to be a very good thing. Ideally, they'd help each other.

He hadn't decided what to do about sex. They both wanted to have it, but that didn't mean that they should. He'd pretty much promised Josie Chance that he wouldn't, and in a town like Shoshone there was zero probability that it would stay a secret.

For the moment he wouldn't worry about it. As he toweled off, he caught the subtle aroma of lentil soup warming on the stove. She must have put the corn bread in the oven as well, because he could smell that, too.

For the first time in months, he felt relaxed and almost peaceful. Tracy knew the worst about him, and yet she was fixing him supper. Better yet, she needed him around because of Dottie. Remembering her panic whenever she thought he might leave made him feel a little bit like her knight in shining armor. His armor might be tarnished, but she'd agreed to look past that for the time being.

By the time he walked into the kitchen wearing some of Regan's clothes but his own jeans and boots, she was in the dining room setting the table. She glanced up and smiled. "Dinner's almost ready, but I was wondering if you'd—"

"Take another look at Dottie?"

"Yeah. Am I being obsessive?"

"Nope." Even if he thought so, he wouldn't have said it. She'd taken on the responsibility of this pregnant mare, and she wouldn't rest easy until the foal had been born and both mother and baby were fine.

He wouldn't totally relax until that moment, either. Although he'd been through a lot of deliveries in his Virginia practice, most involving very valuable foals, this one loomed larger than all the others. He wanted to be Tracy's hero.

Walking outside, he took a deep breath of the warm evening air. The sun had disappeared moments ago, leaving an apricot glow behind. Enough light remained to make out the barn, which was pink with turquoise trim, and the house, painted neon green with orange trim. The orange almost matched the horizon.

Drake remembered his initial impression of this place, the day he and Regan had talked for the first time since the Christmas Eve incident. Regan had cautioned Drake not to make fun of the paint job. Lily was a free spirit who believed in shaking things up. Since that day, Drake had spent enough time here to grow used to the unusual colors, but newcomers always gawked and some of the old-timers muttered about the neighborhood going to hippie hell.

Drake had loyally defended Lily's paint choices to anyone who had criticized them in his presence. Considering his poor reputation around town, he'd wondered lately if maybe his defense had hurt more than helped her cause. So he'd become less vocal about it.

But the pink-and-turquoise barn appealed to him. The colors flew in the face of tradition, and he was all about that these days. His family was steeped in tradition. He might even say mired in it.

As he walked down to the barn, he realized that this

equine-rescue facility made him happy. He'd forced himself not to come here too often because he hadn't wanted to be a pest, but now he had a perfect excuse to hang around and absorb the ambiance of this little five-acre piece of goodness and light.

He envied Regan, who planned to live here for the foreseeable future. He'd continue his vet practice with Nick Chance, and he'd provide free vet care for the animals that Lily took in. Sweet. Regan had found what he wanted in life. Drake was still searching for that perfect fit.

Inside the barn, he hit the switch that turned on some lights installed along the aisle near the floor. Regan said he'd patterned the lighting after what he'd seen in the much bigger barn at the Last Chance Ranch. Drake would have to take Regan's word for it. An invitation to the Last Chance, other than Josie's urging him to go stand on some sacred rock, didn't seem to be in his immediate future.

Familiar aromas greeted him as he walked down the wooden aisle—sweet hay, sun-dried straw, oiled leather and the earthy scent of horses. Would he like to own a barn like this someday? He might, if the horses weren't racing stock being groomed for the track. The intense focus of their lives had too closely mirrored his own, and the pressure had threatened to choke the breath out of him. At the time he hadn't recognized that.

When he came to Dottie's stall, she was quietly munching on the flake of hay she hadn't cared about earlier. She paid little attention to him as he walked into the stall. When he checked her teats, they were dry.

"Okay, pretty girl, what's the story?"

Dottie continued to ignore him as she ate her dinner.

"I hope you realize what a commotion you caused

around here. You scared poor Tracy to death. So now what? Are you gonna make us all wait a week? Two weeks?"

The mare lifted her head long enough to gaze at him. But those liquid brown eyes gave nothing away. Then she went back to her meal.

"A lady of mystery, huh? Okay. I'll go eat my dinner and be back later. I don't quite trust this lull in the action. I think you have more tricks up your sleeve."

Giving Dottie a final pat on the rump, he walked out of the stall and latched it behind him. He could take a blood sample, but in the end it was still a guessing game. If Regan were here, he'd use his intuitive skills and probably pinpoint the moment of birth within a few minutes. That was why he was a great vet and Drake was merely an adequate one.

But he'd bring his A-game to this event. Lacking Regan's horse-whisperer instincts, he'd set his phone alarm to ring on the hour every hour until dawn. If he lost a little sleep, it didn't matter. He was no longer on a rigid schedule.

Tracy had turned on some lights in the house, and the cozy look of it beckoned to him. Funny how much he felt at home, even though both he and Tracy were visitors here. A week from now, regardless of what happened with Dottie, he and Tracy would be gone. Yet at this moment, he felt grounded, as if he finally belonged somewhere. Weird.

When he opened the screen door and walked inside, he had the insane urge to call out *Honey, I'm home!* He didn't, both because it would be lame and because she might think he'd gone completely nuts. She was studying psychology, which logically had to include abnormal psych. He didn't want to be classified with that second bunch.

Even so, he should at least announce his presence, in case she hadn't heard him come in. He didn't want to startle her. "Hey, Tracy!" he called out. "I'm back!"

"Good." Her voice came from the kitchen. "I'll take the corn bread out now."

Damn, but this was homey. He'd deliberately avoided sharing a condo or apartment with a woman because he'd known he wasn't even close to settling down. The thought had always felt stifling. Yet this…was not.

Tracy was in the process of setting the corn-bread pan on the stove when he walked into the kitchen. She glanced over at him, her face flushed with the heat from cooking. Her ponytail was coming loose, and little wisps of dark hair at her nape were damp with sweat. "How's Dottie?"

He longed to get her even hotter and sweatier. It would be so simple to walk over there and gather her into his arms. He couldn't be absolutely sure how she'd react, but he didn't think she'd resist once she got over the initial surprise. Women seemed to like the way he kissed.

She probably thought of him as some sort of Don Juan, though. She eventually might forgive his betrayal of Regan, but he couldn't deny that he was popular with the ladies. At least he had been before coming here. If he and Tracy ended up having sex, it would be a hundred times better if she made the first move.

So instead of crossing the room and kissing her, he stayed where he was and answered her question. "Honestly? If I didn't know better, I'd say that mare's decided not to deliver for a couple of weeks. Her teats are perfectly dry now." He walked over to the sink and started washing up.

"So it's a false alarm." She picked up a knife and cut the corn bread into squares. "I brought you out here for nothing."

"Not at all." And even if Dottie had issued a false alarm, he'd never think this trip was for nothing. He loved being here with Tracy. It was the most fun he'd had since arriving in Jackson Hole. "Something's going on, or she wouldn't have produced that colostrum this afternoon. I still plan to watch her closely tonight."

As she transferred pieces of corn bread into a napkin-draped basket, she paused to look at him. "You'll come and get me if she goes into labor, right?"

"You bet." He was counting on the excitement of the moment to distract him from the temptation she'd present when she was half-awake and wearing something skimpy. "You wouldn't want to miss the main event."

"Absolutely not." She held out the basket of corn bread. "You can take this into the dining room and I'll bring the soup. Oh, I nearly forgot. There's wine. Do you want any? Or a beer?"

He shook his head. He didn't need a fuzzy brain, both because of the mare and because of the hot woman he was determined not to touch until she touched him. "We can save that for a celebration after the foal is born." He wondered if that would be when Tracy let down her hair and her barriers. Maybe. He hoped Dottie would give birth real soon.

"Good idea. I won't have any, either. We should stay sharp. I'll bring us some water."

Drake had to smile as he walked into the dining room. She'd lit the tapers sitting in silver holders in the center of the table. Regan had given Lily those candlesticks, and since then the happy couple had eaten by candlelight almost every evening. Drake was touched that Tracy thought he was worthy of candles.

Place mats had been put down, too, he noticed, and cloth napkins. A plate to hold the soup bowl stood waiting at each place. A butter dish was already on the table. "This looks nice." He positioned the basket of corn bread where they both could reach it.

"I don't entertain often." She walked in with a bowl of steaming soup in each hand and placed them on the table. "Lily and Regan are set up for it, and I decided to make things festive as a way to thank you for donating your time to this effort."

"It's my pleasure." It was the polite thing to say, but the words had never been truer.

"Choose your seat."

He glanced at the table. She'd arranged the place settings so that one of them would be at the head of the table and the other to that person's right. He stood behind the chair at the second spot. "I'll sit here."

She laughed. "I figured you for the head of the table."

"Why?"

"I don't know. You sound like Rhett Butler, and he would take the head of the table."

"I'm happy to destroy another stereotype."

"Then have a seat."

"Not yet. I might not automatically sit at the head of the table, but I'm Southern to the bone, which means I will help you into your chair."

"Oh!" She smiled brightly. "That would be lovely." She paused until he came around. "Sarah Chance would approve of your manners."

"Is that right?" He pulled out Tracy's chair, waited until she was seated, and slid the chair smoothly up to the table, just as he'd been taught as a boy. This close, he was tempted to lean down and kiss the soft skin behind her ear, but she'd probably jump ten feet if he did. Releasing his hold on her chair, he moved to his own and sat down.

Tracy put her napkin in her lap. "Sarah's big on manners, including the old-fashioned things like holding a lady's chair and opening doors. All three of her sons are known for it. The cowhands who work for her are expected to behave that way, too."

"Is she Southern?" He'd pretty much given up on the idea of making friends with Sarah, the matriarch at the Last Chance Ranch. He hadn't met her, but she was reputed to be extremely protective of her extended family, which included Regan. She might approve of Drake's manners, but she certainly wouldn't approve of him.

"No, she was a Yankee originally. She's almost like the queen of this area."

"So I've heard." He understood why Regan hadn't taken him out to the ranch to meet Sarah. He kept hearing about the woman, though, and he couldn't shake the idea that if he had Sarah on his side, everyone else would ease up. He'd had a nice talk with Josie today. Maybe that was a start.

"I've known Sarah forever, so she doesn't intimidate me, but I can understand how she would affect others. She has a regal bearing about her, which makes sense if you know that her mother was a model and probably trained Sarah to have great posture, too."

"Guess so." He spread his napkin over his lap. "Thanks for feeding me."

"You're welcome, but Lily deserves the credit. I don't like to cook, so she made a special effort to leave food for me. Even though it's vegetarian, which I don't normally eat, Lily makes it really taste good. But you know that already because you've had dinner here before." She grabbed her spoon. "And I'm babbling. Sorry."

He had to agree that she *was* babbling, and her breathing was quick and shallow, too. When she looked at him, she never quite met his gaze, and her color was high. Interesting. Was she nervous about serving him a meal? He didn't think so. She'd served him a ton of meals at Spirits and Spurs. Then he thought of another potential reason for her behavior, and his pulse rate climbed.

She scooped up a spoonful of soup and immediately spit it back out. "Hot, hot!" She gulped some water. "Don't try it yet. Let it cool."

"Tracy? Are you okay?"

"Sure." She drank more water. "Just burned my tongue. Should've waited. Silly of me. I'm the one who heated it up, so I should have realized that it was—"

"You're babbling again."

"I am." She kept her gaze on her soup. Her cheeks turned even pinker.

"Why?"

"You…um…affect me when you're this close, especially if I don't have something else to think about, like pregnant mares and such." Her attention remained on her soup. "I tried to convince myself I could handle it fine, but…apparently not. I'm sorry. I mean, we should be able to enjoy a nice meal, but then you helped me into my chair, and I… This is ridiculous."

His heart beat faster and heat surged through his body to settle in his groin. Finally she was ready to admit she craved him as much as he craved her. Hallelujah. "What do you want me to do?" He knew what *he* wanted to do, but she had to make the call.

"Nothing. I don't know what's wrong with me. No guy has ever affected me this way. Just give me a minute."

That threw a bucket of ice water on his libido. In spite of their recent conversation, she still seemed to think wanting him was wrong. He pushed back from the table. "I wouldn't want to make you uncomfortable. I'll take a walk down to the barn. I have my phone. When you're finished eating, text me and I'll come back and have some dinner."

"Wait!"

He heard her chair scrape the floor, knew she'd left the table, but he kept walking. She felt desire for him but wanted nothing from him. He could take a hint. A two-by-four upside the head would be more subtle.

"Drake, I'm sorry!" Her footsteps sounded behind him. "It's just that—"

"You're not ready to trust me?" He turned when he reached the door. She was standing about five feet away, breathing hard. "Is that what you're trying to say, Tracy? Because that's what I'm hearing, and if that's the way you feel, then I'll make sure to keep my distance."

"That's not it!"

"I think it is. Text me when you've finished eating. I promise to stick around until Dottie has her foal, so don't worry about that. This is a big place. We can avoid each other." He walked out the door.

Damn it. Damn it to hell. He'd thought maybe he'd found someone who could help him shed the guilt he'd been carrying around for six months. Instead she'd only made things worse.

6

WELL, SHE'D CERTAINLY loused that up. Tracy stared at the screen door as Drake's words played in a continuous loop in her head. *You're not ready to trust me.*

No one could blame him for coming to that soul-shattering conclusion. She'd admitted to wanting him desperately, and when he'd been ready to do something about it, she'd told him not to. She'd implied that given time, she'd rather squelch this unwelcome lust. No wonder he'd left.

Now she had a decision to make. If she really was scared to death of getting involved with him, all she had to do was leave things as they were. He'd keep far away from her now that she'd thoroughly insulted him and stomped all over his pride.

She paced the living room as she tried to sort through her thoughts. An armed truce sounded awful. Peaceful Kingdom was a happy place, and although she wasn't as into the woo-woo stuff as Lily, she hated to pollute the environment with bad feelings.

Besides, she had a mare in the barn who was about to give birth. If she and Drake were barely speaking, the atmosphere during delivery would be strained. That couldn't be good for any of them.

Something should be done, and she had to do it. She might not be able to repair the damage, but she had to try. That required working through what had happened at dinner so she could explain it to Drake.

She resumed her seat at the table. Maybe revisiting the scene of the crime would help her think. Chewing was supposed to stimulate the brain, so she picked up a piece of corn bread and took a bite.

Obviously she'd responded in a knee-jerk fashion. Until he'd scooted her chair in, she'd managed to keep her sexual response at the level of a low hum. But then he'd come close, very close, and the hum had turned into a rock concert.

When that powerful surge of desire caught her off guard, she'd gone into panic mode. That had resulted in the babbling, which of course he'd noticed. Normally she wasn't prone to it, and he'd been around her enough to know that. He'd asked a direct question, and she'd responded with the truth. So far, not so bad.

But then he'd done the right thing, the gentlemanly thing, and asked if he could help. He'd behaved in the most admirable way possible in such a situation. He hadn't pounced or leered, or any of a million obnoxious responses that other guys might have had to her confession. He'd quietly asked what she wanted him to do, implying that he was willing to do *just about anything.* How great was that?

She'd brushed him off. Why? Closing her eyes, she let her head drop back in despair. She'd brushed him off because she was a big, fat coward. She knew why, but that didn't help a whole lot. She'd still done damage to a well-meaning guy.

Ever since she'd hit puberty, her mother had warned her that wanting a man too much was dangerous. Following that advice, Tracy had made sure to date nice men who didn't particularly turn her on. She'd had a lukewarm physical relationship with two of them. Both men had moved on, which hadn't bothered her at all.

When Drake had first showed up at Spirits and Spurs, red hazard lights had flashed. The closer he'd come, the more she'd been convinced—this was the man her mother had warned her about. And a mother's warning, issued early and often, wasn't easily set aside.

Leaping up from the dinner table and hauling Drake into the bedroom would have felt reckless. It would have been the kind of impetuous behavior guaranteed to create the disaster her mother had predicted.

That was her reason for responding to Drake the way she had—not that she wasn't willing to trust him, but that she needed time to think about the implications first, to assess and to regroup.

Now she'd taken that time, and several things had come to mind. First of all, the man who'd wronged her mother, aka Tracy's father, had neglected to mention that he was married. Drake wasn't married. Not even close. No wives or fiancées waited in the wings, because Regan would have known about them and told her.

And Regan brought up the second point. Drake had won Regan's seal of approval, even though Regan easily could have told her to stay away from Drake. He hadn't because, other than that one slip, Regan believed in the guy.

Last of all, the jerk who had inadvertently become Tracy's father had claimed to have had a vasectomy so he could have unprotected sex with Tracy's mother.

Tracy couldn't imagine Drake lying under those circumstances.

Maybe that was the bottom line for Drake Brewster. He had made a mistake, which meant he was human. It was a dilly of a mistake, but he obviously regretted it deeply. Other than his one false move, which from all indications had been a spur-of-the-moment bad decision, Drake was an honest man.

He was also hot, and she might have blown her chance to find out just how hot. That gave her a selfish motive for fixing what she'd broken. It wouldn't be easy. If she managed to fix it, Drake could still break her heart, and because her feelings for him were intense, it would likely be a nasty break.

She picked up another piece of corn bread. Risking heartbreak was the kind of chance people had to take if they wanted to experience something besides lukewarm sex. Until meeting Drake, she'd wondered if lukewarm was all she was destined to feel.

He'd corrected that misunderstanding. Had he ever. But when given an opportunity to prove that she, too, could have a grand passion, she'd been afraid to let herself go. She was still afraid, but no longer quite so terrified as she had been after the holding-out-her-chair incident. She was nervously ready to suit up and get into the game.

First she needed to check on something, though. She'd already raided Regan's toiletries once, so maybe taking one other item wouldn't hurt. And she'd replace everything, of course. No doubt he'd taken a box to D.C., but Drake said Regan liked backup supplies, so logically another box should be tucked away somewhere.

She found the item in question under the sink. After

opening the box, she carried it to the guest room and set it on the nightstand next to the queen-size bed. Looking at that bed and imagining what might take place there later gave her goose bumps. But she also had to be prepared for rejection. Drake had a perfect right to turn her down.

Back in the dining room, she wolfed down her soup, which was almost cool, before dumping Drake's soup back in the pot and turning it on low. Then she wrapped the remaining corn bread in foil and put it in the oven on warm.

The clock was ticking. He must be wondering when he'd get to eat, but she had more to do before texting him. She located a pen, paper and an envelope and brought them to the table. The note took her longer than she would have liked, but it had to set the tone. Licking the envelope was the worst part of the job. So far no one had come up with envelope-flap glue that didn't taste like motor oil laced with menthol.

She wrote his name on the outside of the envelope and propped it against his water glass. After dishing his soup, she put the corn bread back on the table and ducked into her bedroom. Finally she emerged in her red silk bathrobe with her hair loose, and texted him that she was finished eating.

Time to disappear. She made a beeline for the guest room, barely making it before she heard his booted footsteps on the wooden porch. The screen door creaked open. He must have been hungry.

She lay in his bed in the dark, because dark was how he'd left the room. A light on in there might have alerted him to a change in the situation. Sound carried perfectly in the still house, which allowed her to hear the chair scrape as he sat down at the table.

She held her breath. Paper ripped. He was reading her note, which she remembered in vivid detail.

Dear Drake,
My reaction to you was motivated by fear. I was taught from an early age not to trust men who made me feel as you do, because they would ruin my life. So I've dated only safe guys who didn't arouse scary emotions. I realize now that's a cowardly way to live.

I haven't treated you well. I'd like a chance to do better, but if you still want to keep distance between us, I understand completely. Please let me know if Dottie goes into labor. Sleep well.
Yours, Tracy

How she would have loved to watch his expression as he'd read the note, but short of setting up a remote video feed, that would have been impossible. Thinking of the elaborate spy system she would have set up if she'd had time, she started to giggle and had to use a pillow to muffle the sound.

By the time she settled down again, she could hear the rhythmic sound of his spoon dipping in and out of his soup bowl. That noise stopped and paper crinkled, as if he'd wadded up the note. Then it crinkled again, as if he might be smoothing it out. He sighed.

She'd wanted to give him time to think, time when she wasn't around, just as she'd had when he'd left for the barn. What if he decided she wasn't worth the trouble? Finding her in his bed would not be a pleasant surprise then, would it? He might order her out of his room. At least she'd brought the robe to put on in case that happened.

No matter where she was now or what his decision might be, they couldn't have avoided an awkward moment whenever they'd come face-to-face again. So she'd chosen to create a meeting that was shocking and quick. It might be painful, like ripping off a bandage, or bracing, like cannonballing into a cold swimming hole. Either way, it wouldn't be boring.

If he sent her away, that would be a reasonable payback for how she'd treated him. But because he was seeking forgiveness, she hoped he'd be in a forgiving mood, too. She'd know soon enough. She could hear him loading the dishwasher.

He took some time in the kitchen, which probably meant he was putting away the leftovers and wiping down the counters, exactly as she would have done. And all the while he had to be thinking.

When he left the kitchen, she expected to hear steps coming down the hall toward where she lay trembling, torn between excitement and anxiety. That didn't happen. He walked somewhere else, and she wasn't sure where until the screen door squeaked again. The ornery man was going back down to the barn!

She groaned in frustration. For all she knew he'd sleep down there. It was a warm night. There were saddle blankets he could use if necessary. Because he was an equine vet, he'd probably spent his share of nights in a barn.

After waiting another few minutes to see if he'd come back, she realized her plan wasn't going to work the way she'd envisioned it. So she'd have to come up with a new plan. He'd had his thinking time, and now it was action time. She could still take him by surprise.

A few minutes later she headed out to the barn wearing her red silk robe and her boots. She had a condom tucked in her pocket and a blanket in her arms. If he told her to leave, she'd give him the blanket so he could be more comfortable in his self-imposed exile.

The crescent moon didn't give her much light, but the barn doors were open and the glow from the floor lights saved her from tripping. She'd hate to fall and rip her bathrobe, which had set her back a tidy sum when she'd bought it at a trendy lingerie shop in Jackson.

The robe should have signaled to her that she was ready for a change of attitude. She'd bought it a few months ago when she couldn't stand her old, ratty terry-cloth robe for another second. She'd meant to get a snuggly fake fur to keep her warm on cold winter nights, and instead she'd walked out of the store with this. It made her think of forbidden fantasies, and here she was, walking toward a barn that contained a man who knew all about those.

The closer she got to the open door, the faster her heart raced. She had never propositioned a man. She wasn't even sure if she could carry it off, but she'd walked all the way down here in semidarkness without tripping. Maybe a little adventure suited her, after all.

She ran through some potential greetings. *What's a cowboy like you doing in a barn like this? I'm researching the effects of a roll in the hay. Wanna help? Thought I'd save a horse and ride a cowboy tonight.* The last one was far too specific. She was becoming braver, but not that brave.

As she approached the door, she saw Drake walking down the barn aisle toward her. His face was in shadow. "I thought I heard someone out there."

"Just me." Faced with the actual Drake Brewster coming toward her, she forgot all the suggestive things she'd meant to say. Instead she totally wimped out. "I brought you a blanket." Worse yet, she held it in front of her like a shield. "How's Dottie?"

"No change." He stopped about five feet away from her. "Interesting outfit."

"Yes, well…I was in bed, and I heard you go outside again, so I figured you'd decided to sleep in the barn. And you might need a blanket." Wow, was she a temptress or what? Seduction City.

"Thoughtful of you."

"*Are* you planning to sleep in the barn?"

"Not really. I just decided to do one last check before going to bed. But I appreciate the effort."

"Oh." Shitfire! She could have stayed in his bed and everything would have gone as planned. Instead she was out here wearing boots and a bathrobe with a condom in her pocket. If they walked back to the house together, which now seemed likely, he'd go into his room and discover someone had been sleeping in his bed, and it sure as hell hadn't been Goldilocks.

"Did you *want* me to sleep in the barn?"

"Of course not, especially if there's no change with Dottie. That would be silly."

His gaze traveled over her. "Tracy, what's going on? Why are you out here wearing a red silk bathrobe?"

"How do you know it's silk?" As if that mattered, but she was surprised he'd guessed correctly.

"Silk has a distinctive way of draping a woman's body, especially when she's naked under it."

"You don't know that I'm naked!"

"Yes, I do."

Her cheeks grew hot. "Okay, so I'm naked. So I have a condom in my pocket and I came down here to seduce you. So what?"

"Oh, my God." He started to laugh but clapped a

hand over his mouth immediately. Then he scrubbed that same hand over his face and cleared his throat. "Sorry, sorry. I'm not laughing at you, I promise."

"You are so laughing at me! You think I'm ridiculous. Which I am." She couldn't decide whether to run or stand her ground.

"You most certainly are not ridiculous. You're adorable. And sexy. And…could I please have that blanket?"

"Why?" She eyed him suspiciously.

"Because it's blocking my view."

That sounded promising, although she certainly couldn't claim to have engineered this seduction. If she had any talent for it, she'd have dropped the blanket a long time ago and slowly opened her robe.

He came closer and held out his hand. "Let me have it, please."

She released her death grip on the blanket. He took it from her and hung it over the nearest stall door. Meanwhile she could have started her vamp routine, but no, she just stood there waiting for him to make the next move.

He turned back to her. "That's much better. Now you can proceed."

"To do what?"

"Seduce me."

She gulped.

"It won't be tough to do. Imagining you naked under that silk, especially while you're wearing boots, is almost enough by itself."

"You're still laughing at me."

"Oh, no, I'm not, sweetheart. I'm putty in your hands. Whether you realize it or not, you have all the power. Own it."

7

DRAKE THOUGHT BRIEFLY of the assurances he'd given Josie Chance. But circumstances had changed. Tracy was outgrowing her fears, and he was the lucky bastard who got to be here now that she'd decided to spread her wings.

Or, more accurately, spread the lapels of her red silk robe. Fingers trembling, she untied the sash. Then slowly, ever so slowly, she opened the curtains on a show he would never forget if he lived to be a hundred.

His breath caught as the supple material slid away to reveal her creamy skin, inch by delicious inch. He glimpsed the inner swell of each breast, the valley between her ribs, the tempting indentation of her navel and the V of dark curls between her smooth thighs.

He dared not blink and miss a single moment. She was doing this for him, the man she'd been afraid to trust. And now she was ready to give him…everything. She parted the robe a little more, and her nipples emerged, rosy and tight.

They quivered as she drew in a shaky breath. "Say something."

He wasn't sure his vocal cords would work. "I'm…

speechless." Sure enough, he sounded like a horny bullfrog. Felt like one, too. His cock pressed painfully against the ridge of his fly.

"Short but sweet." She swallowed. "I'll take it."

"Mmm." He'd always been proud of his gift of gab, for having a clever remark in any situation. Not this time. She was beautiful, but he'd been with beautiful women before. Although she'd dazzled him with her body, she'd blown him away with her bravery.

He couldn't imagine the raw courage she'd summoned to come down here wearing nothing but a silk robe and boots. Seeing any woman like that would have turned him on. Being confronted with Tracy in that getup was so unexpected that he clenched his fists against the urge to take her *now.*

But this was her show. That was the whole point, to let her test the limits of her sexuality. He wouldn't rob her of that. So he stood there as his slight tremors betrayed the strain of holding back.

Her gaze traveled over him and lingered on his crotch. When she lifted her head and looked into his eyes, her sultry smile was triumphant. "Parts of you are shouting."

"Yes, ma'am." He desperately wished she'd drop the robe and come closer, but if she wanted to draw out the torture, then somehow he'd keep from going crazy.

She reached into her pocket for the condom and held it out. "Mind this for me, okay?"

"How long?" It wasn't an idle question.

Her voice was as silky as her robe. "We'll see."

He might've groaned then. His brain was feeling fuzzy, and he couldn't be sure what he was doing anymore. He ached as he'd never ached, wondering if she had any idea what it cost him to take the foil packet from her outstretched hand without grabbing her and yanking her into his arms. As she tested her limits, she was sure as hell testing his. He'd never wanted a woman this much without acting on it.

"This is way more fun than I thought it would be." She allowed the robe to slither over her shoulders and drop to the floor of the barn. Then she braced her booted feet slightly apart, placed her hands on her rounded hips and sent him a challenging glance.

"Oh, yeah." He drank in the sight of her looking so strong, so proud. Her skin flushed and her nipples tightened as his gaze moved slowly from the fire in her eyes to her quivering breasts, down to her narrow waist and the womanly flare of her hips. When his attention traveled lower to the juncture of her thighs, heat shot through him at the glisten of moisture there. He wasn't the only one burning with anticipation.

She lifted one hand and crooked her finger. "Slowly."

He nodded, although *slow* didn't describe the way blood pounded through his veins or excitement zinged along every nerve in his body.

"Arms at your sides."

When he opened his mouth to protest, she shook her head. "I'm owning it, Drake."

So she was. He approached with his arms hanging at his sides as she'd instructed.

She held up one hand, palm facing him, like a traffic cop. "Close enough. I'll take it from here. Just… stand there."

He hoped he'd be able to obey that command as she stepped closer, her spicy perfume blending with the scent of aroused woman. At last she touched him, flattening her hands against his shirt, standing on tiptoe, and pressing her plump lips to his. Her mouth was open, her breath sweet and warm, her tongue… Oh, God, her tongue began to tease him, and his arms automatically went around her. It was pure reflex.

She pushed away from him, stepping out of his arms. "No." She sounded breathless. "Just kiss me. That's all."

Judging from her rapid breathing, he thought she might be losing a little of her iron control, but he nodded again and let his arms go limp. One part of him was the complete opposite of limp, though, and if she didn't do something about that soon, he couldn't be responsible for the consequences. She might hold all the cards, but he held the condom.

When she started kissing him again, he gripped the condom so tight the foil edge bit into his fingers. He was only vaguely aware of that, because he was too busy exploring the wonders of her mouth with his tongue, the only part of him she allowed free rein. She sighed and tilted her head, allowing him greater access. Then she moaned a little, and he knew they were making progress toward the goal.

Gently she unfastened his shirt. She made maddeningly slow progress. By the time she pulled it out of his waistband and massaged his bare chest, he was slippery with sweat. She moaned again and dug her fingertips into his pecs. If she didn't undo his jeans soon, he'd have to do it. A man could take only so much.

She was breathing hard, too, and glory be, she unhooked his belt and went to work on his jeans. Fortunately she didn't linger. When she slipped both hands under the waistband of his briefs and cupped him, he had to stop kissing her for fear he'd bite her tongue. It was that intense.

"Tracy, I need you." He could barely get the words

out as he gulped for air. Her hands were stroking, massaging, creating pure havoc.

She wasn't in much better shape. "Okay." Panting, she shoved his briefs down and stepped back. "Put it on. Oh, Lordy, you are something to look at, Drake Brewster."

He'd been told that he was well endowed before, but he'd never been happier for the praise than now. He needed to please this woman as he'd never needed to please anyone before. She would remember tonight for the rest of her life, and he wanted her to remember that it was oh, so good.

He rolled on the condom. "What's the plan?"

"I didn't…get that far in my thinking."

If he'd had the breath to spare, he would have laughed. She'd managed this seduction all the way up to the critical part, but now she was out of ideas. He wasn't, though. He grabbed the blanket where he'd hung it on the stall door and tossed it on a nearby hay bale. "Sit there."

She did. Still wearing his jeans, sort of, he dropped to his knees in front of her. "Scoot forward. Good. Can I touch you now?"

"Oh, yes. Yes, *please*."

"Excellent." He filled both hands with her smooth, hot bottom. "Lean back and brace yourself on your arms."

The motion lifted her breasts, and he was so tempted to nuzzle, to taste. But he had other things to do, very important things that involved making her come. Looking into her eyes, he nudged her thighs a little wider with his hips. "You surely did seduce me, lady."

Her eyes glowed with excitement. "I did, didn't I?"

"Yes, sweetheart, and this is what happens when you

successfully seduce a man." Tightening his grip on her fanny, he probed her heat with his cock. She was so slick, he groaned. "Ready?"

She swallowed. "Yes."

Holding her gaze, he plunged into paradise. And held very still so he wouldn't come. Wow. Perfect.

Her eyes widened.

Instantly remorse hit him. Maybe he should have gone slower. "Did I hurt—"

"No! That was… Oh, Drake, you feel amazing."

He couldn't help but smile at that frank compliment. "Thank you, ma'am." How refreshing to know that Tracy would always tell him the truth, good or bad. This time, the truth was very, very good for his battered ego. "But we're just gettin' started."

"Speak for yourself." She tightened around his happy johnson. "I'm well on my way."

He sucked in a breath. "Easy."

"I've had easy." She squeezed him again. "Go for it, cowboy. And don't spare the horses."

If a man existed who could resist a challenge like that, Drake hadn't met him. He watched the light in her eyes grow brighter as he began to move, steadily increasing the pace until he was thrusting deep and fast. She held his gaze as if daring him to slow, daring him to come.

He would not. Not yet. Not until—there. A flash of sharp pleasure arced in those dark depths, a whimper escaped her parted lips, a tremor massaged his cock as he shot home again, and again. She was close.

His breathing was ragged, but he managed a warning. "I want you to come for me. But don't be loud about it, sweetheart."

She shook her head once, arched upward and came

apart with a low, deep moan that was the sexiest thing he'd ever heard. The sound alone was enough to send him hurtling toward his own climax. He pushed in tight and let go, pulsing in rhythm with her, locked into her body, loving being there.

They stayed like that for several long seconds, neither of them moving, neither of them speaking. But he never stopped looking into her eyes. She made no attempt to hide…anything.

She seemed as caught up in the moment, as stunned by the intensity of it, as he was. Apparently she was brave enough to own the wonder of this moment just as she'd owned her power while seducing him. He'd never been with a woman this honest.

Sure, it scared him. He didn't know if he could handle that level of sharing, but he wanted to give it a try. His superficial way of relating to women was a bad habit that belonged to his past, not his future. She'd demonstrated that she could rid herself of old patterns. He would follow her lead.

When he finally spoke, gratitude tumbled out. "Thank you for walking down to the barn tonight. I expected to go to bed without resolving anything. I thought we'd tackle it in the morning."

She smiled. "We would have tackled it tonight, regardless."

"Oh?"

"If you hadn't headed down here for one last check on Dottie, you would have found me waiting in your bed."

That floored him. "You were in my room? When?"

"The whole time you ate dinner and cleaned up the kitchen. I thought you'd come to bed after that, and I'd…apologize in person."

"I'll be damned." He thought about that some more. "You were in my bed?"

"Yep."

"What were you wearing?" He wanted to complete the mental picture.

"Nothing."

He stared at her. "So we could have been doin' this in a cozy bed instead of in a barn full of horses?"

"Guess so."

"Damnation, woman. You should've given me a shout out or somethin'." But he couldn't help chuckling at the absurdity of it. "This has been memorable and all, but my knees are killing me."

"Then get up, for heaven's sake."

"I like being inside you." He couldn't remember ever admitting that to someone he'd just had sex with. It sounded needy, and he'd never wanted to appear that way.

But he'd said it now because Tracy inspired that kind of truth. Even better, he trusted her not to take advantage of his vulnerability. That was huge.

"That's nice to know, but you'll have to leave sometime. My arms can't hold me up much longer."

"Well, that shines a different light on things. I want you to be comfortable. Obviously we need to get going." He eased away from her. "Stay right there. I'll grab your robe."

Turning away, he used a handkerchief in his hip pocket to dispose of the condom, zipped up his pants and buckled his belt. Out here the cowhands carried bandanas, and if he ended up becoming a Westerner, he'd do the same. Was that his destiny?

He wished he knew, but at the present moment, his destiny wasn't a nagging problem. He was feeling contented, and that was an emotion he hadn't experienced in a while. He planned to enjoy it.

Tracy's robe was right where she'd dropped it, a splash of vivid color on the battered wooden floor. He picked it up and shook it out to get rid of any dust and bits of straw. A robe like this didn't belong on the floor of a barn, but he was mighty glad she'd worn it. He would never forget the picture she'd made coming in through the barn doors clutching that blanket to her chest.

He must have stood there for a minute reminiscing, because suddenly she was at his elbow. "I'll take it."

"I thought you were going to stay right—"

"No." She glanced up at him, her dark eyes sparkling. "You *told* me to stay right there. But I'm in the process of owning my power, so I didn't choose to listen."

He laughed. "Dear God, what sort of monster have I created?"

"The kind who will be lots more fun in bed."

That's when it occurred to him that what had happened between them could happen again. Multiple times, in fact. He'd moved into the guest room in order to keep an eye on a pregnant mare. But that didn't preclude keeping an eye on Tracy, who was fast becoming his favorite subject.

"So that condom you brought down here," he said casually. "Was that a single one you happened to come across, or…"

"There's an entire box sitting on your bedside table."

"Say no more, sweet lady. Let me check on Dottie one last time before we head on up to the house to count condoms."

"We'll still need to set an alarm."

"Absolutely. Dottie needs supervision. But I don't

expect her to need constant supervision. You, on the other hand, very well might."

Tracy laughed, and the sound was light and carefree, the laugh of a woman who'd had good sex and was expecting to have more of it.

Drake wasn't above taking some credit for that. He'd wondered if such intense physical stimulation would sabotage his determination to give Tracy the kind of experience she deserved. But her happiness had been so important that he'd managed to control his urges. She was definitely the kind of woman who was capable of making him a better man.

But he vowed not to think too far ahead. He'd been lucky enough to be in the right place at the right time to spend hours, maybe even days, with Tracy. He wouldn't get greedy, and he wouldn't start creating unrealistic expectations. They were together now, and that was great.

He fastened his shirt snaps as he walked down the aisle toward Dottie's stall. Probably a waste of time. Pretty soon he hoped to be completely naked and rolling around in his bed with Tracy. How funny that she'd lain in wait for him and he'd messed up her plan with his detour to the barn.

Smiling at the image of Tracy lying in his bed while he puttered around in the kitchen, he glanced into Dottie's stall. Then he went very still. She lay on her side in a bed of straw, her flanks heaving. He'd seen this often enough to know what was happening. Dottie was going into labor.

8

WHILE DRAKE ASSEMBLED the necessary supplies from Regan's truck, Tracy hurried back to the house to throw on some clothes and grab her smartphone to take pictures. She didn't want to meet this foal wearing nothing but a red silk robe and boots, and any new baby deserved photos.

Much as she'd looked forward to continuing her sexual adventure with Drake in the privacy of his bedroom, the thrill of an impending new life was damned exciting. Nerve-racking, too. If she'd had a working number for Jerry Rankin, she would have called him now. She was sad that he wouldn't be here.

At least Drake would be, and she had great confidence in him. He was far steadier and competent than she'd given him credit for when they'd first met, but she hadn't understood him then the way she did now. She wanted to learn more, because she suspected he'd acted out of character when he'd had sex with Regan's fiancée. That behavior didn't fit the man she knew.

Pulling on a worn pair of jeans and a T-shirt, she shoved her feet into her boots again. If those boots could talk… She shook her head and smiled. Drake would never let her forget how she showed up in the barn dressed the way she had been. For a brief moment she imagined talking about it years from now.

But that would mean they'd keep in touch. It would mean they'd maintain a relationship where talking about a wild night in the barn would make them laugh instead of cringe in embarrassment. It would mean neither of them would be with other people. It would mean… No, she wouldn't continue that line of thought. What a pointless thing to do at this stage.

She used the flashlight app on her phone to light her way to the barn. She could have done that earlier, but she hadn't wanted to announce her presence prematurely. She'd wanted to surprise him, and by God, she'd done that. In *so* many ways.

She chuckled, feeling a touch of pride as she relived those moments. She'd done it. She'd conquered her fears, at least for tonight, and experienced something remarkable. Lesson learned.

Once inside the barn, she switched off her flashlight app and quickly made her way down to the end stall. It was unlatched. Dottie still lay on her side breathing hard while Drake crouched near her head, stroking her and talking to her.

Tracy couldn't hear the words, but the low rumble of his voice sent warm shivers down her spine. "How's it going?" She hesitated to step into the stall. The process scared her more than a little, even though she wouldn't have missed it for anything.

Drake glanced up, his expression filled with a kindness and empathy that tugged at her heart. "She's coming along. Every time I see this, I thank God I'm not a woman. It's rough duty, giving birth."

"I thank God you're not a woman, too."

He grinned. "I appreciate that. How're you doin'?"

"Couldn't be better." She could elaborate on that and say she couldn't remember the last time she'd felt so alive, but she didn't want to gush, as if she'd never experienced sex that good. Which she hadn't.

His grin widened. "I'd go along with that, sweetheart. In fact, I—" He stopped talking as Dottie stirred and lumbered to her feet. "Guess she needs to move a bit."

"Is that normal?"

"Absolutely." He snapped a lead rope on her halter. "If you'll move back, I'll bring her out and walk her up and down the aisle."

"But what if she has her baby out here on the bare floor?"

"She won't." He started toward the front of the barn. "She'll let me know when she's ready to lie down again."

"Okay." It made Tracy nervous to see Dottie parading around when she needed to be settled on a bed of clean straw near the equipment Drake had laid out.

He turned and led the mare back toward Tracy. "You look worried. That foal isn't going to suddenly drop out of her with no warning, like a gum ball popping out of a machine."

That made her laugh. "I suppose not."

"Ever been in a maternity ward in the hospital?"

"Not as much as you might think. There's a growing tradition around here of having babies at home. But yes, I've been in one a time or two."

"Do you remember seeing pregnant women walking up and down the corridor?"

"I guess I have, now that you mention it."

"Same idea with a horse. Sometimes just lying there isn't the best plan. When a mare's in labor, it can feel better for her if she's able to move around. Isn't that right, Dottie?"

The mare snorted.

"I'll take that as a yes. Need another lap?"

Dottie paused by the stall door.

"Up to you." Drake smiled and stroked the mare's neck.

"You're enjoying this, aren't you?"

He glanced over at Tracy and blinked. "What makes you say that?"

"You're smiling, and you seem very relaxed and happy."

"That's partly your doing, sweetheart. And I could say the same about you."

She blushed. "Point taken."

"But you're right. I am enjoying myself, now that you mention it. Which is interesting, because lately I've been asking myself if I should continue being a vet."

"Why wouldn't you want to be a vet? You're obviously good at it."

"I'm a decent vet." He continued to stroke and scratch Dottie's neck. "Not as gifted as my buddy Regan, but decent."

What an interesting admission. She wondered if she could coax him to say more. "You must be excellent or he wouldn't have left you in charge while he's gone."

"I'm fine for backup. But Regan's understanding of horses is exceptional. I admit I envy that ability." He glanced at her. "I can see the wheels turning."

"So you'll give up rather than compete with him?"

"No, nothing like that. Or I hope that wouldn't be my reason. And if you're dying to ask if my jealousy had something to do with what happened last Christmas…"

"It crossed my mind."

"The answer is yes, probably, to some extent. But it's not that simple."

Tracy didn't think so, either. She was about to ask another question when Dottie snorted even louder than before and stepped back into the stall.

"I think it might be showtime." Drake led her over to the bed of straw and unsnapped the lead rope. Dottie carefully dropped to her knees and rolled to her side. Then she rolled back and forth, groaning.

"Is she okay?"

"I'm sure it hurts, but this is normal." Drake unsnapped his cuffs and folded back his sleeves before putting on clear plastic gloves. "Poor girl. Bet you'll be glad when this is over." He stood back and gave Dottie plenty of room as she continued to grunt and roll.

Tracy hovered by the stall entrance. "Anything I can do?"

"My usual plan is to let nature take its course. If nature flakes out on me, then I'll move in and help things along. But for now, we let Dottie do her thing."

The mare finally stopped rolling and lay in the straw, her flanks heaving. Drake crouched down by her rump. He drew her tail aside and scooped away several handfuls of straw. "Here we go! Come on in here, Tracy. Get a better view."

She crept closer, heart pounding. Drake had done this countless times, so he probably wasn't the least bit worried. But she was the one who'd agreed to take this pregnant mare, and she desperately wanted everything to go well. She was torn between fascination with the process and the urge to bury her head in her arms until it was all over.

"See? Here come the forelegs." Drake's voice vibrated with excitement.

"Feet first?"

"If we're lucky, and it looks as if we are."

Sure enough, two sticks that apparently were legs emerged covered in what looked like a greased, semi-transparent garbage bag. Tracy held her breath.

"There's the nose. See it?"

Tracy leaned closer as a blunt, somewhat head-shaped form followed the spindly legs. "Yeah," she murmured. "Come on, Dottie. You're doing great."

"She is. She's pushing for all she's worth, and… there…the body, the hind legs, and…we're done!"

"What about that slimy thing?"

"We'll see if Dottie wants to handle that part, too. The less interference from me, the better. Let's give her a little more room." Drake edged away a few feet and Tracy followed his example.

Dottie lay still for a moment, still breathing hard. Then she lifted her head and gazed down the length of her body.

"Your foal is right there, girl," Drake crooned. "You did a mighty fine job. Want to finish up?"

As if she'd understood every word, Dottie maneuvered until she could lick the foal.

"Incredible." Tracy watched as the little creature gradually was freed of its covering. "It looks like her!"

"It does, indeed." Drake moved closer. "Will you let me take care of the cord, sweetie? That's a good girl." He handled the job with brisk efficiency and then checked between the foal's legs. "Colt."

"A son. Dottie has a son." Tracy couldn't help thinking of how proud Jerry Rankin would be. She'd make it her job to track him down. He should at least have visiting privileges.

Drake gathered up his instruments. "Glad I didn't

have to use most of these. When everything goes according to plan, I don't. This birth was pure pleasure."

"I'm glad, for many reasons." Tracy straightened. "And I don't know what I would have done without you here. The minute she started rolling around, I'd have been beside myself."

He shrugged. "You would have called the guy from Jackson."

"And he would have taken a good hour to get here. By then it would have been all over. Even if it had gone well, I wouldn't have known whether it was going well or not. I would have been a basket case." She gazed at him. "Minimize your contribution if you must, but I won't."

He gave her a lopsided smile. "You sound serious about that."

"I am." She didn't return his smile. "You rode in here like a knight in shining armor and saved the day. I'm incredibly grateful that you did, and I'm prepared to let people around here know that they've judged you unfairly."

"Whoa, whoa! You're going to start a campaign to get the residents of this town to *like* me? That would be embarrassing as hell. Don't you dare."

"I'll be subtle about it."

"I don't know how subtle you can be once they figure out we spent the night together."

She frowned. "You make that sound as if you're leaving after tonight."

"For your sake, I probably should. Maybe we can convince everyone I was only here for the birth of the foal and we were too busy taking care of that to get horizontal."

"I don't care if they know we got horizontal, although technically, that hasn't happened yet. I'm still hoping."

He chuckled and glanced up at the rafters. "Oh, Tracy. You do have a way about you."

"You, too. And a killer accent."

His green eyes danced as he met her gaze. "And you accuse *me* of being charming. If you keep making remarks like that, you'll make it impossible for me to resist you."

"Booya!"

"Tracy..." He laughed and shook his head.

"And I do want to set people straight about you. I wish they could have seen you tonight with Dottie. These are horse people, Drake. They'd respect the way you dealt with her, how patient you've been the whole time. It would go a long way toward repairing the damage. Please don't tell me I can't mention what you've done here tonight."

His eyebrows lifted. "*All* of what I've done?"

"No, of course not. The vet part. Not the action on the hay bale. That's our business."

"Good luck with that. Apparently you've forgotten that I have a reputation around these parts, and everyone will assume I won you over with lots of good sex, and that's the only reason you've become my biggest fan all of a sudden."

"But *I* seduced *you.*"

"Are you going to tell them that?"

She had to admit that didn't sound like a good idea. "I'd like to keep sex out of the discussion. This is about you getting a fair shake in this town because you're not the villain everyone thinks you are."

"They know Regan has forgiven me, right?"

"Well, yeah."

He spread his arms. "There you go. They know the wronged party has moved past the incident, but that doesn't matter. They think Regan is going too easy on me." He paused. "You thought so."

"I know, but that was before—"

"Tracy, it's a wonderful impulse, but I don't think having you sing my praises is going to help, especially because you're the town sweetheart and they'll assume I've despoiled you."

"Despoiled? Who uses that word anymore?"

"Me. It's one of my closely guarded secrets. I actually liked my English classes. I dug Shakespeare and even thought the sonnets were cool. I, um, have been known to write my own poetry. Which no one has ever seen, by the way." He peered at her as if he'd just confessed to occasionally committing murder.

She was stunned, both by the fact he was a closet romantic and that he'd never revealed it before. "No one?"

"Nope."

"Where do you keep it?"

"I have some journals in the cabin."

"Would you…let me read them?"

He gazed at her for a long time. "I don't know. Maybe. Let me think about it."

"Okay." At least he hadn't flatly refused.

He broke eye contact and turned his attention to Dottie and her foal. "You know, if we're not careful, we'll miss the magic when the little guy first gets to his feet."

She took her cue. He was through delving into his most personal issues for now. "Can't have that! I specifically brought my phone to record it."

"Then get ready, because his momma's looking to get up, and once she does, she'll coax her son to do the same."

Tracy focused her lens on the foal. "He seems so fragile. Can he really stand on those legs?"

"He has to if he wants to eat, and believe you me, he wants to eat. That'll be his primary goal for quite a while. It's the way everything's set up. Foals have to stand to eat, which in the wild means they'll soon be ready to run if a predator comes along."

"I'm glad that won't be a problem for Sprinkles."

"Sprinkles? Is that his name?"

"I think it is." She held the phone steady and snapped a couple of shots of the foal lying in the straw. "He looks like vanilla ice cream with sprinkles."

"So he does." Drake sounded amused.

"But you have a vote. If you have a name to propose, go right ahead. Without you, he might not even be here."

"I like Sprinkles. Do you think we need to give Regan and Lily a vote?"

"Maybe, but let's not. Let's just announce that his name is Sprinkles. We were here at the critical moment, so I think that gives us naming privileges." As she gazed at her phone's screen, Dottie's nose appeared. She nudged the foal. "Is this it?"

"This is it." Drake came to stand next to her. "You'll text these to me, right?"

"You bet." She took shot after shot as Dottie coaxed her wobbly foal to test those toothpick legs against the pull of gravity.

She didn't realize she was cheering softly until Drake joined in. They stood there like a couple of proud parents urging a toddler to walk. When he was finally standing on those impossibly long legs, they both uttered a muted cheer, one guaranteed not to startle the little guy and cause him to lose his balance.

Tracy got a few more shots of Sprinkles nursing before she turned off her camera. "So sweet. Should we give them some privacy?"

"Not quite yet. I have to stick around and make sure Dottie passes the placenta, but if you're tired, go on back up to the house."

She shook her head. "If you're staying, I'm staying."

"It won't be very interesting from here on out. The drama is over."

"I'll get to be with you, right?"

"Yes, but I won't be a lot of fun. I need to monitor these two and make sure everything's fine, so if you brought another condom down, I wouldn't be able to—"

"Are you suggesting that all I can think about when I'm with you is sex?"

He gave her a lazy grin. "Just for the record, I wouldn't blame you for that. It's quite a compliment, when you stop to think about it."

"Well, just for the record, I would love to stay down here and talk with you, even if we can't have sex."

He met her gaze. "That's an even bigger compliment. Thank you, Tracy."

"You're welcome. I'll go get the blanket and make us a nice place to sit. And then we can discuss why you're considering giving up your profession."

He groaned at that, but she ignored him. Drake Brewster needed to exorcise his demons, and she was just the person to help him do it.

9

Drake had groaned partly because he thought Tracy expected him to. Secretly he was relieved to have someone willing to discuss what he should do with his life. The men in his family weren't supposed to have doubts, and if they did, they knocked back a few shots of bourbon and forgot about their worries. As the only son of a man who'd always been cloaked in absolute certainty, Drake had never felt free to be unsure.

While he examined mother and foal for any signs of stress, Tracy arranged their seating. He came out to discover she'd doubled the blanket and laid it alongside the outer wall of the stall. She sat on one side of it, her arms wrapped around her bent knees.

She freed one hand to pat the spot next to her. "Take a load off, cowboy."

"I love having you call me that." He dropped down beside her and sat cross-legged. "But much as I like it, I don't qualify."

"Sure you do." She glanced over at him. "You know your way around horses and you look good in the clothes. You'll pass."

The woman sure could make him laugh. "But I can't

twirl a rope and I've never ridden in a Western saddle. Just English."

"We can fix that tomorrow." She picked up her phone and looked at the time. "Or more accurately, today. But you are missing one critical component of cowboyness."

"I'm probably missing several, but what one are you thinking about?" Feet in front of him, he relaxed against the wooden wall behind them. Tonight he'd made love to a woman and watched over the delivery of a healthy foal. Good stuff.

"You don't have a hat. Or if you do, I've never seen it on you."

He turned his head to look at her. She looked right back, her dark eyes warm, her expression open and accepting. That made him feel like a million bucks. "You're right. I don't own a cowboy hat."

"Why not?"

He couldn't help smiling. She was so damned cute. She'd put her hair back in its ponytail, probably so it wouldn't be in her way during the foaling. "I thought we were going to discuss my next career move."

"We can in a minute, but I'm curious about the hat thing. I've watched plenty of folks come out to this part of the world, and if they like it here, they usually pick up a hat, even if they're not planning to stay. You haven't bought one."

"I guess it's a fair question." He savored the feeling of being able to talk to her without worrying what she'd think. "I believe a hat signifies something important, and as I said, I don't qualify."

She took some time to absorb that. "Regan would probably teach you to rope, and two of these horses need to be ridden, so you could check that box fairly easily, too."

"I hadn't thought of asking Regan to teach me roping. Might be fun."

"Then you could get a hat."

Resting his head against the wall and closing his eyes, he thought about it, but even if he learned to throw a rope and spent some time in a Western saddle, he still couldn't picture himself wearing the hat. "Don't think so. A baseball cap is all I need."

"A cowboy hat is more practical. It shades your eyes and the back of your head. Plus it looks really cool."

"I know, but..." He tried to identify where his resistance came from, because she was right about the practical side of a Western hat. When it suddenly hit him, he sucked in a breath. Yeah, that was it.

"What?"

"When I was a kid, I liked cowboy movies. I even watched the old ones on cable, the ones where you could tell the good guys because they wore the white hats."

She didn't say anything, but her hand found his. She interlaced their fingers and held on.

"I admired everything about those guys. They were champions of the weak, they were honest to a fault, and...loyal to their friends." It physically hurt his throat to say that last part, but he forced himself.

She squeezed his hand.

"I don't deserve to wear that hat, Tracy." When he felt her move and let go of his hand, he opened his eyes.

She quickly straddled his knees and took his face in both hands. "Yes, you do." And she kissed him.

It was the sweetest, most loving gesture any woman had ever made to him. It spoke of caring and empathy, of encouragement and respect. He wrapped both arms around her and simply held her as he received her blessing—he couldn't think of a better word for it—in the spirit it was intended. This wasn't about heat and hunger. It was about redemption.

Slowly she ended the kiss and settled back on his knees. He opened his eyes to find her watching him, her smile soft. "What do you say now, cowboy?"

"Okay." His voice was still hoarse with emotion. "I'll consider getting a hat."

She shook her head. "Not good enough. *Considering* means you're still in the thinking stage."

"What is this, a project?"

"I think it is, yes. You would look great in a hat, and I know exactly what we're going to do."

"Oh?" He liked the way she'd said *we,* as if they shared this project. "And what are *we* going to do, Miss Tracy?"

"We're going shopping."

"Oh, no, we're not. If you help me pick out a hat in the Shoshone General Store, the gossip will fly. It may anyway, but that would ramp it up considerably. I can hear it now. *Nice hat. Understand Tracy picked it out for you. How are things going between you guys?* Wink, wink, nudge, nudge."

"I wasn't thinking we'd buy it here. I have to work from eleven to five tomorrow. Then I need to feed the critters, but after that, assuming Dottie and Sprinkles are doing fine, we'll take a quick drive to Jackson. The stores are keeping summer hours. We can make it there before they close and be home again in a jiffy." She grinned. "With a hat."

She looked so proud of her idea that he couldn't imagine saying no. "All right. I'll drive us into Jackson."

"Yay!"

Here she'd given him a gift by proposing this trip, and yet she acted as if he'd given her one by agreeing to go. He knew himself. Left to his own devices, he'd never buy a hat, even if he thought he was worthy of one. "But only if Dottie and Sprinkles are doin' fine."

"They will be." She climbed off him. "Let's take a look and see how they're doing now."

"Good call. Maybe Dottie's delivered the placenta by now." He hoped so. He couldn't speak for Tracy, but he was tired. She had to be, too.

Tracy stood and peered over the chest-high enclosure. "Aw, Drake. They're sleeping."

He joined her, and it was the most natural thing in the world to put his arm around her as they gazed at the tender scene in the stall. Sprinkles had curled up in the shelter of his mother's body, and both mare and foal were asleep.

Watching them, he felt a sense of accomplishment, and with it came another epiphany. He really did love working with horses. Whether he continued as a vet or not, he needed horses in his life. He might not be the horse whisperer Regan was, but he treasured working with them, anyway.

"That's just precious," Tracy murmured.

Precious wasn't a word he generally used, but they were darned cute. Sharing the moment with Tracy was pretty special, too, almost as if they were proud parents peeking into the nursery. He hated to disturb the magic of holding her against his side while they contemplated the miracle of a newborn foal, but she would want a picture of this. He should probably remind her to take one. She seemed mesmerized by the scene, though. Then she slid her arm around his waist and laid her head on his shoulder.

His chest tightened with an emotion he wasn't all that

familiar with. To hell with the picture. If she didn't mention it, he wouldn't either. He'd rather stay right like this.

In fact, he wouldn't move if someone offered him a million bucks. Tracy had told him without words that she didn't just lust after him anymore. She might still display that hair-trigger response under the right circumstances, but at the moment, she was communicating clearly that she *liked* him.

Earlier in the evening they'd become lovers, and that had been a big turning point in their relationship. But in the past few hours something more had passed between them, and they'd become friends. He valued the second stage even more than the first one, and he'd been crazy about that first one.

She snuggled closer. "I should get a picture."

"Guess so."

"But I hate to move."

"Me, too."

"This has been an awesome night, Drake. The kind of night that I'll remember for a long time."

"So will I." He kissed the top of her head. "Thank you."

She sighed happily. "I should thank *you,* but then we'd start that silly thing where we compete to see who gets in the last thank-you."

"How do you know we'd do that?" He rested his cheek on the top of her head. "Maybe you'd say, *No, I should thank you,* and I'd say, *You're right. You should.*"

"I doubt it. That's not you."

"Try me."

"Okay, I will. No, Drake, I should be thanking *you,* because you're so wonderful and generous and—"

"Yep, I surely am. I'm amazing. In fact, I'm so special I think I'll get me a hat."

She started laughing, which broke up their cozy little moment, but he was okay with that. They were both getting slaphappy from fatigue. With any luck, Dottie had passed the placenta and he and Tracy could go to bed. That was an enticing prospect. He didn't want to fall asleep and miss all the fun they could have.

Back in the stall, he located the placenta and tossed it into the bucket he'd brought for it. Dottie and Sprinkles continued to snooze as Tracy took a few more pictures.

Then she turned. "Are we ready to go?"

"Whenever you are." He peeled off his gloves and set the bucket outside the stall. He'd deal with that later. "They'll be fine for a few hours."

She covered a yawn and glanced at her phone. "We have another three hours before it's feeding time again."

"Then let's close up and head out." Moments later they'd latched both the back and front doors of the barn. He caught her hand in his as they walked up to the house in the slight chill. Stars winked overhead and the crescent moon had already set. "I'll set my alarm and feed," he said. "You have to be at work by eleven, but I can nap."

"That's not right. Feeding the critters is what Lily and Regan are paying me for."

"Yes, but circumstances have changed, so we have to be flexible. Besides, if you don't sleep in, you'll be too tired to go hat shopping."

"You drive a tough bargain, Brewster." She covered her mouth with her free hand as another yawn overtook her.

That second yawn convinced him that he should rethink his original plan for what would happen when they got back to the house. "Listen, maybe you should go back to your room so you can get some decent rest."

"What?" She pulled him to a halt. "Are you kicking me out of your room?"

"Of course not! But you're obviously tired, and if we both end up in my room, I may not be able to let you go straight to sleep, which you should, because you need your—"

"Shut up, cowboy."

"Excuse me?"

"Just be quiet until we get to your room, okay? And then the only things I want to hear out of you are gasps and moans of ecstasy. None of this *you need your rest* garbage. Understood?"

"Yes, ma'am." Suddenly he wasn't the least bit tired.

"I guess you can also say *yes, ma'am* now and then, because that Southern drawl turns me on like you wouldn't believe. No more being solicitous, though. I've been waiting to climb into bed with you for hours. Hay bales are fine once in a while, but I wouldn't want a steady diet of having sex on them."

Neither would he, but he didn't say so. He was saving his breath for all those gasps and moans of ecstasy she'd promised him. Apparently the switch Tracy had flipped to give herself a change of attitude had been permanently turned on. And he was loving it.

"I will, however, let you feed the critters so I can sleep in. You make an excellent point about the shopping trip, and I need to be sharp for that. There's an art to choosing the right hat, especially the first one. Eventually you'll get a feel for how to choose them on your own."

He grinned. "Yes, ma'am."

"That's what I like. A Southern gentleman in an agreeable mood. I can't wait to get you naked."

He was laughing, now, because he so enjoyed listening to her being sassy. But as they climbed the steps together and went into the house, he realized that he'd semicommitted to staying at least through tomorrow night. He doubted they'd come home from a hat-shopping trip and not want to celebrate the event appropriately, which would be in his bed.

But if Dottie and Sprinkles continued to do well, he had no official reason to stay after that. The mare had foaled and Tracy was no longer afraid of her sexuality. If he stayed beyond tomorrow night, word would surely get out.

After that, he could reasonably predict that someone, most likely Josie, would demand to know his intentions. After all, he'd told her he wouldn't be getting involved with Tracy. Unfortunately, he had no idea what his intentions were.

At least he had no idea for the future. The present was crystal clear, especially after Tracy drew him into the guest bedroom and clothes began flying everywhere. He couldn't have talked, even if she hadn't forbid him to. He was too busy kissing whatever wonders he uncovered.

He was particularly focused on her plump breasts. He'd denied himself the pleasure of touching and licking them when he'd made love to her in the barn, but he planned to correct that omission now. Once they were both stripped down to nothing, he tumbled her back onto the bed, cupped that glorious bounty in both hands, and feasted.

Moaning, she arched into his caress, which sent desire shooting through his veins. He couldn't seem to get enough of her. After putting up with a blanket tossed onto a hay bale, having her stretched out on the bed, where he had access to every bit of her, made him determined not to miss a single inch of soft, moist skin.

She was delicious everywhere, but when he slid down between her thighs and tasted her essence, desire ripped through him with a tsunami-like force. She writhed beneath him as she responded to the lap of his tongue and the thrust of his fingers. She came, and then she came again, her cries filling the room.

He loved hearing those lusty sounds, loved knowing she could make all the noise she wanted this time. He lingered in that sweet valley as she trembled in the aftermath. Her scent intoxicated him, and although his cock was stiff as granite, although his balls ached for release, he leaned forward and swiped his tongue over her pulsing center. Maybe once more.

She gasped and clutched his head as she struggled for breath. "Come…here." She tugged.

He eased up her sweat-dampened body and hovered over her, his forearms taking most of his weight.

She looked up at him, her dark eyes glazed with pleasure. "That was…" She smiled. *"Good."*

"I'm glad." He leaned down and brushed his mouth over hers so she could share the taste. Then he watched as she licked her lips. He had to clench his jaw against the urge to come. Once he had himself under control, he cleared his throat. "Can I talk, now?"

"Uh-huh." She dragged in air. "But first, get the box."

He didn't have to ask what she meant. There was only one box that mattered, the one that had been sitting on the nightstand when they'd walked into the room. Fortunately he could reach it without much effort. He set it down between her breasts. "Here."

She pulled a packet out and handed it to him. "Here."

Grinning, he pushed himself to a sitting position straddling her thighs, ripped open the packet and handed her the unwrapped condom. “Here.” This was fun. He picked up the box and leaned slightly forward so he could return it to the nightstand while putting his cock within her reach.

He’d thought he was being so clever, so cute. Then she fumbled the job. Not completely, because she got the thing on him, but in the process he had flashbacks to his teen years when he’d had the control of a gnat. Giggling hysterically might have been part of her problem. He didn’t think it was so damn funny, and neither would she if this condom application went bad.

Finally she snapped it in place. “There.”

He spoke through gritted teeth. “Thanks.”

“Your face is all scrunched up.”

“No kidding.”

“Did I get it on right? Maybe I should adjust—”

“Don’t touch.”

“If you say so.” Laughter rippled through her voice. “Are we going to do this, then?”

“In a minute.”

“Okay.”

Gradually the pounding in his groin let up enough that he unclenched his jaw and opened his eyes.

She stared up at him, all innocence except for the sparkle of mischief lurking in her eyes.

“Tracy, did you do that on purpose?”

Her smile confirmed his suspicions. “You started it,” she said. “I just ended it.”

“You almost *did* end it.” He moved between her soft thighs, grateful that he’d held on, in spite of her. His reward would be worth everything she’d put him through.

“Just proving a point.”

"What point?" He knew the territory well, now, and he found her slick heat without effort. After two orgasms, she was drenched. He held back, poised at her entrance, knowing that once he thrust deep, his brain would cease to function, and he wanted to hear this.

"A cowboy only fires when ready. More evidence that you qualify."

"Damnation, woman! You're makin' this up as you go along."

"Ask any cowboy. They'll say it's true."

"I guarantee they would, sweetheart. No man would admit to anything less, cowboy or stockbroker."

She ran her hands down his back and bracketed his hips. "Just want to make sure you're still getting that hat."

"I don't know. You'd better check out my other qualifications before we go shopping."

"Such as?"

He surged forward, burying himself in her hot channel as she gasped in surprise. Breathing hard, he gazed down at her. "Is that the cowboy way?"

She gulped. "Yes."

"How about this?" He began a slow, deliberate rhythm and watched the fire build in her eyes. "Is that how cowboys do it?"

"Uh-huh."

"Then what?" He shifted his angle and picked up the pace. "Like this?"

"Oh, *yeah.*" She clutched his hips and held on as her breasts jiggled with the impact of each thrust. "Just like that."

He scooped one arm under her bottom and lifted her just enough to let him go deeper. "Then maybe this."

She didn't answer him this time, but her body did. The first spasm rolled over his cock, then the second.

"Come for me, Tracy." He felt her give way. "That's it, darlin'. *Now.*"

She erupted in his arms, and he followed her right down that tumbling waterfall of sensation. His cries blended with hers as he surrendered to a climax that shook him to his soul. If this was the cowboy way, he was all for it.

10

TRACY FELL ASLEEP in Drake's arms, his body still locked securely with hers. Obviously that situation had changed at some point, because when her phone alarm went off, she was by herself in his bed. She stretched and foolishly wished he'd been there beside her when she'd opened her eyes.

That wouldn't have worked out too well, though. She was still naked, and thoughts of him brought a rush of arousal to all the places he'd loved so energetically hours earlier. If he'd been there, she would have been tempted to replay some of those excellent moments.

But she had to go to work. As she sat up, she noticed a note anchored by the box of condoms sitting on the nightstand. He'd scribbled it in haste and he wrote in cursive, not the neat block letters she'd noticed many men preferred. His handwriting was horrible, and she had to squint to figure out some of the words, but she managed it.

Dottie and Sprinkles doing great. Critters all fed. Coffee in the carafe if you want it. Drove home for a few things. Back around noon. Will start feeding at five.

See you after work. I just realized I don't know where you live. I mean normally.

He'd signed it *D.* No tender closing. The man had admitted to writing poetry, but there wasn't anything poetic about this note. If she'd hoped for something sweet, something to let her know...what? That he was madly in love with her? That would be a little quick, now, wouldn't it? She'd be suspicious of a love note this soon.

Or so she told herself. Still, the utilitarian message he'd left, and the very fact he hadn't waited until she woke up to drive away, didn't make her feel all warm and fuzzy. She wouldn't have minded if he'd signed his note *Warmly* or *Fondly.* He'd been both warm and fond in the barn and in this bed.

He'd been one hot commodity, too. Whew. If he'd been popular with women in the past, and she believed that he had, then experience counted for something. He'd given her more pleasure in a few hours than her other two serious boyfriends had given her...ever. They'd never come close to making her yell. In this room, in this bed, with Drake, she'd yelled. Loudly.

Maybe loud yelling didn't translate into flowery love notes. If she had to choose, she'd take sex that prompted shouts of joy over those notes. No contest there. Plus he had asked where she lived, which had a promising ring to it, as if he might want to continue seeing her after the house-sitting gig ended.

After all they'd shared, she found it odd that he didn't know that simple fact about her. She rented a small apartment above Spirits and Spurs from Josie. Josie had lived there originally, and after she'd moved to the Last Chance, Caro Davis had stepped in to help run the bar. Caro had also rented the apartment because it was so close to work.

Now married, Caro and former Chicago Cubs star Logan Carswell traveled the country, using Logan's invested earnings to do good works. Logan ran baseball clinics for disadvantaged kids and Caro supervised quilting circles in senior centers.

Tracy had grabbed the apartment the minute Caro had moved out. She loved living in the middle of the tiny town where she'd grown up. Before she started her shift, she'd check on her houseplants. She glanced at the digital clock on her phone. Time to get moving.

She'd rather not have to explain being late. She wasn't good at lying, and because of her caretaking chores at Peaceful Kingdom, she couldn't use oversleeping as a legitimate excuse. That would imply she'd neglected the animals.

After quickly making the bed, she returned to her own room to shower and dress. Lily and Regan's bed was a king and more suited for wild sex, but Tracy had made a decision to keep the action in the guest room. That seemed more respectful. Drake hadn't questioned her choice, and she'd bet that he'd agree with her. Southern manners and all that.

Having him gone felt strange, which wasn't the least bit logical. He hadn't arrived to check on Dottie until late in the afternoon, so he'd been on the premises less than twenty-four hours. It seemed longer, no doubt because of all they'd experienced. And all they'd talked about.

She hoped he wouldn't back out of the shopping trip. She'd never known a man who loved to buy clothes, and a hat was an article of clothing. For Drake, though, it was far more than that. She'd stumbled into that discussion out of pure curiosity, and thank goodness she had. He'd helped her leap the boundaries of her comfort zone, and maybe she could help him forgive himself enough to buy a hat.

Holding that thought, she hurried down to the barn to make sure Dottie and Sprinkles were doing fine. They were snuggled together, both sound asleep, so she hopped in her little white truck and drove to Spirits and Spurs. It wasn't a muscular truck, but it ran well and people in Shoshone tended to drive pickups. She felt more a part of the community having a truck instead of a sedan.

She adored this quaint town with its one stoplight and a typical main street lined with a few established businesses. Shoshone had a diner, a general store, a gas station, a real-estate office, an ice-cream parlor and the bar. Folks who needed to do serious shopping went to Jackson about an hour away, just as she and Drake planned to do tonight.

Congratulating herself on coming up with a plan that would give them some anonymity on their outing, she pulled into the side parking lot next to Spirits and Spurs. Josie's truck was there, so her employer must have decided to work on the books today. Maybe she'd brought Archie in. Tracy adored that little towhead. Archie was the only person in the world who could turn Jack Chance into mush. It was fun to watch.

She entered the bar through the front door, which all the employees did except Josie. The building was old and the design was quirky. The only back door opened straight into Josie's office. That meant at closing time all the garbage had to be taken through there, and all food supplies came in through her office, too.

Josie kept talking about remodeling, but that would require some structural changes that would permanently alter the look and feel of the bar. Nobody wanted that.

Some said that the "spirits" who'd inspired Josie to change the name of the bar would stage a revolt if she remodeled. It was said that the bar was haunted by the ghosts of miners and cowboys who'd patronized it during its century-long existence. Tracy had never seen a ghost, but she knew people who swore that they had, including Josie.

The bar wasn't busy at eleven in the morning, either with live guests or dearly departed ones. The lunch rush would start in another hour. Archie's cheerful little voice piped up from the office and Tracy smiled. She'd take a minute to say hello before starting her shift.

At age two and a half, Archie was speaking in complete sentences and getting into everything. Tracy admired Josie for bringing him to her office, where he could quickly create chaos if she turned her back on him for even a second. But Josie seemed to have a sixth sense about that.

Peeking through the office door, Tracy discovered her boss wasn't trying to work, after all. She sat at her desk with Archie on her lap while he colored enthusiastically on blank sheets of paper Josie had provided.

"Looks like Rembrandt in training," Tracy said.

Josie glanced up. "Maybe. I'm thinking he's more of an impressionist."

Archie finished drawing with a purple crayon and held up his picture. "I made a *doggie.*"

Tracy gave him thumbs-up. "You totally did, Archie!"

The little boy turned the paper around and nodded with satisfaction at what he saw. "Yup. I totally did." He mimicked Tracy's thumbs-up before grabbing another piece of paper so he could start his next masterpiece.

Josie sent Tracy a look. "Does that attitude remind you of anybody?"

"Yep." Tracy smiled.

"It's as if Jack spit him right out of his mouth."

Archie looked up and giggled. "You're silly, Mommy!"

"I get it from you, you little munchkin." Josie blew a raspberry against his cheek.

He giggled some more. "Stop it, Mommy. I gotta work."

"Yeah, me, too," Tracy said. "See you guys later." She turned to leave.

"Just a sec, Tracy. I wanted to ask you about something."

With a sense of foreboding, Tracy faced her boss. "What's that?" But she knew.

"I understand you have a pregnant mare out at Peaceful Kingdom."

Tracy gulped. Then she stammered. All in all, she reacted exactly like someone who had been doing something clandestine. And the whole story was about to come out.

"I took her in yesterday. How did you know?"

Something flickered in Josie's blue eyes. "A guy named Jerry Rankin came into the bar last night to ask around and find out if anyone knew of a job."

"He came here? Do you have a contact number for him?" Maybe this wasn't such a disaster, after all, if Josie had a number for Jerry.

"He's at the Last Chance. Jack put him on the payroll temporarily. He wasn't happy that the guy dumped a mare about to foal on an unsuspecting house sitter. Jerry admitted he knew the foal could come any minute, which was one of the main reasons he brought her to you."

"He knew that? I wish he'd told me."

"He was afraid if he did, you wouldn't take her. In his defense, he didn't fully understand the awkward situation he was sticking you with. He just knew he didn't have the resources to deal with it. Jack wanted me to ask you about the mare when you came in today."

"Well, she's fine." Tracy felt her cheeks warm. "She delivered her foal last night."

Josie swore, and then quickly covered Archie's ears, as if she could keep him from hearing. "Sorry, munchkin."

"It's okay, Mommy."

"So she foaled." The sharpness in Josie's blue eyes didn't match her casual pose. "But surely you didn't try to handle that yourself."

"No, but since I'd taken in an animal against Regan and Lily's instructions, I didn't want to call the vet in Jackson because that would cost a bunch of money."

"You called Drake Brewster."

"Yes." Tracy took a shaky breath. "He did a terrific job, Josie. He's a good guy who made a terrible mistake. I think maybe we should all—"

"I agree with you."

"You *do?* I thought everybody at the Last Chance hated Drake."

Archie held up another picture that looked pretty much like the previous one. "I made a kitty!"

Tracy summoned up a cheerful comment. "You did, Archie! That's a great kitty!"

Archie shrugged. "I know." He grabbed another sheet of paper.

Josie glanced down at her son. "You know what,

buddy? I think you need to relocate to the bar. You can show Steve your pictures, okay? I'm sure he'd love to see your work."

"Okay." Archie seemed perfectly happy to attract a new audience.

Josie gathered his supplies and took him by the hand. "Don't go away," she said to Tracy as she herded the little boy out the door. "I'll be right back once I get him settled with Steve."

"My shift's about to start." Steve could handle the bartending duties for a while, but Tracy liked to organize her supplies before the rush began and she and Steve were both frantic to fill orders. Besides, she didn't look forward to the coming discussion.

"I know, but hardly anyone's out there. And this is important."

That was what Tracy was afraid of. She didn't want to have an *important* discussion about Drake.

Josie came back in, and instead of sitting behind her desk, she leaned against the front of it. "I won't kid you. Drake doesn't have a lot of fans out at the ranch. But I always think there are two sides to every story, so yesterday I paid him a visit. That's when I first found out about the pregnant mare. Jerry Rankin only confirmed what I already knew."

"You went to see Drake?" Drake had failed to mention that important incident. It wasn't quite lying, but it wasn't exactly being open, either. Her stomach churned.

"I'm guessing from your expression that he didn't tell you about that. Good for him. I specifically asked him not to, because I knew you wouldn't appreciate that I'd gone over there."

"Why would I mind? In fact, I'm glad you were willing to make friends with him." So Drake had been keeping his word to Josie by not saying anything. Tracy felt a little better, but she wondered why Josie had made him promise to keep quiet. She wasn't sure she wanted to know.

"I am willing to be his friend on the condition that he doesn't do something stupid regarding you. You were my main motivation for going over there."

Tracy groaned. "Josie…"

"Okay, I'm guilty of meddling. I admit it. But I could tell you were fascinated with him, and he doesn't have a good record when it comes to women."

"He made *one* mistake."

"Maybe that's true, but I've met the man. He's charming as hell. I understand the type, because Jack's a lot like him, and years ago, Jack had a terrible record when it came to women."

"But look how well that all turned out for you and Jack!"

Josie took a deep breath. "I said Drake reminds me of Jack, but he's different in two important ways. Jack had roots. No matter what, he wasn't going anywhere. After his dad died, Jack had focus, too, because he had to step up and keep the ranch on an even keel. By Drake's own admission, he doesn't have any direction, but he's not planning to go back to Virginia, so he has no roots, either."

"That doesn't mean he won't get those things." Tracy hated hearing what she knew was the truth. She'd even told herself that Drake could end up breaking her heart and that she was okay with taking the risk. But hearing it spoken aloud by Josie, a woman whose judgment she trusted, made her wonder how okay she would really be if Drake left her high and dry. And he might.

"Maybe he'll settle into a groove eventually," Josie

said. "But he's not a very good bet right now when he's flailing around. I went over there basically to ask him to leave you alone. He said he'd already planned to do that."

"Josie!" Tracy's cheeks grew hot with a combination of humiliation and anger. Josie was her boss, so she had to be careful not to be disrespectful, but…how dare she do that!

As for Drake, although he'd kept his word about not mentioning Josie's visit, he hadn't kept the other part of the bargain. Thinking back on the course of events, she couldn't really blame him. She'd made the first move, and it had been a doozy.

"I knew you'd be fit to be tied if you found out I warned him off. I didn't ever plan to tell you, but now that I know Drake's probably going to be over there a lot, it's only fair you know what was said. I knew if the mare went into labor you'd call Drake. I hoped that wouldn't happen, but after listening to Jerry Rankin, I had a bad feeling that it *would*."

Tracy had no idea what to say. Josie's worst fears had come true. She'd become involved with Drake, and maybe it would end up in a mess. But Drake had given her the courage to reach out for the passion she'd been denying herself out of fear. She cherished that he'd given her permission to be sexually adventuresome, but it wasn't the kind of thing she was ready to tell Josie.

Josie's expression was filled with compassion. "The thing is, I don't…I don't want you to get hurt."

"I appreciate that." Tracy knew her friend's motives were pure, but she'd left Tracy's shiny new view of life somewhat tarnished. Not completely, but she didn't feel as joyous as she had earlier this morning. She wished Drake hadn't assured Josie he would stay clear. But she tried to imagine how she'd have felt if he'd told her then what he'd said to Josie. What if he'd rejected her because of that?

She would have been crushed. If her first attempt at seducing a man had ended in failure, she might not have worked up the courage to try it again. Drake had been in a no-win situation. He could either honor his word to Josie or help a repressed woman break away from her self-imposed restrictions.

He'd chosen to help her. That had to be worth something. Of course he'd enjoyed himself, too, so his decision hadn't been totally unselfish.

"I should probably apologize for prying into your business," Josie said. "But I think of you as a little sister. I've known you ever since you were a kid. You've had your share of lumps, and Drake is just not… He's just not the man I would trust to make you happy. I wish he could be, but I don't think so. Not right now, anyway."

"You're probably right. He is in a transitional period, and I can see him breaking a woman's heart without ever meaning to do it. He's gorgeous and women find him irresistible." She hesitated, but there was no point in being coy. "Me included."

"I know, honey, and I don't blame you for that. He's one hot guy. All I can say is, be careful. Be very careful."

"I will." But she hadn't been at all careful so far.

Josie pushed away from the desk. "I'd better go fetch my son and let you get to work."

"Yeah." Tracy's throat felt tight.

"If there's anything I can do, let me know. If the foal's been born, then you probably don't need Drake to monitor the situation anymore. Jack could do it. He'd be glad to, in fact."

"That's very generous. I'll let you know." But inside she was loudly protesting that Drake was the man for the job. She didn't want Jack or anyone else taking care of Dottie and Sprinkles.

She and Drake should do it. They'd been there for the birth, and they were the obvious ones to handle the next few days as mother and son became stronger. All four of them had shared a bonding experience, and Tracy didn't want it to be over. Not yet.

Besides, tonight she was taking Drake out hat shopping. Buying him a hat wasn't going to miraculously give him answers for how to live his life. She knew that. But she thought it might be a start.

11

DRAKE WAS STANDING at the island in the kitchen chopping veggies for Wilbur and Harley when he heard Tracy's little white truck pull up outside. Two of his poetry journals sat on the small kitchen table. He'd gone back to the cabin for clothes, and after much inner debate, he'd brought his journals, too.

The decision hadn't been easy. Right before driving away, he'd turned off the engine, taken the journals out of the SUV and put them back in the cabin. Then he'd called himself a lily-livered coward and thrown them onto the front seat, where his duffel sat filled with clean clothes.

That had been another difficult call. He didn't know yet whether he was staying for more than one night. He'd finally decided on clothing for two days, hardly enough to make it seem he was moving in for the duration. If Tracy wanted him to stay longer, he'd run the washing machine. He hoped he'd end up doing that. He ought to wash Regan's stuff, no matter how things worked out…or didn't.

Tonight while they were in Jackson, he'd pick up replacements for the toiletries he'd used. Tracy might decide against telling Regan and Lily that he'd slept over. He'd respect her wishes on that.

All he knew was that the sound of her truck set his blood to pumping, and when she opened the front door, he had to stop himself from going to meet her. But he had a sharp knife in one hand and a head of cauliflower in the other. He stayed where he was and kept chopping. "I'm in here!"

When she walked through the kitchen doorway, he could tell something was on her mind. He'd fantasized that she'd come over and lay one on him in greeting, but it didn't look as if that dream would come true. "Tough day?"

She managed a smile, but it lacked sparkle. "Not exactly. Let me get rid of my purse and I'll help you." She walked over to the kitchen table.

He held his breath.

"What's this? Are these your…" Her voice trailed off.

When he glanced over, she'd picked up the top journal and opened it.

"You don't have to read them now." He was sweating, and not because the room was particularly hot. "In fact, you don't have to read them at all. It was an afterthought to bring them." Then he cursed under his breath. "Actually it wasn't an afterthought. That was one of the reasons I drove back home this morning."

She glanced up, her eyes shining. "Drake, this first one is beautiful."

"I…um…thanks." Dear God, he was blushing. He could feel it.

"It's as if I'm there in the pasture with you in the early morning light, with dew on the grass, and the horses chasing each other, *their hooves tossing diamonds through sunbeams.* I love that!"

He swallowed. "This is way more embarrassin' than I thought it would be."

"Please don't be embarrassed." She closed the journal and held it against her chest. "You can't know how honored I am that you're willing to let me read what you've written. But you'll have to help me with some of it. Your handwriting is atrocious."

He chuckled and the knot of tension in his stomach eased. "Thank God for bad handwriting. This moment was just cryin' out for some comic relief."

"Bringing the journals was very brave." She walked toward him, still holding the journal close.

Holding it against her heart. Her reaction left no doubt that she understood what showing her those journals had cost him, would continue to cost him as she read through them. "I decided if you could step out of your comfort zone, then so could I."

She came right up to him, then. Still holding the book clutched against her breast, she wrapped one arm around his neck. "Lean toward me, cowboy. I want to kiss you hello."

He put down the knife and the head of cauliflower. "My hands are wet."

She smiled. "I didn't ask you to hold on to me. I'll hold on to you. Just lean down like I asked you to. Last night you put me in charge, and I've discovered I like that. A lot."

"I really have created a monster." But he rested his wet hands on the counter and bent toward her as instructed, so that his mouth was available for her hello kiss, the one he'd thought he wouldn't get.

Ah, but he got it now. She started out soft and light, but before long she'd invaded his mouth with her sassy tongue, and he'd returned the favor. When she began to suck on his tongue, his blood flowed south to the area he would love to have her suck on next.

They hadn't gotten around to that particular game last night, and from the way she was kissing him, he'd bet money she was thinking about it now. He considered wiping his hands on his jeans so he could grab hold of her and carry her down the hall. Or hoist her up on the kitchen island. It was sturdy enough.

Just when he'd lifted his damp palms from the counter to take action, she broke away and stepped back. He opened his eyes, hoping to see her put down the book and unbutton her blouse. Or put down the book so he could undress her.

Instead she continued to hold it tight against her heaving bosom. "We can't right now."

The sound of their breathing was loud in the otherwise silent kitchen. He finally did wipe his hands on his jeans. "The way I'm feeling, it wouldn't take long."

Fire burned in her dark eyes, and her moist lips were temptingly parted as she gulped in air. Then slowly her gaze lowered to his protruding fly. Her voice was pure temptation. "Promise?"

His heartbeat went from fast to rocket speed. He didn't pretend to misunderstand. He couldn't even bring himself to turn down her unspoken offer. He'd been semiaroused all day thinking about her, and one kiss had tipped the balance. He ached with a fierceness that could last a while, unless…unless he surrendered. He looked into her eyes. "Promise."

Her slow smile of anticipation was all any man could wish for. She'd not only offered. She wanted to. Setting the journal on a tall stool next to the island, she knelt in front of him and reached for his zipper. Blood sang in his ears as she drew it down. She found the opening in his briefs and freed his eager penis.

Trembling, he braced himself for the first slide of her mouth. Fast was one thing. Coming the second she began was not his idea of cool.

As she wrapped her fingers around his girth, she lifted her head and looked up at him. "You have a beautiful cock, Drake Brewster."

Once again, she'd left him speechless. That soft groan had probably come from him, though. His brain lacked a normal blood supply, so he couldn't be sure of anything.

She gave him that sultry smile again. "I look forward to paying my respects to it." With that, she dipped her head and took him in.

The woman didn't mess around. She took him deep, so deep that the sensitive tip bumped the back of her throat. He gasped and fought the urge to come. He was so glad he fought that urge, so glad he'd held on for the next part.

That first move was only the beginning of the ride. Next she used her tongue to massage the front ridge. After that she hollowed her cheeks and slid her mouth up and down in a rhythm guaranteed to make him a happy man. And all the while she used both hands to squeeze, stroke and pet him until he was delirious with pleasure.

He shoved his hands into her glossy hair and sent hairpins flying. His moans increased as she moved faster and sucked harder. At last those moans blended into one triumphant cry as he erupted. As his cock pulsed in the warm haven of her mouth, his lust-soaked brain swirled with one overarching thought—he'd never had sex this good.

She stayed with him to the end, her swallows the kind of erotic sound men dream of. Shuddering with the force of his orgasm, he gripped the edge of the kitchen island for support.

Gently she rearranged his briefs and carefully pulled the zipper back in place. “There.”

His laugh was more of a croak, but he mentally saluted her for getting in one more cheeky comment relating to their joke from last night. Besides being an enthusiastic lover, she was just plain fun. When he'd first met her at the Spirits and Spurs, he hadn't guessed that. Then again, she'd disapproved of him. Judging from what had just happened, she no longer did.

He recovered enough to help her to her feet. “You're incredible.”

“You inspire me.” She picked up his journal and held it as before, pressed against her heart.

He met her gaze. “If my poetry affects you that way, I'll devote my life to it.”

“Let's put it this way—your poems didn't hurt your cause any. Women are suckers for a poetry-writing man. I'm surprised you've never shown it to other women.”

“Maybe I should have trusted them more, but I didn't.”

She studied him for several seconds. “Why me?”

“I've asked myself the same thing.” He cupped her face in both hands and looked into the unexplored depths of those beautiful eyes. “For some reason I feel safe with you. I didn't expect I ever would, especially after our blowup at the dinner table. But you explained why that happened, and then…then you put yourself out there, took the risk.” He smiled. “I guess you could say you put your money where your mouth is. Not everyone has the guts to do that.”

She wrapped her arms around his waist. "I didn't used to. You came along at the perfect time, when I was ready to grow. You sprinkled on some fertilizer, and I blossomed."

He grinned. "Are you telling me I'm full of shit?"

"Yeah." She laughed and gave him a squeeze. "And that was exactly what I needed, apparently. So what do you say? Ready to finish feeding the critters and go buy a hat?"

"If I wasn't before, I am now. If I'm worthy of what you just did, I'm sure as hell worthy of a hat."

"Excellent. Then let's get to it."

Less than an hour later, they'd fed everyone and made sure Dottie and Sprinkles were progressing as expected. Tracy had fixed the hair arrangement he'd destroyed and settled into the passenger seat of his SUV.

She'd wanted to bring one of his journals for the road, but he'd talked her out of it. He couldn't handle having her read snippets of his work to him while they sailed down the highway. And she would have. He'd already figured that out.

When they were finally headed toward Jackson, she leaned back into the leather seat, anticipation glowing in her eyes. "If you want, we can grab something quick for dinner before we look for hats."

He set the SUV on cruise control. The sun was low on the horizon and traffic was light. Easy trip. "I do want food at some point. A really good orgasm makes a man hungry, and you, ma'am, gave me a really good orgasm."

"Glad to hear it. You probably won't believe this, but I've never initiated something like that. I'd do it if a guy asked me, but I wasn't bold enough to suggest it on my own, especially in a kitchen."

He couldn't resist teasing her. "How about in a dining room? Is that any better?" She started to laugh, and he kept going. "What about the laundry room? Or the hallway? I personally think a blow job in the hallway would be—"

"Stop!" She punched him playfully on the arm. "I just meant that I've never had oral sex anywhere except in a bedroom."

"Are you talking about you doing it to him or him doing it to you?"

"Both. Either. Only in bedrooms."

"We have to remedy *that.* I didn't realize last night was a damned cliché."

"Trust me, it wasn't."

"You're sure?" He shot her another look and discovered that her cheeks were pink. "I mean, we were in a bed, so how special could it be for you? Been there, done that."

"Not with such…finesse."

"Ah." He liked the sound of that.

"Or concentration. I've never come twice in a row during oral sex."

"Then maybe it wasn't such a cliché after all."

"You're fishing for compliments!"

He shook his head, although he totally was. With great effort he managed not to laugh. "I just don't want to be redundant."

"You are absolutely fishing, but I don't mind telling you that the oral sex with you is the best I've ever had."

Now that was enough to make a man's chest puff out, for sure. "I'm glad to hear that. I—"

"And now that I've stroked your male ego, it's—"

"Stroked my ego? Do you mean you were lying?"

"Not at all. You rocked my world in a way no man

ever has, but if you can fish for compliments, so can I. How would you rate my blow job?"

He almost drove off the road. "*Rate?* What do you mean, *rate?*"

"On a scale of one to ten. Obviously you've had much more experience than I have, so I don't expect you to score me at the top. I can put you at the top of my chart, because, to be honest, you don't have much competition."

"So I'm in a race with losers?"

"Not losers. Just men who were unimaginative in bed, and like me, probably didn't have a lot of experience. Since you've had plenty of experience, I'd be curious how I did with that episode in the kitchen."

The discussion was making him cranky. "First of all, you make me sound as if I've had dozens of women, which I haven't."

"Okay, how many?"

"A gentleman doesn't discuss specifics with a lady."

"Ballpark figure, then. More or less than twenty?"

"I'm not answering that." Because he couldn't. He'd have to sort through his entire sexual history, which would take some time. But he was afraid it was more than twenty, and that…sounded like a man who had superficial affairs.

At this moment, he didn't want to confirm what Tracy probably already suspected. He'd never had a serious relationship. Not ever.

"I'll assume it's more than twenty," she said, "because if it had been less, you would have said so. Okay, forget about the count. Let's get back to rating my performance in the kitchen. You can tell me the truth. As I said, I don't expect to outrank everyone. I'm too inexperienced for that."

"Damn it, it's not a sport."

"You're afraid to hurt my feelings. Really, you won't."

Just the opposite, he thought. He was afraid to tell her how strongly she affected him, for fear she'd make assumptions about a future that was unclear to him.

He began by hedging. "If I tell you the truth, I don't want you to put too much importance on it."

"Was I that terrible?"

"No," he said quietly. "You were that wonderful."

She was quiet for several seconds. "Thank you for telling me. That's nice to know."

"Tracy, I'm at a very uncertain point in my life. You're the best thing that's ever happened to me. You're an exciting lover, someone I trust with my deepest secrets, and you make me laugh more than anyone I know. You're perfect. But I may not be ready for you."

Another long silence. "That's pretty close to what Josie said today."

"Josie? You talked to her?" He envisioned their current discussion going quickly downhill. Maybe this was why she'd come home looking frazzled. Finding his journal had caught her attention, and the sexual chemistry between them had distracted her even more. But now they were getting down to it. "What did she say?"

"Kind of what you said, that you don't have a clue what you'll end up doing with your life, and that a person in your position isn't ready for a relationship with someone like me."

"Josie's a very smart lady. You should probably listen to her."

"I found out she asked you to stay away from me, and you told her you'd already decided to do that."

He stared at the road ahead. "That was the plan. Then you showed up in a red silk bathrobe and boots."

"I know, and I don't blame you for going back on your promise to Josie. But she knows about the mare and foal now. She pointed out that Jack could probably handle them from here on out. You're under no obligation to stay if you think it would be easier on you if you left."

His jaw tightened. "Not easier on me. Probably easier on you, though."

"So you're ready to make that decision for me, just like Josie?"

"Tracy, you're rooted to this place. I'm not. I worry about how it will affect you if I end up leaving, after all."

"Well, don't worry about that! Just don't!"

He glanced at her in surprise. "I can't help it. I care about you."

"I understand that. But you have to try." She sounded resolute. "You and Josie have to quit worrying about how I'll survive if you and I don't work out. Let me worry about that, okay?"

"But—"

"I'm serious, Drake. You're the most exciting man I've ever met. If I want to enjoy every possible minute with you, if I want to say damn the torpedoes, full speed ahead, that's my privilege."

He thought about that. "I guess it is."

"It sure as hell is. I want you to stay at Peaceful Kingdom until Regan and Lily come home. If you're still here at that point, I'm inviting you to share my apartment, which, to answer the question in your note, is above Spirits and Spurs."

His brain was still spinning from her unexpected determination to carry on, no matter what. But he managed an appropriate response. "That sounds cozy."

"It is. However, if we don't get that far, then please know that I'll be fine. I'll be grateful for what we've shared, and I won't wail and gnash my teeth when you leave."

He risked another quick glance at her face, to see if he saw any humor there. He did, so he decided to nourish it. "Not even a little wailing and gnashing?"

"Oh, all right. A little bit. After all, I'll miss the sex."

"Yeah. Me, too." He reached over and took her hand. "Me, too." He'd love to think that they'd ease into a lasting relationship, but in his present situation, that seemed so unlikely. Yet she'd told him exactly what she wanted from him—as much fun as he could provide until it was time to leave. He'd do that for her. But he'd still worry.

12

TRACY SUGGESTED A little hamburger joint she'd tried on her last trip to Jackson, because for the rest of the week they'd be eating vegetarian meals.

"You could also come into the bar when I'm working during the dinner hour this week," Tracy said as they finished their burgers and sipped the rest of their draft beer. "I'll serve you up a juicy hamburger even better than this, and this was darned good."

"It was."

"Thank you for buying me dinner, Drake." He'd already paid the bill, but neither of them had made a move to leave. Sitting and talking had been nice.

"It's been my pleasure, ma'am." He picked up his remaining pub fry. "When's your next evening shift?"

"Tomorrow night. Maybe you should come in."

He chewed slowly. "Depends on whether you think Josie will be there. Did you tell her I'm staying at Peaceful Kingdom?"

"No. I should have." She felt like a wuss for listening to all of Josie's warnings without admitting they were superfluous now. The horse was out of the barn, so to speak.

"You don't have to if you'd rather not. It's really none of her business."

"She said that, too, but I'm not sure she believes it. Josie's protective of the people she loves."

"Nothing wrong with that." He shoved back his empty plate. "As long as we're getting this all out on the table, I'll tell you that Regan was convinced you and I would get together while they were gone."

"Why would he assume that?"

"I admitted that I thought you were hot."

"You did?" She flushed with pleasure. "I didn't realize that. You never really flirted with me."

"Tracy, I never flirted with *anybody* in Shoshone. When you're the guy who seduced his best friend's fiancée, and you're in that guy's hometown, you don't flirt. Period."

"Come on. It hasn't been *that* bad."

"Wanna bet? Husbands would give me the stink eye if I so much as glanced in the direction of their wives. I gave up looking at women, at least most of the time. I still watched you behind the bar when I thought nobody was payin' attention."

"I watched you, too."

"Yeah?" He looked pleased. "And here I thought you hated my guts." He polished off his beer.

"I tried to, but the minute I laid eyes on you, I got all hot and bothered. I started taking more time with my hair and makeup before going in to work, in case you'd show up at the bar."

"All I can say is, you always looked great. You were a bright spot in my life, even if I didn't think I had a chance with you."

"And see what's happened."

He reached over and laced his fingers through hers. “I’m a lucky guy. Thanks for givin’ me that chance.”

“Glad I did.” Tracy gazed at him across the checkered tablecloth and finally found the courage to ask the question that mattered the most, in her mind, at least. “Did you love her?”

He blinked. “Love who?” The confusion in his expression slowly cleared. “Oh. You mean Jeannette.”

“Yes.”

“It’s not an easy question to answer.”

“Then never mind,” Tracy said quickly. “You don’t have to answer it now. You don’t ever have to answer it.”

“But you want to know.”

She couldn’t lie. “Yes.”

“Because if I secretly loved her all along, that makes what I did a little easier to swallow, right?” He caressed her palm with his thumb.

She wondered if he even realized he was doing it. He was a naturally sensual man who enjoyed touching people. She’d benefited greatly from that. Now she wished she hadn’t brought up Jeannette, but she’d started the discussion, so she couldn’t drop it now. “If you loved her, what happened would be more understandable, I guess.”

“Yes, I loved Jeannette. Still do.”

It was the answer that would help absolve him, so why did it hurt so much when he said it? Tracy reminded herself that she’d asked, and she didn’t want him to lie, so if she didn’t like the answer, too bad. She started to pull her hand away.

He tightened his grip and held on. “Tracy, don’t. Let me explain. I’ve known Jeannette since we were kids. We’ve been buddies. I never dated her. We went to the University of Virginia, and that’s where I met Regan.

He and I got along great, so of course I introduced him to my pal Jeannette. They sort of drifted into a relationship."

Tracy's mood improved, but she still wondered if Drake was a little bit in love with his childhood friend. "That doesn't sound very romantic."

"It didn't seem like it to me, either, but they both insisted they were blissfully happy. They had it all—great careers, promising future, yada yada yada. Regan loves being a vet, no matter what the circumstances. I liked it okay, but I never loved the job the way he does, maybe because it was my parents' idea. They always wanted me to open a practice specializing in thoroughbred racehorses. They were paying the bills, and I took the path of least resistance."

She suspected he'd been under way more pressure than he was letting on. Although she could be wrong, she had a feeling his entire life had been laid out for him, and he'd been expected to follow the yellow brick road, no questions asked. "Were you writing, then?"

"Oh, sure, but I wasn't going to make a living writing poetry, especially if I never told anybody I was doin' it."

"Well, there's that. But you're right. Most poets have day jobs."

"I know, and I thought being a vet could be my day job. But I wasn't just an equine vet. I was a vet for animals worth millions. I thought I'd be thrilled with the prestige, but I wasn't. I hated the pressure."

Because you're a poet. "But not Regan?"

"He's like Teflon. It just rolled off of him. He has this inner core of certainty, no matter what he does. I envied how he had everything goin' his way when I so obviously didn't have a clue. Instead of trying to get my act together, which looked impossible, I threw a rock into the calm pool of his perfect life, because that was easy."

She gazed at him in admiration. "But Drake, you figured out why you did it. Most people aren't willing to do that. And you've made amends. On top of everything else, Regan's life wasn't as perfect as it looked. If you hadn't thrown that rock, he wouldn't be here. He wouldn't have found Lily and Peaceful Kingdom. He loves her and he loves that place."

"True, and I feel a little better when I think about that. But I can't say Jeannette and I are friends anymore. I tried to justify what we did by continuing to see her, but neither of us could get past the guilt. We ended the affair, but our friendship died with it. What a waste."

"Have you contacted her since you came out here?" Tracy had to ask. He'd rebuilt the friendship with Regan, and he could do the same with Jeannette. Once the guilt was gone, maybe they'd discover they really did love each other. That made her stomach clench, but she'd be incredibly selfish not to suggest that he try to repair his relationship with a woman he'd known for years.

"I haven't contacted her, but that's a good idea. Maybe I could get her to come out here for a few days. She could talk to Regan, then, too. I'd ask him, first, though, before I asked her to come."

"Definitely. I think Lily would be okay with it. She's all about mending fences, but still. Jeannette was his fiancée. You don't want to put Lily in an awkward position." *Or me.* But she had no claim to Drake and no right to feel jealous of Jeannette. If the thought of Jeannette showing up in Jackson Hole made her feel sick to her stomach, she'd have to get over it.

"Thanks for the suggestion." Drake smiled and

squeezed her hand again. "Have I told you how great you are?"

"Maybe not when we have all our clothes on."

"Then let me say it now, when we're fully dressed and sitting in a public place where there's no chance we'll be getting naked anytime soon. You're terrific. You—"

"Miss Tracy, Miss Tracy!"

Tracy yanked her hand free and turned toward the little redhead racing toward her. Sarah Bianca Chance, aka SB, was in the restaurant. Because she was only three, she undoubtedly hadn't arrived alone.

SB threw herself into Tracy's arms. "Guess what? Me, Mommy and Daddy saw a movie! Not my brother. He's too little. We didn't get popcorn but we're gonna get *hamburgers*." Then she turned to stare at Drake. "Who's that?"

"That's Mr. Drake, SB." A very pregnant Morgan Chance, her red hair a shade darker than her daughter's, walked up to the table followed by her husband, Gabe. "Hi, Trace. Nice to see you." Morgan's voice was cool and her expression remained carefully neutral.

That alone told Tracy how upset she must be, because Morgan's face was always animated and her blue-green eyes constantly sparkled with delight. She didn't look the least bit delighted now. She'd probably seen Drake and Tracy holding hands, too. Tracy was afraid she'd just been branded a traitor.

Drake got to his feet immediately and held out his hand to Morgan. "I'm honored to finally meet one of Regan's sisters."

Morgan shook his hand, but she made it brief. "This is my husband, Gabe."

Gabe stepped forward, and he wasn't smiling, either.

"Brewster." He shook Drake's hand with a little more force than necessary. Then he moved back, smoothed two fingers over his sandy mustache and glanced around the restaurant as if desperately searching for an appropriate comment. "Kind of crowded tonight."

"It is." Tracy stood, too. "But we're about to leave if you want this table."

"That's okay," Morgan said. "I like to be by the window. Gabe, would you please go ask the hostess to put us on the list for a window table? And take SB with you?"

"Sure thing." Gabe looked relieved as he held out his hand to SB. "Come on, peanut. We need to ask her about crayons."

"Right!" The little girl hopped up and down. "I want to color!" She hurried over to her father and skipped along by his side.

Morgan watched them leave before turning back to Tracy. "Well, this is awkward. I didn't know you two were…seeing each other."

"It's a long story," Tracy said. "I took in a pregnant mare yesterday and she delivered last night, so rather than pay for a vet, I asked Drake to come over. Regan said I should call on him in an emergency."

"I vaguely remember hearing about that, but…" She glanced from Tracy to Drake. "This doesn't look like a veterinary emergency. It looks like a date."

"Tracy's been workin' hard," Drake said. "I thought she could use a little break, so we—"

"He's staying with me at Peaceful Kingdom." Tracy looked Morgan squarely in the eye. "There's no point in trying to hide it. And he's not there just because of the mare and foal, although I appreciate the huge help he's been. We've discovered we really like each other."

Morgan nodded. "Okay, then." She gazed at both of

them for a moment longer. "I'd better go find Gabe and SB. You two have a nice night." She still didn't smile.

Neither did Drake, but he'd been raised to be a gentleman, so Tracy wasn't surprised when he responded with his typical *thank you, ma'am.* If he'd had a hat on, he could have touched its brim as another gesture of respect. Now more than ever she wanted him to have that hat. If he had to put up with being snubbed, at least he could walk proudly and wear a big hat.

She stood beside him as Morgan walked away. "Sorry about that. I should have remembered that Morgan and Gabe like this place, too, but I still can't believe they showed up tonight, and while we were here, too! Another ten minutes and we would have been gone."

Drake glanced down at her, warm concern in his gaze. "I'm not the least bit sorry about it for my sake. But you just announced to the world that we're sleepin' together. I'm honored that you did, but you blew me away, sayin' that."

"Folks might assume it, anyway, once Morgan reports that we were eating a meal together and holding hands."

"Because of my reputation." He scowled. "You're probably right, damn it."

"Frankly, I'm relieved we don't have to sneak around. I'd rather take the offensive and get it out in the open instead of having people talk behind our backs. Now, shall we go? Or do you want to stand here and give me a big old kiss in front of everybody?"

He grinned at her. "While that has enormous appeal, if we're going to make that dramatic gesture, we should do it somewhere more fittin', like in the middle of Shoshone's main street."

"I like that idea! Save it for later. For now, we need to

go get you a hat." She took his hand. "We'll pass them again on our way to the door. Break out that fabulous smile of yours."

"I will if you will."

"You've got it, cowboy." Her fingers firmly laced through his, she walked with her back straight and her head high. When they reached the cluster of diners waiting for tables, she beamed at Morgan, Gabe and SB. "Great to see you!"

"It's been a real pleasure." Drake's voice oozed Southern charm.

At first Morgan had watched them approach with cold disdain, but after they'd greeted her warmly, something shifted in her expression. Unless Tracy was mistaken, Morgan's blue-green eyes now reflected a new emotion—grudging respect.

"That was entertainin'." Drake continued to hold her hand as they strolled around the Jackson town square toward the Western wear store. "I don't imagine we'll have nearly as much fun in the store."

"You might be surprised."

"How so?"

"I predict you'll go in a Southern gentleman and you'll come out a cowboy."

"They'll teach me to rope in there, too? Now that's a bargain."

"They won't teach you to rope, but once you have a hat, you'll look like you can rope. Then you'll be more motivated to learn to rope so you'll match your hat."

Drake laughed. "That's way too complicated for this Southern boy. I may not be ready for this hat, after all."

She hoped he was only kidding. "Don't wimp out on me now, Brewster."

"I won't." He released her hand and wrapped an arm

around her shoulders as they approached the store with its windows full of mannequins wearing Western outfits. "I've seen the light. Any man lucky enough to be sharin' a bed with you had better own a decent hat." He reached out and opened the glass door for her.

She smiled at him as she walked past. "Or an indecent one."

"Better watch out, sweetheart. You're playin' with fire."

"I surely hope so." Catching his hand, she led him over to the shelves filled with Western hats. "What strikes your fancy?"

He took his time looking over the display. "It needs to be black."

"I hope that doesn't have anything to do with your story about white hats and black hats." She was only half teasing.

"No, it doesn't." He picked up a black Stetson by the brim. "Much as I loved those movies, white hats make no sense. They'll just get dirty."

"And they don't look nearly as sexy as black."

He smiled at her. "Lord knows I want to look sexy for you." And he put on the hat.

Tracy caught her breath. Whether by accident or instinct, he'd chosen the perfect hat. He'd also managed to put it on at exactly the right angle. The brim shadowed his eyes just enough to make him look even more manly, if that was even possible.

He gazed at her from under that brim. "Is that sexy enough for you?"

She swallowed. "I think…it might be overkill."

13

ILLOGICAL THOUGH IT might be, Drake felt different wearing the hat. He'd never have bought it without Tracy's urging, without her belief in him. She'd given him a renewed faith in his essential decency, and then she'd made the hat into a symbol, one he could relate to. One he could wear, for God's sake. How great was that? He owed her, big-time.

Wearing it out of that store, he wasn't convinced that he'd been magically transformed into a cowboy. That would be delusional. But he did feel like a better man.

He might never learn how to twirl a rope, but he would live up to what the hat stood for. He would never again attempt to ease his own pain by causing pain to those he loved. He was better than that.

Tracy kept staring at him, so he was pretty sure the hat was working for her, too. He took hold of her hand again as they stood on the sidewalk outside the store. "Anything else you want to do while we're in town, little lady?"

She laughed, which made her eyes light up and her cheeks rosy. "Just because you have a hat doesn't mean you have to talk like John Wayne."

He loved seeing her like that, so he continued the riff. "Oh, I think it does. And look. Now I'm bowlegged." He managed a pigeon-toed stance that was fairly convincing. "I'm also hankerin' for a cold sarsaparilla and a tin plate full of beans."

"Stop, just stop!"

But she was still bubbling over with laughter, so of course he didn't stop. "If I could find me a nice long piece of straw, I do believe I'd chew on it."

Giggling, she shook her head. "You're ridiculous."

"And here I thought the hat was supposed to make me sexy. Maybe I should return it and get my money back." He started to take it off.

"Don't you dare remove that hat, cowboy, or I'll have to hurt you."

"Whoa!" He crammed it back on his head so the brim made his ears stick out. "I sure hope you're not packin', little lady, or I might have to vamoose."

Grinning, she stepped back and surveyed him. "You have totally screwed up your sexy, but I think it's salvageable. Come here and lean down. Let me fix you."

He did as she asked because he had to agree there was way too much space between them.

Lifting the hat slightly, she set it back on his head more as he'd had it the first time. "There."

"I like it when you say that word." He straightened. "It makes me think of you…naked." He cupped the back of her head. "I might have to kiss you in the middle of Jackson instead of waiting until we get to Shoshone."

"I'm not sure that's a good idea."

"Why? Is there a law against it around here?"

"No, but—"

"Then let's do it." But the minute he started the maneuver, he understood the problem. Damned if his hat wasn't in the way. He angled his head one way, then the other. "How the hell can I do this without poking your eye out?"

"Nudge it back like this." Tracy reached up and pushed it slightly back on his forehead.

"Ah." Simple and elegant. He could finally achieve the desired connection with her smiling mouth. As always, making that connection felt like coming home. He settled in with a sigh. It wouldn't be a long kiss, just enough to hold him until they got back to the house.

She wound her arms around his neck and pressed against him with a carefully controlled passion that matched his own. It was an open-mouthed kiss with a restrained use of tongues, a PG-13 kind of kiss suitable for a public street corner. But any kiss involving Tracy could swing into X-rated territory if he didn't watch himself. He ended it before he forgot where he was and embarrassed them both.

Drawing back, he smiled down at her. "Nice."

"Yeah." She reached up and pulled his hat back where it had been. "Now take me home, cowboy. I want to have my way with you."

He didn't need more motivation than that. They were back in the SUV and on the road in no time. He started to take his hat off, because it seemed silly to keep it on for the drive home.

She put a hand on his arm, stopping him. "Leave it on. For me."

He settled it back on his head.

"Do you like it?" she asked. "I hope you do, because it wasn't cheap."

"Yeah, I do like it. A lot." He glanced over at her. "Thank you for talkin' me into it."

"You're welcome."

He returned his attention to the road, but from the corner of his eye he could see that she was staring at him. "Are you fixated on my hat?"

"A little. But I'm also thinking about what you said tonight at dinner, about not loving your job, although you do seem to like working with horses."

"Apparently I like it fine when the horses aren't valuable thoroughbreds. I had fun supervising Dottie's foaling."

"So did I." Her voice rippled with amusement.

"I wasn't talking about the sex!"

"I know. Sorry. Couldn't resist. So you had fun supervising the foaling."

"I did. I was working with a beautiful, but essentially ordinary, horse. Dottie's not going to run in the Derby. Neither is Sprinkles. I finally recognized that night that I *do* want horses in my life, just not under the conditions I had before. I also like the idea that we were there for Dottie when she had nowhere else to go."

"So you like the rescue angle?"

"It's brilliant. I hope the computer game Lily developed continues to pay those nice royalties so she can afford to keep Peaceful Kingdom goin' forever."

"So do I, but even if the royalties dry up, she'll find another way to pay for it. She'll organize fund-raisers of some kind or look for wealthy investors. She's committed to the horses. So's Regan."

Drake nodded. "You're right. She'll move heaven and earth if she has to."

"You could do that, too."

He looked at her in confusion. "Help her raise money? I suppose I could."

"No, I mean raise money for your own rescue operation. You're a charmer, Drake. You'd be great at running a horse-adoption facility. Fund-raising would be a snap for someone with your personality."

The suggestion caught him completely by surprise. "I don't… Wow, I'd never thought about *me* doin' it."

"Think about it. You'd be a natural."

Slowly the possibility took hold of his imagination. "I was planning to sell my share of the practice, anyway. I could use that as seed money, maybe a down payment on a location."

"There you go."

His brain clicked into high gear. "You know where something like that is needed?"

"Everywhere."

"That's true, but I was thinking of Virginia. Racehorses are worth a ton of money until they're not. There may already be equine rescues for racing thoroughbreds, but it's a big industry. They could probably use another one."

"And you already have the vet skills. You wouldn't have to worry about getting a volunteer for that."

"No, and thanks to my practice, I have a network of wealthy people who might be looking for a tax credit or a write-off. Tracy, this might actually work." Excitement fizzed in his veins until he realized the big drawback to his plan. She wouldn't be part of it.

Not that she couldn't be, but he couldn't ask her to leave this town and the people who had practically raised her. Shoshone already had an equine-adoption facility. The town was small and didn't need another one. Nick and Regan had the vet situation covered, and all they might require in the future was a part-time employee, somebody like Jerry Rankin.

"You're quiet over there."

"Just thinkin'."

"If you don't mind thinking out loud, I'd love hearing whatever plans you're cooking up for this new place. It'll be wonderful, Drake. You might even have time to do some writing on the side."

"I might." He decided to test her reaction to an alternative. "I wonder if maybe I should consider a different location, something closer to this area."

"Why? All your connections are back there, and you know thoroughbreds so well. You're uniquely qualified to set up a rescue and adoption facility for racehorses."

He knew he was on shaky ground, but he'd give it a shot. "You thought this up. It seems like you should be involved, somehow."

She was silent for quite a while.

"Tracy? You okay over there?"

"Yes."

"Look, I realize we haven't known each other very long, but speaking strictly for myself, I'd like to see where this relationship might go. If I head off to Virginia, we won't get that chance."

Her voice was soft, but filled with sincerity. "You shouldn't base your decision on me."

"But—"

"Seriously, Drake." Her voice grew stronger. "You haven't said it in so many words, but I get the impression you've been doing what other people want for a long time. You should do what's best for you now."

"What if being with you is what's best for me? You need to be here. I get it. So if I choose to work around your needs, what's so terrible about that?"

"I'm not sure I can explain, but it doesn't feel right to me. It feels as if you're contorting your plans to fit mine instead of going straight toward your goal."

"Hell, I wouldn't even have a goal if you hadn't suggested it!" The truth was, he wanted everything. He could envision the rescue operation in Virginia perfectly. She was right that it suited him right down to the ground. But he wanted to spend more time with her and find out if they had the kind of special something that would take them through the next fifty years. He thought they might.

Yet she was the town sweetheart, rooted firmly in this community, watched over by the likes of Josie and Jack Chance. She'd told him how much she loved it here, so coaxing her to move back east would be extremely selfish.

He might be able to do it because she liked him and she liked the sex. She might think that would make up for all she'd lose by leaving here. But it would be like yanking a beautiful wildflower out of the ground and then wondering why it wilted and died.

He had to think about this some more. He didn't want to ruin the time they had together at Peaceful Kingdom by arguing about it, either. "It's a great idea," he said at last. "I want to mull it over for a while before making any firm decisions."

"Would you care to translate that? It sounds like doublespeak."

He chuckled. She wouldn't let him get away with anything, which was one of her traits he cherished the most. "Okay. I love havin' sex with you and we have the house to ourselves for at least another five nights. Let's not mess that up with deep, philosophical discussions about the future. Let's live for the present."

She didn't answer right away, but eventually she did. "Okay."

"Excellent."

"I want you to leave your hat on."

"I am leaving it on. I have it on right this minute per your specific request."

"I mean leave it on after you've taken everything else off."

He laughed. "So when we get home, you want me naked except for my hat?"

"That's what I'm saying. You were turned on by my boots. I'm turned on by your hat."

"Fair enough."

"So you'll do it?"

"I'll do it, although I can't picture how it will work."

"That's okay. I can."

TRACY HAD A very clear picture of what she wanted, and she kept it firmly in mind as they drove the rest of the way home. They talked about Dottie and Sprinkles. She told him that Josie had suggested Jack could take over from this point, but she was prepared to tell Josie that wouldn't be necessary. She'd call her boss in the morning.

But even as she said that, she knew Josie wouldn't need a call. She had Morgan, who might have already spread the word that Tracy was sleeping with none other than the evil Drake Brewster. Josie might not like hearing the news, but at least she wouldn't have the kind of fit Morgan might have expected.

They talked about Dottie and Sprinkles for the rest of the trip. Drake wanted to let both of them out into the pasture tomorrow with some supervision, and he expected the new foal's first outing to go fine. Tracy wished she had a proper video camera instead of just her phone, but she'd make do.

While she kept up her end of the conversation, she hadn't stopped thinking about Drake's equine rescue in

Virginia. Establishing it there had been his instinctive response, and it was the right one. That first poem of his told her how much he loved his native state, even if he hadn't loved his life there.

He needed to go back and create a different life, maybe even with Jeannette. Accepting that he would not stay here wasn't easy. It hurt like hell. But she wouldn't let his infatuation with her ruin what could be an exciting future.

She was convinced it was only infatuation, or perhaps even transference, a term she'd learned today while she caught up on her psych coursework during breaks at Spirits and Spurs. He wasn't a client by any stretch. If he had been, then having sex with him would have been highly unprofessional.

But she had urged him to talk about his problems, and he'd gained insight into his issues. That kind of intimate discussion, she'd learned, could cause people to imagine they'd fallen for the therapist. That might explain why Drake couldn't imagine going to Virginia without her.

She, on the other hand, had no such excuse. She was head over heels for the guy. Though it had happened quickly, she'd talked with enough women in this town to know that when lightning struck, time was irrelevant.

She was in love, but she'd never tell him. Instead she'd do everything in her power to guarantee his future happiness. Unfortunately for her, that meant encouraging him to leave.

Knowing the likely outcome of this brief affair made every minute bittersweet, but she didn't want him to know that, either. She'd keep it light and fun. That was the gift they would give to each other, and she wanted him to have good memories. As would she. The best memories ever.

After they pulled into the front yard, she let Drake help her out of the SUV because the poor guy felt guilty if he didn't perform those courtesies for a woman. They walked hand in hand down to the barn so they could assure themselves that Dottie and Sprinkles were fine.

They were. Once again they were curled up together fast asleep.

Drake put his arm around Tracy's shoulders as they watched the mare and foal. "Is it just me, or is this like when the parents come home from a night out and go check on the kids?"

"It does feel like that, doesn't it?" Her heart ached a little knowing that wasn't in the cards for them, but then, she'd never really thought it would be.

"Well, the kids are fine. Let's go." Squeezing her shoulder, he released her and held her hand as they walked out of the barn and latched the door behind them.

As they started back to the house, Tracy glanced up at the moon, which was a smidgen fuller tonight. "It was about this same time when I walked down here in my silk robe and boots."

"Are you saying it's only been twenty-four hours since then?"

"Yep." Their boots crunched on the bare dirt.

"Hard to believe. I feel as if I've known you forever."

"I know what you mean." In her case, she'd been waiting for him forever. He was the man destined to set her free from her mother's rigid rules. Whatever happened, she'd have that to remember him by. Maybe another lover as exciting as Drake would come along. She doubted it, but a miracle might happen.

"I'll never forget how you looked clutching that blanket."

"I was grateful for something to hold on to. I was shaking like a leaf."

"I wasn't all that steady, myself."

"Really?" He was so completely male and self-assured, especially wearing his new hat. "After all the experience you've had?"

"I wish you'd quit referring to that. It's not important."

"Of course it is! Practice makes perfect."

With a soft growl of frustration, he grabbed her and swung her around to face him. "Then how do you explain that when you make love with me, you are absolutely perfect? No one's ever satisfied me more than you do."

She was gratified to hear it, although she couldn't quite believe it was true. "Maybe you're easily satisfied."

He blew out an impatient breath. "It's the exact opposite. That's why my relationships usually last a few months, at most. I've never been engaged. Never seriously thought about it."

"There could be a lot of reasons for that." Her textbooks would probably list at least ten.

"Or maybe there's only one reason. Maybe nobody's ever been right for me and I'm not right for them. Maybe when two people *are* right for each other, it doesn't matter a damn bit whether they're experienced or not. They're operating from an instinct older than history, and when they come together, it's magic."

She gazed up at him. She wanted to memorize this moment when a gorgeous cowboy with the soul of a poet spoke to her of magic while stars sparkled in the sky above him and a crescent moon hung golden with promise.

He could be trying to convince himself that she was special because he needed that right now. She'd learned enough about psychology to understand that and not get her hopes up. But if she thought she'd find another man like this, she was kidding herself.

"You're magic," she murmured. "I love being with you, Drake Brewster."

"Good." He tipped back his hat as if he'd been doing it all his life. "Then let's keep it that way." This time his kiss wasn't quite so sweet or quite so restrained.

14

DRAKE KISSED TRACY until she melted like butter and they very nearly had sex in the yard. But he wasn't willing to lie in the dirt no matter how much he wanted her—and he didn't have condoms with him, either.

Getting into the house and down the hall to his bedroom was a challenge because they couldn't stop kissing and working each other out of their clothes. Well, except for his hat. It fell off three times, and Tracy always retrieved it and placed it back on his head.

They left a trail of clothes through the house and flung away the last of them as they stumbled through the door into his room. Thank God he'd left a light on, which kept them from running into the furniture. Drake grabbed a condom from the open box because he expected they'd dive straight into bed, but Tracy had other ideas.

She whirled out of his arms and stood there panting. "Hold still for a minute."

"Why?" He already had the packet and the condom in his hand, ready for action.

She gulped in air. "I want to…look at…my naked cowboy."

He was having trouble breathing, too, and he didn't want to stand around when they could be doing something more interesting. "You've seen me naked before."

"Not when you're wearing a hat." She edged toward the bed. "Stay right there. Let me get in first."

He groaned. "Tracy…"

"Humor me."

Of course he would. She could ask him to stand on his head and twirl that hat with his toes and he'd do it, or try his damnedest, because…well, because he was in love with her. Might as well face the fact.

He'd imagined himself to be in love a few times, but those relationships hadn't been anything like this—a mixture of tenderness, deep connection, wild sex and hilarity. He never wanted it to end. Impossible though it seemed, it appeared that Tracy was his first love.

But right now she was frustrating the hell out of him. His pride and joy ached something fierce, but she had a fantasy in her head that meant delaying the action. He should be rejoicing that he was part of her fantasy, but right now, all he wanted was to—

"Okay." She stretched out on the bed and propped up her head with a couple of pillows. "Pull your hat down a little lower. Perfect. You look like one badass cowboy."

"One very aroused cowboy."

"I can see that." Her gaze flicked to his johnson. "Nice."

"I could hang my hat on it."

Her lips twitched. "Don't do that. Leave your hat on and crawl toward me from the foot of the bed."

"Do you want to give me dialogue to go along with this performance, or should I make something up?"

"Make it up. Just don't call me *little lady*."

He had no idea what a badass cowboy would say in

a situation like this. In the movies he'd loved as a kid, the cowboys never even kissed the women they loved, let alone talked sexy while naked except for a hat. But he'd give it his best shot.

He looked into her eyes. Telling her he loved her would probably freak her out. So instead he'd concentrate on bringing the heat.

Keeping a firm hold on the condom, he braced his other hand on the bottom edge of the mattress. Then he let his gaze travel over her body with deliberate intent. She was already trembling and flushed with anticipation, but his intimate survey stepped up the pace of her breathing. Good. It certainly stepped up the pace of his.

He pitched his voice low. "You're right accommodatin', sweetheart." He rolled the condom on one-handed. Experience counted for something, after all. "It's not every day a man finds a juicy woman without a stitch on lyin' in his bed just waitin' for it." Sliding forward, he rested one knee on the bed. "And I'm here to give you what you want, darlin'."

She swallowed. "Good."

"Oh, it will be good. Very good. I can promise you that." He moved closer and put his other knee on the bed. "I'm gonna give it to you till you can't see straight."

"I'll bet you will, cowboy." Her eyes darkened.

"And then you'll beg for more."

"Mmm." Her breasts quivered with each ragged breath.

"Now spread those pretty legs, darlin'. I'm coming in."

With a soft moan of surrender, she parted her silky thighs.

Holding her gaze, he eased into position, his cock brushing her soft folds, probing gently. Ah, so slick. So hot. She clutched his hips, her fingertips pressing, urging him forward.

He resisted, ramping up the tension, making them both want it even more. By now he knew not to mess with the hat, even though it meant he couldn't lean down and kiss her. She didn't want his kiss right now. She wanted to be taken by a cowboy.

"I think you're ready for me, sweetheart." He held himself very still, poised on the brink of heaven.

She trembled and tried to pull him toward her. "Yes."

He eased in a fraction, but no more. "I think you're aching for me."

"Yes." Her grip tightened.

"Ask me for it."

Her breath caught. "Please."

"Beg me."

"Please."

He shoved deep and she cried out, convulsing around him, arching into her first climax, bathing him with her nectar. He began thrusting, fast and hard, riding the crest of her orgasm as she gasped his name over and over.

She sank back to the mattress, the tremors fading. Panting, she gazed up at him, her eyes wild, her skin damp, her body shaking.

He slowed his movements, but didn't stop. "Again." He threw it out as a challenge, wondering if she'd tell him no.

She sucked in a breath, but she didn't disagree. She wanted adventure, this lover of his. Still locked inside her, he sat back, slipped his hands under her knees, and brought her legs up until her feet rested on his shoulders.

Her eyes widened, and then she smiled and looked him over. She seemed to take it all in—his hat, his heaving chest glistening with sweat, and the place where his cock was buried deep inside her. "Love the view."

His gaze swept downward. "Me, too." As he began a slow, easy rhythm, he was treated to the quiver of her breasts each time he pushed home, and the erotic sight of his cock moving in and out as he created the connection they both craved.

She flattened her palms against the mattress and lifted to meet each stroke. Her breathing quickened. She was getting close. He could see it in her eyes, feel it in the way she shuddered.

Reaching between her thighs, he massaged her pressure point with his thumb. She moaned and contracted around his aching cock. Then her body tightened, lifted and hurled her into another climax that made her yell and tested his control almost beyond endurance.

Yet he controlled himself. Gently lowering her feet, he eased back down so they were face-to-face, chest to chest. "Wrap your legs around me."

She was still breathing hard, still quaking from aftershocks, but she did as he asked. Then she put her arms around him, too.

He settled in, his hips between her thighs and his cock securely locked in place. He stayed like that, letting her catch her breath, letting him curb his urge to come.

At last her breathing slowed and he didn't feel quite so much like a rocket about to launch. Looking into her eyes, he saw a reflection of his own turbulent thoughts. He had to believe that she wanted what he wanted, a chance to explore what they'd found together. But she seemed afraid to hope.

Maybe, if he loved her well enough, he could change

that. He combed her hair back from her face. "I'm takin' off the hat."

"Okay." Her tiny smile said that she understood. Enough was enough. "I'll do it." Reaching up, she lifted it from his head and laid it brim-side up on the bed next to them. "Thank you for indulging me."

"It was my pleasure, ma'am." Leaning down, he feathered a kiss against her lips as he began to move.

Her breath was warm against his mouth. "I don't think so. You haven't come, yet."

He ran his tongue over her lower lip as he accelerated just a little. Damn, but loving her felt good. "I get pleasure when I give it to you."

"Then it's my turn to give you some." She rose to meet his next thrust.

He liked that a whole lot. The climax he'd been holding back shouldered its way forward, demanding to be turned loose. "I was thinkin' we'd give some to each other."

"Maybe." She matched his rhythm. "But this one's for you."

Lifting his head, he gazed into her eyes as he moved faster. "For us."

Moisture gathered in her eyes. "Drake…"

"Shh. It'll be fine, darlin'." He kissed her again, so softly, even though his body strained toward release. "It'll be just fine." Then he watched her eyes as he pushed home again, and again, and again.

At last he saw flames leap in those dark depths and her body began to hum beneath his. "That's it. Let go."

"Oh, Drake. *Drake.*" Closing her eyes, she came apart in his arms. Tears leaked from the corners of her eyes as she came in a rush.

Her contractions rolled over his cock, dragging him

closer, and closer… Now. *Now.* With a bellow of surrender, he drove into her one last time and came harder than he ever had in his life. As he held on to her and gasped for breath, he was sure of only one thing.

He'd found what he wanted with Tracy, and he wouldn't give that up without a fight.

TRACY DECIDED TO take Drake's advice to heart and live in the present. And the present was darned good as they turned Dottie and Sprinkles loose in the pasture the next morning. A few feet away from the mare and foal, Tracy stood beside Drake, smartphone at the ready, watching to see what mother and son would do.

The foal seemed a little dazed by the grass and the sunlight and stood quietly for a moment looking bewildered. He took a few steps, and when that went well, he walked a little faster. Dottie followed as Sprinkles' fast walk became a trot. Then, as if he'd determined that being outside was fun, he took off running, his little tail held high. His mother chased after him, dodging and weaving whenever Sprinkles abruptly changed direction.

"Oh, my gosh!" Laughing with delight, Tracy turned on the video feature and followed the little guy with her phone. "He's so stinkin' *cute.*"

"When you're right, you're right. Look at him go! He's trying to outrun her, the little squirt." Drake sounded like a proud parent.

Tracy kept filming. "Now I don't know which I love more, the moment Dottie gave birth, or right now, when that baby finally gets out in the world."

"They're both damned special."

"Yep." Tracy lowered the phone when Sprinkles took

a break to nurse. "How would you feel about inviting Jerry Rankin over to see them?"

"That's up to you."

"I don't know." She glanced at him and smiled. "Love that hat."

"So you've said."

"I feel as if Jerry should see this. But if I invite him, he might decide to drop by more often, and then…"

"Goodbye, privacy."

"Yes. Maybe I won't invite him yet."

"That's fine, but I should warn you that I made a couple of calls while you were in the shower."

"You did?" She could guess whom he'd called. "And?"

"Regan said he and Lily were fine with inviting Jeannette out here, and Jeannette is checking into flights."

"That's great!" She hoped that sounded sincere. She wanted it to be sincere.

He studied her. "Is it?"

"Of course it is." She almost wished he hadn't bought the hat after all. That thought was unworthy of her, but damn it, Jeannette would love his new look. What woman wouldn't? "You three need to patch things up."

"I agree, but… Listen, Jeannette is a good friend. That's *all.*"

"I know! And it's wonderful that she's planning to fly out here." She desperately wanted to change the subject. "Did Regan say when they'd be coming home?"

"Yeah, they decided not to stay longer, after all. Turns out he'd already heard about the mare and foal. And us."

"Oh." Tracy sought out the frolicking colt, hoping the sight would lift her suddenly sagging spirits. It did, at least for a couple of seconds. "From Morgan, I assume."

"Yep."

She glanced back at Drake. "How come you didn't tell me all this sooner? I've been out of the shower for a good thirty minutes."

"You were so excited about lettin' Dottie and Sprinkles out, and I didn't want to spoil that moment with… whatever's going on. I'm really not sure what *is* going on between you and me, to be honest."

"Was Regan upset about any of it?"

"Didn't seem to be."

"But still, they're coming home instead of staying."

"He said they should do that, anyway. The Chances are hosting an engagement party for them next weekend, and they decided it wasn't cool to sail in on the eve of the party."

"Oh, right. I forgot about that. Well, then. Regan and Lily will be back in four days. Did…did Jeannette say when she might arrive?" She hated that she'd stumbled with that question.

His calling Jeannette had been her brilliant idea, too. Talk about shooting herself in the foot. He might end up back with Jeannette, but she'd been hoping for several more days alone with him before forcing herself to give him up.

"She'll have to get a few things under control at the firm, so she estimated the soonest she could be here was day after tomorrow."

Tracy's time with Drake was shrinking by the second. "What sort of firm? I don't think anyone ever told me what she does."

"She's a lawyer. A very good one, in fact."

Of course she was a crackerjack lawyer, damn it. No doubt she was stunningly beautiful, too, and Tracy was officially jealous as hell. Pulling herself up short, she vowed to stop letting negative thoughts get the better of her.

Jeannette might well be perfect for Drake. She could help him with any legal issues when he set up his equine rescue in Virginia. She'd also have valuable contacts with wealthy people who might contribute money to the cause.

She dredged up her best smile for Drake. "I look forward to meeting her."

"I want you to. Then you can see for yourself that we're just friends. What happened between us shouldn't have. I hope that we can—" The rumble of a powerful pickup cut into the quiet of the summer morning. Drake glanced toward the front gate. "Looks like somebody's payin' us a visit."

Tracy turned as a cherry-red dually truck drove into the yard. And the morning had started out with such promise before it took a nosedive. She didn't feel even slightly ready to face the man who drove that truck. She sighed.

"I take it you know who it is?"

"Unfortunately, I do. I suppose after telling Morgan and Gabe about us last night, I should have expected this."

"Who is it?"

"Jack Chance."

15

Drake straightened his shoulders. "I've heard plenty about the guy. It's about time I met him." He was glad Tracy had talked him into the hat. As they walked toward the big red truck, he pulled the brim a little lower over his eyes. He was willing to bet that Jack Chance wore a black hat.

Had he had someone to take that wager, he would have won it. Jack climbed down from the cab wearing a hat that looked remarkably like Drake's. So Jack had good taste.

Instead of coming toward them, Jack rounded the front bumper and opened the passenger door. Drake had never been so glad to see anyone as he was to see Josie getting out of the passenger side. Then again, he hadn't followed the program. He'd slept with Tracy. Josie might not be on his team anymore.

As Josie and Jack walked toward them, Drake couldn't help thinking of the gunfight at the OK Corral. Josie and Jack weren't smiling—never a good sign.

Then Drake remembered how Tracy had handled the encounter with Morgan and Gabe. He would behave like the Southern gentleman he'd been trained to be, with a slight Western twist now that he had a hat.

He smiled and held out his hand to Jack as if he'd known him for years. "I'm real glad you two came by. We just let Dottie and her foal out in the pasture. You might want to take a look. He's cute as the dickens."

Jack shook his hand without missing a beat. His grip was strong but not a bone-crusher. "We'd be happy to. Nothing like a newborn colt to make a person smile." But Jack was not smiling.

Josie was, though. "I can hardly wait to see him." She wore a brown Stetson and her blond hair was gathered into a single braid as it had been when Drake had talked with her.

He couldn't believe that had been a mere two days ago. It felt as if months had passed since then.

"That's one of the reasons we're here," Josie said. "Let's go see the little guy."

Drake took note that it was only *one of the reasons.* He exchanged a quick glance with Tracy before they all walked back up to the pasture. She shrugged.

"The place is coming along." Jack looked around as he and Josie walked a little ahead of Drake and Tracy.

"I didn't see it before the transformation," Drake said, "but Regan told me about the work everyone did to make it a viable operation."

"Regan and Lily get most of the credit," Josie said. "They worked so hard, and I'm glad they took this trip. They both deserve a break from the routine. I'm glad you were available to house-sit for them, Tracy."

"Me, too, although they may not thank me for taking in a pregnant mare."

Jack cleared his throat. "That's one of the things I want to talk to you about."

"That I overstepped my authority? I know that I—"

"She had no choice." Drake spoke without hesitation. "She was faced with an animal in dire straits. She did the right thing."

Jack glanced at him, and for the first time he *almost* smiled. "Easy, Brewster. I wasn't criticizing her decision. I absolutely agree it was the right one. If there's any blame, it belongs to Jerry Rankin. I'm trying to decide whether he deserves the job I've given him. He put Tracy in a helluva position. Nice hat, by the way. Looks new."

"Thanks. It is." And that, Drake thought, was why Jack Chance was the reigning prince around here. He projected authority with his big red truck and his take-charge attitude, but then, just when you were ready to hate the guy for throwing his weight around, he disarmed you with an obviously sincere compliment about your new hat.

Josie had mentioned that she thought Drake and Jack would get along. Drake wasn't sure about that, but it would be interesting to find out. Much depended on Jack's other reasons for driving over to Peaceful Kingdom. At least Drake had put him on notice that nobody was going to chastise Tracy while he was around.

"Jerry's a poor old guy who ended up in a bad situation," Tracy said. "Do you know he can't read?"

"I found that out." Jack paused as they reached the pasture fence. Then he leaned on it and gazed at Dottie chasing after Sprinkles. "Now that's a real good-looking horse. If her foals typically looked like that one, I can see why Jerry made some money."

Tracy joined him at the fence. "But if his wife was his business manager, after she died he couldn't handle things the way he used to. I think she helped him disguise his illiteracy so he could keep his job and sell Appaloosas on the side."

Drake admired the way she stuck up for Jerry. Her compassion was another thing he loved about her. The list kept growing.

Jack nodded. "Yeah, I think that's true. I'm just not sure he's the right fit for the Last Chance. I'll keep him on for a while, but he's a little overwhelmed by the size and scope of the place. However…" He turned and leaned his back against the fence and propped one booted foot on the bottom rail as he surveyed Peaceful Kingdom.

Tracy smiled. "Nice try, but you're talking to the wrong person. Regan and Lily have to make that decision."

"She's right, Jack," Josie said. "Don't go trying to strike a deal with Tracy. Honestly. You would have made a great politician."

Jack didn't disagree. "Hey, she's met the guy. She could be his character reference."

Drake couldn't help laughing at that. "Wouldn't you be the logical character reference? She saw Jerry for about twenty minutes, tops. He's workin' at your ranch. You know him better than she does."

"Yes, but if I talk him up, Regan and Lily will figure out I'm trying to unload him, which I am. Whereas Tracy has nothing to gain or lose if she talks him up. She'll have a much better chance of convincing them to take on Jerry than I will. They'll suspect me of ulterior motives."

Josie shook her head. "Which you have coming out your ears. So, are we done with this topic?"

"That depends." Jack glanced at Tracy. "Will you

please put in a good word for old Jerry with Regan and Lily?"

She grinned at him. "Yes, Jack, I will. I really think he'd make a great employee here."

"Thank you. So do I. And that frees us up to discuss a more sensitive topic." He looked straight at Drake.

Drake tensed.

Tracy had obviously seen Jack's look, because she pushed away from the fence and faced him, her jaw tight. "Jack, you know I think a lot of you, but if you're going to say anything negative about Drake, then, with all due respect, I'll have to ask you to get back in your truck and drive away."

Drake was touched by her loyalty, but he couldn't ask her to fight his battles. He stepped forward. "I appreciate that more than I can say, but if Jack wants to have it out with me, we should. Maybe it'll clear the air. I'm sick of having the most prominent family in Shoshone treat me like a leper."

"A leper?" Jack looked wounded. "I hardly think that's fair, Brewster. We've been polite. From a distance."

"Which is exactly how they used to treat lepers, Chance!"

"Oh, for God's sake." Josie blew out a breath. "Drake, we came over this morning to invite you to Regan and Lily's engagement party next weekend."

Drake was stunned into silence.

"I was working up to that," Jack grumbled. "Then everybody jumped on me."

Drake still couldn't get his head around it. "You're inviting me to a party…at the Last Chance Ranch?"

"Yes." Josie's tone was friendly but efficient. "It starts at one, and we'll be serving an outdoor barbecue. You can bring a gift if you'd like, but it's certainly not—"

"You bet I'll bring a gift! Regan's my best friend!" Belatedly he realized he wasn't exactly displaying his Southern gentleman's manners. "I appreciate the invitation. Thank you."

"It required a big family meeting," Jack said.

"Jack." Josie gave him a look of warning.

"Well, it did."

"We don't need to discuss it, though."

"Oh, please do." Drake was fascinated. "I've never been the subject of a big family meetin' before. I want to hear about it."

Jack seemed all too willing to share. "See, Morgan was on the phone with everybody last night, carrying on about the incident at the hamburger joint. So my mom, Sarah Chance Beckett to you, called a family meeting early this morning because she said we couldn't keep this up. Regan's been saying you're an okay guy, and now Tracy seems to think so, too, so we voted, and…" He shrugged. "Looks like you're in. Congratulations."

"I'll be damned." He glanced over at Tracy. "Will you be my date for this shindig?"

To his surprise, she hesitated. "I'd be glad to, but don't forget that Jeannette will probably still be here then. You might rather take her, instead."

"If it comes to that, I'll take both of you."

Tracy's cheeks turned pink. "No, that's okay. I can get there on my own."

He realized that suggesting all three of them go together might not have been his brightest idea.

Then Jack spoke up again. "Who's Jeannette?" He looked from Drake to Tracy. "The name sounds familiar, but I can't place her."

Josie cleared her throat nervously. "Are we talking about Regan's Jeannette? Wait, I don't mean that like it sounded. She's not *Regan's* Jeannette anymore, obviously. But is she the woman I'm thinking of? Because if she is, then—"

"Yes, it's that Jeannette, and I invited her to come here for a visit," Drake said. "I cleared it with Regan and Lily, first, of course."

Jack stared at him in obvious disbelief. "Brewster, I was just thinking that maybe I might like you, and now I discover to my great disappointment that you have shit for brains. Are you telling me that you have invited Regan's ex-fiancée to Jackson Hole?"

"It was my idea," Tracy said. "Well, not the inviting part, but having Drake call her was my idea. They've been buddies since they were kids, and now they're not friends anymore. That's a shame."

"Of course they're not friends!" Jack scowled at Drake. "You slept with her! You can't be friends with someone you…" He shot a glance in Josie's direction. "Well, yes, you can, but not in this case. This is a particularly screwed-up case. You really invited her here? Really?"

"Yes, I did."

"Can you uninvite her?"

"No, I can't. She's probably already booked a flight. She should be here in a couple of days."

Jack groaned. "We're just now getting used to *you,* and you bring the other half of the triangle into town?" His scowl deepened. "Hold it. Scratch that. You can't have two halves of a triangle. It would be the other third of the triangle, but who the hell gives a damn about geometry at a time like this? Brewster, you suck."

"He does *not.*" Tracy got right in Jack's face. "I started all of this by saying he should get in touch with her, but if he thinks it's an even better idea to bring her out here so that she can clear the air with Regan, and

Regan and Lily agree to it, then it's a done deal. You don't have to meet Jeannette, so it's none. Of. Your. Business." She held his gaze with defiance radiating from every part of her trembling body.

Jack blinked. "Oh." He adjusted the angle of his hat so it sat back a little more on his head. "You have a point." He looked over at Drake. "Sorry, Brewster. Sometimes I forget I'm not the king. Fortunately I have people more than willing to remind me of that."

Drake was blown away, both by Tracy's fierce defense of him and Jack's instant capitulation. "Apology accepted."

Jack held out his hand and Drake shook it. Then Jack glanced at Josie. "Think we should mosey on home, now?"

She rolled her eyes. "Not yet, Your Majesty. Drake needs to know whether Jeannette is welcome at the party. I'd be happy to have her. I'll bet Regan will want her there. But if you're going to treat her like a leper, too, then—"

"Oh, God. Here we go with the leper thing again." Jack sighed and faced Drake again. "Please bring whoever you want to the party, Brewster." He looked to Josie for approval. "Is that okay?"

She smiled. "That's fine. Let's go home."

"Yeah, let's do. I'm exhausted."

Josie came over and hugged Tracy. Then she sent a cautious smile Drake's way. "See you two later."

Jack gave Drake one last glance. "I really do like the hat. It suits you." Then he slung an arm around Josie's waist and they headed back to the big red truck.

Once they were out of hearing range, Drake turned to Tracy and cupped her face in both hands. "I don't know what to say. You were incredible. It's not even your fight, but you stood up for me." His gaze searched hers and found what he was looking for. She loved him. He knew it more surely than he knew his own name. "Tracy, I'm in love with you, and I think you're in—"

"Drake, you can't trust what you're feeling now."

"The hell I can't. I've never met a woman I've wanted this much, and not just sexually, although that part is beyond amazing. That's rare, by the way. Take my word for it because I'm the one who's supposed to be the experienced person in this group."

"Okay, I believe you, but—"

He tightened his grip and poured out his heart. "I want *you,* Tracy. All of you—your compassion, your loyalty, your crazy fantasies, your great laugh, your quirky sense of humor, which is so much like mine it's scary. But mostly I want that certain something we share, as if we've known each other forever, as if we *will* know each other forever. I want to be with you, Tracy. Whatever it takes, I want to be with you."

"Oh, Drake…" Her eyes grew moist. "I wish it could be that simple."

"It is simple. We'll make it that way. We'll—damn, there's my phone." And it was Jeannette's ring. Terrible timing. He decided to let it go to voice mail.

But Tracy gently took his hands from her face and stepped away from him. "Take the call. It might be Jeannette."

"I don't care. I'll get it later."

"Take the call."

The moment was spoiled, anyway, so he reached for the phone in his pocket. It had stopped ringing, but then his text message signal chimed. He opened the message. When he lifted his head, Tracy was watching him, a question in her eyes.

He knew the news would mean their time alone was pretty much over. “Jeannette finished work ahead of schedule and she’s flying in tonight. Come with me to the airport. I want her to meet you. I want her to meet the woman I—”

“No, Drake.” She shook her head. “For one thing, I have to work tonight. For another, you two need time alone.”

“We can talk on the way back from the airport. I’ll come by Spirits and Spurs.”

“Please don’t.” Panic gripped her. She didn’t want to face what could end up being the love of Drake’s life while she was in a public situation where she couldn’t escape. “She’ll be tired, and I’ll be busy. It wouldn’t be a good beginning for either of us.”

“I guess not.”

“Just take her back to your cabin. I’ll meet her…later. Now let’s go round up the horses and put them back in the barn before Sprinkles wears Dottie to a frazzle.”

He agreed, and while they did, he found himself regretting that he’d invited Jeannette to Jackson Hole. Maybe it would end up okay, but he had a bad feeling that her visit threatened to ruin everything.

16

TRACY THOUGHT SHE'D prepared herself to get through this night. She'd worked especially hard at Spirits and Spurs and had even stayed later than she needed to while she polished every item behind the bar until the area gleamed. She would hear from Drake the next day, and that was fine.

He and Jeannette had plenty to talk about. They'd stay up late, so he wouldn't come back to Peaceful Kingdom in the middle of the night. But just in case, she left the front door unlocked because she'd never given him a key.

She was almost sure he wouldn't come over, though. He and Jeannette would both be tired from the emotional stress of seeing each other and working through their issues. She couldn't really believe he would just leave Jeannette and come back here.

Logically, he'd offer her his bed in the cabin, and… he'd take the sofa. Tracy did her best to picture Drake on that sofa, but the image of them sharing a bed wouldn't go away, no matter how she tried to banish it.

Drake had claimed to love her, although she was afraid to believe it. But if *he* believed it, then he wouldn't share a bed with Jeannette, not even just to sleep. Or would he? Tracy thought of how long Drake and Jeannette had been friends. If you knew someone that well, would you even think twice about sleeping in the same bed? Maybe not. And it would be *fine.*

No, it wouldn't, damn it. She didn't want any other woman waking up beside Drake, whether they'd had sex or not. She slept in Regan and Lily's king-size bed that night, unwilling to stay in the room that contained so many hot memories of Drake.

Or rather, she *didn't* sleep. All she could do was lie there and stare into the darkness, torturing herself as she wondered what was happening in Drake's cabin. She'd never spent such a miserable night in her life.

Finally, when it was barely light out, she crawled out of bed, dressed in old jeans and a T-shirt, and staggered into the kitchen to make coffee. She might as well jack herself up with caffeine, because today didn't promise to be any better, stress-wise, and coffee would have to substitute for sleep.

As the coffee brewed, she paced the kitchen in her bare feet and reminded herself that no one was to blame for her misery except her. She'd taken in the pregnant mare against orders. She'd elected to call Drake, and then she'd invited him to stay.

Oh, but it got worse. She'd initiated the sex. If she hadn't gone to the barn that night, he wouldn't have made the first move. Not with all the guilt he'd carried about Regan and Jeannette.

Tension would have remained high, but they wouldn't have spent all that lovely time in bed together. She wouldn't have taken him hat shopping. She wouldn't have fallen in love with him. She didn't regret any of it, but man, payback was a bitch.

She was pouring her first cup of coffee when the front door opened. Her stomach pitched. If he'd brought Jeannette over here without warning her, without giving her a chance to shower and fix her hair and put on makeup, she'd *kill* him.

Heart pounding, she finger combed her unbound hair and tugged down the hem of her T-shirt, but she was positive that she looked like hell. Couldn't be helped.

He walked into the kitchen looking at least as ragged as she felt, although he had one thing going for him. He'd worn his hat. But he was in desperate need of a shave, and his Western shirt—the same one he'd left in—was badly wrinkled. He regarded her through bloodshot eyes, and his voice was hoarse, as if he'd used it a lot in the past few hours. "I love you."

She felt as if a gigantic vacuum had sucked the air out of the room. "Drake, you may think—"

"I don't *think,* Tracy. I *know.* Just like I know you love me, but I don't want to stand here and argue about it. Put somethin' on your feet. We're taking a ride."

She struggled to breathe. "Who's we? Is Jeannette with you?"

"No. She's asleep in the cabin."

Okay. That helped. She took a shaky breath.

"We stayed up most of the night talkin'—about us, about Regan, but mostly about you." He sounded tired. "I was pretty damned sure how I felt, but after all those hours of goin' over it with Jeannette, every doubt is gone. Go get your shoes. Or your boots. Whatever."

"Where are we going?"

"I'll tell you on the way."

"There's coffee if you want some." She gestured to the pot.

"That'll be nice to have, at that. I'll fix us a thermos."

"I'll be right back." She hurried into the bedroom and put on some sneakers. Her boots had a strong association for him, and she didn't want to cloud the issue of whether he was in love with her by causing him to think about sex.

When she returned to the kitchen, he picked up the thermos. "Let's go. We need to be back in time to feed the critters."

She nodded. Whatever he was up to, he seemed to have taken all the factors into consideration. He helped her into his dusty black SUV, but that was the only time he tried to touch her. He behaved like a man on a mission, a man who wouldn't allow himself to be distracted until he'd achieved his goal.

This was a side of Drake she'd never seen before. He'd always seemed so laid-back with his Southern accent and his tendency to joke about nearly everything. That Drake wasn't driving the SUV and pushing the speed limit. Fortunately nobody else was on the road at this hour.

To her surprise, he seemed to be going toward the Last Chance. But that would also take them past the cabin where Jeannette lay sleeping. "You're not taking me to see Jeannette, are you? Because I'd rather not go over there looking like I'd been pulled backward through a knothole, and I'm sure she wouldn't appreciate seeing me before she has a chance to—"

"I'm takin' you to a place Josie mentioned to me a while ago. After you and I came to an impasse yesterday, I called her and got directions. I wasn't sure whether I'd need them or not, but it seemed like a good plan to have in my hip pocket."

"Are we going to that flat rock, the one that's supposed to be sacred to the Shoshone tribe?"

"That's it. Have you been there?"

"No. It's on Chance land, so I'd have to ask first, and I just never… To tell you the truth, I would have felt funny telling them I wanted to go stand on their rock to clear my mind."

"You have my permission to feel as funny as you want, because that's exactly what we're gonna do. I'm runnin' out of ways to convince you that what we have is the real deal, so we'll give this a shot."

"You're, um, driving kind of fast."

"I want to get there before the sun comes up."

"Okay." She settled back in her seat and decided not to talk to him for the rest of the trip. If he insisted on barreling down the highway, she didn't want to interfere with his concentration. "I'll watch for cops."

"Thanks." He floored it, and they came to the Last Chance turnoff in no time at all.

The road was unpaved and known for being an axle-breaker, so he slowed down. Drake swore each time the SUV bottomed out. "Jack needs to maintain his damned road."

"He leaves it this way on purpose."

"You're kiddin' me."

"No. It's how his father chose to discourage trespassers. Other family members take a different view, and they've argued about it for years. It's still like this, so I guess Jack's winning."

"Bully for him." Drake hit another pothole and cussed again. "Wouldn't hurt to have a few lights out here, either."

Tracy smiled. Drake was used to the manicured pastures and well-maintained roads of Virginia farms. He was wearing an awesome Western hat and he had fully subscribed to the cowboy code of honor, but at heart he was a Southern gentleman. She cherished that about him. It was part of who he was.

But she wasn't questioning her feelings for him. He thought he could convince her of his sincerity by standing on a piece of granite at sunrise. It was the kind of scenario that would appeal to the soul of a poet. She cherished that about him, too.

They rounded a curve and the ranch buildings came into view. Drake whistled under his breath and slowed down. "Now that's impressive." He brought the SUV to a stop and switched off the headlights.

"Uh-huh." In the predawn light, the immense two-story log house loomed even bigger than in broad daylight. Faint light glowed in a couple of the windows. The occupants might be starting their day.

"I like the way the wings are angled." Drake leaned on the steering wheel and peered at the house. "Like they're welcomin' you to come and sit a spell."

"I think so, too. Jack's grandparents started with just that center section, and then the two wings were added later. My favorite part is the porch that runs the length of the whole thing."

"Mine, too. The rockers remind me of porches in the South."

"People sit on porches out here, too."

"Obviously." Drake's gaze took in the rest of the buildings, which included the original barn, the tractor barn, the bunkhouse and several corrals. "Quite an operation. Probably worth millions."

"It is, but they have no plans to sell, and the overhead has to be huge. Josie says that Jack works hard to make sure the place stays in the black."

"I can believe it." Drake looked at Tracy. "But fascinatin' as all that is, we have a date with the sun." Stepping on the gas, he turned left and followed another dirt road that wound westward through ranch land and brought them closer to the mountains.

He took this road more slowly. "Keep an eye out for the rock."

"I will."

"It'll be on the right. It's supposed to be the size of a parking spot."

"So I've heard. Let's put down the windows now that dust won't come billowing in."

"Sure. Sorry about the wild ride. Just wanted to get here in time." He lowered the front windows and cool morning air wafted in, along with the occasional chirp of a bird.

Tracy drew in a deep breath. The scent of dew-soaked grass and a whiff of evergreens across a meadow calmed her. "Ah. Nice."

"I know you love it here."

"Of course I do. Who wouldn't?" But something in the way he'd said it told her it was more than an idle comment. "To be fair, I haven't been out of the state, so I don't know what other places are like. Oh, I did take one short trip to Idaho with some friends from high school, but that barely counts since it's just across the border."

"If you had to live in just one place, this isn't a bad choice."

"Probably not. Wait, slow down! It's right up ahead! I saw something sparkle in your headlights. Everybody says it sparkles in the light. The quartz in the granite makes it do that."

He slowed the SUV to a crawl. "Okay, I see it. Josie said I could park beside it. The ground's packed down from all the folks who've parked there."

"Can you pull in so your headlights shine on it? I

want to see the sparkling effect again. This is cool. Now I wish I hadn't been so shy about asking to come out here."

Drake maneuvered the SUV until the headlights were focused directly on the slab of gray rock with veins of white quartz running through it. "How's that?"

"Perfect. It's as if teenaged girls were out here playing with glitter."

"I'll leave the lights on. We won't be here that long."

"Okay." Tracy reached for her door handle.

"Hang on. I'll come get you. And I'm leavin' this." He took off his hat and laid it on the dash.

She sat patiently and waited for him to come around. He really was cute about that. Even though she was a fully liberated woman, she enjoyed his gestures because he'd never implied that she *couldn't* do those things for herself. He just liked making her feel special.

He thoroughly succeeded at that. As he helped her out of the SUV, she felt like a princess being escorted to the ball. Hand in hand, they walked up to the rock, which jutted out of the earth about two feet.

Tracy surveyed the granite. "So we just climb up on it?"

"Josie said it's supposed to work better if you take off your shoes."

"Then let's do it. It would be silly to come all the way out here and not do it right." She let go of Drake's hand, sat on the rock and pulled off her sneakers. She hadn't bothered with socks.

He followed suit and took off his boots and socks. "I'll go up first." Bracing his palm on the rock, he vaulted up.

"Nice job."

"I was on the gymnastics team in high school."

"There are so many things I don't know about you."

He held out his hand. "But you know the important things."

She thought about that as she placed her hand in his and he pulled her up. He was right. She knew enough to love the man he was and the man he would become. Once he began devoting his time to equine rescue, he would blossom as his innate kindness was allowed to flourish. She wished that she could read the poems he would write then.

He led her over to the center of the rock. "So, what do you think?"

She paid attention to the feel of the rock under her feet. "It's warmer than I thought it would be." Glancing down, she smiled. "I feel as if I'm standing on the Milky Way."

"And I feel as if…I'm standing…with the woman I'm supposed to be with…forever."

She looked into his eyes and tried to tell herself that he was confused, but he didn't look confused. There was no teasing in those green depths. The self-mockery was gone, too. In its place gleamed the clear certainty of a man who knew what he wanted. And he wanted her.

A burst of energy radiated from the spot where his hand clasped hers. It flowed through her body in a tingling river of sensation. She almost expected to begin sparkling like the rock at her feet.

"I love you." His voice was as steady as his gaze. "No matter what happens between us, no matter whether you choose to be with me or not, that isn't going to change."

Warmth filled her, then, and with that warmth came precious knowledge. He loved her. *He loved her.*

He stared at her, and then he sucked in a breath. "You believe me."

"Yes." She couldn't stop smiling.

"You believe me!" He scooped her up and twirled them around. "Thank God. Oh, thank God." Setting her down again, he held her face with both hands. "Tracy Gibbons, will you marry me?"

"Yes."

"We can live anywhere you want. You love this place, and I want you to be happy, so I—"

"Don't be silly." She wrapped her arms around his waist. "We're moving to Virginia, and we're starting an equine-rescue facility, and I'm going to get my psychology degree, and we are going to have a fabulous life."

"Wow. But I'll give you plenty of time to rethink that when you're not standing on a magic rock."

"It's not the rock. It's you. I told you that you are magic. Drake, I don't care where we live! That wasn't my problem at all! I was just afraid you had deluded yourself that you loved me because I was the person who helped you figure out some things. In psychology they call that transference, and I—"

"Good grief." He smiled and shook his head. "I had no idea that's what you thought. I've heard of transference. I took an introductory psych class as a freshman."

"It's a legitimate concern!"

His gaze warmed. "It is if you love someone so much that you want to keep them from makin' a big mistake, even if you'll suffer the consequences."

She basked in the love glowing in his expression. "That would be me," she said softly, "loving you that much."

"I know." And he kissed her.

It was an easy, gentle kiss, but he packed plenty of love into it. Then he added just enough sizzle to remind her of the heat they shared.

With a soft groan, he lifted his mouth from hers. "I wish we didn't have to leave."

"But we do. The critters."

"One more and we'll go." He started to kiss her again, but then he stopped abruptly. "Oh, Tracy. Open your eyes."

She did and was surprised at how well she could see him. Then she realized why. "The sun's coming up."

"It surely is. Let's watch it."

"Absolutely, after you drove like a maniac to get here in time."

"A maniac? Is that any way to talk to the love of your life?"

"It was kind of exciting. You were being all manly and intense."

"That's better. Manly and intense, huh?"

"Yes, but don't let it go to your head."

"That's exactly where it's going, sweetheart. I may need to buy me a bigger hat."

She was happy to discover that the silly side of him hadn't disappeared. Feeling her world click into place, she nestled against his side as a rim of gold slid over the horizon. "It's a new day."

"It's the best day of my life."

"Mine, too." Then she smiled to herself. *So far.*

Epilogue

JEANNETTE TRENTON PACED the living room of Drake's small cabin, across from the boundary of the Last Chance Ranch. Regan, her ex-fiancé, had wanted to honeymoon at the ranch, but she'd convinced him they should fly to Paris. Instead, they'd had no wedding and no honeymoon because she'd cheated with Regan's best friend. Her parents' nonrefundable deposits on the expensive venue, gourmet food and top-notch entertainment had gone down the drain.

Seven months later her folks were still angry, although they claimed to have gotten past it. Jeannette couldn't tell which they'd hated more, being embarrassed in front of their high-society friends or losing all that money. She'd also shocked them to their toes. Their perfect daughter, who'd never given them a moment's worry, had made a public and very humiliating mistake.

Jeannette regretted causing them pain, which couldn't be helped now. She had offered to pay back the money, but they'd refused to take it, as if they didn't want to give her a chance to redeem herself. Apparently she wouldn't be forgiven for a long, long time.

She had a little more hope that Regan might forgive

her, though. Four days ago she'd flown to Jackson Hole at Drake's invitation, and wow, it had felt great to see him and find out they hadn't ruined their friendship, after all. The first hour or so had been pretty damned awkward, but then Drake had cracked a joke and just like that, the tension had evaporated.

In a few minutes she'd face her second big challenge, seeing Regan for the first time since he'd moved out of their condo seven months ago. He and Drake were coming over for what Drake had insisted on calling a reunion. She'd love to believe it could be that, but oh, God, was she a nervous wreck.

It helped that Drake and Regan had each found someone. Drake had moved into Tracy's apartment above Spirits and Spurs, leaving this little cabin available for her. The location was good, if remote and a tiny bit scary. She wasn't used to hearing wolves howl at night or raccoons rattling the garbage cans.

Tracy and Lily weren't coming along for this initial encounter, and Jeannette thought that was just as well. No telling how the meeting would go.

Still, Regan and Drake had patched up their friendship, and she'd almost achieved normalcy with Drake. She had her moments of embarrassment and regret, and she'd bet he did, too, but mostly they'd returned to the easy banter they used to enjoy.

That left Regan, the injured party. Seven months ago he hadn't given her the chance to apologize, or even to talk about what had happened. He'd left Virginia as if his tail had caught fire. She couldn't blame him.

But Drake said Regan was no longer bitter or angry, and she hoped to hell that was true. She was about to find out. She heard Drake's SUV pulling up, and she took a deep breath.

The sound of their laughter as they joked with each other outside made her smile. She used to love listening to them kid around. She hadn't realized how much she'd missed that until now.

One of them rapped on the door, and she hurried over to open it. For one awful moment, they all stood and stared at each other. Then Regan stepped forward and gathered her into his arms. "It's good to see you." His voice was gruff with emotion as he gave her a tight hug.

"Same here." Relief brought tears to her eyes, but she blinked them away. Crying would make them all uncomfortable. As she and Regan moved apart, she took a quick survey of her ex and smiled. "You look good. Happy."

"I am."

She could see the joy shining in his eyes. "I'm so glad, Regan. So glad for you."

"Yeah, yeah, we're all glad," Drake said. "Life's a bowl of cherries, but let's don't be standin' in the door and lettin' in flies." He shooed them both inside. "We need to pop the top on some beers and get this party *started*."

She laughed. "I found some Cheetos at the Shoshone General Store." Back in college that had been their favorite snack food.

"Perfect." Regan grinned at her. "Can't beat Cheetos and beer."

And good friends. But she didn't say that. Back in the day, they never would have indulged in sentimentality. She wasn't about to screw up their reunion with embarrassing sappiness. Yet this was her chance to apologize, and she wasn't going to chicken out on that. "Regan, please let me say that I am so—"

"I know you are." His gaze was filled with warmth

and understanding. "Me, too. I wasn't the right guy for you."

Her smile trembled. "I don't know if there is one."

"Sure there is. Just keep looking."

"And we'll help scout him out for you." Drake passed around the beer as Jeannette dumped Cheetos into a bowl. "In the meantime, here's to the Awesome Three from U of V."

Bottles clinked and they took hefty swallows of their beer, and then spread out in the tiny living room, like old times. They talked about movies and politics, about what books were worth reading and what TV shows should be canceled for their sheer stupidity.

Jeannette soaked up the atmosphere of good cheer and knew that yes, everything would be okay. Their friendship would survive. As for her love life, she didn't much care about that right now. She had her friends back, and that was more than enough.

* * * * *

Riding Home

Dear Reader,

When I first set foot on the Last Chance Ranch in 2010, I had no idea that one day I'd be welcoming you to the sixteenth book in the series! I know some of you have been with me for the whole ride, and some might be joining me for the first time. Either way, I've worked hard to make sure that each story stands alone. Whether you're a long-time Sons of Chance fan or just beginning to get into the series, you won't get lost, I promise!

After all these books, *Riding Home* seems like an appropriate title. Each time I go back to the Last Chance Ranch, I feel as if I'm coming home. The two-story log ranch house is as familiar as my own house. The Chance family members are friends, and I'm quite attached to the horses, too!

I know from your emails and comments on Facebook that many of you feel the same way. If you read both *Riding High* and *Riding Hard* you know whose story this has to be. Regan O'Connelli and Drake Brewster have found their soul mates, and I think Jeannette Trenton, despite her issues, deserves a shot. I've put her in the path of Zach Powell, a recent hire at the ranch, but he has some demons of his own.

So let's see how they handle the situation, shall we? Of course you'll get to hang out with the rest of the gang at the ranch. Jack Chance can't let a book go by without making his presence known, and Mary Lou always has a fresh pot of coffee available for anyone who shows up in her kitchen. Grab yourself a mug and make yourself at home!

Cosily yours,

Vicki

DEDICATION

To my wonderful readers—
You've taken the Sons of Chance into your hearts,
and your enthusiasm touches me!

Prologue

From the diary of Eleanor Chance
August 15, 1990

WHEN YOUR CHILD MARRIES, you instantly become related to a whole lot more folks. Sometimes that's a lovely thing and sometimes it's not. But in the case of our only son, Jonathan, marrying Sarah Gillespie eight years ago, we lucked out. Judy and Bill are salt-of-the-earth.

When I told Judy that, she called it a supreme compliment. She's lived in Shoshone for more than thirty years, but some locals still think of her as an uppity Easterner. I admit when she first arrived she caused quite a stir, and people around here have long memories.

She blew in from New York City, flush with money from her modeling career and wearing pricey designer outfits. She immediately bought a small ranch and hired one of Jackson Hole's most eligible bachelors, Bill Gillespie, to help run it. We all predicted they'd get married, which they did, and within a year little Sarah was born.

But then Judy made the mistake of announcing she'd only have one child in order to keep her figure. That didn't sit well with the town busybodies. Personally, I didn't give a hoot. She had the right to make that decision for herself.

I liked her from the get-go. She was generous with her money, always willing to support local charity efforts, and she worked right alongside Bill as they turned their place into a cute little guest ranch. She worked hard to make the place cozy and profitable until they chose to sell and move into town.

Judy came over today so she, Sarah and I could have a confab about Jack's twelfth birthday party next month. Judy keeps trying to get that boy to warm up to her, but Jack's a funny one. He's never quite recovered after his mother left when he was a toddler.

Consequently he got it into his head that because Sarah is not his "real" mother, he has no right to claim Judy as his grandmother. He thinks his brothers are the only ones who deserve that privilege. No amount of reasoning works with him. Next to the word *stubborn* in the dictionary is a picture of my grandson Jack.

But Judy keeps trying, and the birthday present she's bought for Jack is a perfect example. She asked a rare book dealer in New York to track down an autographed copy of one of Jack's favorite Louis L'Amour titles. I don't even want to know what she paid for it, and Jack won't realize the effort and expense involved, but I'm sure he'll treasure the book. Maybe someday he'll realize what a gift of love it is.

In any case, I'll be forever grateful that Judy chose Wyoming as her landing spot after she left modeling. Besides giving birth to the amazing Sarah, she's also been an asset to the community. In my opinion, we could use a few more Easterners blowing into town to shake things up and keep us from getting too set in our ways.

1

Last Chance Ranch
Present day

ON HIS KNEES inside an empty stall, Zach Powell concentrated on nailing a loose board in place. Except for one horse with medical issues, Zach was alone in the barn. Or so he thought until he stopped hammering and heard the echo of footsteps.

Whoever was wandering around wasn't wearing cowboy boots, either. Boots made a distinctive *clump-clump* sound on the wooden barn floor, whereas this was a sharper *click-click*. After spending years in L.A. courtrooms, Zach was familiar with that noise.

For some reason, this woman was wearing stilettos in the barn. He'd only been working here a few weeks, but he hadn't seen a woman in stilettos anywhere on the ranch, let alone in the barn. He was curious enough to stand up and take a look.

She was five stalls down and totally focused on Ink Spot, a black-and-white Paint who'd been kept in because of a recent sprain. Tall, slender and blond, the woman wore cream-colored dress pants and a lemon-yellow blouse, probably silk. The shoes that peeked out were also yellow and probably designer, judging from the rest of her ensemble—gold bangles on her wrists and gold hoop earrings. No doubt her short, sleek haircut was courtesy of a pricey salon.

She looked completely out of place here, except for the way she stroked the horse's nose. Whoever she was, she knew horses, which made her outfit even more puzzling. She touched the horse with great affection, reaching up to scratch under his forelock as she murmured softly.

Something about the way she communed with Ink Spot told Zach that she wasn't eager for company. He should just finish up his hammering and leave by the back door. On the other hand, she didn't look very happy. Zach knew all about unhappiness.

She'd been so motivated to seek the comfort of horses that she'd risked her expensive outfit by coming out to the barn. That meant she must be really upset, and by speaking to her, he could be intruding on a private moment. Plus, they didn't know each other.

He'd about decided to go back to his hammering when she turned toward him. "You're probably wondering what the hell I'm doin' here dressed like a Sunday school teacher."

No Sunday school teacher he'd ever known had looked like that, but the Southern accent clued him in. This had to be Jeannette Trenton from Virginia. Everybody on the ranch knew her story, even a new hire like Zach.

Last year she'd been Regan O'Connelli's fiancée, but then she'd cheated on him with Regan's best friend, Drake Brewster. Consequently Regan had left Virginia and moved to Wyoming. He was related by blood or marriage to quite a few Chance family members, and they'd all been incensed about Drake and Jeannette's betrayal.

Since then Regan had found a new love, Lily King. Then Drake had shown up to make amends, and in the process he'd become chummy with a local woman, Tracy Gibbons. Drake had also invited Jeannette to Wyoming so the three former friends could bury the hatchet. They seemed to have done that, but members of the Chance family weren't so quick to forgive and forget.

Zach could imagine why Jeannette had come out to be with the horses for a while. Even in his brief time here, he'd figured out that angering a Chance, or someone connected to a Chance, was a huge mistake. He gave both Drake and Jeannette props for braving that disapproval in order to repair their friendship with Regan.

So this was the woman at the heart of the controversy. He had no trouble picturing that, because she was stunning. Apparently she'd known that he'd been staring. Maybe she was used to men looking at her, because if she'd been attractive in profile, she was breathtaking full-on. Those green eyes were showstoppers, not to mention her kissable mouth.

He cleared his throat. "Um, I didn't mean to bother you. I heard you come in, and I thought maybe..." What? His mind went blank. Pretty embarrassing for someone who used to make his living as an entertainment lawyer, someone who'd dealt with A-list actors, directors and producers every day. She didn't have to know that, though. He wasn't that guy anymore.

"I was tryin' to help with the food for Regan and

Lily's engagement party, but…" She gestured to her blouse. "As you can see, kitchen duty is not my talent."

He walked closer. Yeah, now he noticed flecks of something that could be meringue or white frosting on the front of her blouse. "It sort of matches your pants."

That brought out a sad little smile. "You know, I told them that very thing, but they were all worried about the blouse, which I surely appreciated, but they don't have time to mess around with a klutz like me. I'd already dropped a bowl of chocolate chips. I thought I could frost that danged cake. I swear, how hard can that be? Turns out it's harder than it looks on TV."

He couldn't help smiling back. "Everything's harder than it looks on TV."

"Isn't that the God's truth? Anyway, I decided to make myself scarce and just naturally gravitated to the barn."

"I completely understand. You obviously know your way around horses."

"My folks raise them." She turned back to the horse. "Who is this, by the way?"

"Ink Spot. He's nursing a sprain, so he didn't get to go out."

"His bad luck, but my good luck. I wasn't thinkin' the horses would be out in the pasture, but of course they would be on a fine day like this. Back home they tend to bring them into the air-conditioning in the heat of the day." She stroked the gelding's neck. "And who would you be?"

Because she wasn't looking at him, he didn't immediately understand she was asking for his name. But he'd already supplied the horse's name, so she had to mean him. "I'm Zach. Zach Powell."

She continued to caress the horse. "I suppose you know who I am." Her version of *I* sounded more like *ah.*

"I didn't until I heard your accent."

She was quiet for a moment. "It's real strange, knowin' that people talk about you behind your back. Of course, people do that all the time. You just don't know it for sure. In this case, I do."

"For what it's worth, I have no stake in this situation. I started working here last month and I'm not related to any of the players." He could add that his law training predisposed him to remain impartial until he'd heard all sides of a story. But for now, he was just a cowhand, and that suited him fine.

"You're new here?" She glanced at him with a spark of interest in her eyes. "Where'd you come from?"

"California."

"Then I'm pleased to meet you, Zach Powell. I have to say you're the first person who hasn't looked at me with thinly disguised suspicion, like I might suddenly sprout horns and a tail. Well, I take that back. Sarah Chance seems willin' to suspend judgment, and her cook, Mary Lou, is friendly. But Regan's sisters…" She sighed.

"Not welcoming?"

"No, and I can't say as I blame them. I don't have a brother, or a sister, either, for that matter. But if I did, I'd probably behave exactly the same way. They're loyal and I admire that. I just…don't know what to do."

"Well…" Zach hesitated. He had some thoughts, but it wasn't his place to make suggestions.

Her gaze sharpened. "What? If you have ideas, speak up. I could use some advice."

"All right. You look great, but you don't exactly blend into the scenery."

"Don't think I don't know it." She glanced down at her outfit. "My mother taught me that wearin' nice clothes is respectful, plus I'd heard that the Jackson Hole area was filled with celebrities so I thought this ranch might be dress-for-dinner sophisticated. I should have asked Drake more questions before I flew out here." She swept a hand down her body. "Everything I packed is like this."

"And Drake didn't say anything once he found that out?"

"We haven't discussed my wardrobe choices. The poor man is so in love with Tracy he wouldn't notice if I ran around naked. Same thing with Regan."

Zach would certainly notice. Thanks to her comment, he was picturing that scenario in vivid detail. He tried to erase the image, but his libido wouldn't cooperate. He hadn't been involved with anyone for months and had thought he didn't miss sex all that much. Judging from the stirring in his groin, he'd missed it more than he'd realized.

To take his mind off the subject, he focused on a potential solution to her problem. "You need to go shopping."

"I think you're right, but I don't know the area. Where should I go?"

"Shoshone has a few shops, but if you want to get what you need, you'd better go to Jackson."

She took a deep breath. "Then I'll just head to Jackson, I guess. Do you recommend any particular stores? No, wait, never mind. I can figure it out. You've been a big help already, and I—"

"I get off at five. Give me time to shower and change, and I'll drive you up there. We can take my truck. Everything stays open late for the tourist trade."

Her shoulders sagged in relief. "That sounds fantastic, but are you sure it's not too much trouble?"

"No trouble at all. I could use a couple of things myself."

"Then I'll pay for gas."

He smiled. "Not necessary."

"No, seriously. And I'll buy dinner. It's the least I can do."

He started to argue with her. He hadn't dated since making this drastic change in his lifestyle. Previously he'd been the high roller who picked up the tab, and having her pay for gas and food felt weird. His wages at the Last Chance were a joke compared with what he used to make in Hollywood, but he'd invested well and didn't ever have to work again if he chose not to.

Unless he planned to explain that, though, he might want to keep his mouth shut and accept her offer. "Okay, thank you. That would be very nice."

"I'm staying at the Bunk and Grub. Do you know it?"

"Yep. Nice bed-and-breakfast down the road."

"It is. Very nice. At first I was in the cabin Drake rented, and he said I was welcome to it now that he's moved in with Tracy. But it's kind of remote, and I'm a city girl. I'm not all that brave when it comes to things like...well, grizzlies."

"Don't blame you. I'm really careful out at my campsite. I keep everything bears might want locked up tight inside the Airstream."

She blinked. "Campsite? You don't live in the bunkhouse?"

"Oh, they offered to put me there. But then I'd have to store the Airstream, and besides, I like living in it. So Jack gave me permission to park down beside the creek that runs through the property."

"Jack Chance?"

He laughed. "The one and only. A legend in his own time."

"So I hear. I haven't officially made his acquaintance. Do you get any electricity down there?"

"I have a little generator. Don't run it much. Mostly I cook over the campfire and I have a solar water setup outside for taking showers."

"Sounds primitive." But instead of looking appalled, which would make sense given her city-girl orientation, she seemed intrigued.

"It works for me." Then it occurred to him that he'd just painted a picture of *him* naked. From the gleam in her eyes, could she be enjoying the image of him standing under that solar shower? Hmm. "So how long will you be sticking around?" He was suddenly more interested in that.

Her jaw tightened. "I'm determined to stay until after the engagement party, no matter how unwelcome I may be." Then she clapped a hand over her mouth. "Did I just say that out loud?"

"You did, but you said it to the right person. I'm not here to judge. I'll bet socializing with this crowd is a bit uncomfortable for you."

"You don't know the half of it. But like I said, I can't blame them at all. I'll tough it out because I want to give Regan and Lily a big hug on their special day. That's important to me."

He wondered if Drake's new romance bothered her. She might have been hooked on the guy and now he'd moved on. "So the party's tomorrow night. Are you leaving Sunday?"

"I didn't want to run off like my danged tail was on fire, so the plan is to fly out Monday."

"I see." Not much time to get to know each other. That was sort of disappointing given that some mutual attraction seemed to be developing.

"And I need to get back to my job."

"Doing what?"

"I'm a lawyer."

"Is that so?" He should get an Academy Award for his casual response. Inside he was laughing his head off. He'd worked so hard to leave that profession behind, and now he was making goo-goo eyes at a member of the clan. The last person in the world he'd ever date would be another lawyer. "What's your specialty?"

"Do you need legal advice?"

"No."

"I ask because usually when I mention that I'm a lawyer people's eyes glaze over. But if they have a legal issue, then they want to know what kind of lawyer I am, either because they might hire me or, in some cases, they're after free advice."

"I know." Whoops. "I mean, I'll bet. But I don't need a lawyer." Not in any sense. "I was just curious. Anyway, you have to survive until Monday."

"I do, but I'm sure more appropriate clothes will help me with that. That's so obvious I can't believe I didn't think of it, although I wouldn't know where to go. The party's being held outside, so jeans would be good."

"And boots." Zach glanced down at her yellow shoes.

"Guess so. These aren't going to work for a barbeque." She lifted one foot to peer at the sole. There wasn't much surface area to the bottom of her stiletto, but the little that existed was dotted with smashed chocolate chips, dirt and bits of straw. "Good Lord." She groaned. "I probably tracked chocolate chips all over Sarah's hardwood floor on my way out."

"Probably."

"Worse yet, the housekeeper is one of Regan's sisters. Cassidy idolizes that brother of hers. She's already wantin' to snatch me bald-headed, and now she'll have to clean up my trail of chocolate. I'll have to go back inside and apologize to her. To all of them." She glanced up at Zach. "You must think I'm a total screwup, but I swear I'm not. At least not normally."

"I believe you."

"Do you?" She met his gaze. "I don't know why. I'm the woman who cheated on my fiancé with his best friend. Then I showed up here in designer clothes more suitable to a country club than a ranch, and obviously I made a mess of things in the kitchen." Her voice caught. "If that's not a description of a screwup, I don't know what is."

She seemed to be on the verge of tears and he considered pulling her into his arms and letting her have a good cry on his shoulder. She probably needed to release some of that tension that had her wound way too tight. But they'd just met, and he also sensed a Southern reserve in her. If he coaxed her into crying it out, she might be horribly embarrassed afterward.

Besides, if she were going back inside to apologize for the chocolate on the floor, she wouldn't want to have red, puffy eyes. He'd only known her a short time, but he could already tell she wouldn't want her vulnerability made public. Unfortunately, her natural reserve might be working against her, too.

So he settled on words of encouragement to shore her up instead of physical contact that would make her lose her cool. "You can't be a total screwup. You flew out here and made peace with your ex. That took diplomacy and guts. Even though you know nothing about cooking, you volunteered to help prepare the food for tomorrow's party while working with women who aren't all in your corner. That takes nerves of steel. I'm just a bystander to this drama, but from my perspective, you're pretty damned incredible."

She stared at him for a long time, her eyes growing suspiciously bright. Then she sniffed and used her thumbs to flick away the moisture gathering on her lower lashes. "Thank you. You can't know how much that means to me."

"Oh, I have some idea. I'm a recovering perfectionist."

Her smile trembled. "I'm just a plain old perfectionist. Maybe on the drive to Jackson you can tell me how to get rid of that tendency because it's a royal pain in the ass."

"I hate to be the bearer of bad news, but you never get rid of it."

"That is bad news."

"But you might be able to cut it down to size."

"Then I want to know how to do that." She held out her hand. "Until tonight. I'm looking forward to it."

"Me, too." He clasped her hand and his adrenaline spiked. Her grip was firm but her skin was petal-soft. He forced himself to let go when all he wanted to do was draw her closer…and closer yet.

Awareness flashed in her green eyes. "See you later, Zach Powell." Turning abruptly, she walked out of the barn without looking back.

He was grateful for that, because he couldn't seem to move. He stood there like a fool and watched until she was out of sight. His visceral reaction to her had him by the throat, or more accurately, by the gonads.

But she didn't need a lover right now. She needed a

friend. Even if she had been in the market for a lover, she worked in the profession he'd vowed to avoid. So he'd help her shop, share a nice dinner and that would be that.

2

ALTHOUGH IT WASN'T quite five-thirty, Jeannette came downstairs to wait for Zach in the Bunk and Grub's parlor. Usually someone was in there reading or knitting or texting, but the room was empty. Then she remembered that the other guests were probably gathering on the back porch for the B and B's scheduled happy hour.

She'd attended that event the previous night and had enjoyed herself until she'd received a text from work. Then she'd gone back to her room so she could straighten out an issue at the office, and by the time she'd finished, happy hour had ended. The porch had been deserted.

For a little while, though, she'd been a welcome part of a social occasion. The guests were all from someplace else so no one knew that she was persona non grata in Shoshone. She could go back there now, reconnect with those nice people and have some wine while she waited for Zach. The young woman at the reception desk near the front door could come and get her when he arrived.

But even though that was a pleasant idea, she'd rather stay here and watch for him. She didn't care if she looked eager for the trip to Jackson and the chance to be with him again. She *was* eager. He was her new friend.

In addition to that, he was a beautiful man. At first glance she'd noticed his broad shoulders and lean hips. She'd registered his confident stance. But when he'd moved closer she'd been captivated by the expression in his cloud-gray eyes. His Stetson had shaded his face slightly, but shade couldn't mute the intelligence and compassion in those eyes.

Sure, male appreciation had flickered in his gaze. That was fine. She wouldn't complain about getting that look, which hadn't been sleazy in the least. But it was his sincere compliment that had blown her away. His empathy for her situation was greater than she'd felt from anyone since she'd arrived. Much as she understood everyone's reaction to her, she'd desperately needed someone like Zach to show up.

Bolstered by his understanding and his praise of her courage, she'd managed to walk back into the ranch house with her head high. She'd apologized for her clumsiness and inexperience in the kitchen. She'd apologized specifically to Cassidy for the chocolate smeared on the hardwood floors in both the hall and the living room.

Had it still been there, she would have gotten down on her hands and knees and cleaned it up herself. But the chocolate had been gone—no doubt someone had seen the chaos she'd left in her wake and reported it to Cassidy.

Jeannette didn't want to think about the comments that must have flown around as the floor was cleaned. Yet when she'd come back into the kitchen, everyone had been perfectly nice to her, including Cassidy. She gave them all credit for that.

But there hadn't been a lot of warmth coming her way, and she'd caught a few exchanged glances that had made her stomach twist. Maybe if she'd gotten to know them prior to the Christmas Eve drama, this situation wouldn't be so awkward. But during her engagement to Regan, she'd only met his parents. There hadn't been time to fly out to Jackson Hole to see his sisters.

Now they were obviously only being nice for Regan's sake, which was admirable. But if they could somehow manage to see past her awful mistake and get to know and like her as a person… No, that was probably asking way too much under the circumstances. She couldn't help longing for it, though.

Before she'd left the kitchen, she'd mentioned the clothes issue and had acknowledged that hers weren't suited to the weekend's activities. She'd told them about the planned shopping trip with Zach, which had caused a few more exchanged glances.

She hoped that eighteen-year-old Cassidy didn't have a crush on Zach. Jeannette didn't want her to be jealous on top of everything else. Cassidy was the only single woman on the ranch, but Zach was too old for her. Jeannette wasn't good with ages, but the crinkles at the corners of his amazing eyes put him at somewhere past thirty.

And that made him the perfect age for her, since she'd just hit the big three-oh this year. Not that she had any business comparing ages as if they had a future together. He seemed very happy to be a ranch hand in Wyoming living in his Airstream. She was very happy as an attorney in Virginia.

But that hadn't kept her from fantasizing about him

taking his solar shower in front of God and everybody. Or replaying his kind words to her right before she'd left the barn. In her fantasy they ended the moment with a kiss instead of a civilized handshake.

She was intensely grateful for his encouragement and help, and their relationship would probably only be a platonic one, but he was very handsome. She'd been doing penance for her sins ever since she and Drake had admitted they weren't right for each other. She hadn't gone on a date since, which had been almost eight months.

Maybe she could be forgiven for having inappropriate thoughts about Zach. She wondered if his sensitive behavior had nudged her libido because it telegraphed his potential as a wonderful lover. It was a logical conclusion.

Any man who'd take the time to listen to a woman's troubles and offer to help her solve them would likely also be committed to giving his sexual partner pleasure. He would employ all the skills he possessed in that endeavor. He wouldn't rest until she was utterly and completely satisfied.

Oh, Lord. That concept made her hot. She got up from the sofa and began to pace the small parlor. She'd better rein in her fantasies before he arrived because a man like him would sense her reaction. That would be plain embarrassing.

The receptionist, a slim brunette, left her desk and walked into the parlor. "Happy hour is about to start," she said. "Would you like a glass of wine while you wait? I can bring it to you."

"No, thanks. But that's very sweet." Jeannette estimated the girl was about Cassidy's age and conscientious about her job.

"I like your outfit."

"Thank you." Jeannette had chosen the least dressy combination she'd brought, but even so the ankle pants were beige linen and the black blouse was silk. At least she'd tied the shirttails at the waist in a faux casual way. Her black Ferragamo mules added a good three inches to her height. She'd left off the bangle bracelets and wore the smallest gold hoops she owned. "I'm afraid my clothes don't fit in very well, though."

"They would if you were staying in Jackson. It's more cosmopolitan there. Are you sure you wouldn't like some wine? When Pam's not here, it's my job to make sure the guests are happy."

"She's not?" Jeannette had thought the B and B owner would be on the back porch serving drinks as she had the night before.

"She's spending the night with her husband. Good thing I'm over twenty-one so I can serve liquor." The girl smiled.

"Where's her husband?" Vaguely Jeannette remembered a ring on Pam Mulholland's left hand, but she hadn't seen a husband around.

"Over at the Last Chance. He's the foreman there. Emmett Sterling."

"I did not know about that."

"Some people think it's strange because she didn't take his name and they each kept their own place, but I think it's cool. Well, I'd better head back there before they get restless." With a grin, she whirled around and left the parlor.

No sooner had she disappeared than Zach walked in the front door. For a brief moment he paused to gaze at her, and the air between them seemed to crackle. Damn, he looked good—clean white Western shirt, snug jeans, polished boots and a light gray Stetson pulled low over his eyes.

She took a deep breath and drew in the spicy scent of his cologne. A little spot of dried blood on his chin indicated that he'd nicked himself while shaving. How endearing. Maybe he was a little bit excited about this shopping excursion, too.

He cleared his throat. "You look great."

"For a greenhorn." She picked up her black cloth shoulder bag from the sofa.

"No, just plain great." He walked into the parlor. "I almost hate to take you shopping for jeans when what you have on suits you so well."

"But as we discussed, it's impractical for a ranch barbeque. And although no one's offered to take me out on a horse, I couldn't ride like this, either. Besides…I want to fit in."

"Then let's go." He ushered her through the front door and down the sidewalk to his truck, which turned out to be muscular, black and dusty. "I would apologize for the state of my truck, but it's always like this. Black is the wrong color if you live at the end of a dirt road."

"But aren't dirt roads inevitable if you work on a ranch?"

"As it turns out, yes. I didn't take that into consideration when I bought this baby." He walked with her to the passenger side and opened the door. "At least the inside's clean."

"Nice." The smell of new leather greeted her as she climbed in and buckled up. The seat rivaled the comfort of her Mercedes back home. He'd splurged on this vehicle, and recently, too. She didn't know how much ranch hands made these days, but the job must pay better than she thought or maybe he'd come in to some money. Or he could be up to his ears in debt.

He settled himself behind the wheel, closed his door and started the engine. The truck's deep-throated rumble was decidedly masculine. So was the man sitting next to her, and his cologne tantalized her even more in the enclosed space of the air-conditioned cab.

She tried to remember the last time she'd ridden in a truck. Even though her parents raised horses, the valuable Thoroughbreds were always transported by professionals in semis. Her family drove luxury cars. Even if she had been a passenger in a pickup a time or two, she certainly hadn't been chauffeured by a Stetson-wearing cowboy.

When she'd imagined this trip to Jackson, she hadn't anticipated that Zach's truck would provide a sensually rewarding experience. She'd assumed he'd have an ordinary truck, maybe one with some rattles and worn upholstery. Instead they cruised down the highway effortlessly.

He glanced at her. "How did things go in the house when you went back?"

"Fine. No one's ever been rude to me, but I can tell they're only being nice because they're decent people and they love Regan. So do I, but I doubt they'd believe me if I said so."

He was quiet for a moment. "You're still in love with him?"

"Not *in* love, but I love him as a friend."

"Oh." He didn't sound convinced. "I'm not sure I understand how that works."

"You've never had a close woman friend, someone you loved but weren't in love with?"

"I'd have to think about that. My close relationships

with women always seem to have a sexual undertone. Then when we act on that, we have an affair, and after it ends, we're usually not that close anymore."

She wasn't surprised that he ended up in bed with his women friends. One look at his classic profile as he drove this massive truck got her engines running. His hair was a soft brown with enough curl to curve around his ears. She even liked the shape of those ears. Women would naturally want to get their hands on this guy.

"That's the way it often goes," she said. "I'm the last person to brag about my relationship skills. I used to be so proud of my situation with Regan and Drake. I had love and sex with Regan and cherished Drake as a close friend. But a bottle of wine and general dissatisfaction with the status quo ruined everything."

"If you could go back and change that, would you?"

"Good question." She settled into her comfy leather seat. "If you'd asked me that last January, I would have said yes, in a heartbeat. But now I realize the status quo wasn't right, and goin' to bed with Drake was probably my subconscious effort to change it. Regan and I didn't have the bone-deep passion and commitment that would carry us through fifty or sixty years of marriage."

"Did you have it with Drake?"

"God, no!" She laughed at the thought. Talking about this with someone who wouldn't judge was a huge relief. "He had his own reasons for shaking things up, but an undying love for me wasn't one of them."

"He told you that?"

"More or less. I admitted the same thing to him. We were a sorry pair, all right. I should have broken up with Regan instead of getting smashed and having sex with his best friend. But wedding plans have a life of their own. My parents had made a sizable, nonrefundable down payment on the venue. The wedding party had been chosen, and the dresses and tuxes had been ordered."

"You felt trapped."

"Yes." She heard something in his voice. "From the way you said that, I'm guessing you know what that's like."

"Absolutely."

"Did you almost marry the wrong person, too?" That would explain his empathetic response.

"Nope. But I know what it feels like to be going down a road and realize it's the wrong one, but you can't get a handle on how to change it."

"How so?"

He smiled. "Not now. I want to hear your story."

She made a note to ask later. "There's not much more to tell. Drake and I caused a scandal. My folks pretend they've forgiven me, but they haven't. I think Regan has, though. And Drake, Regan and I are *almost* back to normal. I wish Regan's extended family could let it go, but…they may not. I'll have to live with that."

"I predict they'll warm up."

"If I wear different clothes?"

"Won't hurt."

"I found out something right before you picked me up. I thought by staying at the Bunk and Grub, I'd escaped the Chance family's influence."

He looked over at her. "You didn't know that Pam was married to Emmett?"

"Why would I? They don't even live together!"

"Which is apparently how they like it. They married late in life, so they each need their space, except for… well, the obvious."

"Right." And here they were focusing once again

on the topic of sex. The cab was roomy, but not so big that she didn't feel his energy across the console. He was a potent guy.

"Pam is also Nick Chance's aunt."

"She is?" Jeannette sighed. "And Regan joined Nick's veterinary practice when he moved out here, so that explains why Pam has been friendly and polite, but never warm. I thought she was simply being professional, but no, she's part of Team Chance. Oh, well."

"What about Drake? You shouldn't be dealing with this alone. Is he getting the cold shoulder, too?"

"Oh, probably to some extent, but he's been here longer, and now he's involved with Tracy, who's very popular, I gather. They may be giving him a pass because Tracy likes him." Her phone chirped, indicating she had a text. "Will you excuse me a minute? I should get that. It might be from work."

"On a Friday night?"

"Oh, yeah. My assistant is dedicated."

"By all means, see what's up."

Jeannette checked her phone, hoping for good news from Erin, her paralegal assistant. Instead Erin confirmed that they had a big hole in their research on the current case. She promised to work through the weekend to plug that hole, which made Jeannette feel guilty. She should be there helping Erin dig up the information they needed to build a solid defense.

But she wasn't there, and so all she could do was text her sincere thanks for Erin's effort. With a sigh, she put her phone back in her purse. Maybe she should change her flight and go back on Sunday, after all.

"Problems?"

"I was afraid we hadn't thoroughly researched a contract dispute, and sure enough, we haven't. The client expects an open-and-shut case, but at this point, there's no guarantee that we'll prevail."

"Tell me about it."

"Why?"

"I might be able to help."

She was touched, but if he made his living as a cowhand, he wouldn't be of much use in this capacity. She didn't want to insult him, though. "I can describe the case, and I appreciate your offer, but I'm not sure that you—"

"I may not be able to help considering that you're in Virginia and every state is different. But it's worth a shot. Contract law has similarities all over the country."

"Yes, but I still don't think—"

"Look, nobody besides Jack knows this, and I'd rather not broadcast it if you don't mind, but...I was an entertainment lawyer in Hollywood for thirteen years. Contract law is my specialty."

She stared at him. "Well, that sure as hell explains this fancy truck."

3

JEANNETTE OUTLINED THE CASE, which involved a contract for the sale of a registered Thoroughbred foal. Even though he'd never dealt with the intricacies of Thoroughbred racing, he knew contract law. He grasped the essentials fairly quickly and they debated the merits of the case all the way to Jackson.

He'd thought his interest in contract law was dead. Maybe not. The lively discussion with Jeannette was more fun than it should have been if he'd abandoned his profession. In his heart he knew he hadn't totally given up on practicing law.

But his job at the Last Chance satisfied something basic in his nature. He loved working with the horses, repairing things around the ranch, even shoveling shit. The idea of going back to a desk job didn't appeal to him at all.

Before they'd reached the outskirts of Jackson, Jeannette had texted several suggestions to her assistant, Erin, and had received an enthusiastic response. Jeannette laughed and turned to Zach. "She wants to know if I've stumbled upon a hidden law library up in the hinterlands."

He couldn't pretend that wasn't gratifying. "Just tell her you met a burned-out lawyer who still has a few tricks up his sleeve. Maybe none of them will pan out, either. You have a complicated deal there."

Jeannette sent the message and got back an instant reply. "She says I should lasso you and bring you back to Virginia as…" She stopped.

"As what?" Luck was with him and he found a parking space on the square near the Western-wear store. He pulled into it.

"Never mind."

"No fair." He shut off the engine and turned to her. "What did she say?"

Even at this hour, the summer sky was bright, so her blush was easy to see. "As my, um, love slave."

He laughed. "How did she come up with that? I thought we were talking about lawyerly things."

"I might have said that I met a sexy burned-out lawyer."

"Oh, yeah?" More and more, he regretted that she was leaving on Monday.

"You know you are, Zach. I mean, look at this truck. It oozes testosterone."

"Well, that's good. A manly truck was what I was going for. I just didn't figure on the dust." He surveyed the crowded square. "Which will it be, food or shopping?"

"Food. I'll shop better on a full stomach. Besides, now that I know about your background, I have millions of questions about why you're here and not there."

"It's simple."

"I doubt it."

He opened his door. "I promise you it is, but now that you know I have resources, will you let me buy dinner?"

"Absolutely not. If your suggestions work, then you saved my bacon on this case."

"Don't jump to any conclusions. I might have sent you and your assistant down the wrong bunny trail."

"Or not. Assuming you set us on the right track, I owe you way more than a dinner."

"Oh?" He couldn't resist teasing her. After all, she was the one who'd called him sexy. "And what exactly did you have in mind that would repay that enormous debt?"

She met his gaze with a deadpan expression. "My eternal gratitude."

"*Damn*. Guess I'm not quite sexy enough, even driving this big-ass truck."

"Hold on." Her green eyes danced with mischief. "You don't know what my eternal gratitude might inspire me to do."

Lust arrowed through him and centered in his crotch. He took a steadying breath. "Good point. Guess I'd better take your eternal gratitude for now and see how things work out. Let's find some food."

Twenty minutes later they were finally seated in a little Italian restaurant a block off the main square. It was the only place that didn't have a two-hour wait. He should have anticipated that Jackson would be hopping on a Friday night in August, which was still officially tourist season. At least a table for two was easier to snag than if they'd had a larger party.

He ordered a bottle of Chianti and poured them each a full glass. They were on the far side of the square from the Western-wear store and the truck. By the time they ate, walked back around the square and shopped for her clothes, he'd be fine to drive.

Picking up his glass, he raised it in her direction. "Here's to settling your case in your client's favor."

"I'll drink to that." She touched her glass to his and took a long swallow.

He watched her slender throat move, forgetting to drink his wine. All he could think about was pressing his mouth to that ivory skin and driving her wild with his kisses. She'd told her assistant he was sexy. He really wanted to prove that assumption.

"Zach? Are you okay?"

He snapped out of his sexual daze. "Great. Just great."

"You haven't touched your wine."

"I was waiting for you."

"Am I the taste tester? If I keel over, you'll know not to drink it?"

"No, I… Ah, to hell with it. You're beautiful, Jeannette. I've been trying to ignore that, but then you went and told your assistant that I'm sexy. That sort of changed the game for me."

She put down her wine and gazed at him across the small table. "Okay, I'll admit that you fascinate me, especially now that I know you had this whole other life before becoming a cowboy. What happened? Why did you give it up?"

"If I tell you that, I'm liable to lose some of my sexy quotient."

That made her laugh. "I doubt it. Come on. We have time before our meal arrives, and I really want to know."

He sighed. "Okay, might as well ruin my image sooner than later. I'd been dissatisfied for quite a while, although I wouldn't admit it to myself. Couldn't see myself walking away from all that money."

"That's understandable."

"Nice try. But it's not understandable when you figure I'd socked away enough to live comfortably for the rest of my life."

Her eyes widened.

"*Please* don't be impressed."

"I'll be impressed if I want to."

"No, seriously, don't be. You can make crazy money in Hollywood. But it's a hectic life and your values can easily get skewed."

"Sure, for the stars, but—"

"For anyone working in the business. I wasn't morally bankrupt, at least not completely, but I was the contract lawyer for someone who was. He was a horse's ass who never showed up at the set on time or else he'd be drunk, stoned or both. The studio finally fired him, but I got him the money, anyway. Millions. He sent me a case of Dom Pérignon and a pricey call girl."

"Wow."

"For the record, I kept the champagne but sent the call girl home."

"You must be a damned good lawyer."

"Used to be. Past tense."

"That seems like a shame." She picked up her wine and gazed at him over the rim of the glass. "All that education and experience, going to waste."

"You're not the first person to mention that."

"I mean, sure, I can understand wanting to leave L.A. if you were burned out from that lifestyle, but you could set up shop somewhere else, especially if you have savings."

"Just can't get excited about doing that."

"So you became a ranch hand, instead. Why?"

He sipped his wine as he thought how to answer without sounding starry-eyed. "I've been around Hollywood enough to know that the cowboy fantasy is a myth created by books and movies. But it's a good myth, and it has some basis in fact."

"Maybe it does." Her green gaze became thoughtful. "Regan once said the guys he met at the Last Chance lived up to the image of what a cowboy should be—brave, honest, protective. I'm not surprised he's happy to be part of that mystique. He's all of those things." Regret shone in her eyes. "He didn't deserve—"

"Hey." He leaned toward her. "He didn't deserve ending up with the wrong person, either. Because of your actions, he didn't. I propose a moratorium on guilt, at least for tonight."

"Okay, but that goes for you, too. I hope you're not still feeling guilty about the money you won for that actor."

He thought about that. "I am, but you're right. I need to lose the guilt. It's over. Can't do anything about it now."

"Right."

"Anyway, the reason I wanted to become a ranch hand is that cowboys are considered heroic, and I wanted to feel like that." He shrugged. "Stupid, huh?"

She shook her head. "No," she said softly. "Sweet."

"Ugh. No man wants to be called sweet. The sweet guy is the best friend of the dude who gets the girl. Everybody who watches movies knows that."

"That depends. Sometimes the sweet guy has a very good chance of gettin' the girl."

"He does?" Zach tried to read her expression to see if she was teasing him or not. The light had faded outside and the restaurant was lit by little candles that cast shadows everywhere.

"I'd say so." She drained her wineglass and put it

down carefully on the table. "I've been under a lot of stress lately, but bein' with you is the most fun I've had in a long, long time."

"Then I'm glad I suggested this."

"Life's not so fun when you don't like yourself very much. Sometimes I don't know if people really are disapproving of me or if I'm projecting my own feelings onto them. But I've never sensed disapproval from you."

"Like I said, it's not my place to judge."

"Yes, but not judging is a neutral position. You go beyond that to offer support to the person with difficulties—namely, me."

"Maybe because I know what it's like to live with regrets, especially for those of us who expect a lot of ourselves."

She took a deep breath. "It *sucks*."

"Yeah."

She regarded him silently for a moment. "I've only known you for a little while, but I think we have a lot in common. The lawyer thing took me by surprise, but now it makes even more sense that we click."

"Yeah." He grimaced. "Rotten timing for two people to click."

"Tell me about it."

He looked into her eyes, and his breath caught as he recognized longing…and heat. Oh, yeah, lust simmered just beneath the surface, and he responded, despite himself. A wise man would look away, pick up his wineglass, change the topic.

But he'd been a fool for less important things. His heart pumped faster. "Or maybe it's the perfect time." He reached across the table and took her hand. She sucked in a breath. Clasping her hand between both of his, he massaged her soft skin. "If you could have anything you wanted right now, what would it be?"

"Oh, Zach. Don't ask me that."

"I am asking. Tell me."

She took a shaky breath. "I would love…a break from all of this drama…with someone who's not a part of it."

"Like me." His body warmed, tightened.

"Yes, but—"

"I can do that. Let me give you that tonight."

Her eyes glowed with excitement for a brief second, and then she closed them and shook her head. "I don't want to make another mistake."

"How can it be a mistake? You're free. I'm free. No one ever has to know."

She opened her eyes and met his gaze.

"This is between you and me." He tightened his grip on her hand. "It's our business. Nobody else's. I'm a lawyer. I understand confidentiality."

Her smile trembled. "I'm sure you do." She sounded breathless.

"Just say yes and leave the rest to me."

"I'm so tempted…."

"Let yourself be tempted. Let yourself go."

She stared at him for a long time as a blush crept over her cheeks. "Okay."

"Okay." Now he was starting to shake. "Are you still hungry?"

"No." She swallowed. "To be honest, I haven't wanted a man this much in…I don't know how long."

"Then let's get—" Belatedly he remembered the original reason for this trip. "Wait. You still need those clothes."

"I'll be a power shopper."

"Sounds good. Let's head out." He reluctantly let go of her hand and signaled for the waitress.

She hurried over. "Your order should be ready any minute. We're a little backed up in the kitchen."

"Actually, we're going to have to leave."

"I can have it packaged to go, then."

"Fine." He hadn't figured out the details of the evening yet, so maybe that would work.

"Just give me a few more minutes." The waitress left.

Jeannette scooted back her chair. "I have an idea. You wait for our dinner and the check and I'll head on over to the Western-wear store you pointed out. No need to bore you with the shopping."

He couldn't imagine being bored as long as she was around. But she was right about conserving time. "All right."

She reached for her purse. "Dinner's still on me, so I'll just—"

"You will *not* leave money for the bill."

She paused in the middle of digging for her wallet and gave him a tiny smile. "Okay, I won't. And FYI, your take-charge attitude is very sexy."

Lust slammed into him so hard it was a wonder he didn't gasp out loud. Getting through the shopping would be tough, but if they didn't handle that now, they never would.

"Meet you at the store."

"See you then." The minute she walked away from the table he pulled out his phone. He'd made the transition from mover and shaker to good ol' boy, but that didn't mean he'd forgotten how a mover and shaker handled situations like this. If Jeannette liked his take-charge attitude, she was gonna love the idea he'd just come up with.

Because of the number of tourists in town, he had to make several calls, but within ten minutes he'd booked a luxury suite at one of Jackson's finest hotels. He hadn't experienced that brand of pampering since leaving L.A. and he hadn't missed it at all. But then, he hadn't entertained a woman since then, either.

When the waitress arrived with their takeout order, he paid for the meal they wouldn't be eating and returned the bag with his apologies. He gave her an extra large tip and hoped she'd find a home for that food. He wasn't going to haul doggie bags into a five-star hotel with excellent room service.

By the time he left the restaurant and started toward the clothing store, he was feeling in control of the proceedings. A gorgeous woman had agreed to spend the night with him and that was reason to celebrate.

Oh, hell. He stepped to the edge of the sidewalk so he wouldn't block traffic and pulled out his phone again, doing a quick web search. Fortunately there was a drugstore a couple of blocks away. He made the journey in record time and tossed the small bag into the truck before heading back toward the Western-wear store.

Jeannette was checking out when he walked in. She glanced up. "Hi. I was beginning to think I'd lost you."

"Not a chance."

She handed her credit card to the clerk. "What took so long?"

"I'll tell you on the way." He joined her at the checkout counter. "Find everything?" Looked like it, judging from two large bags sitting there.

"I did."

"Boots?"

"Yep."

"Hat?"

"I love my hat. It's white straw. I think you'll like it." She signed the credit-card slip and tucked the receipt in the bag. "Ready?"

"More than you know." He was on fire for her. "I'll take those bags."

"Thank you." She hesitated. "So now…"

"You said you liked my take-charge attitude."

"I do."

"So I've taken charge."

4

JEANNETTE FELT ENERGY pouring from Zach as he helped her into the truck. Then he took her bags and stowed them in the covered truck bed. Finally he climbed into the driver's seat and closed the door.

But instead of buckling himself in, he laid his hat on the dashboard, turned toward her and unfastened her seat belt.

She gasped at the unexpected move. "Aren't we leavin'?" She thought he was as eager to get on with the evening as she was.

"In a minute." He cupped her cheek in one large hand. "I need to do something first."

She looked into his eyes, warm with emotion. He planned to kiss her, and how she longed for that. But she was afraid once they started kissing, they would never stop. "Maybe we shouldn't…" She lost track of what she'd meant to say as he stroked his thumb gently over her cheekbone. His touch was heaven.

"Yes, we should. We're about to become lovers, but we haven't even kissed."

"Except we're in the middle of the town square."

"I know." He leaned closer. "We'll be fine."

"What if we get carried away?"

The corners of his beautiful mouth tilted. "*I* won't."

"You might. I'm a pretty awesome kisser."

"Prove it."

She never could resist a challenge. She craved the feel of those sculpted lips on hers even if they were taking a risk making out in a public place. "All right." She grasped his head in both hands. His hair was exactly as soft and silky as she'd imagined. "Come here, you."

He was extremely obliging. In the very next second he covered her mouth with his. Too late, she discovered that she might be the one who would get carried away. She was in the presence of a master.

From that first velvet contact, he was fully in charge. Her world narrowed to the pressure of his lips, the glide of his tongue, the warmth of his breath. His kiss tasted like all the decadent pleasures she'd dreamed of having with a man and had never quite had.

And she wanted those promised pleasures. Her body ached for them. She tried to get closer and came up against the console. She moaned in frustration and writhed against the supple leather of the seat. She needed…more.

Slowly, with obvious reluctance, he eased away. But then he returned to nibble and lick as if he couldn't make himself abandon her mouth. She didn't want him to, either.

"We have to go," he murmured between quick kisses.

"Not yet." She pulled him back for another deep, passionate round that left her panties wet and her heart racing.

When he finally broke away, he was breathing hard. "We really have to go."

"I know, but..." She tried to tug him down again. "One more for the road."

He resisted her efforts and loosened her grip. "Buckle up. We're getting out of here."

With a sigh, she leaned back and buckled herself in as instructed.

"You were right, by the way. You're a pretty awesome kisser." He started the truck, checked his mirrors and backed out of the parking space.

"Ditto. Um, I suspect you have everything figured out, but where are we going?"

"I booked us a room." He said it casually as he navigated through traffic with practiced ease.

She shivered in excitement. "I should help you pay for—"

"Don't even think about it."

"Okay." She wanted to ask where this room was, but figured he wanted to surprise her. Considering his previous job and the luxury of his truck, she didn't think they'd end up at the cheap sleep.

Watching him drive the huge truck with quiet confidence was very arousing, as was this latest gesture of his. She'd made a veiled request for a sexy time-out, and he'd handled the details. In doing that, he'd increased his hotness by at least a thousand percent.

"That's what took me so long while you were shopping. Well, that and my own shopping."

"Right." She had trouble making casual conversation when her body was humming with anticipation, but she gave it her best effort. "You said you had to pick up a few things, but I thought you meant clothes from the Western-wear store."

"Not clothes."

"Then what...? *Oh*." The electricity arcing between

them was almost visible. "Is there anything you haven't thought of?"

"You'll have to do without makeup in the morning."

In the morning. They'd make love all night. She had trouble sitting still. "That's what you think." She always kept an emergency makeup kit in her shoulder bag.

Judging from the looks of the entrance where he turned in, they were staying in a luxury resort. "You sure know how to dazzle a girl." If she sounded a little breathless, she figured she had cause.

"I'm under a time constraint. If I don't dazzle you now, I might never get a chance."

"Trust me, you're way up there on the dazzle meter."

"Good to know." He pulled under the portico for valet parking.

While a doorman helped her out of the truck, Zach retrieved her shopping bags from the back. She'd never checked into a hotel with only two shopping bags, but Zach treated the experience calmly, as if he did it all the time. She suspected he was giving her a glimpse of the L.A. lawyer he used to be.

He might be used to swanky one-nighters, but she wasn't. She'd certainly stayed in plenty of hotels like this, though. Her parents wouldn't accept anything less when they traveled.

But tonight she was checking in with a guy wearing jeans, boots and a Stetson. He was an irresistible combination of sophistication and down-home earthiness. His assumption that this was all perfectly normal made her wonder about his past.

Maybe she'd ask him. Then again, maybe she wouldn't. It didn't matter. This was one night, not the start of something significant.

Once she and Zach stepped into the glittering elevator, he transferred both shopping bags to one hand so he could pull her close for a quick kiss. "Is this working for you?"

"If you mean am I impressed out of my mind, yes, it's workin' for me."

"Good." He gazed down at her as the elevator kept climbing. "In case I forget to say it, thank you for deciding you'd like to spend the night with me."

"You're welcome, but I have the feeling I'll be the one feeling thankful when this is all over." The elevator pinged to a stop and she noticed they were on the top floor. "You rented the *penthouse?*"

"It was all they had."

"Zach!" She stepped out of the elevator and her wedge heels sank into thick carpet. Ahead of her, double doors stood open and she walked into a living area furnished in sleek leather and polished wood. The lamps may have been on a dimmer switch since the light was muted and atmospheric. Floor-to-ceiling windows looked out on the lights of Jackson and shadowy mountains in the distance. "This must have cost a fortune."

"I don't care."

She glanced at a wet bar on the far side of the room. Champagne sat in an ice bucket on the granite counter, along with two crystal flutes and an elegantly arranged cheese-and-fruit platter. She turned back to him. "Seems a shame it's only for one night," she said softly.

He dropped the bags at his feet and sent his hat twirling toward a lamp. It landed precisely on the finial. He walked toward her, his gaze intent. "Then we'd better make the most of it."

If she'd been prone to swooning, she might have done it then. No man had ever treated her like this, as if she were everything he ever wanted, as if every moment they were together was more precious than his next breath. Such a fantasy couldn't last, of course, but it might hold up for a few hours. Then she'd have her unspoiled memory to relive as she reentered the real world.

She spread her arms. "I'm yours for the night. What do you want to do first?"

He laughed. "If you have to ask, then you haven't been paying attention."

"I don't have to ask." If he could act with flair, so could she. "Stop right there."

He paused. "I had in mind something involving bodily contact."

"Me, too, but let's build up to it."

"I've been doing that ever since you agreed with me in the restaurant that this is the perfect time. Before that, if I'm being honest. When you came into the barn this morning you mentioned that Regan and Drake wouldn't notice if you ran around naked."

"I guess I said something like that."

"You said exactly that, and immediately I pictured you that way."

The luxurious setting, the stress of the past eight months and the gorgeous man standing before her made for an electric combination. She was ready to kick over the traces. "Then let me make that picture a reality, cowboy."

He started forward. "I can help."

"No." She held up her hand to stop him. "You'll get the full effect if you stay where you are and watch."

He swallowed and clenched his fists, as if he had to do that to control himself. "Okay."

Knowing how much he wanted to touch her gave her courage to put on a show for him. She'd never felt inclined to do that for a man. But Zach, with his classy ideas and his passionate kisses, inspired her to new heights of sensuality.

Standing in the living room of this expensive suite made the adventure even more exotic. She wasn't in a bedroom doing this, but in an elegant living area with floor-to-ceiling windows. They were too high up for anyone to see in, but stripping down here felt much more risqué than if she were in a smaller room with the drapes closed.

She started by untying her shirttails. She didn't rush it, either. From there she unfastened the mother-of-pearl buttons down the front. Although she'd had the blouse for a long time, she'd never appreciated the sensuality of sliding those buttons free, one by one.

Zach's chest rose and fell more rapidly with each button. When at last she slipped the blouse from her shoulders and let it drift to the carpet, he moaned. That sound caused her nipples to tighten.

Instinct made her touch herself through her black lace bra. She stroked in a circular motion and watched his eyes darken to the color of storm clouds as he focused on her lazy caress. Then she cupped her breasts and in one dramatic gesture, opened the front clasp and shrugged out of the garment. It, too, fell to the floor at her feet.

The sound of his ragged breathing filled the silence, but he stayed where he was, muscles rigid and hands fisted at his sides. The material of his fly strained over his growing erection, and his gaze was so very hot.

She'd never felt so powerful in her life. She nudged off her shoes and unbuttoned her pants. Her hands trembled, not from nervousness, but from the adrenaline rush of knowing she was driving Zach crazy.

She was no expert at this striptease routine, but it

didn't matter. For one night she could do anything and be anything she wanted. Just as he'd said in the restaurant, it was their business. Nobody else's. That kind of freedom was a whole new experience for her, but she was catching on fast.

Peeling down her pants, she eventually kicked them aside and stood before him wearing only a tiny scrap of black lace. His attention was riveted on that lacy triangle. She knew he wanted it off, but she had other ideas.

She'd never done this, either. But she'd never have a better reason than now, in this luxury suite with this fascinating man who was almost a stranger. She slipped her hand inside her panties.

Zach sucked in a breath.

"I won't make myself come." She hardly recognized her own voice. It was low and sultry, the voice of a temptress. "I'll let you do that."

"Please." He sounded desperate.

She continued to fondle herself. "Tell me what you want."

"You know." The words came out tight and hard.

"Tell me."

"I want to put my mouth where your hand is. I want to make you come. God, Jeannette…"

"That could be nice."

His jaw tightened. "I promise it will be."

She withdrew her hand and deliberately licked her fingers. "Will I get to return the favor?"

He groaned. "*Yes*, so now can I—"

"Yes, you may." And she slipped off her drenched panties and kicked them away.

He wasted no time. In two strides he was there, kneeling at her feet, splaying his hands over her bottom as he nuzzled his way to the epicenter of all her pleasure. She'd known from the way he kissed that he'd be amazing at this, too.

But as he loved her, as her legs threatened to give way and she clutched his shoulders for support, the word *amazing* didn't begin to describe the sensations rocketing through her. He took charge once more, and she was helpless to control her response.

Her gasps became whimpers, and her whimpers grew in volume. When he paused, she wailed in frustration. His soft laughter told her he was teasing her, testing her. She failed the test because she shamelessly begged for more.

He gave more, of course. He was only giving as good as he'd gotten, gently torturing her as she'd tortured him. But in the end, he finished what he'd started and she came in a glorious cascade of pleasure. So good. So very good.

He guided her trembling body down to the thick carpet. Dazed by the force of her climax, sounds traveled to her as if she were underwater. She vaguely registered the clink of his belt buckle, the rasp of his zipper and the crinkle of foil.

His mouth found hers, and he tasted of sex. He kissed her for a long time before raising his head. "You don't have to do anything," he murmured. "Just lie there. But I need…" He eased between her thighs and the blunt tip of his cock sought the hot, quivering spot he'd loved so thoroughly with his mouth. "This." He slid deep with a heartfelt sigh. "Oh, yeah. This."

Little shock waves of delight zinged through her as he locked himself in tight. Then he began to stroke in and out and she didn't even have to think about it. She wrapped her arms around him and lifted to meet each thrust.

"Ah, Jeannette," he murmured in her ear as he increased his speed, "you're with me."

"Yes." She matched his pace and felt another orgasm building.

"I can't… I don't think I can wait."

"Don't wait." Sliding her hands down, she gripped his firm buns, pressing her fingertips into his solid muscles as he pumped steadily. His rhythmic movements excited her even more. "I'm right behind you."

He began to pant. "Damn, you feel incredible. If you didn't feel so great I could hold off, but I…I can't… I have to… I'm…" With a soft curse, he moved faster yet.

His excitement fueled hers. She kept up with him as he pounded into her, and when at last he cried out and drove home, she erupted at the moment his spasms hit. She held on tight as his body shook in time with hers. His groan of satisfaction brought her overwhelming joy, the kind of incandescent happiness that made her toes curl.

She had no idea how long they lay on the floor, but she had no inclination to move. She'd slept on beds that weren't as cushioned as this carpet.

Eventually Zach propped himself on his forearms and gazed down at her with a smile. "You know, this is funny."

She reached up and traced that smile with her fingertip. "Why?"

"I booked this room so our first time together could be on a high-end mattress on a king-size bed. And look at where we are."

"Are you complaining?"

"Never." He leaned down and kissed her on the nose. "But since we've had the floor experience, I vote we conduct the next round in bed."

"And when do you anticipate the next round will start?"

Levering himself higher, he swept a glance down her naked body. He rested on one arm and cupped her breast. Her nipple responded to the lazy brush of his thumb. "Might not be long."

Deep within her body, she felt the twitch of his cock.

He continued to play with her breasts, and the twitch came again. "Might not be long at all." He looked into her eyes. "If we don't have much time together, I don't want to waste any of it."

"I don't, either." But now she saw the fatal flaw in his otherwise excellent plan. They'd created a ticking clock, not unlike lovers had in wartime, where every moment could be their last. That might make this time with Zach seem more significant than it was. She'd have to guard against that kind of delusional thinking.

5

ZACH TALKED JEANNETTE into staying put while he disposed of the condom in the half bath off the living room. He buttoned and zipped his jeans but decided to take off his belt and his boots. They would only be in the way for his next maneuver. Glancing around, he located the bedroom door.

After his somewhat ungentlemanly behavior, taking her on the living room floor, he hoped to redeem himself by masterfully carrying her into the bedroom. He was pretty sure he could manage it. He'd always kept in shape, and he'd just spent a month doing manual labor. But when he crouched down and started to scoop her up, she protested.

"Never mind. I can walk."

"But then I don't get to show off my cowboy muscles. After shoveling out stalls for a month, I'm practically Mr. Universe. Come on. I've always wanted to try it. Humor me."

She smiled and wrapped her arms around his neck. "Okay, if it'll make you happy."

"It will. I might even beat my chest afterward."

"Oh, good. That would be fun to watch. I'd think it would hurt, though."

"Don't know. Never tried it. I'm new at this he-man stuff." From gym workouts and slinging hay bales, he'd learned to lift with his legs. He stood without too much wobbling, and there he was, holding a naked Jeannette in his arms. What a great feeling. "I like this."

She nestled close and gazed up at him. "There's a certain Tarzan-and-Jane quality to it."

"Yeah." When he'd made his living with his brain, he'd kept his gym membership so his suits fit better. But he liked having the strength to pick up his lady love and carry her off like a conquering hero. Very retro and not particularly enlightened, but he couldn't deny the satisfaction of being able to do it.

"Are you takin' me somewhere? Or did you just want to stand here a while?"

"Oh, I'm definitely taking you somewhere." He headed for it with what he considered a purposeful stride.

He laid Jeannette on the chocolate-brown comforter and stood back to admire the view.

"Isn't this the part where you beat your chest?"

"I'm over the Tarzan thing. Now I feel like Rhett Butler carrying Scarlett up the staircase."

"Just so you don't expect me to make a dress out of the curtains. I can't sew. In fact, I'm a washout at domestic chores. Cooking, cleaning, sewing—I'm clueless."

"I don't expect you to make a dress out of the curtains. In fact, that would probably get us permanently banned from this hotel chain." He sat on the edge of the bed and allowed his gaze to travel deliberately over her creamy skin. Under his scrutiny, she flushed a tempting pink. He loved that he could make that happen.

"What *do* you expect?" She asked the question with a twinkle in her eye.

"I have no expectations." He flattened his palms on either side of her head as he leaned closer. "Only give what you feel like giving."

She cupped the back of his head. "I feel like givin' you a big ol' kiss. How's that?"

"I'd like that."

She guided him down, and he delved into the richness of her mouth. In seconds his cock was hard. And he'd left the box of condoms in the other room. He hadn't planned that very well.

He lifted his mouth with great reluctance. "I want you again, but I left the—"

"Never mind."

"But—"

"You promised I could return the favor." And she reached down and unfastened the metal button of his jeans.

A man would be a fool to argue with a proposition like that, and he was no fool.

She pushed gently at his chest. "Just lie back and let me make you feel real good."

The words were seductive enough, but when delivered with a Southern accent…he was a stick of dynamite ready to explode and she'd barely touched him. Stretching out on the comforter, he prayed that he wouldn't embarrass himself by coming right away.

He closed his eyes and gritted his teeth as she fumbled with his zipper and his briefs, but he understood the problem. It was generally better to take the clothes off *before* expansion began. Now that he was fully erect, dealing with the zipper was tricky.

But she finally accomplished her mission. And oh, dear God, the sensation when she wrapped her warm fingers around his shaft made his eyes roll back in his head. He groaned and tightened his jaw against a climax that was perilously close.

"You're gorgeous, you know." She squeezed his cock gently with one hand and reached to cup his aching balls with the other.

"Mmm." It was the best response he could make under the circumstances. Not that he was complaining about the circumstances. These were most excellent circumstances.

He was just worried that… Sweet Jesus, she was using her mouth. She knew how to do that, too. She understood the male anatomy very well, apparently. He clutched two handfuls of the comforter and gasped for breath.

"Good?"

"Yeah." He dragged in more air, but it wasn't enough to carry him through the next deep groan as she took him all the way to the back of her throat. When she flattened her tongue against the ridge on the underside of his cock and began to bob her head in a steady rhythm, he knew the end was near.

Sure enough, she increased the pressure. More, a little more…ahhhh. He surrendered. Loudly. His moans grew even louder as she continued to suck on his pulsing cock. He'd never come so hard or so long, and she'd swallowed every drop.

As he lay there panting, she carefully tucked his family jewels back in his briefs before buttoning and zipping his jeans. Then she crawled up to place a flavorful kiss on his mouth before drawing back again.

He opened his eyes to find her chin propped on her fist as she watched him. He searched for what to say, but nothing in his vocabulary was good enough. "I'm speechless," he murmured. "That was…" He shook his head. "I can't think of a word."

"Super?"

"Better."

"Super-duper?"

"Better."

She smiled. "There's nothing better than super-duper. That's the highest level of excellence there is. Everybody knows that."

He tucked his hand behind his head so he could see her better. "Then let's say super-duper to the millionth power."

"Now you're just being silly."

"Hell, no. There was nothing silly about what you just did. My heart's still going a mile a minute."

"That's what I wanted. To give you a joyride."

"Oh, you did. But I wonder if I'll ever move again."

"You're just low on energy because we haven't eaten."

"That's true." His conscience pricked him. "Are you hungry now?"

She nodded.

"I gave away our Italian meal."

"I wondered where it was."

"I couldn't see hauling cold pasta up to the penthouse. There's a cheese tray sitting on the wet bar, but I think we need more than that. Let's order room service."

"I'll go find the menu. You stay here and recover from your super-duper blow job." She started to move away.

He caught her wrist and tugged her back. “No, I’ll go.”

“Why should you? I’m perfectly capable.”

“I know you are. But I carried you in here in true manly fashion. If you just walk back into the living room, you’ll cancel my heroic effort.”

“So I’m supposed to lie here like Cleopatra on her barge while you fetch everything?”

“Yes.” Taking a deep breath, he pushed himself to a sitting position. “That’s exactly what you should do. While I’m at it I’ll bring in the champagne bucket, the flutes and the cheese platter.”

“We’re goin’ to eat and drink in bed?”

“I thought we would. Is that a problem?”

“We might make a mess.”

“We might.” He suspected he’d just uncovered one of her perfectionist tendencies, one that wouldn’t risk eating in bed and getting food on the sheets. “Would that bother you?”

She hesitated, but then a defiant light flared in her green eyes. “No. No, it won’t.”

“Are you sure? Because we don’t have to. If you really want to eat at the table in the living room, I won’t make you stay here. I was sort of teasing, anyway.”

“I *want* to eat in bed. That was the old me popping up, the one who always has to eat at an actual table, the one who worries about food stains on sheets, whether they’re mine or they belong to a hotel. The new me, or at least the *tonight* version of me, doesn’t care about those things. Bring it on.”

“Okay.” He wished that they had more than one night together. He’d like to watch this transformation continue. “Then I’ll be back in a flash with everything we need.”

“In one trip?”

"Sure."

"This I've got to see."

"Prepare to be amazed." He slid off the bed and stood. He was still a little wrecked, but she was probably right about needing food. He wanted to keep up his strength. The night was young.

As he walked out of the bedroom, he marveled that he would be spending the entire night alone in this suite with Jeannette. He had trouble believing they'd just met, because he felt as if he'd known her a long time. Some said if you found the right person, you'd know it instantly.

He wasn't sure he agreed with that, but if there were any truth to the idea, then he'd experienced that immediate recognition with Jeannette. Even her body was familiar to him. He'd teetered on the brink of insanity during her striptease, but every time she'd revealed another lovely part, he'd thought, *Oh, yeah, there you are.*

Weird. But they only had this one night, and she was going home Monday. He needed to remember that. There was no reason to believe she'd changed her mind. This wasn't a movie where she'd get all sappy and run back to him right before she boarded her plane.

He found the room-service menu on a large desk in a far corner of the living room. Tucking the leather-bound menu under his arm, he surveyed the cheese platter, the champagne bucket, the crystal flutes and the box of condoms. He could do this. He'd seen a movie where the guy carried flutes without using his hands—except he wouldn't make the mistake the guy had.

He shoved a flute in each of his hip pockets. Then he tucked the condom box under one arm, grabbed the champagne bucket and picked up the cheese tray.

When he walked into the bedroom with all of it, she laughed. "That's awesome, but where are the flutes?"

He turned to show her.

"Oh, my God! Like in *Sabrina*."

"That's the one. I just have to remember not to sit down."

"I love that movie. Both the original and the remake."

"Me, too." He set the ice bucket on the nightstand and put the cheese platter on the bed. After placing the box of condoms on the nightstand, he handed her the menu before pulling the flutes out of his back pockets. "Safe. Want some champagne?"

"I'd love some." She studied the menu, but did not, however, pick up any of the cheese.

He peeled the foil off the champagne bottle. "Grab a flute, will you? I don't know if this will foam or not."

"Okay." She laid down the menu and picked up one of the glasses. "Maybe we should do this in the bathroom."

He glanced at her. Old habits were hard to break, but he had an inspiration on how to confront this one and have fun doing it. At least he'd have fun. "I have a better idea. Lie down while you're holding the glass."

"Lie down?"

"Yeah." He cautiously twisted the metal wire holding the cork in place. Sometimes the bottles blew once that was gone. He'd rather this one didn't.

"If you say so." She moved the cheese platter to the other side of the bed and stretched out. "Where should I hold it?"

"Oh, let's see." Before he finished taking off the wire, he guided her hand until the flute was poised about three inches above her navel. "That should do it."

"I think I know where this is headed."

"Too obvious?"

"If you want to drip champagne on me you could do it after you've poured it."

"But then there's no adventure." He took off the wire and the cork stayed put. Using the small towel the hotel had provided, he placed it over the cork and put one knee on the bed so he could open the bottle close to where she held the glass.

"If you get the sheets soaked you're sleeping on this side."

"I don't know about you, but I don't plan to do much sleeping tonight." To his intense disappointment, the cork popped out and he didn't get a drop of champagne on her luscious body. He'd have to be a little sloppy when he poured it, then.

Tossing the towel and cork aside, he leaned down and carefully poured champagne into the flute. He kept pouring.

"Zach, that's enough. Zach!" she yelped as the bubbly liquid trickled over the top of the glass and spilled onto her silky skin. "I *knew* you would do this. I knew it."

"And you were right! Here, let me have that glass before you spill all over yourself."

"Very funny. This champagne is cold, Zach. Extremely cold."

"Let's see if I can warm you up." After setting down her glass on the nightstand, he climbed onto the bed.

"I hope you're getting a charge out of this."

"I am. So will you." He began to lick the champagne where it had pooled in her navel.

"That's...different."

"I'm just getting started." He licked his way up to

her breasts. "Darn, no champagne. Let me fix that." He picked up the flute and dribbled some onto her.

She gasped. "Still cold."

"I'm working on that." He licked away the little trails of liquid. A subtle change in her breathing told him she was starting to get into this.

Picking up the glass again, he took a sip of champagne and held it on his tongue while he cupped her breast. Slowly he drew her nipple into his mouth and began to suck until the bubbles danced against her sensitive skin.

"Oh!" She quivered in reaction.

Swallowing the champagne, he took another small sip and treated her other nipple to the same experience. As he sucked, he reached between her thighs. She must like this, if her slick heat was any indication. And he'd saved the best for last.

Taking in a last mouthful, he slid down between her thighs. She knew what he was up to, because she opened to him with a little moan of welcome. Sliding his hands under her bottom, he lifted her to the angle he needed. He lost some of the champagne in his quest but he still had enough to create a fizzy sensation at that tender spot guaranteed to bring her to the edge.

As the bubbles worked their magic, he pushed two fingers deep and stroked her, lazily at first. As she caught fire, he picked up the pace. Within seconds she arched into his caress with a wild cry and the taste of her climax mingled with the tang of champagne.

She sank back to the mattress and murmured a soft oath.

After kissing his way back up her slightly sticky body, he gazed into her flushed face. "Is there a problem?"

Her breathing was still ragged. "You bet there is."

"You didn't enjoy that?"

"You know I did."

"Then what's the matter?"

"I'll never be able to drink champagne again without remembering this."

"Oh." He smiled. "Sorry."

"No, you're not."

"You're right, I'm not. I'm human. I want to leave you with some indelible memories. So shoot me."

"I'll find a way to get you back. I'll make sure I leave you with some indelible memories, too."

He looked into her green eyes and knew they'd haunt him long after she was gone. "Trust me, you already have."

6

ON SOME LEVEL Jeannette knew they were playing a dangerous game that could end in emotional disaster. If she'd had any sense, she'd have rejected his idea of one spectacular night together. But she hadn't been able to make herself do the sensible thing.

She'd spent her life being sensible, until the incident with Drake. Letting herself be sucked into that drama had taught her that she was itching to live a far less ordered life. But she wasn't willing to repeat the kind of behavior that had wrecked long-standing friendships. From now on she'd consider whether her choices would impact others.

Spending the night at this hotel affected only two people—herself and Zach. Apparently he was ready to teach her how to be less sensible, as evidenced by the adventure with champagne. She tingled with anticipation as she imagined what other surprises he had in store.

Their order of club sandwiches and fries arrived quickly. She'd overridden Zach's suggestion that they choose a gourmet dinner with the argument that it would take longer to prepare. He'd grumbled a bit but once she'd agreed to eat the meal in bed, he'd been fine with it.

She'd put on the complimentary hotel bathrobe while they waited for the bellman to bring a dinner cart. The bellman left the cart in the living room because Jeannette hadn't wanted to advertise that they would eat in bed.

Zach began unbuttoning his shirt. "No reason for me to stay dressed anymore, right?"

"Um, yes, there is." She watched the shirt come off and gulped. "Are you planning to eat naked?" He hadn't been kidding about the muscles he'd developed shoveling out stalls.

"Why not? Aren't you?"

"I hadn't decided."

"That's part of the fun of eating in bed. Then if we take a notion, we don't have to fool with clothes." He sat on the nearest upholstered chair and pulled off his socks, which made his powerful biceps flex.

"Take a notion? That sounds like cowboy talk." Jeannette longed to touch him. She wanted to lick, rub and caress every inch of his muscled torso.

"I know." He grinned. "It's not enough to wear the clothes. You gotta talk the talk." He stood and casually unbuttoned his jeans.

She, on the other hand, was becoming more agitated by the second. She took a steadying breath. "Zach, I think we really need to eat these sandwiches."

"I was planning on it." His zipper rasped.

"It may have escaped your notice, but I've been naked practically since we arrived in this suite. You've probably become used to the idea."

"I wouldn't say I'm *used* to it. Looking at you still gets me hot."

"Exactly, but maybe not as fiercely as when I first stripped. You, on the other hand, have been mostly clothed."

"I'm about to remedy that." He started to shove both jeans and briefs down.

"Wait."

"Wait?"

"I don't think you took my meaning. If you shuck those clothes, I can't be responsible for my actions."

A slow grin spread across his handsome face. "I do like the sound of that."

"But I really need to eat some dinner."

"Oh. So you're trying to tell me that the sight of my naked body will be so arousing that you won't be able to concentrate on your meal?"

"I am saying that, yes."

"Huh." He seemed quite pleased with the thought. "Do you need me to put my shirt back on?"

"That's not necessary." And it would be a crime against nature. Now that she'd seen him without it, she thought he should make going shirtless a permanent wardrobe choice. "But if you could leave your jeans on until we finish the meal, I'd be very grateful."

"I can do that." He zipped up and fastened the button at his waist. "Better?"

"Yes."

"I guess I thought, since you'd already been up close and personal with what's inside these jeans, it wouldn't matter whether I wore them or not."

"It matters."

"Okay, then. Ready to retire to the bedroom?"

"Yes, but I have another request."

"If you want to leave your bathrobe on, that's fine. I understand your point about needing food."

"I think we also need a distraction. Let's see what movies are available."

He gazed at her. "So you want to sit in bed eating sandwiches and watching movies? Like we're roommates hanging out together?"

"At least until we finish the meal."

"Are you a fast eater?"

"Zach!"

"Well, you said you're a power shopper, so it's a reasonable question."

"I'm not goin' to rush through dinner so we can have sex." At least not on purpose. But she really did want to get her hands on that lovely torso of his. She wanted to run her fingers through the chest hair that swirled around his nipples and formed a sexy line that disappeared under his waistband. After the meal was over, he could take off those jeans, too. And then she'd—

"Jeannette?"

"What?" She felt her cheeks heat. She'd been caught ogling.

"I asked what kind of movie you wanted to watch."

"Oh, a comedy."

"Then let's see what's on." He walked to the desk, grabbed a movie guide and flipped through it. "Would you believe the *Sabrina* remake is on right now?"

"Then let's watch that."

He handed her the movie guide. "You're in charge of that. I'll bring in the cart."

"I know this isn't what you envisioned, but—"

"Don't worry about it. My little fantasy will come later. I ordered us chocolate mousse for dessert."

"You didn't tell me that."

"My little surprise."

And that was exactly why she needed to spend the

night with this man. He was determined to blast her right out of her comfort zone. "I suppose you want to eat that in bed, too."

"And off each other."

He must be having an effect on her, because she was ready to forget about their club sandwiches and go straight to dessert. But she'd requested a movie with dinner. After consulting the movie guide, she turned on the huge flat screen in the bedroom and clicked through the offerings until she found the listing for *Sabrina.*

If she were to apply the story line to her situation with Zach, she'd have to reverse the roles. She was more of a nose-to-the-grindstone type, while Zach was the impulsive one, at least now that he'd stopped practicing law to become a cowboy.

She still struggled with the idea that he'd abandoned his profession. Society desperately needed lawyers who weren't focused on earning big fees and winning high-profile cases. He could be as low-key and altruistic as he wanted, but to deprive the world of his ability as a principled lawyer—that seemed wrong.

"Got it cued up?"

"I do."

"I'll put the cart on my side of the bed." He started around to the far side.

"Hold it. That's the part that wasn't baptized with champagne. I'll take that side and you can have the other one."

He shrugged and steered the cart back around to the other side. "I'm good with either. I don't mind a few champagne splatters. Speaking of that, do you want more?"

"How do you mean that, exactly?"

His sexy mouth lifted at the corners. "How do you

want me to mean it? You might complain about spills, but I seem to recall that you had a really good time with the bubbly."

He would have to mention that episode, which reminded her of how his mouth had felt when he… She called a halt to those erotic thoughts. If she started remembering all the pleasure he'd given her since they'd checked into this suite, she would die of starvation. She'd die happy, but still…a woman could not live on sex alone.

She gazed at this arousing, imaginative, challenging man. He would never let her get away with being stuffy and boring. He'd bring out the vixen in her. He'd awaken the rebel who wasn't satisfied with the status quo even when she pretended to be coloring inside the lines.

She faced him across the wide expanse of the king-size mattress. "I had a great time with you and the bubbly, as we established earlier. I have a feelin' that before the meal is over, you'll have changed my relationship with chocolate mousse, too."

"It's my sincerest wish."

"I figured as much. For now, though, I'd like some champagne in a glass, please."

"I can do that."

He was as good as his word. Once they were settled on the bed, he handed her a glass of champagne without dribbling any on her. It wouldn't have worked, anyway, because she'd decided to keep the bathrobe on while they ate.

"Aren't you warm in that bulky thing?" He sounded disappointed that she was so covered up.

"Not really." She wasn't warm. She was hot, and not because the room temperature was too high. Every time she glanced at him propped against a mound of pillows, a shirtless fantasy man if she'd ever seen one, she wanted to jump his bones.

She considered asking him to put his shirt back on after all, but he looked so comfy. And so tanned. He must have spent part of his time outdoors soaking up the Wyoming sunshine. Dear God, he was gorgeous. She forced herself to look away before she ruined the program she'd been so committed to.

They each balanced their plates on their laps as they watched the movie. She noticed they laughed in the same places. When Greg Kinnear sat on the glasses tucked in his back pocket, they looked at each other and grinned.

"You know what?" Zach kept his attention on the screen as he picked up a fry from his plate.

"What?"

"This is fun." He popped the fry in his mouth.

"I think so, too." She watched him while pretending she wasn't. He was absorbed in the movie.

"I mean, really fun. I got so tired of the Hollywood scene that I didn't want to watch movies anymore. And I love movies. It's the reason I got into entertainment law in the first place."

Her heart twisted when she thought of his broken dreams. He must have imagined that working in Hollywood as a lawyer would make him happy. For some people, it might, but it seemed he wasn't suited to the frenetic pace or the pressure to make piles of money. "Then I'm glad we're doing this."

"Me, too. But just so you know, I'm still thinking about you over there naked under your bathrobe. That might be why this is so fun. It's like an X-rated version of a sleepover."

"I like that."

"So do I." He continued to watch the movie and eat his fries. When he was finished and had set his plate on the nightstand, he spoke again. "Is it okay if we pause the movie for a minute? This next part is great but I wanted to say something that's been on my mind."

"Sure." She put her empty plate on the nightstand, too, picked up the remote and clicked the pause button before turning to him. "What?"

"I've been thinking about the things you said earlier, about having women friends I loved but didn't sleep with. I'm not sure I've had close women friends, period. If I slept with them, sex was the focus, not friendship."

"That's too bad."

"It is, I guess, but I'm still not sure the concept works, at least for a man. There's always a sexual component. I mean, you had these two great guys as friends, but look what happened."

She sighed. "I know. Point taken."

"Maybe now you can be friends with them, but will you really be that close? Regan has a fiancée, and Drake moved in with Tracy. You may always be friends with those guys, but best buds? I'm not so sure."

"You're right, of course. Lily is great, and I'm sure Tracy is cool with me, too, but…yeah. It won't be the same. Lily will be Regan's best friend and Tracy will be Drake's. That's the way it should be. I'll fit in a different category of friend—still close, but not as close."

"That's where I was going with this. I never thought about it before, but that's what has been missing from every relationship I've had with a woman. We were lovers, but we weren't necessarily friends. And that was my fault."

She couldn't let him shoulder the blame. "I doubt

it was entirely your fault. Each person has a part in building—"

"No, it was my fault, and I'll tell you why. We never did stuff like this." He swept a hand around the room.

"Sure you did. You obviously are used to sharing a meal in bed with a woman."

"But not while we were watching TV. Do you see the difference? We're just sitting here and watching something instead of turning the meal into a sexual adventure. We found a movie we both liked and it's been fun watching it together, right?"

"It has, but I can't believe you didn't watch movies with the women in your life."

"Of course I did, but hardly ever for the pure fun of it. We knew too much about the industry, so we'd fall into the trap of criticizing this or that, and the joy would seep right out of the experience. Bad, bad habit."

"And not much fun, really."

"Not much." He met her gaze. "And another thing. What we're doing right now, talking about things that matter. I never used to do that with them."

"Why not?"

"I don't know. Maybe…hell, it's obvious, isn't it? I couldn't bitch about my frustrations with my job, because that would be a total buzzkill and destroy my precious image. So I clammed up about the one thing that was driving me nuts."

"And they didn't get to see the real you."

"Right." He stared at her, his gray eyes thoughtful. "And now that you say that, I'll bet I didn't get to see the real them, either. Lots of people wear masks in Hollywood. I did. I was the successful lawyer who drove a Lamborghini."

"Pricey car."

"No kidding. If you think that truck oozes testosterone, you should have seen my black Lamborghini. If I'd really fixed myself, I would have bought a used pickup. Maybe a faded brown one."

She reached over and stroked his cheek. "Don't be so hard on yourself, Zach. It's a beautiful truck. You don't have to deny yourself all the perks."

"But it's impractical as hell." He caught her hand and pressed a kiss into her palm. Then he laced his fingers through hers. "If you're going to drive on ranch roads, you need a truck the color of dirt."

"That's not you, either. You have too much energy to drive a truck the color of dirt."

"Jack has a red truck. It doesn't show the dirt nearly as much as mine." He gazed at her. "And speaking of the ranch, I didn't think through this hotel stay very well."

"I don't know." She smiled at him. "I think it's worked out very well."

"Up to now, you bet. But I'm afraid I fell back into my old way of thinking once I booked a luxury hotel. I'm no longer a lawyer who can reschedule his morning appointments. I'm a ranch hand, and I have to be back on the job at dawn."

"Right." She glanced at the time on the bedside clock and discovered it was past midnight. "And we're an hour away from Shoshone."

He nodded. "Besides that, I'll need to factor in dropping you at the B and B."

"What you're saying is that we don't have much more time here."

"Sadly, no."

"Zach, I just thought of something. I can take a nap at the Bunk and Grub, but you have to work. When will you sleep?"

"I get off at two tomorrow, so I can grab a quick nap before the party at five."

"That doesn't seem like enough time."

He grinned. "Ask me if I care."

"I care. Let's leave now so you can grab at least an hour or two before you have to head to work."

"Let's not." He reached over and loosened the belt of her robe.

Her heart started thudding faster. "Are you still fixated on that chocolate mousse?"

"Oddly enough, I'm not. I'm more in the mood for good, old-fashioned sex." He looked into her eyes. "Would that be okay with you?"

Her breath caught. The emotion in his gaze matched the warmth she was feeling. It was no longer simply lust between them. Something more was going on. Considering that fact, playing around with chocolate mousse might be a safer option than face-to-face lovemaking.

Funny how the issue of stepping out of her comfort zone had just shifted to include missionary-position sex with a man who was supposed to be essentially a one-night stand. "Yes," she said. "Totally okay with me."

7

ZACH LEFT THE bed so he could get out of the rest of his clothes. If he'd started this meal the way he'd intended, he wouldn't have to do that, but if he'd started the meal naked, they would have been rolling around in that bed in no time. Wearing the jeans had been a good thing, a lesson in postponing sex so he could actually get to know a woman. And himself.

The more he got to know Jeannette, the more he chafed against their abbreviated time together. But he'd worry about that later. At the moment he had no worries whatsoever, because she was waiting for him in that big bed.

He rolled on a condom before he joined her there, because he wouldn't be playing any games this time. Games were fun when you had all the time in the world, but he and Jeannette didn't. Despite having fun doing it on the floor and the various oral variations that had followed, he secretly loved this way the best.

As he climbed back into bed and moved between her thighs, he realized that he'd denied himself this favorite position most of the time. He'd been afraid his partners would find it unimaginative and boring. Luckily Jeannette didn't look bored.

Her green eyes were bright as she slid both hands up his chest and around his neck. "Welcome."

"You don't think this is clichéd?"

Her laughter was breathless. "You *have* been in Hollywood too long."

"Yeah." He would get down to business in a minute. First he wanted to remain braced above her so he could watch her skin flush as the tip of his cock nudged her entrance.

"Mmm." She lifted her hips and took him in a fraction more.

Adrenaline shot through him, tempting him to accept her unspoken invitation to thrust deep. But he was still enjoying his view. Her breasts quivered with every rapid breath she took and her nipples were tight buds of arousal. "I'd almost forgotten how much I like having sex like this."

"I do, too." She kneaded his shoulders. "I like watching your eyes change color."

"They do?" No one had ever told him that.

"Uh-huh. Light to dark."

He pushed in farther. "So do yours."

"Not…surprised." She flattened her hands against his chest. "You feel good."

"Where?"

"Here." She rubbed his pecs.

"Here?" He rotated his hips.

Her eyes flashed green fire. Then she clutched his hips, wrapped her legs around his and lifted up, taking him all the way. *"There."*

If he'd had any breath left, he would have laughed, but she'd taken it all away with that feisty move. If he'd thought he was in control, she'd just proved him wrong. He didn't care. He was exactly where he wanted to be, buried to the hilt in her warmth.

Settling down on his forearms, he gazed into her eyes and gulped in air. "Nice move."

"You were dawdlin'."

"My apologies." He was securely anchored and he loved the feeling, but he thought they both might benefit from a looser situation. "Gonna let me move?"

She smiled. "Only if you promise to be nice."

He leaned down, his mouth hovering over hers. "What's nice?"

"You know perfectly well."

He touched his mouth to hers and slid his tongue inside. After stroking back and forth a few times, he lifted his head. "Like that?"

"You're gettin' the idea, cowboy."

"Then ease up so I can be nice where it counts."

She relaxed her grip but kept her legs wrapped around his.

Propping himself up a little more so he could watch her expression, he began a slow rhythm. "How's that?"

"It'll do."

God, but she made him smile. The heat in her gaze told him that she liked it better than she was letting on, but he loved her saucy attitude. Here he'd been worried that missionary-position sex would be a cliché.

He doubted that sex would ever be a cliché when he made love to Jeannette. They brought out the playfulness in each other. Teasing her and being teased back was as natural as breathing.

And speaking of breathing, hers was getting a little rapid, as if she might be excited. Imagine that. Shifting his angle, he drove in deeper, with a slightly faster pace. "Like that?"

"For…the time bein'…" Her little whimper gave her away.

"I think you're getting hot." He sure as hell was. The blood rushed in his ears and his cock wanted more, and faster yet. So he gave his bad boy what it longed for, and thrust in time with a wild, primitive beat.

Her lips parted and her gaze took on the intensity of her looming orgasm. He watched avidly as her expression signaled that her moment was near. Oh, yeah. This was why he loved this position.

"I think you're gonna come," he murmured softly. He stroked swiftly, his attention on her eyes. "You're gonna come right…*now.*" He pushed deep and she closed her eyes and arched upward with a helpless cry of surrender. It was the sweetest sound, the greatest gift.

With a groan, he unleashed the climax he'd barely been able to contain. Gasping, he pulsed within her and thanked his lucky stars that this woman had entered his life. If he had his way, it would be for more than one night.

When his breathing had slowed, he kissed her softly. "Beautiful." For him that was a global statement that covered her and the sex they'd just shared.

"It was." Her eyes fluttered open. "But now we should probably—"

"In a little bit. Don't go anywhere. I'll be right back." Reluctantly he eased away from her, sat up and swung his feet to the floor.

"But I should get up, too." She pushed herself to a sitting position.

"Not yet. Please." He stood and turned to her. "Just stay there, okay?"

She hesitated before sliding back down. "All right."

"Great." He hurried into the bathroom while he wondered how in hell he could avoid the separation that was about to happen. He'd see what they might be able to work out, because he wasn't ready for this to be over.

When he came back into the room, she was lying on her side, her head propped on a pillow as she gazed at him. He climbed in and mirrored her position. "I can't speak for you, but I'm not ready to end this."

She sighed. "Neither am I, but I don't know what else to do. I'm not going to risk sneakin' you up to my room at the Bunk and Grub."

"You could stay in my Airstream." He figured she'd say no, but he had to put it out there.

She regarded him silently for several long seconds. "That wouldn't do my reputation any good."

"Probably not." He couldn't very well deny it. "Okay, forget that idea. But I just…" He cupped her cheek. "I just hate to think you'll be so close, and yet so far."

"I know. I'll be thinkin' of you the whole time."

"Same here."

She sighed again. "And we'll both be miserable."

"I'll try not to be, but yeah, I'll pretty much hate seeing you at the party and knowing I can't be with you after it's over."

"Come to think of it, my reputation isn't in very good shape as it is."

Maybe all wasn't lost, then, but a sense of fairness made him remind her of her original goal. "I thought you were trying to fix that."

She pressed his hand against her cheek. "I was, until we had this time together. The people that matter most to me, Regan and Drake, won't care if I spend the rest of the weekend with you. As for everybody else, their good opinion doesn't seem so important if you and I have to suffer in order to earn it."

"Are you sure about this? I don't want to let you in for more of what you've been through."

She gazed at him. "When I weigh that against us having more time together, their disapproval doesn't matter so much anymore."

"Ah, Jeannette." He gathered her close and combed his fingers through her hair. "I'm trying not to think of how selfish I'm being by wanting to take you back with me."

"But I want to go." She hugged him tight. "I'm dyin' of curiosity about that solar shower."

Laughing, he rolled her to her back. "You'll love it. We'll take a shower together when I come back from work, before we get dressed for the party."

"Which I now have a date for, right?"

"You most certainly do."

"We should get started back, then, so we can pick up my stuff and my car before you have to go to work."

"We will." He reached for a condom on the night-stand. "But first we need one for the road."

AN HOUR LATER, they were headed back to Shoshone, and he was glad he'd only had a few drops of champagne licked from Jeannette's sweet body. His head was clear and his imagination was busily concocting scenarios of what would happen when they reached his campsite. Jeannette seemed determined that he'd get an hour or so of sleep, but he doubted it. Traffic was light, which allowed him to jack up his speed.

"You should sleep on the way home," he told her.

"Not on your life. We need some tunes, is what we need." She leaned over and switched on the radio. His favorite classic rock station came on with a number by Billy Joel. "Do you mean to tell me you don't have a country station locked in to go with your big bad truck?"

"Sorry. If you want country, you can search around and find some."

"What if I like this?"

He glanced over at her. "Then I guess we're good." Were they ever. Each similarity they discovered underlined how good they would be together. He wondered if she'd noticed that. "I figured you'd like the newer stuff."

"I like some of it, but my parents were older when they had me, so they played this kind of music all the time. I grew up on it."

"So did I, although my parents weren't terribly old when they had me. If you went to school with Regan and Drake, you must be what, thirty?"

"A lady doesn't discuss her age."

"If you won't discuss it, I'll have to conclude that you went back to college after working several dead-end jobs and you're now pushing forty."

"I am not!"

"Okay, I'll go first. I'm thirty-six." When he was with her, though, he felt like a teenager with his first crush.

"That old, huh?"

"That old. When I graduated from law school, you were a wet-behind-the-ears freshman in college. It's a wonder we connect at all."

"Sarcasm."

"Do you think?"

"In actuality, a thirty-six-year-old man is about right for a thirty-year-old woman. Women mature faster than men."

He decided to ignore that comment. “So you admit to being thirty?”

“I do. I was supposed to be married by now. I was on track for it, too.”

“If you were supposed to be married by now, what about me? I’m way past the age when I should have found the perfect woman and settled down.”

“Come to think of it, you are old to never have been married. Are you divorced?”

“Nope.”

“Why not?”

He laughed. “Because I didn’t get married. It’s kind of hard to get a divorce from a wife you’ve never had.”

“I said that wrong. Let’s try that again. Why haven’t you ever been married?”

“Damn, now you sound like my mother. She’s been pestering me for years about that.”

“And what do you tell her?”

He focused on the white dividing line rolling past. “I tell her the same thing I’ll tell you. I haven’t found the right person.” A small voice whispered that he might have found her now, but that was a ridiculously premature idea. “I did get engaged once, but we both figured out it wouldn’t work and broke up.”

“Smart. Regan and I should have done that. But on the other hand, if we had, I never would have met you. I’m glad for whatever circumstances brought us together.”

“Me, too.” More than she’d ever know, probably. “I take it your parents were pushing you to get married, too. Expecting you to give them grandkids and all that.”

“Get married, yes. That’s generally what Southern girls are supposed to do. I don’t think they were particularly eager for grandchildren, though. They didn't intend to have me in the first place."

"Oh."

She sighed. "Blame the late hour. I didn't mean to blurt that out. Please don't think I dwell on it, or think of myself as some kind of mistake. Once they had me, they were very proud of me and what I accomplished."

"As well they should be." But his heart ached for her. No wonder she'd tried to be Miss Perfect all her life. She'd been trying to justify her right to exist.

He had the crazy urge to coax her away from Virginia and what sounded like a toxic situation. Maybe she wasn't all that happy at work. "Tell me about your job."

She seemed grateful for a change of subject. "It's terrific. My firm has a lot of clients who own and race Thoroughbreds. Sale contracts get complicated, especially for a foal that might go on to be a Derby winner. Everyone's always looking for the next Triple Crown hopeful. Very high-pressure, but I love it."

"And the horses can't show up drunk or stoned. That would be a plus."

She laughed. "Some of the owners might, though. Wherever there's money, there's excess. I'm sure I don't have to tell you that."

"Sure don't."

"I'm about to make partner." She said it softly, but with a touch of pride.

"No kidding? That's great!" Not for him, obviously. His tentative idea that she might consider moving to Jackson Hole and open a practice seemed doomed from the start.

If she'd worked her tail off for this firm and was about to be offered a partnership, she wouldn't want to give that up without a really good reason. He was willing to try to provide her with a reason, but that was a tall order, even though he'd stretched their one-night-stand into a three-day affair. A long-distance relationship was an option, but he'd never been a fan of those. He'd seen too many Hollywood couples break up because they didn't spend enough time together.

"My folks are happy about the partnership."

"I'll bet." Yeah, they would be. They might have suffered through botched wedding plans, but they could take solace in their daughter's professional success. Zach didn't think he'd like them very much.

Even if they hadn't planned to have Jeannette, why tell her so? Only selfishness, insensitivity or both would motivate a parent to blab something like that to a kid. He didn't have much patience with either, especially when he witnessed the fallout—a woman who thought she had to do everything just right.

Then "Jailhouse Rock" came on, and Jeannette started singing along. He thought that was so cute that he joined in, and soon the two of them were belting out the song at the top of their lungs. They both made love better than they sang, but it didn't matter. Cruising down the highway in the wee hours of the morning, singing along with Elvis, he couldn't remember when he'd ever been happier.

She knew the Buddy Holly song that came on next, too, and they ended up singing like fools for the rest of the trip. He'd made the drive from Shoshone to Jackson several times in the month he'd lived here, but it had never seemed as short as it did tonight. Logically he should be exhausted, but being with Jeannette gave him a second wind.

The streets of Shoshone were deserted at this hour, but when Zach came to the intersection, the light turned red. "It always does this. Jack says Elmer Crookshanks, the guy with the gas station on the corner, has a sensor so you have to stop and look over at his station."

"You could run it."

"I could, but Elmer used to have a traffic camera hooked up, too. Jack swears he made him take it down, but I've heard others say it's still running. Might as well sit here until it turns green."

"This is a quirky little town." She looked over at the Spirits and Spurs. The neon sign depicting a cowboy on a bucking bronco had been turned off. "That bar looks like fun."

"Supposedly it's haunted. That's why Josie calls it the Spirits and Spurs. Kind of an inside joke."

"I met Josie today while we were working in the kitchen. Pretty lady, long blond braid."

"That's her."

"I didn't realize she owns the local bar."

"Didn't Regan or Drake give you a cheat sheet?"

"Like I said, they've both been involved with the new women in their lives, and I'm fine with that. I'll muddle through."

"You're not going to have to muddle anymore. Before we go to the party, I'll give you a rundown."

"That would be great." She paused. "We won't be in danger of upstaging Regan and Lily, will we? I'd never want to do that."

"I'll clue Jack in before I leave work so he can pass the word around. And we'll keep a low profile." He wasn't sure if that would work considering the gossip that had been swirling before. That gossip would erupt when people found out she'd left the Bunk and Grub to stay with him. But he'd do his damnedest. Her major concern might be for Regan and Lily, but his first concern was for her.

One dim light shone from a front window of the Victorian house that Pam Mulholland had turned into a bed-and-breakfast. Jeannette had him wait while she went in and quickly packed her things and left a note at the reception desk. She didn't waste time. She was in and out with no visible signs that anyone had heard her.

He watched her sling her suitcase in the backseat of her rental car. Then he pulled forward so she could follow him out of the small parking lot. From the moment she'd left the cab of his truck, he'd missed her.

Once she was behind him, he took the road out of town toward the ranch. She'd driven it before, but he kept tabs on his rearview mirror, anyway, to make sure her headlights were reflected there. His protective instincts had developed without him realizing it. Now, they weren't together and he had to think about whether she was safe back there.

The dirt road into the ranch property had been washboard-rough ever since he'd arrived a month ago. The family had an ongoing debate about it, with Jack insisting it stay that way because his dad had intended to make visiting difficult. His two brothers believed that customers for the registered Paints the Chances sold would appreciate a paved entrance to the property.

Zach's truck had no problem with the road, but he winced as Jeannette's rental car bounced around. He went slowly, even though he was eager to get her ensconced in the Airstream. They drove past the massive ranch house, a two-story log structure with a central section and two wings set at an angle, like arms reaching out.

The house was dark, the ranch buildings lit with

a few dusk-to-dawn lamps. Otherwise the place was quiet. In a couple of hours, though, as the sun peeked over the horizon, the hustle and bustle would begin.

Normally Zach looked forward to that time of day, but maybe he could be forgiven if he'd rather stay in the Airstream with Jeannette this morning. He wouldn't do it, though. Once she was tucked into bed, he'd head back to the ranch to work his shift.

The road to his campsite was filled with even more ruts. Maybe he should have told her to park at the ranch and then join him in his truck, but her car would create more gossip. This was better. They'd be tucked away, out of sight and maybe out of mind.

He didn't really believe that, but at least he'd be on hand to shield her from whatever came her way. Maybe nothing would. The Last Chance had been established as a place where people and animals really could have one last chance to set things right. Jeannette had come to Jackson Hole for that very purpose.

At last he turned on a smaller dirt road and within minutes saw the silver gleam of his trailer in the moonlight. He parked and hopped out so he could guide her to a parking spot where the ground was firm.

She pulled in, shut off the motor and got out of the car. "It's so quiet. But it smells great, like Christmas trees. Wait, I can hear the water. That's the stream, right?"

"That's the stream." He pulled her close because he couldn't help himself. He wanted to surround her with whatever security he could provide.

An owl hooted, and she shivered. "I should warn you that I've never camped before."

"That's okay. You'll love it." He had no basis for saying that, and maybe it was wishful thinking on his part.

"Will you stay until it gets light?"

"Yes." He could tell she was nervous, but she would get over it. He'd make love to her in his double bed under the curved roof of his Airstream with the windows open so they could hear the night sounds while they enjoyed each other.

He wanted her to fall in love with the woods the way he had. He couldn't explain why that was so important to him. He only knew that it was.

8

When Jeannette had agreed to this plan, she'd only thought about being with Zach in his cozy little trailer. She'd thought about the solar shower, mostly in terms of watching him take one. She hadn't thought about the bears.

She didn't want to mention them now, either, and look like a total wuss. At least Zach would stay until the sun started to rise. He had to be at work by dawn, but that was a flexible description. He wasn't punching a time clock.

Although she wasn't clear on bear behavior, she thought they were mostly nocturnal. Even if they weren't, a bear would be much scarier in the dark than in broad daylight. She could see a bear coming when the sun was out, and she had her phone.

Zach continued to hold her close, probably because she was still shivering a little. "Ready to check out the Airstream?"

"Yep."

He released her. "I'll unlock the tailgate so you can haul the shopping bags in. I'll handle your suitcase."

"Okay." It wasn't cold at all, and moonlight lit up

the clearing pretty well. She shouldn't be scared, but as she followed him to the back of the truck, she started to shiver again. "How's the phone reception out here?"

"Not that great. It's sporadic on the ranch property." He pulled the tailgate down. "Sometimes it's great and sometimes not. This area is kind of a dead spot. If you need to make a call, your best bet is to try when you're up at the house."

Crap. "Oh, well. Not important."

He unhooked the bungee cord holding the two shopping bags and handed both of them to her. Then he closed the tailgate with a clang. "Do you need to make a call?"

"Not right now." She'd been listening intently for the sound of pine needles crunching under heavy paws. She had no idea what kind of noise an approaching bear would make, but if she heard any shuffling or crunching, she was diving into Zach's truck. It seemed more bear-proof than her flimsy rental car.

"You could try texting if you want to reach your assistant. That might work."

"Sure. I'll do that later." She'd let him think that contacting Erin was the only reason she'd need a phone out here. Something rustled in the wild bushes growing among the trees. She froze. "Wh-what was that?"

"I don't know." He walked toward her car, obviously unconcerned. "Maybe a raccoon. Maybe a skunk."

"A *skunk?*" She mostly didn't want to be eaten by a bear, but she had no interest in being sprayed by a skunk, either. "Let's get inside."

"Most things around here won't bother you if you don't mess with them." He pulled her suitcase out of the backseat and closed the door. Then he held out his hand. "Come on. Check out the silver bullet."

"Is that its name?" She felt better the minute he laced his strong fingers through hers.

"Not this one, specifically. People call Airstreams silver bullets for obvious reasons."

"It sure is shiny."

"It was a lot shinier before I pulled it over those dirt roads. Fortunately we had some rain and that washed it down some."

She heard the pride in his voice and guessed that he was excited to show off his trailer. "Is it old? I know these used to be popular a long time ago."

"It's new. I thought about buying a restored one, but I'm a beginner at this RV thing and I needed a manual and a warranty. My grandparents had one of these, and I used to love going on road trips with them, so it's all about the nostalgia." He squeezed her hand and let go. "Need to get my keys out."

"Sure." She looked around as he went up the small steps and unlocked the door, but whatever had rustled before wasn't doing it anymore. She couldn't get over the feeling that unseen eyes were watching her, though. Made sense. She was in the wilds with wild creatures. Of course they'd be watching.

Zach walked into the trailer, set down her bag and flicked a light switch.

She didn't wait for an invitation to follow him. She stayed right on his heels. Whatever had rustled in the bushes could be right on *her* heels for all she knew.

He turned and bumped into her. "Oops. Sorry. Didn't realize you were so close. So this is… Oh, hey, did you hear that?"

"What?" Shopping bags held in front of her as some kind of barrier, she whirled to face the door in case that bushes-rustling animal was climbing the steps. She saw nothing in the light spilling out the door.

"Be real quiet. Maybe we'll hear it again."

Although she had a strong urge to close that door, she didn't. She also tried to be quiet, but her heart pounded loud enough to drown out anything they might be listening for. She'd have to count on Zach to be her ears right now. "Hear what?" she whispered.

"Wolves."

She swallowed a little whimper of anxiety. "Are they close?" She knew logically a wolf wasn't any danger to people, but still. If one walked up those steps and looked her in the eye, she'd have trouble being calm about it. She was used to horse farms that hadn't seen a bear or a wolf in generations.

"Not very. Maybe they won't howl again. Go ahead and make yourself at home."

"Okay." She set her shopping bags on either side of her and tried not to rattle them too loud.

Then the sound came again. Now she recognized it as a howl, and every hair on her body stood on end.

"Did you hear that?" Zach's low voice vibrated with excitement.

"Yes." Another howl from a different direction seemed to answer the one that had come before it.

"What a treat. Howling wolves on your first night." Zach wrapped his arms around her waist and pulled her back against his solid warmth.

The first wolf howled again.

"They're talking," he murmured.

"About what?" Now that Zach had both arms around her and she knew a wolf wouldn't come charging in the door, she relaxed a little. Their calls to each other off in the distance were kind of cool. If the wolves stayed there, they could make as much noise as they wanted.

"Possibly they're announcing their presence to keep one pack from encroaching on another pack's territory."

"How do they know where the boundaries are?"

"The alpha males mark their territory by peeing on trees and rocks."

"Oh."

"They're fascinating creatures. Loyal, brave, smart. I've always loved them."

"I can tell." The longer they stood there listening to the wolves howl with her backside pressed up against his groin, the more she became aware of his interest in other subjects besides wolves.

Sliding both hands up to cup her breasts, he leaned down and nuzzled behind her ear. "I've never had a pretty lady in my arms while the wolves howled. I think it's bringing out the beast in me."

"Is that so?" Camping in the woods might have some advantages—she hadn't considered that it might awaken his inner alpha male. The howling wolves had stirred her up some, too, especially when she'd realized he was getting hard.

But she felt some responsibility for seeing that he rested for the hour or so before he had to leave. She captured his hands and held them still. "You really should take a quick nap."

"No, thanks." Escaping her grip easily, he drew back her collar and nipped the sensitive skin of her neck.

It didn't hurt, but it sure as heck turned her on, especially after listening to those wolves. She moaned softly.

"I'm going to take that as a yes." He reached for the front button of her slacks. "But stop me if that isn't what you meant."

"Zach, you really should..." She didn't finish the weak protest because he'd slipped his hand inside her panties and discovered for himself that her answer was yes to whatever he had in mind.

His husky murmur of appreciation aroused her even more. His voice rasped in the stillness. "Kick off your shoes."

She understood why. He had no intention of taking her back to his tiny bedroom. He wanted her to strip right here, in the open doorway.

Apparently lust trumped modesty and her fear of wild animals, because she was going to let him do that. Once she was naked from the waist down, she wasn't surprised when he turned her toward a counter beside the door and asked her to brace her hands on it.

Her pulse beat frantically as she imagined having sex in a doorway open to the night air. No one could see or hear them, no one but the creatures of the forest. That seemed even more erotic. She had her own wild animal here in the trailer with her, and acting out his fantasy excited her more than he knew.

The condom box just happened to be in one of the shopping bags at her feet, and he wasted no time finding it. Cool air touched her bare bottom and the hot, moist place where he would soon bury his cock. She shivered, this time in anticipation instead of fear.

"Mmm, Jeannette." His breathing was ragged as he grasped her hips. "You drive me crazy." He probed once and sucked in a breath. "You're so wet." In one swift movement, he filled her, his groan thick with desire.

She gasped with pleasure as his cock twitched and his thighs brushed hers.

Supporting her and helping her balance, he eased back and slid home again. This time his groan was louder. "It feels too good." His voice was tight with strain. "I want it too much."

Her chest heaved as she struggled for air. "Go... for it."

"I...I have to." He began to stroke slowly at first, but that pace didn't last long. Soon he was pumping wildly as his thighs slapped hers. His noisy gusts of breath turned into stifled sounds punctuated with hoarse swearwords.

His frenzy fueled hers and she hurtled toward her climax. When their movements had reached a fever pitch, he slipped one hand forward to cup her, holding her for his thrusts as he massaged her trigger point.

She came before he did, panting and whimpering as her release surged through her. Her knees might have given way if he hadn't gripped her tight, one hand at her hip and one between her legs. Then he drove home one last time with a bellow of triumph. His body shuddered against hers and he swore once more as he pulsed within her.

They stayed like that for several long seconds until their breathing no longer sounded like the tortured gasps of two long-distance runners.

Zach spoke first. "Wow."

"Yeah."

"Intense."

"Uh-huh."

"If I let go, will you fall down?"

She took inventory. Her legs felt rubbery but she had a tight grip on the counter. "No."

"I'll go slow."

"Please do." She felt a sense of loss as he withdrew. Now that they weren't making so much noise, she heard a cricket tuning up outside. The owl hooted again. Some creature moved through the bushes.

But she experienced the sounds differently now. Pushing herself upright, she turned toward the open door and unbuttoned her blouse. The breeze felt heavenly on her overheated body, so she took off both her blouse and her bra.

Standing naked in front of the open doorway, she no longer felt so alien, so out of place. Sure, she'd freak out if a bear came wandering by. She might be ready to embrace nature, but she also would continue to have a healthy respect for it.

"If you'd let me, I'd take a picture of you like that."

She didn't turn around. "Well, I won't let you."

"Then I'll take a mental picture." Once again he came up behind her and gathered her close. "I've never seen anything so beautiful as you standing naked in the open doorway of my trailer."

"Well, I was danged hot, and there's a nice breeze."

"Logical. Is that all there is to it?"

"No." She leaned her head against his shoulder. "Thank you for what just happened."

"Hey, I'm the one full of gratitude. I honestly didn't think you'd agree. You seemed really nervous when we arrived, but I wanted to hear the wolves, and I was hoping you'd be open to the mysterious beauty of the place."

"I *was* nervous at first. But then the wolves started howlin', and you got turned on, which turned me on, and one thing led to another."

He laughed and gave her a hug. "It sure did."

"We behaved a little bit like animals do."

"I know. That's what I wanted."

"And because you wanted that, I began to want it, and now…it's as if some switch was tripped when we had sex that way, with the door open to the night. I feel as if I'm just another animal out here in the forest. It's kind of nice. Liberating."

He sighed. "That's great. I can't tell you how happy that makes me."

"That doesn't mean I'm ready to get up close and personal with a bear, though. I'm still scared of them."

"That's okay. I'd rather you didn't decide to get chummy with a bear. But like I said, I haven't seen one yet, and I've camped here for a month. For you to catch a glimpse of one in the next two days would be astounding."

"I don't know, Zach. Astounding things keep happening to me. But I could pass on seeing a bear." Now that she was braver, though, she wouldn't mind seeing one from a great distance.

"It's getting lighter out there. Can you tell? Before the outline of the Tetons wasn't clear, but now it is."

"That means you need to leave in a little while."

"Yeah. I was on probation for my first two weeks until they decided whether or not I could cut it around here. Now that I've been put on permanently, I don't want to screw that up by coming in late."

"Then show me around, tell me anything I need to know about this trailer and take off, cowboy."

"Okay." He gave her a quick hug and released her. "We can start by closing this door. No one will come out here at night, but during the day, it's possible somebody could show up. After all, this is Chance land." He pulled the door closed and twisted the dead bolt. "I'll lock you in when I leave."

"Are you worried about someone coming in?"

"Not a person. The crime rate's really low in the Shoshone area. But raccoons can be tricky. They use those little hands of theirs like you wouldn't believe. If I don't lock the door, they might figure out how to open it."

"I'll remember that."

"They're mostly nocturnal, so it's not a huge risk during the day, but I'm in the habit of locking the door just in case."

"Understood."

"Hang on a minute. I'm going to get you something." He walked back toward what she'd identified as the bedroom.

"If it's a weapon of some kind, I don't want it." She took in the extensive wood paneling covering many of the surfaces. Although the shape of the Airstream was nothing like a boat, she was reminded of sailing on her parents' yacht.

"It's not a weapon." He ducked through the bedroom doorway, although the door was merely a navy curtain secured with a tailored band of material. When he came back, he held out a navy bathrobe. "This is mine, and if you'd put it on, I'd be appreciative."

"All right." The bathrobe engulfed her, but it carried his spicy scent, so she didn't mind its enormous size. At least it didn't drag on the floor. He'd chosen knee-length, which was ankle-length on her. She belted it securely and rolled up the sleeves. "Better?"

He smiled. "I'm not sure. You look damned cute in it, so even though you're covered up, I want to do you."

"I could lock myself in the bathroom and we could talk through the door."

"Nah. I'll be strong. The robe does help. Just not enough. I'm not sure anything would, to tell the truth. I have a serious case of lust for you, Jeannette Trenton."

"That cuts both ways, Zach Powell."

"That's something. At least we're in the same fix."

His gaze was warm and he seemed to lose his place in the conversation.

Through the window, she could see the sky was turning the color of his gray eyes. "You were going to acquaint me with the silver bullet," she prompted.

"Yes. Yes, I was." He gestured toward the end opposite his bedroom. "That's the sitting area. A tabletop folds down and it becomes the dining room." Once again, he became lost staring at her.

"Lord, boy, you need sleep. You keep spacin' out on me." She should feel guilty that she'd been part of the scenario that had kept him from sleeping, but she knew he wouldn't have given that up for anything.

He shook his head as if to clear it. "I'll be fine. Where was I?"

"The couch is there, and a table folds down so you can eat there, too. I already know the bedroom's at the other end, and I can see the kitchen's in the middle. I assume the bathroom is, too."

"Right. There's food in the refrigerator. If you get hungry, help yourself."

"What about you? I completely forgot about your breakfast!"

"I'll grab something during a break at the ranch. The hands keep snacks in the bunkhouse. They're great guys and they've told me I'm welcome to it."

"You really love it here, don't you?"

"I do."

"And you don't miss the intellectual challenge of your legal practice?"

"Not at all."

She caught the flicker in his gray eyes. He might be telling himself he didn't miss it, but he'd been totally involved in the case she'd presented to him during the drive to Jackson. Now wasn't the time to argue that point, though.

"I expect you to sleep most of the time I'm gone, though."

She laughed. "Are you ordering me to bed?"

"I wish I could, and then follow you in there. In fact, if you wouldn't mind tucking yourself in right now while I'm being noble and strong, I won't be tempted to kiss you goodbye."

She met his gaze. He yearned for more time together and so did she. After what they'd shared, a kiss goodbye would be a natural thing to do, but one kiss would turn into twenty, and he'd be late to work.

"I'll see you later, Zach."

"See you later, Jeannette."

She turned and walked back toward the curtained doorway. It was a little goodbye, not the big one that would come in a couple of days. If she had trouble parting from him now, what would Monday be like?

9

ZACH PUT IN a couple of hours doing the usual morning chores, feeding horses and mucking out stalls. That kind of manual labor allowed him to think. The more he considered the step that he and Jeannette had taken by sharing living quarters this weekend, the more he realized he needed to inform Jack ASAP.

Jeannette had left a note at the Bunk and Grub, so word might eventually filter to the ranch. But Pam was spending the night in Emmett's little house and might have decided to stay until after the party. The grapevine wouldn't be working as efficiently as it might otherwise.

Zach felt an obligation both to Jeannette and the Chance family to make sure the new arrangement didn't catch everyone by surprise, especially in the middle of what was supposed to be Regan and Lily's show. Jeannette had mentioned that she didn't want to mess up their party by creating gossip. As the head of the family, Jack should be notified, and soon.

Fortunately Jack was on the premises this morning. The Last Chance was throwing a party tonight, and as the host, Jack was supervising every aspect of it. According to the old-timers, he'd gone through a period when he didn't want to have anything to do with parties or the planning of them.

But marriage and fatherhood had changed him and now he wanted to know every last detail, to the point that some complained that he'd overcorrected. As for Zach, he was thrilled the guy was on hand today so they could discuss Jeannette.

He found the eldest Chance brother helping the ranch hands set up a platform that would serve as a bandstand and dance floor. Judging from the conversation, the platform had been erected and dismantled several times in the past few years. It looked a little the worse for wear.

"It'll be fine for one more event." A hammer held loosely in one hand, Jack was talking with Watkins, a stocky ranch hand with a carefully waxed handlebar mustache. Watkins would be playing guitar for the event, along with a younger hand named Trey.

"I'm not convinced," Watkins said. "Trey and me, we invested in new speakers and they're heavier than the ones we used to have. Plus once people start dancing, if they stomp around like usual, they'll stress those joints."

"It's gonna work," Jack said. "After this party, we'll turn it into firewood and start over, but this is the last event of the season and I hate like hell to invest in a new platform that will just sit all winter in the tractor barn. And we're running out of time." He caught sight of Zach standing nearby. "What do you think, Powell?"

He shrugged. "I'm no expert."

Jack walked over to him and lowered his voice. "You've eyeballed contracts for rock concerts. You must have an opinion about the logistics, even for something piddly like this deal. Give me what you got, man."

After assessing the platform and thinking about the

potential dangers, Zach shrugged. "Like I said, this isn't my area, but I've seen what can happen when things go wrong. In your shoes, I wouldn't risk it. I'd call in all the hands if you have to so you can build a new platform."

"You're right. I know you're right. I've just been trying to convince myself by trying to convince Watkins." He adjusted the fit of his black Stetson before calling out to the hands. "We're starting over! Watkins, head into town and rustle us up some wood."

The stocky cowboy grinned. "Good decision, boss."

"It's an expensive decision, and we'll need everybody's help." He turned to another cowhand. "Shorty, put out the word. We need a new platform by five." Then he turned to Zach. "How are you with a hammer and saw?"

"Not bad. I'll help. But that wasn't why I came looking for you."

Jack's gaze narrowed. "I hope you're not giving me your notice. I realize you're overeducated for this job, but I like you and I'm hoping you stick it out."

"I plan to stick it out. This isn't about me. It's about Jeannette Trenton."

Jack's expression became unreadable. "What about her?"

"She's staying in my Airstream for the weekend."

"She's *what?*"

"I invited her and she accepted. Do you have a problem with that?"

"I don't know yet. The words are still making their way from my ears to my brain. Wasn't she at the Bunk and Grub or did I make that up?"

"She was at the Bunk and Grub, but she…I mean *we* decided she'd enjoy…uh, that is, we thought—"

"Easy, cowboy. Don't strain your brain." Jack tipped

his hat back and scrubbed a hand over his face. "I'm putting it all together, now. Josie told me that you and Jeannette were heading off to Jackson so she could buy more appropriate clothes for this weekend. I guess that shopping trip went well, huh?"

"She's a lawyer. I'm a lawyer. We have a lot in common."

"I can see that."

"Anyway, I just wanted you to know."

Jack nodded. "Thanks."

"And she'll be coming to the party with me."

"I figured as much. Is she still leaving town on Monday?"

"Far as I know." His chest tightened at the thought.

"You just said you plan to stick it out here, so I'll take that to mean you won't be running off to Virginia anytime soon."

"Definitely not."

Jack tapped the hammer handle against his thigh. "Okay, then." He turned toward the platform. "Might as well start turning this into kindling. We'll be needing it come December. Ever wintered in snow country?"

"Nope."

"When six-foot drifts block the front door and the wind chill is forty below, a man finds out what he's made of."

"Good." Zach grinned at him. "I'm looking forward to it."

ZACH'S DOUBLE BED tucked under the paneled curve of the Airstream's roof combined with the closed blinds over the windows gave the nook a cavelike quality that made her think of hibernating bears. His soft sheets and light blanket carried the scent of his aftershave. Although she was exhausted, she couldn't go to sleep right away. She kept thinking of Zach and all they'd shared.

Eventually she did fall asleep, though, and when she woke up she spent a couple of seconds trying to figure out where she was. Her nose registered the answer first. She was in Zach's bed, in Zach's silver bullet of a trailer, in a wooded area of the Last Chance Ranch.

The bedroom was tiny and didn't have space for much more than the bed, but a small ledge on the door wall held a clock. Nearly one in the afternoon. Zach got off work at two. Picturing him coming through the front door in another hour or so sent a jolt of anticipation through her.

Meeting him had changed everything, and seemed to be changing her, too. She never would have guessed she'd agree to make love in front of a door open to the wilds of Wyoming. Remembering it made her laugh in delight. She could take a solar shower with him this afternoon, no problem.

His solid presence gave her courage in so many ways. Until he'd come on the scene, she'd dreaded Regan and Lily's engagement party even though attending seemed like the right thing to do. She was still such an outsider that she'd expected to struggle through the evening. Having Zach by her side would make all the difference.

Thinking of the coolness that had surrounded them when they'd made love in the wee morning hours made her aware that the air was close and warm. Getting to her knees on the bed, she pulled up the blinds on all three windows that wrapped around the front of the trailer. Then she cranked each one open.

Ah. A breeze filled the bedroom with the aroma of evergreens. Birds chirped in the trees, and the burble of the stream created a scene right out of a nature video.

She could see why Zach loved it here, but the weather wouldn't always be this gorgeous.

She'd researched Jackson Hole after becoming engaged to Regan because he'd talked about taking her to the ranch. Summers had sounded great and this visit had convinced her how wonderful they could be. But winters were seriously frigid and snowy in this area. She wondered how Zach planned to deal with snow, ice and subzero weather.

Maybe he hadn't thought of that, yet. He seemed to be living his new life day-by-day, which interested her. She'd always been a planner, but he didn't seem to have definite plans for the future.

Her stomach rumbled. Zach would probably eat lunch at the ranch, so since she was hungry, she should feed herself before he came back. Besides, she was curious about the trailer. Now that she was more rested, she wanted to explore it, although that exploration wouldn't take long.

Grabbing Zach's bathrobe from where she'd left it at the end of the bed, she put it on. He had said that people sometimes showed up here during daylight hours. She didn't want to be seen wandering around his trailer stark naked.

She expected to find her clothes scattered on the floor where she'd shed them, but apparently Zach had gathered them before leaving. They lay folded on her suitcase, which stood right where he'd left it when they first came in. Both shopping bags sat beside the suitcase.

She knew for a fact Zach was glad she'd moved in for the weekend, but she didn't want him tripping over her things. With the limited space in the trailer, she wasn't sure what she would do with the suitcase, the bags or her clothes. She'd figure something out after lunch.

The blinds had been pulled up in the kitchen and living/dining area, so she opened those windows, too. Sunlight filtered through the trees, creating a dappled pattern on the walls, floor and built-in furniture. She noticed a rainbow dancing along one wall and traced it to a sun catcher Zach had hung from the ceiling near one of the windows. It shivered in the breeze.

A small plaque on another wall depicted a rustic log cabin and the words *Happiness is a cabin in the woods.* She wondered if he hoped to buy or build a cabin eventually somewhere in the area. That would answer the question of how he'd get through the winters, and it also told her he'd found his bliss in Jackson Hole.

Out of habit, she picked up her purse from the counter and pulled out her phone. To her surprise, there was a text from Zach. Now she remembered that they'd exchanged numbers on the way home from Jackson, in between belting out rock tunes.

Apparently he'd been asked to stay later to help build a new dance platform for the party tonight. He'd be back in time to shower and change. She hoped he was holding up okay without sleep. A nap would have helped, although knowing him, he might not have agreed to sleep when they could make love instead.

No text from Erin, though, so the research on the case must be going better thanks to Zach's suggestions. The law office seemed a million miles away as she tucked her phone back in her purse. In two short steps she stood in front of the cupboards and the refrigerator. Compact living took some getting used to.

She hoped to find food items that wouldn't take major cooking skills. She'd already screwed up a kitchen experience once on this trip and she didn't relish doing it again here. This place belonged to a guy, so she thought her chances were good that simple food would be available.

The kitchen yielded a jar of peanut butter, smooth, the way she liked it, apricot jam, also a favorite of hers, and a loaf of bread. His coffeepot was simple enough to operate, and before long she'd pulled down the collapsible dining table and was eating her first meal in his silver bullet.

This setting was seductive, making her want to walk in the woods after lunch and read a book while sitting next to the stream. Unlike Zach, she still needed to earn a living, but she'd saved some money, too. If she scaled back her lifestyle, she could take a part-time job and still make ends meet.

If she stayed here long enough, would she lose all ambition the way Zach seemed to have done? She didn't want to find out. She'd worked too long and hard to achieve her success, and a partnership was something she'd envisioned from the beginning. It was within reach. She wanted that validation.

But thinking of reading beside the stream reminded her that a book would be nice to have while she ate. Leaving the table, she walked three steps to his bookshelf. Maybe the Airstream reminded her of a boat partly because everything had to be secured against falling in transit. Railings kept both food and cookware in the cupboards, and reading material from falling off the bookshelf.

She browsed his selection of action/adventure novels and decided against those. He had a few mysteries that interested her. He also had trail guides and a selection of outdoor living magazines. His manual for the

Airstream was tucked in with the magazines, which made her smile.

Behind the magazines she discovered something surprising, though. In spite of his firm statement that he had no interest in practicing law, he'd bought a study guide for passing the Wyoming bar exam. It looked and smelled brand-new. She paged through it, hoping to find some jotted notes or a dog-eared page, anything to indicate he'd spent time with the material. Nothing.

Yet he'd bought it. She clung to that thought as evidence that he might yet resume the profession he'd trained for. Replacing the study guide exactly as she'd found it, she took a paperback mystery from the shelf and returned to the table.

The book stayed closed as she wrestled with her thoughts. It shouldn't matter to her whether Zach abandoned his career. He obviously intended to stay in this area, and whether he worked as a lawyer or a ranch hand wouldn't affect her one bit.

But that wasn't the whole story, and she knew it. She believed that everyone came into this world with certain gifts, and using them fully contributed to a satisfying life. That's what she wanted for herself and for anyone sharing her journey.

In discussing her Thoroughbred-foal case with him, she'd discovered that he had a mind perfectly suited to the intricacies of contract law. She knew that because she had the same gift. Physically they were a great match, but they were also in tune mentally. No wonder they'd bonded so fast.

Sure, circumstances might keep them apart, namely his decision to live here and her career opportunities in Virginia. But that problem wasn't the biggest sticking point between them. She purely hated that he was wasting his potential.

She'd agreed to this sexual adventure because she'd desperately needed a night of fantasy and Zach had been eager to share that with her. Now the adventure would last longer than one night, but the boundaries hadn't really changed. She was still leaving on Monday.

They could continue having great sex until she left and keep those boundaries in place. Until finding that study guide, she'd expected to do exactly that. She hadn't intended to involve herself in his future.

But now she planned to open up this can of worms. If he loved working on the ranch, great. Surely he could satisfy that urge and still use his top-notch legal mind in some capacity. If he chose not to, well, that was his right, of course.

If she were more Zen maybe she'd be able to accept it. She wasn't Zen. Before she left on Monday, they were going to talk about that study guide. Maybe the discussion would blow up in her face, but she had to give it a shot.

As she finished her PB and J and sipped her coffee, she decided to choose that moment very carefully. So much could depend on how such a discussion ended. She certainly wouldn't hit him with it when he walked in the door this afternoon.

Between now and then she had some tidying up to do. Rolling back the sleeves of his bathrobe a couple more turns, she washed up her lunch dishes. Then she tackled the suitcase and shopping-bag situation.

Miracle of miracles, she found two empty drawers in the hallway. She transferred the contents of her suitcase and the bags to the large drawers. She put the box of condoms on the ledge in the bedroom next to the clock.

She'd brought a pair of flip-flops, and she put those on while she carried her empty suitcase to the car.

Zach pulled up just as she opened the back door of her rental car to hoist the suitcase inside. He hopped out and rounded the front of his truck. "I hope this isn't what it looks like." His tone was joking, but there was a slight frown denting the space between his eyebrows.

"The suitcase is empty."

"That's good news." The frown disappeared and he nudged back his hat. "For a minute there I wondered if you were moving out."

"Nope." She closed the door and walked over to him. "Just tryin' to keep the floor clear of obstacles."

He smiled. "Good thinking." Hooking his finger in the bathrobe's tie, he tugged her closer and loosened the tie in the process. "Missed you."

"I missed you, too." She'd noticed sawdust on his jeans, which matched the heady aroma of freshly cut lumber and manly sweat. Her body responded with astounding speed. "You're early."

"We finished up sooner than expected." He slid both hands inside the bathrobe, loosening the tie completely as he drew her into his arms. "So I hotfooted it home only to find you slinging your suitcase into your car. I immediately started coming up with what I could say or do to keep you from taking off."

She wound her arms around his neck and nestled against him. The cool metal of his belt buckle pressed against her warm skin. "Like what?"

"Like telling you how much fun you're going to have under my solar shower." He massaged her bottom.

"I will?"

"Guaranteed. If you haven't been soaped, sponged

and rinsed off by Zach Powell, you have no idea what you're missing."

"Can't wait."

"I'm afraid you'll have to." He lowered his head and gave her a kiss that included a very erotic use of his tongue. Finally he lifted his mouth a fraction from hers. "The thing is," he murmured, "because I'm back early, we have some time to kill before we shower. And I have some ideas about that, too."

"I'll just bet you do."

"How do you like my bed?"

"Love it."

"I predict you'll love it even more with a couple of enhancements."

"Which are?"

"Me and a condom."

10

ZACH RELISHED EVERY HOT, heavy-breathing moment with Jeannette in his double bed, even if they were a little cramped and he bumped his head. Twice. That was the number of times she'd come, and he was so involved in her enthusiastic response that he forgot the space constraints.

He came soon after her second orgasm, which canceled out the pain in his head right quick. Eventually he had to exit the bedroom and go into the airplane-sized bathroom to dispose of the condom. Knowing the solar shower was next on the agenda, he grabbed a couple of towels on his way back.

He walked in to find her lying there all pink and mussed from their great sex. She rolled to her side and smiled at him. He realized then that he was well and truly screwed, and not in the way he would have preferred.

Weeks, months, maybe years would go by before he could sleep in that bed without being reminded of Jeannette. The hot sex was part of it, but he loved the way she looked lying there, especially at this very moment, her green eyes smoky and her body relaxed and languid.

Despite knowing the memories would haunt him, he would give anything not to have this party obligation. Although every intimate second he spent with her dug the hole deeper, he longed to hide away with this woman. They wouldn't have to make love constantly. He was willing to take time out to eat and talk. In fact, talking to her was one of the best parts.

In short, he was falling in love. And that was why he was screwed six ways to Sunday. He wasn't right for her and she wasn't right for him. They'd both known it in advance, and like a fool, he'd thought he could handle this temporary arrangement.

Well, he'd just have to, wouldn't he? Not much choice in the matter. He wasn't going to ask her to give up all she'd worked for in Virginia to start over in Jackson Hole so she could hang out with him. He knew what it took to build a practice from scratch. She'd be justified in laughing at the idea.

Maybe the party was a good thing. It would get them out of here for a few hours so he could pull back emotionally. He adopted the drill-sergeant voice he'd learned from watching movies. "Time to hit the showers, Trenton!"

"Aye, aye, sir." She gave him a sloppy salute and stayed where she was.

"I said move it!"

"Somebody turned my bones to rubber, sir."

"Tell me who that son of a bitch was and I'll have him thrown in the brig!"

"Only if you'll throw me in there, too, sir. I want him to do it again."

His cock stirred. "Trust me, he wants to." His voice grew husky. "But he promised to take you to a party."

"I know." She sighed. "And the party's important. I need to get into that shower."

"It'll be a very good shower." He waggled his eyebrows.

"I see." She sat up and swung her feet to the floor. "You're turning me into a libertine, Zach Powell. All I can think of is having sex with you in all sorts of imaginative ways."

"I'll take that as a compliment."

"You should. You're looking at a type-A personality who always puts business before pleasure."

"It takes one to know one."

She shook her head. "If you were that way once, you're not now."

"You'd be surprised. I could revert in no time." That was one of the reasons he wouldn't go back to practicing law. He was a recovering type-A personality, if there were such a thing.

"Does it make you nervous to be around someone like me, then?"

"A little bit." He grinned. "But then I can get you naked and make you come, and we're all good."

"So that's your method." She stood and walked toward him. "FYI, it works like a charm."

"For now, anyway." He didn't kid himself. He knew when she was back in lawyer mode that his strategy would be less effective. He'd caught her at a time when she needed the distraction he was willing to provide. "Ready for the solar-shower experience?"

"Why not? What should I bring?"

"Just your sweet body. You can put on your flip-flops if you want. I'm used to walking barefoot on the ground, but you're not. The soap and sponges are already out there."

"We're leaving the trailer wearing nothing? I thought you said it was always possible someone would come by."

"Normally that's true, but everyone and his dog is working furiously to get ready for the party. They're either setting up tables and chairs, fixing food or getting dressed. No one has time to take a trip out to check on you and me."

"What about some stranger?"

"We're on private property. A stranger would be trespassing, and Jack doesn't tolerate trespassers. He takes his stewardship of this land very seriously. Not much happens on the Last Chance that escapes his notice."

"Including me staying out here with you?"

"I told him about that this morning."

She looked wary. "What did he say?"

"Not much. He was surprised at first, but in the long run, I think he figures it's our business." He thought about whether to add any more, and decided she might be reassured if he mentioned what else had been said. "He wanted to make sure I wouldn't be heading for Virginia in the near future. I said there was no chance of that."

"Of course not. I can tell how much you love it here."

"Anyway, Jack understands this deal between us is temporary."

"That's good."

"I thought so. I didn't want any speculation on anyone's part. Jack will probably inform Josie, and the word will get out."

"At least I know Regan will be fine with it."

Zach started to say that he couldn't care less. He'd been the one to offer Jeannette support when Regan had been otherwise occupied, so the guy was in no position to say anything about the situation now. But he thought better of saying so. "But if we don't take showers, we'll never get there, which would not be a good thing."

"Right. Lead the way."

He grabbed his keys on the way out the door and locked up after them to make sure nothing got in while they were engrossed in the shower. He'd checked the time and they had some leeway. They could have some fun with the shower.

The relaxation they'd both felt after rolling around on his bed had disappeared during their discussion. The shower would be another tension reliever. Nothing like warm water, a smooth bar of soap and a soft sponge to make them both feel great.

He was proud of this shower setup. The Airstream had one, but he was always knocking his knees and elbows against the wall in there. His solar shower gave him all the room he needed, and it didn't use any energy other than sunlight.

He'd built a wooden drainage platform and positioned it under the bag of water hanging from a tree branch, and the trench he'd dug carried water away so he didn't end up with a mud hole. A bamboo shower caddy hanging from the trunk of the tree held his soap, shampoo and a sponge.

Jeannette surveyed his creation. "This is amazing, Zach. Everyone should have something like this."

"That would be great except not everyone has acres of private land surrounding them, and come winter, I won't be using this anymore."

"I've wondered what will happen with you and this trailer after the first snow."

"I'm working on that. I have some ideas. I've only been here a month."

"I know. And for the summer, you're in great shape. So what happens first with this shower situation?"

"Do you want to wash your hair? I recommend it because I don't have a shower cap."

She peered at his shampoo. "Okay, sure. Not my brand, but it'll do."

The scene seemed somewhat unreal. He'd been out here nearly every afternoon for a month and had begun taking the routine for granted. Seeing Jeannette standing there in all her glory put a whole new erotic spin on things. He had a little trouble concentrating on the task at hand.

She peered at him. "So what next?"

"I have to get you wet."

Her green eyes sparkled. "That's usually no problem."

Lust hardened his cock. "Uh, with water."

"Oh, *that's* what you're talking about. You'll have to be more specific."

He cleared his throat. "I'll try to remember that. First thing, get up on the platform."

"With or without flip-flops?"

"Without. I sanded the wood until it was like satin. You'll like standing on it."

"Gotcha." She stepped out of her rubber sandals and onto the platform. "You're right. This feels great under my toes. Now what?"

"I'll release some water from the bag. Get under it and use your hands to work it through your hair and spread it over your body."

"Sounds kinky."

"It's not when I do it."

"You don't have a little solo fun in this shower?"

"No. I'm outside, for God's sake. I'm not going to..."

"Then we won't be fooling around out here?"

He realized all the plans he had for her. They would still be outside, and he'd specifically imagined using the sponge to make her a happy woman. "I didn't say that."

"But you don't fool around alone."

"That's different."

"Why?"

He stared at her as he tried to come up with a reasonable explanation as to why he was perfectly willing to make her come during this shower experience, but he'd never considered taking his own pleasure that way.

"You don't have an answer, do you?"

"No."

"Then here's the deal. You can play around with me all you want, but then you have to let me have the same liberties. Because I'm getting into this outdoor recreation plan. Now that you've convinced me we won't be observed except for the birds and the bees, I'm all for it."

"Then so am I." Hell, why quibble? He had her here for a very short time, and he might as well get as much enjoyment out of those precious hours as possible.

She gazed up at the spigot. "Now that we've settled that, turn on the water. And don't use too much."

"I won't." He opened the valve.

"I want plenty left for my turn with you."

That comment distracted him so much that he forgot to turn off the water.

"Zach!"

He shut it off again.

"That was too much water. I know it was."

"Maybe."

"I'm guessing I should wash my hair before you move in with whatever you have in mind. Otherwise I'll get soap in my eyes."

He grinned. His seductive operation was being taken over by this newly liberated woman and he was fine with that. "Sure. Get some suds in your hair and then I'll give you more water to wash them out." Then he had a thought. "Or I could wash your hair."

She paused with her hand cupped, shampoo pooled in her palm. "I suppose you could. Do you want to?"

"Silly question." He stepped onto the platform, took her hand and transferred the slippery shampoo to his palm. Standing behind her, his body brushing hers, he began working the lather into her hair. "Are your eyes closed?" He didn't want to get soap in them.

"Yes."

"Well, tip your head back some more to make sure nothing runs into them." He massaged her scalp with the tips of his fingers. "Am I doing it right? I've never washed anyone's hair but mine."

"You're doing…great." Her words tumbled out along with a soft purr of contentment.

"Don't know why I never have. This is fun. Especially naked."

"Mmm."

"Eyes still closed?" He leaned over her shoulder to make sure and discovered her nipples were tight with arousal. He was turning her on by washing her hair. He'd had no clue that would happen.

He hated to rinse her hair and break the mood he had going. Figuring that shampoo wasn't much different from liquid soap, he stroked the lather over her shoulders. Next he covered her breasts with his hands and massaged in slow circles.

She moaned softly and leaned against him, which brought her sleek behind in contact with his increasingly rigid cock. Sweet torture. He reached a hand between her thighs and caressed her with deliberate intent.

Her breathing changed as she rose on her toes and rocked her hips forward, inviting him deeper. Ah, there. Curving his fingers to stroke her G-spot brought a throaty groan of delight.

Her moist channel flexed and he pressed his thumb on her sensitive nub. For one moment she was as taut as a bow, poised on the brink, and then she came, his name on her lips as her body surrendered to the surge of her orgasm.

He held her until she stopped shaking. Continuing to support her with one hand, he reached for the valve that sent a spray of warm water onto them. "Keep your eyes shut," he murmured as he worked the suds from her hair. He followed the trail of lather down her body, wiping it away with his wet hands.

He let the water run to make sure the shampoo was all gone. He wouldn't have enough for his shower, but he didn't care. When he was convinced she was rinsed clean, he reached for the valve, but she chose that moment to turn in his arms and wrap her fingers around his cock.

Droplets clung to her eyelashes as she gazed up at him. Her mouth curved seductively. "My turn." She began to slide her fingers rapidly up and down as warm water sluiced over them, aiding her cause.

There couldn't be much water left and this was a far better use of it than any shower would ever be. He'd been aroused ever since he'd started washing her hair. He would come quickly. She held his gaze as she stroked, and his climax arrived right before the water ran out. Shuddering, he pulled her slick body close.

He had no wish to let her go, but they couldn't stand

out here forever. With great reluctance he sighed and released her. He'd lost track of the time, but judging from the lengthening shadows, they needed to move along.

She gave him a lazy smile. "I liked that."

"Me, too."

She noticed the empty water bag. "It's all gone and you didn't get your shower."

"I'll take one inside." His voice was husky, his body still humming. If they didn't have to leave he'd invite her back to bed. But they had places to go and people to see.

"I love your solar shower."

He reached out and combed a damp strand of hair back from her cheek. "I knew you would."

"Tomorrow, you get to be first. And I'll wash *your* hair. I promise it will turn you on like you wouldn't believe."

He chuckled. "Yeah, like my libido needs a boost. I've never had so much sex in my life. Never wanted to. But with you, I can't seem to get enough. You're amazing."

Her expression grew serious. "It's not me. It's the tickin' clock."

He didn't want to believe that, but he didn't feel like arguing about it, either. "Oh, I'm pretty sure it's you. Clocks do nothing for me whatsoever."

"You know what I mean." She smiled. "We—"

"Shh." He laid a finger over her mouth. "I do know, and I think you're wrong, but let's debate it later, preferably in bed after we're sweaty and satisfied. Right now, we're expected at an engagement party. You don't want to miss it."

"Guess not."

"If you don't go to the party, you can't show off the

clothes you bought in Jackson." He picked up her flip-flops and knelt down to slip them on her feet.

"When you do that, you make me feel like Cinderella."

He stood and held out his hand. "And you make me feel like Prince Charming. Will you dance with me at the ball, princess?"

"Do you dance?" She seemed intrigued with the idea.

"Jack expects all his cowhands to know how. He claims it's an important part of the cowboy way and should be encouraged whenever possible. Fortunately I had that covered before I hired on." He gazed at her. "Do *you* dance?"

"I'm a Southern belle. I had a comin'-out party. Of course I dance."

"Then we're good. But let's not stay until the clock strikes twelve, okay?"

"Will you turn into a pumpkin?"

"No. I'll turn into a frustrated cowboy with an erection. I'm in danger of that right now, in fact. Let's get you back to the trailer and into those new clothes."

She laughed. "Okay."

As they walked over to the trailer hand-in-hand, he wished they hadn't done a riff on that particular fairy tale. It was all about a ticking clock.

11

ZACH DIDN'T HAVE full-length mirrors in his trailer, but he convinced her she looked like a cowgirl in her new outfit of jeans and a white stretchy knit top that showed off a little cleavage. "A sexy cowgirl, at that," he said with a smile.

"Thank you." She watched him finish getting dressed in the living room. It was the only place big enough to accomplish the task, so she'd dressed while he'd showered in the minuscule bathroom. "But I don't want to seem as if I'm tryin' too hard. My mama used to caution me about it. I have that tendency."

His jaw tightened. "We all try too hard sometimes." He fastened the last few snaps on his dove-grey Western shirt. "I'm not sure it helps to point it out."

She thought about that. "I suppose not. I guess she meant well, but I used to get a knot in my stomach when she said I was tryin' too hard."

"How's your stomach feeling now?" He unfastened his jeans and tucked his shirttails inside.

"Warm and happy. All of me is warm and happy watchin' you get dressed. The only thing that would be better is watching you get undressed."

He sighed as he buckled his belt. "Don't I wish you could be doing that right now." He opened a cupboard and pulled out what looked like a new black Stetson and put it on. "Ready?"

"Sure." Oh, yeah, she was, but not to be with a bunch of other people. She wanted to have this broad-shouldered, sweet-smelling man all to herself. "Nice hat."

"It's my party hat. The gray one's for going into town, and the brown one's for getting dusty working on the ranch. This one's special."

"That's a reason for me to be excited about going tonight, then. You look mighty fine, cowboy."

He touched the brim of his hat. "Thank you, ma'am."

"Did you practice that?"

He grinned. "I might have a time or two, after I bought my first hat."

"Well, it's extremely effective. It made my little heart flutter."

"Interesting. Did it have any effect on the rest of you?"

She ran a finger down his chest and batted her eyelashes. "*May*-be. Wanna find out?"

"Yes, damn it." With a growl, he set his hands on her shoulders and turned her toward the door. "Get on out of here before I forget all my good intentions."

Laughing, she opened the trailer door and walked down the steps.

He locked up the Airstream but still managed to get the door of his truck open before she reached it. "I do love the fit of those jeans, lady. And the little sparkles on the back pockets make me think of things I shouldn't, at least for now. Have you ever line danced?"

"No, why?"

"Because if you decide to try it tonight, you'll drive

the guys crazy when you wiggle those rhinestones." He winked and closed the door.

After he rounded the truck and climbed behind the wheel, she glanced at him. "You're good for my ego."

"You're good for mine." He closed the door and buckled up. "I feel like the luckiest guy on the planet tonight." He started the powerful engine and backed the truck around.

"Oh, Lord, I just thought of something."

He stepped on the brakes. "What?"

"I didn't get Lily and Regan anything. I probably should have. It's an engagement party, so I should be bringing them an engagement present. I should have thought of that while we were in Jackson, but I didn't. I was too focused on—"

"Jeannette, it's okay." He put a hand on her thigh and gave it a squeeze. "Just tell them you wanted to ask what they needed and you'll send them a gift from Virginia."

"I know, but I don't even have a card! If I had a card, I could write something like that in it, but I didn't even get that far in my thinking. Sheesh."

Zach put the truck in Reverse. "Let's go see what I have. I'm thinking that I bought a box of note cards a while ago, a mixture for various occasions. I don't write to people much, but every now and then I get the urge."

Somehow, she doubted that he'd happen to have a note card that said Congratulations on Your Engagement. But he was being sweet and understanding, so she'd go back in the trailer with him and see what he had available.

Once they were back in the Airstream, he pulled open a drawer. "Yeah, here's the box." He opened it. "There's one left, but it won't work."

"Why not?"

Laughing, he handed her the card.

The message on the front read In Deepest Sympathy. "I see what you mean." She grinned. "But don't give up. We could tear off the front if the message inside is ambiguous." She opened the card. "'May your memories comfort you in your hour of grief.'" She looked at Zach and they both started laughing like crazy people.

"Oh, yeah." He gasped for breath. "Use the inside part. That's *so* much better!"

"I can think of some couples this card would be great for." She wiped tears from her eyes.

"But not this one. Sorry I haven't solved your problem."

"Yes, you have." She smiled at him. "You made me laugh about it and gave me some perspective. So I don't have a gift and I don't have a card. But I'm here to give them a hug and wish them well in person, so what's the point in a card? And I'm the gift!"

"Yes, you are." He gazed at her with a soft light in his eyes. "You're one hell of a gift. Let's go to that party."

THEY'D BEEN RUNNING behind to begin with, and the issue with the card made them later yet, but Zach watched in admiration as Jeannette shrugged off any trace of discomfort. She stepped right into the party atmosphere with her head high and a bright smile on her face. He stood back while she had a private moment with the honored guests.

Regan and Lily made a striking couple, with his Italian background and her fiery red hair that never seemed quite tidy. Jeannette greeted Regan with a hug. Zach squelched his automatic twinge of jealousy. She'd been Regan's lover once, but now Zach was the fortunate man who shared a bed with her this weekend.

She was blossoming right before his eyes. Although he was happy for her, he struggled with the knowledge that she'd go on blossoming after she left him. Someone else would be around for that and yet he'd helped influence this massive change. That didn't seem fair.

But if he cared about her, and he definitely did, then he should forget about what was fair for him and concentrate on what was right for her. Then he could send her back to Virginia with a glad heart. He wasn't convinced he was that noble, though.

Regan laughed at whatever Jeannette was saying, and Zach felt another twinge. Envy gripped him instead of jealousy as he thought of all the years Regan had known Jeannette and all the memories they shared. She'd probably reminded him of some funny incident just now.

Then Jeannette hugged Lily. After more laughter, the two women started chatting. Zach caught a few words of it and realized they were talking about wedding dresses and veils. Regan's eyes glazed over.

That was Zach's cue to step up and shake the guy's hand. "I'm happy for you. Lily seems like a wonderful woman."

"She has to be if she's willing to put up with the likes of me." Regan turned slightly away from the two women and lowered his voice. "I heard that Jeannette's staying with you for the weekend."

He met Regan's dark gaze. "She is."

"In the Airstream?"

"Yes." Zach braced himself. The guy was the guest of honor, but he'd better watch what he said about Jeannette or things would get ugly fast.

"That's so…" Regan shook his head.

"So what?"

"Out of character."

"Is it?" Zach's hands flexed.

"Take it easy, Powell. I don't mean that as an insult to her or your Airstream. But Jeannette doesn't camp. Or didn't camp." He glanced back in the direction of his bride-to-be and his ex. "Maybe she's changed."

"Could be. I didn't know her before."

"She seems different tonight, more relaxed. The Jeannette I knew would have been mortified to show up without a card or a gift. Instead she made a joke of it."

"Oh?"

"She told us that at the last minute you rummaged around looking for something and came up with a sympathy card."

"That's what you were laughing about?"

"Yeah. I thought it was hilarious, and so did she—and that surprised the hell out of me. It's good to see her loosening up."

Zach nodded, because he really wasn't sure what to say to that. Fortunately he'd lost the urge to sock Regan in the jaw. Jeannette's ex seemed to genuinely care about her, in spite of what they'd been through.

"Hey, is this a private conversation, or can I join in?" The speaker had a definite Southern drawl.

"Hey, Drake!" Regan gave the newcomer the kind of back-thumping hug that demonstrated affection while asserting manliness. "You know Zach Powell, right? Jack hired him about a month ago."

Drake held out his hand. "Drake Brewster from Virginia. We've never met, but the rumor mills run twenty-four-seven in this town. I saw you with Jeannette a while ago and knew immediately who you were."

Zach accepted the man's firm handshake, thinking this had to be the strangest grouping ever. Here they stood, each of them with an intimate connection to Jeannette. But they couldn't very well mention *that.* He wouldn't, anyway. He searched for some sports-related topic but drew a blank.

Drake had a beer in one hand, but he seemed to be completely sober and every inch the Southern gentleman. The beer didn't seem quite right. It should have been a mint julep, except the Last Chance didn't tend to serve those.

He drew closer to Zach. "This is none of my damn business, but is Jeannette really stayin' in your Airstream for the weekend?"

"Yes." He took a deep breath and hoped Drake would mind his manners, too.

The Southerner glanced over at Regan. "Can you beat that? Our Jeannette camping out?"

Zach would have loved to take issue with the *our Jeannette* part of that comment, but technically Drake and Regan had more right to claim her than he did. They'd both known her since she was eighteen. He'd known her since yesterday.

"It's hard to picture her in a trailer." Regan shrugged. "But I think it's great."

"Oh, so do I. It's just surprisin'." He raised his beer bottle in Zach's direction. "My hat's off to the man who convinced Jeannette Trenton to camp in the woods."

"She's really fine with it." Zach wanted to give credit where credit was due. These guys didn't seem to know anything about Jeannette's spirit of adventure.

Drake's eyes widened. "Seriously?"

"She thought it would be fun." In his opinion, it had shot way past fun and moved into life-changing territory.

"I'll be damned." Drake gazed at Zach with obvious

respect. “My hat’s still off to you, because somehow you inspired her to consider that option.”

“I think she was ready to make some changes. I was just in the right place at the right time.”

Drake laughed. “That’s soundin’ like Lily. Doesn’t that sound like her, Regan? ‘When the student is ready, the teacher will appear’ and all that New Age mumbo jumbo.”

“Hey, that’s my fiancée you’re talking about.” But Regan laughed as if he hadn’t taken any offence to Drake’s comments.

Drake smiled. “I know she is, and I love her to pieces—in a purely platonic way, naturally.”

“Naturally.”

Zach was fascinated by the dynamic between the two friends. They’d been through hell and back with each other. Drake had seduced Regan’s fiancée. And yet they’d rebuilt their trust to the point they could joke about how much Drake loved Lily, but only as a friend.

Zach thought of his conversation with Jeannette on the topic. He still thought it was a tricky juggling act, but maybe a true friendship with a woman who wasn’t also a lover might actually be possible. Now that he was out of the hotbed of L.A., he might be able to explore the concept.

A woman called Drake’s name and Drake glanced in that direction. “Whoops, gotta go. Tracy’s summoning me, and when that woman summons, I respond immediately. Life’s easier that way.”

Regan laughed. “Wise man.” Then he turned to Zach. “What do you say we talk Lily and Jeannette into hitting the buffet table? And I don’t know about you, but I could use a beer.”

“Sounds good.” Zach relaxed. He’d wondered if he’d

have to run interference for Jeannette tonight, but Regan's invitation to share dinner had handled that neatly.

Regan might have been preoccupied with his fiancée and wedding plans during the past week, but tonight he seemed keenly aware that Jeannette needed his sponsorship in order to be accepted into this crowd. To Zach's relief, Regan was ready to give it.

During the meal Zach got to know and admire Lily King, who ran an equine rescue operation on the outskirts of Shoshone. She and Regan had become acquainted when he'd volunteered his vet services there. Zach quickly learned that Lily was way smarter than he was and more generous toward others, too. He put her on his mental list of potential women friends.

And it seemed that once Lily realized Jeannette hadn't truly been accepted by Regan's sisters, she appointed herself the official Jeannette Trenton ambassador. Zach sipped his beer and watched Lily casually bring Jeannette into a group that included two of Regan's sisters, Morgan and Tyler.

Regan followed Zach's gaze. "Lily's working it."

"She sure as hell is. I'm impressed."

"I've tried talking to Morgan and Tyler, but they just brush me off. They want to be affronted on my behalf, and that's that. I was hoping my folks would make it out for this party and they'd talk to my sisters, but at the last minute my mom got the flu so they canceled. Lily will be a big help, though. She's all about peace, love and forgiveness."

"You found yourself a gem, O'Connelli."

"I did. So what about you and Jeannette? Looks like you two get along great."

Zach continued to watch the group of women. Jeannette appeared to be having a good time. "We do get along, but she's about to make partner with her law firm."

"Is she?" Regan grinned. "That's terrific. She didn't tell me that. I'll be sure to congratulate her."

"It is terrific." Zach swallowed another mouthful of beer. "But that means her life is very solid back there. And I've finally found the place I've been looking for. You live here, so I'm sure you know what I'm talking about. This place gets in your blood."

"It does, which means she could learn to love it, too. Talk her into moving. She's a go-getter. Tell her to set up a law office in Shoshone. We could use one."

Zach considered the very tempting idea. But finally he shook his head. "I can't ask her to give up a partnership she's been working toward for years. She wants it. I think…" He caught himself before he said any more. Probably better not to discuss his theories with Regan.

"Of course she wants it." Regan also continued to watch the group of women talking and laughing. "She's desperate to please her parents."

Zach blew out a breath. "She mentioned something about that."

"I've interacted with Dick and Eunice Trenton over the years, and it's obvious they're more interested in their racing stable than in their daughter. I get the impression she's been tolerated instead of cherished."

"I'm afraid you're right."

"It's a defining part of her story. Because she inconvenienced her parents, she has to be the perfect child. I'm sure they gave her hell over the broken engagement."

Zach nodded. "Sounded like it to me. Unforgiving people with high expectations."

"That's why I was so glad when she blew off the card

and present thing. That was a real step forward." Regan turned toward Zach. "If you had anything to do with that, then I have to say you're a good influence on her."

"Maybe I played some small part." He met Regan's gaze. "But that doesn't mean she'd give up the opportunity to make partner so she could come out here and build a practice from the ground up in a little town like Shoshone. Nothing high-profile about that move. I can't see her doing it."

"Depends on how much she wants to be with you."

Zach took a deep breath. "That's the million-dollar question, isn't it?"

12

JEANNETTE REALIZED WHAT Lily was doing and she thoroughly appreciated it. For the first time since she'd arrived in Shoshone, she had a friendly conversation with Morgan Chance. She made friends with Morgan's two children, both redheads like Morgan, and discussed the real estate business in Shoshone, which was Morgan's field.

She was a little more nervous about talking with Tyler, Regan's twin sister, because she'd heard what a close bond twins could have. Tyler's dark eyes and hair reminded her so much of Regan that she felt as if she knew her and they were already friends. Yet they weren't, and Tyler could be carrying a lot of resentment.

Lily's warm presence helped enormously, though, and soon Tyler opened up. Her former job as an activities director for a cruise line meant she'd traveled the world, including places Jeannette had visited with her parents. Tyler's enthusiasm for beautiful spots like Florence and Santorini melted any remaining tension. Soon all the women at the table were busy planning their dream vacations.

Unfortunately Cassidy, Regan's eighteen-year-old

sister, wasn't sitting with them. She'd made no effort to be friendly and probably wouldn't be easy to win over, but Jeannette was encouraged by the interaction with Morgan and Tyler. Cassidy would just take a little longer. If only Jeannette had more time…but she didn't.

In about thirty-six hours, she'd be on a plane to Virginia. Would she be back? That was hard to say. She loved Regan like a brother and his sisters were a hoot, but popping in and out of Jackson Hole might not be as easy as she'd like to imagine.

Drake wouldn't be in town much longer, either. He and Tracy had decided to move to Virginia. Drake planned to establish an equine rescue facility for Thoroughbred racehorses, and Tracy had just been admitted to the University of Virginia and had been able to transfer some of her online credits in psychology. Jeannette looked forward to visiting them.

Flying to Jackson Hole involved a much bigger commitment though. And then there was the issue of Zach. She couldn't come to Shoshone and pretend Zach didn't live here, too. She'd be looking for him around every corner. She'd want to know whether he'd found the woman of his dreams.

Ugh. That was a depressing thought. Yet he was a virile, lovable man who deserved to have a woman in his life. Once she left town, he'd probably start looking for someone who fancied a cabin in the woods.

As if her thoughts had drawn him to her, he approached the group of women gathered around a picnic table, a group she'd become a part of in the past half hour. She was proud of that, but she was glad to see Zach. She'd missed him.

"I don't want to interrupt," he said, "but the guitar

players are tuning up and I'd like to borrow Jeannette for a dance."

Morgan laughed. "If the dancing's about to start, we'll all be out there, even the kids. A Last Chance party is about the food and the dancing." She turned to Lily. "Speaking of that, aren't you and Regan supposed to start this thing off?"

"I think that's a wedding tradition, not an engagement party tradition." Lily shrugged. "But what do I know? I've never been engaged before, let alone married."

"Regan and Lily probably should start the dancin'," Jeannette said. Then she realized maybe she shouldn't have stated that so directly. "At least that's how we do it in Virginia. Y'all might do it differently out here."

"See, I thought that was how it should go." Morgan made a shooing motion with her hands. "Go get your man, Lily, and boogie on out there so the rest of us can join in. My dancing feet are itching to see some action."

"Okay." Lily left her seat. "But don't leave us out there alone for too long, please. Regan and I are kind of new to this Last Chance dancing tradition. Compared to you guys, we might suck."

"Hey," Tyler said, "if my hubby can learn to hang with these folks, anybody can. You'll be fine." She glanced at Zach. "I'll bet Jack asked if you could dance when he hired you. Am I right?"

"You would be right."

"And can you?" Morgan asked.

"I should be able to manage, at least for a number or two."

Morgan looked doubtful. "We're talking about country swing, not hip-hop. Isn't that mostly what they do over in L.A.?"

"There's a fair amount of that, sure. But along the way I picked up a little country swing."

Jeannette wondered if anyone else caught the gleam in Zach's eyes as he said that. She'd spent enough time with him to know that expression meant he relished the challenge of whatever activity was coming up next, whether it was dancing or making love. And if he danced the way he made love, he'd be amazing at it.

She got up from the table and turned to Morgan and Tyler. "Thanks for the conversation. It's always fun to talk about travel plans."

Morgan smiled. "I'm glad we got to know you a little better."

"Me, too." Tyler stood and held out her hand. "Be sure and send me a postcard if you get to Dubrovnik. It's a cool little city."

"I will. Thanks." Jeannette squeezed Tyler's hand. "See you both on the dance floor."

As she walked away with Zach, he leaned closer. "Feeling better about the O'Connelli sisters?"

"Those two, for sure. Lily deserves the credit. She broke the ice, and believe me, there was some ice that needed to be broken."

"Lily's great, isn't she? From what I hear, she could have chosen to make a lot of money designing computer games up in Silicon Valley, but instead she decided to operate an equine rescue facility in Shoshone."

"That's admirable." Jeannette could see why Zach would be all in favor of a move like that. "Did she like designing computer games?"

"I think she liked it okay, but it didn't satisfy her the way the horse operation does."

"Then I'm glad she found what works for her. It's so important to enjoy what you do."

"Absolutely."

If they'd been alone instead of heading for the dance floor, she might have used that as a jumping-off point for a discussion about the Wyoming bar-exam study guide he'd bought. But this wasn't the time or place for that.

The pair of guitarists opened with a Tim McGraw number that didn't seem too taxing for Regan and Lily as they two-stepped around the dance floor. Jeannette couldn't remember ever dancing much when she'd dated Regan, but he seemed to be having a great time. Lily brought out his playful side. Apparently she and Regan had been too much alike to cause sparks to fly.

Jeannette had been taught ballroom dancing as a debutante, and the dance instructor had added a few lessons in country swing for the fun of it. Watching Regan and Lily confirmed that she'd be fine out there. The catchy music had her tapping her toe.

She leaned toward Zach. "Those guitarists are good. Who are they?"

"Two of the ranch hands."

"They're not professionals?"

"Not officially, although they've made some demos and something might come of that. I've sent some tracks to a few of my friends in the business."

"That's terrific, Zach. Sometimes all it takes is the right connections."

"The thing is, they both love working on this ranch. I don't know if either of them really wants to perform full-time. Tyler sings with them sometimes, and I know she's not interested in living that life."

"Yes, but they're *good.* If they have the talent, then—"

"Not everyone wants to take it to the next level."

She didn't want to argue that point. She didn't want to argue at all, in fact. "So what are their names?" She was curious in case someday one of them became famous.

"Watkins is the older guy with the handlebar mustache. He has a first name, but nobody uses it. Trey Wheeler's the younger one. He's engaged to Elle, that blonde standing across the platform from us."

Jeannette located the woman he was talking about. Tall and athletic-looking, she was dressed like everyone else in jeans and a casual shirt. But there was nothing casual in the way she focused on Trey playing that guitar. "She's crazy about him. She's practically glowing with pride. That's very cute."

"He's crazy about her, too. She's a ski instructor at one of the resorts. Trey said this is the first summer she's stayed in Jackson Hole instead of flying down to Argentina to work during their winter months. Obviously she didn't want to leave him to go down there."

"Obviously." Jeannette couldn't help thinking there was a subtext to all the information Zach had given her about people who'd changed their lives for the sake of love.

She also wondered if Elle missed skiing while she stayed here to be with Trey. Sure, couples sometimes had to make sacrifices in order to be together. Would she? If Zach asked her to leave Virginia to be with him, would she consider it?

The answer wasn't simple. She wouldn't give up practicing law to be with him, and she couldn't imagine working in a law office every day and coming home to someone who had turned his back on that profession. Sooner or later that would become an issue between them.

They had to talk about it, and postponing that discussion weighed heavier with every passing moment. She took a deep breath to release some of her tension. The scent of recently cut lumber was strong here, and she guessed by the unmarred surface of the plywood platform that this had been the project that Zach had helped with this afternoon.

That thought reminded her that he still hadn't had any sleep. Until he had, she couldn't pester the poor guy with questions about his future. She leaned closer. "How are you holdin' up?"

"Great."

"I just happened to think…do you have to work tomorrow?"

"Yeah. I'm a new hire, so I work Sundays."

"At dawn?"

He chuckled. "That's when the animals get up."

"Whew. Then let's not stay long. I'm surprised you're upright, now that I think about it. Do you need coffee?"

"Dancing with you will be way more effective than caffeine for jump-starting my engine."

She smiled up at him. "What a nice thing to say."

"What a nice thing to do." He glanced at the dance floor. "More folks are joining in. Let's go." He took her hand and led her up the steps.

"What about my hat? Should I take it off?"

"Not unless you want to. I can work around your hat."

"Then I'll leave it on." She was pleased with the white straw hat and felt more country wearing it.

Anticipation raced through her at the prospect of dancing with Zach. She remembered how much she used to love dancing, but she hadn't made it a priority in a long while. She'd concentrated on work and forgotten how to relax.

Zach drew her into his arms, and from the moment he started to move, she knew dancing with him would be wonderful. He had an excellent sense of rhythm and dear God, did he know how to lead. His partner could be a mediocre dancer and Zach would make her look as if she should be a contestant on *Dancing with the Stars.*

As they circled the floor and he twirled her first one way and then another, she laughed from the sheer joy of it. She'd never had this much fun dancing with a guy. The song ended, and she gazed up at him, breathless with pleasure. "I know you must be tired, but can we do that once more?"

His grin flashed. "Yes, ma'am, we sure can."

"You're very good at this."

"You inspire me."

She met his gaze. "I think we inspire each other."

His expression grew serious as he brushed a thumb tenderly over her cheek. "Hold that thought."

Then the music began again and they were off, dancing together as if they'd been doing it for years. Yet she knew it was Zach making it seem that way. He was far more talented than he'd let on.

Other dancers called out encouragement and praise. Jeannette had never danced with someone who took such control of the floor, and it was a heady experience. Jack and Josie Chance whirled by and Jack gave them a thumbs-up.

"Looks like I won't lose my job for being a washout at dancing," Zach murmured.

"You were never in danger of that, were you?" She ducked under his arm as he turned her in another perfect spin.

He caught her expertly around the waist. “Nope. I won a couple of country swing dance competitions last year.”

“You sandbagger!”

“Keep that under your hat.” He guided her through another tricky maneuver.

“I will. Your secrets are safe with me.”

He twirled her again and pulled her in close. “My secrets aren’t my biggest concern.”

She spun out and came back in tight against him. “What is?”

“My heart.”

That left her speechless. They finished the dance, but those words, spoken casually, echoed between them. She didn’t think they’d been meant casually at all.

Still trying to catch her breath from the pace of the dance, she flattened her palms against his chest and felt the rapid beat of his heart, the one he was hoping would be safe with her. This temporary relationship didn’t feel so temporary now. Lifting her gaze, she looked into eyes filled with intensity. “We should go.”

“Yes, we should.”

“We need to make the rounds and say goodbye.”

“Absolutely.”

Together they satisfied that obligation. They spoke with Lily and Regan before moving on to Morgan and her husband, Gabe. They caught Tyler right before she went up to sing, and Jeannette apologized for leaving without hearing her.

Everyone knew that Zach had to work in the morning, so no one expressed surprise that they were heading out. Jeannette could sense their quiet speculation, though. No doubt many of them had noticed the bond developing and wondered what would happen when she left for Virginia.

Last of all they searched out Jack and Josie. The Chances were conveniently talking with Jack's mother, Sarah, so they could thank her, too. Elegant without seeming formal, Sarah was dressed in jeans and a tailored shirt. She wore her silver hair in a simple pageboy and favored Native American jewelry.

As they were starting to move away, Sarah laid a hand on Jeannette's arm. "As I recall, tomorrow's your last day here."

"That's right." Jeannette fought the sinking feeling that statement brought.

"Zach will be tied up all day, of course, and you may want to spend the time enjoying his campsite. It's beautiful out there, but if you'd like to take a ride tomorrow afternoon, I'd be happy to show you around the property. On horseback is really the only way to see it."

Jeannette couldn't have been more surprised if Sarah had announced she'd be performing a fan dance later on in the evening. Everyone acknowledged Sarah Chance as the reigning queen of Shoshone, including a wide swath of countryside surrounding the little town. To be invited on a trail ride with her was almost like being granted an audience at Buckingham Palace.

A person didn't turn down an invitation like that. A Southern-born woman like Jeannette most certainly didn't. "I would love to," she said. "What time would you like me to come over?"

"Around two would be perfect. You're probably used to an English saddle, but would a Western one be okay for a couple of hours?"

"I'm sure it would. I'll be here. Thank you, that will be a perfect thing for my last day."

"I thought it might." Sarah held out her hand. "Until then."

As Jeannette took the older woman's hand, she felt the steely determination in that grip. Regan had told her all about Sarah Chance. The woman was a survivor. She'd lost her husband five years ago, but she'd carried on with the help of her three sons. Then she'd found a new love, Peter Beckett, and they'd married the previous summer.

Jeannette had no idea why Sarah had invited her on a trail ride, but the outing could prove to be educational. As Jeannette plotted out her future, which had changed dramatically since the events of the previous Christmas, she was more than willing to soak up wisdom wherever she could find it.

13

On the way back to the Airstream, Zach thought of all he wanted to say to Jeannette, but he wasn't sure how to say it or even if he should try. He'd already been fairly certain he was falling for her, but holding her in his arms while they danced had clinched it for him. She seemed to feel the same way, judging from the way her eyes had sparkled and her cheeks had flushed with pleasure.

Regan's words kept running through his head. *Depends on how much she wants to be with you.* That was the part that worried him. They'd had a great time together, but he didn't know if that was enough to offset her desire to stay with the Virginia law firm and make her parents proud.

They rode back with the windows down, and because the road was rough, he had to take it slow. Night sounds filtered into the truck's cab. Crickets chirped from the bushes along the roadside and occasionally the hoot of an owl would drift from the nearby woods. The wolves were quiet tonight, but he heard the yip of coyotes.

"I guess you know how much I like it here," he said at last.

"I do, and I understand. It's beautiful."

He wasn't sure how to take that. Everyone said Jackson Hole was beautiful, but not everyone was willing to move there so they could soak up that beauty year-round. He had no idea how to begin this conversation. How in the hell could he ask her to give up everything to come out here and start over?

Finally he decided to wait until they got back to the Airstream. But he wouldn't broach the subject while they were in bed together. That wasn't fair. He wouldn't use the passion they shared to influence her to say something tonight that she'd regret in the morning.

Maybe he should just make love to her, go to sleep and tackle this tomorrow. That would be far more logical, except that he wasn't in the mood to be logical. He used to pride himself on his practical thinking, but emotion and exhaustion had him by the throat right now and he needed some idea of where he stood with her.

"I have a couple of folding chairs stashed under the trailer," he said. "Would you like to sit outside for a little while? Maybe we'll hear the wolves again."

"That sounds nice."

He loved the way she said the word *nice* with a long *i* sound instead of a short one. Now every time he heard a woman with a Southern accent, he'd think of Jeannette. Hell, every time he heard wolves howl, he'd think of her, and every time he danced the two-step, and every time he ate a club sandwich or watched *Sabrina.*

Except he wouldn't watch that movie again if she left for good. That was one thing he could eliminate from his life to decrease the pain. He might give up club sandwiches, too, and champagne. But that wouldn't be enough to mute the effect of losing her. He'd have to sell the Airstream.

When he thought of how she'd burrowed into his life in such a short time, he swallowed a groan of dismay. Somehow he had to convince her that she belonged with him. The alternative—that she would leave and he'd never see her again—was unacceptable.

He pulled into the campsite, shut off the engine and climbed out of the cab. She was out before he made it around to the other side. And then suddenly he was holding her, because he couldn't help it.

"I don't want you to leave." The words came out before he could stop them. "I want to find a way for us to be together."

She held on tight, her voice muffled against his chest. "Then we have to talk about something I found in your trailer. I'd meant to put it off until you got some sleep, but I guess we have to do this now."

He drew back to stare at her in the pale light of the moon. "Something you found in my trailer? What in God's name could that be?"

"The study guide for passing the Wyoming bar."

"What?" He laughed in disbelief. "Why would you want to talk about that?"

"I need to know why you bought it."

It was a perfectly good question, though he didn't have a neat answer. "I don't know. It doesn't matter. Listen, Regan said something tonight that got me to thinking, and I—"

"It does matter, Zach. What made you buy that study guide?"

He realized she'd push until he offered an explanation. That wouldn't come easily, because he'd never examined his motivation for buying the book. "I suppose I thought of it as a backup plan." He looked into her face, which was mostly in shadows.

"I found it while I was browsing through your bookshelf looking for something to read."

"I haven't really looked at it."

"I could see that. But when I found it, I had this crazy idea that you hadn't totally given up on practicing law."

"Actually, I have." He could guess that wasn't what she wanted to hear, but he wanted them to be straight with each other. "I bought that not long after I moved here. I got hired on at the Last Chance, but Jack gave me a two-week trial before he put me on permanently. I loved it here so much that I figured if Jack fired me, I would study for the bar and work as an attorney if I had to, just so I could stay in Jackson Hole."

"Then you never intend to get back into it?"

He rubbed the small of her back. How he loved touching her, and he could feel that privilege slipping away. "I'm afraid of what practicing law does to me. Once I step into that world, I could get sucked back into a frame of mind where I have to be the best. I was so damned competitive, Jeannette. I kept score with materialistic things. I don't ever want to be that person again."

"Do you think I'm like that?"

"No. No! I'm not condemning you or what you do. It's me that has the problem with the profession, not you."

"But you're in a different environment now, and you've had that revelation." She gazed up at him. "Surely it would be different here."

He sighed. "And if it's not, I've poisoned the well. I've ruined what I love about being here. I don't want to risk it. The peace of mind I've found working at the Last Chance is like nothing I've ever known before."

"Zach, I really think—"

"What about this? What if you started a law practice in Shoshone? Regan said the town could really use one. I know what I'm asking. You're about to make partner, and you've spent years working for it, but..." His throat tightened. "I want you to stay. I'm trying to come up with a way it might work for you."

"But you see, it wouldn't." Her soft words cut deeper than any knife possibly could.

The rejection hit hard. Her reasons might only make that rejection worse, but he had to have them spelled out, anyway. "Is it because you don't want to give up your practice in Virginia?"

"That's part of it."

"If it's a money issue, I could back you while you get established here."

"I'm not worried about the money. I've saved, too. Not as much as you, but I could ride out the lean times until I built up a client list."

"I don't suppose your parents would like the idea of you moving out here."

She hesitated. "No, probably not."

"Is that the problem?"

She slipped out of his arms and walked a few feet away. "My relationship with them is...complicated. I'm sure you've figured that out. Since being in Jackson Hole, and specifically spending time with you, I've started looking at things differently. I thank you for that. But my problems with my parents aren't what's standing in the way of us being together."

"Then what is?"

She turned to face him. "You are."

"Me? I'm trying to find a solution so we *can* be together!"

"But without changing anything in your life. I'd do all the changing."

He rubbed the back of his neck. She had a point. "Are you thinking I should offer to move back there?"

"Although that would be imminently fair, I wouldn't ask it of you. Ironically, you're more attached to this place than I am to Virginia." She took a deep breath. "I'll admit it might be good for me to put some distance between me and my parents. I love them, but that doesn't mean I should live in the same town with them."

Hope surged anew. "I'm glad to hear you say that."

"But neither should I live in the same town with you."

"Why the hell not?"

"Because you have a fine legal mind, and you're about to let it rot. I realize that's your privilege, but I don't want to be around to see that happen."

His emotions were all over the place, but the one that shouldered its way forward at the moment was anger. "You're making this far more dramatic than it is. People switch jobs all the time. No big deal."

"It is if all you're doing is runnin' away from yourself."

His jaw tightened. "That's not how I see it."

"What if your services as a lawyer would be useful to this community? You said yourself that Regan thinks Shoshone could use a lawyer. How about you?"

"And give up what I'm doing now?"

"You wouldn't have to. You could manage both. Your ability with legal issues is exceptional, whether you admit it or not. I could tell that even with the short discussion we had on the way to Jackson."

He gazed at her in silence.

"You have a gift, Zach. Maybe you didn't use that gift wisely in L.A. Maybe you let circumstances control you instead of takin' control yourself. I've heard that the Last Chance Ranch helps people work through that kind of issue."

"Exactly. And that's what I love about the place. I figured out that I'm happy working as a ranch hand. It suits me fine."

She regarded him quietly. "I'm sure it does, for now. If you stick with this program, it'll suit you better and better, I suppose. Eventually your legal knowledge will become outdated and maybe you'll even lose your analytical edge because you're not sharpenin' it on a regular basis. But you used to love that analytical work, didn't you?"

"A long time ago. Before I let the glitz and glamour get the best of me."

"Do you hear yourself? You *let* that happen. You don't have to let it happen again. It's more temptin' to be a hotshot when you're twenty-five than when you're thirty-five."

"I don't know about that. Look at that big-ass truck I bought."

"Damn it, Zach! You're like a dog with a bone. You are capable of making different choices this time around!"

He took off his hat and tunneled his fingers through his hair. "You don't understand what you're asking of me."

"Oh, yes I do. I'm askin' you to be true to who you are, to embrace all sides of yourself."

"What if I'm supposed to be a ranch hand? Because I'm telling you, this job fits me like a glove. I'm happy to drive to the ranch every day. The working conditions are great. I don't have to wear fancy clothes and I love being around horses."

"But I also listened to you throwing out creative ideas for handlin' my case. You cited legal precedent from memory. I knew then I'd met a lawyer who spends time as a ranch hand, not a ranch hand who dabbles in the law."

"And you accuse *me* of being stubborn. You've got it in your head that practicing law is my destiny and you won't rest until I agree to do it!"

She sighed. "Actually, the defense rests as of now. I can see we're not gettin' anywhere. We're both tired. And you probably need to think some more about this."

He opened his mouth to say that he didn't have to think about anything. He loved ranch work and that was what he intended to do for the foreseeable future.

"I would save my rebuttal if I were you, counselor."

In spite of the tense situation, that made him smile. "Why?"

"Because you really do need to take a recess and give yourself a chance to think about the evidence I've presented. In the meantime, I have a suggestion for what we can do during that recess."

His startled laughter woke some birds in a nearby tree and they fluttered restlessly. "Are you saying what I think you are?"

"That I want to go inside and make love? Yes, I do."

"I thought we were fighting."

"Debatin'."

"Whatever. We sure as hell aren't agreeing on anything. I doubt sex will change that, either."

"It won't." She said it matter-of-factly. "But it'll be fun and relaxin'. Then we can get some sleep and review the situation tomorrow."

"I don't know what kind of lawyer I was." He closed

the gap between them and drew her into his arms. "But I can testify that you're an excellent one."

"Thank you." She wound her arms around his neck. "If I do say so myself, I am. Now let's get movin', cowboy."

They made it inside the Airstream in record time and left a trail of clothes on their way back to the bedroom. Zach leaned against the wall and got rid of his boots before helping Jeannette tug hers off. They each shucked their jeans and underwear and tumbled naked and laughing onto the double bed.

Holding her felt so amazing. Kissing her was the second-best activity he'd ever known. Then he rolled on a condom and settled into the best activity ever. When his cock was buried deep in her warmth, all was right in his world.

Pausing to savor the moment, he looked into her green eyes. "You sure are something, Jeannette Trenton."

She smiled as she ran her hands down his back to clutch his hips. "So are you, Zach Powell."

"Not every woman would invite a man to bed under these circumstances."

"I'm not every woman."

"No, you're certainly not." He leaned down and kissed her with all the longing in his heart as he began to love her with slow, sure strokes.

She answered his kiss and she answered the urging of his body as she rose to meet each firm thrust. They were so good together. Their disagreement faded until there was only this…sweet friction creating mutual pleasure.

As his breathing quickened, he lifted his mouth from hers. She moaned and pressed her fingertips into the small of his back. "I'm close," she murmured.

"I know." He shifted his angle and increased the pace as she tightened around his aching cock. "I can feel it." He'd ride out her orgasm so he could give her a second one. Then he'd claim his own.

Gasping, she arched upward, on the brink of surrender. "Come with me."

"No." But apparently his body had other ideas, because it clenched in readiness. "You deserve more than one—"

"Please."

He struggled to hold back. "Not yet."

"But this feels so *right*." She began to pant. "I want you with me. Please let go!"

Her desperate plea snapped his control. With a deep groan, he pounded into her, unleashing his passion with a ferocity that shocked him. What had begun as a friendly roll in the hay had transformed into something far more intense.

Squeezing his eyes shut, he came in a rush while her climax rolled over his pulsing cock. Gasping, he cried out her name and shuddered against her, caught in a whirlpool of sensation that rivaled anything he'd known.

When he stopped shaking, when at last he could draw a steady breath, he opened his eyes and gazed down at her. "That was…" He had no words.

"I know." Her expression was tender as she cupped his face in both hands. "I know."

Earlier tonight he'd suspected the stakes were going up in this relationship. Now he found himself looking into the eyes of the only woman he would ever want by his side. The stakes had just shot through the roof.

14

JEANNETTE WOKE TO bright sunshine, the sound of birds outside the open window and a hastily scribbled note on Zach's pillow. The down pillow—of course he would have bought the best—retained the impression of his head, but it was cool to the touch. Jeannette glanced at the clock and realized he'd been gone for hours.

Had to leave for work, the note said. *Will be back after 5. Z.* Using only his initial suggested a certain intimacy, but he hadn't added a closing endearment or even *XXOO*. Had she been the one writing the note to him, she would have had trouble with a closing, too.

Thinking that she loved him after such a short time sounded delusional. Yet she couldn't come up with any other word that described the bone-deep emotion that gripped her whenever she thought of Zach. She cared in a way that couldn't be explained given their brief acquaintance.

Sure, the sex had been great from the beginning, and they'd had a lot of it. But it had never been only about sex, although she'd tried to tell herself that. The term *making love* wasn't a euphemism in this case, at least not for her.

She'd felt a deeper connection from the moment they'd met in the barn. She'd always prided herself on being logical, but the feelings that had developed so quickly between them defied common sense. She sensed that Zach might be struggling with the same question of emotion versus logic.

Glancing at the clock, she was shocked to discover it was after ten. Normally she was too type A to sleep this late, especially in a strange bed. Zach must have left with the stealth of a cat burglar, which was amazing considering his size and the tight quarters. He'd even managed to open some windows without making noise.

She could picture him taking great care not to disturb her, though. She wondered if he'd set a mental alarm clock in order to wake up on time. She could have done that, too, but she'd had no obligation other than her ride with Sarah at two, so she hadn't bothered.

The concept of leisure was foreign to her, but apparently she'd adapted well enough to sleep late this morning. Stretching languidly, she climbed out of bed, pulled on Zach's enormous bathrobe and padded into the living room. Once again, Zach had picked up the discarded clothes. Hers were folded neatly on the living room couch.

Rainbows danced on the wall. She peered out the window. Something moved in the trees, and a thrill of apprehension zipped up her spine until she identified the shapes of deer.

She counted three as they moved through the trees, no doubt headed down to the stream for a drink. If she lived in a cabin in the woods, she'd be treated to sightings of wildlife on a regular basis. More than that, her growing self-reliance would be nurtured in a setting like this.

Standing in the living room of Zach's Airstream, she came to a decision—and a pretty darned big one, too. She wanted to leave Virginia, regardless of how her relationship with Zach turned out. Whether she'd end up here was a question mark, but she needed a complete change of scenery and some geographical distance from her parents.

She wasn't sure how much their expectations ruled her behavior, but she suspected it was a lot. Whenever she'd thought of the partnership she'd been working so hard for, she'd imagined how pleased they'd be. The partnership had been a prize to lay at their feet, not something she craved for herself.

Without this trip to Jackson Hole and meeting Zach, she might never have gained that insight. Ironically, watching him avoid his issues had brought hers into sharper contrast. She might be able to retain her budding feeling of independence without moving, but changing her environment would help enormously. If she stayed there, she might fall back into old, familiar patterns.

Which was exactly why Zach didn't want to practice law. She sucked in a quick breath. Okay, she got it now. He'd made changes in his life, changes he didn't want to reverse. He was afraid practicing law might coax him into old habits.

Although she could look at the man he was now and be certain that wouldn't happen, he couldn't see that. Telling him he'd be fine working as a lawyer wouldn't convince him any more than someone telling her that she'd function just as well living a few miles away from her parents' horse farm. She'd rather play it safe and leave. Zach would rather play it safe and be a ranch hand.

Of course their situations weren't identical. She'd always be her parents' daughter, which meant she had to deal with those dynamics even if she were living somewhere else. Zach had completely severed his ties with his profession, something he'd once loved and probably still did on some level. There was the rub.

Groaning in frustration, she sank down to the small couch in his living room. Understanding him didn't make the problems go away. If anything, they seemed more daunting than ever. She'd thought to use lawyerly logic on him, but that wasn't going to do a damn bit of good.

After another leisurely breakfast of coffee and PB-and-J sandwiches, she cleaned up the kitchen and made Zach's bed. Taking plenty of time for these simple chores felt relaxing, but she could feel the beginnings of restlessness.

She texted Erin to find out how her research was going but didn't get an immediate answer. Maybe Erin was taking a few hours off. After all, it was Sunday. But Jeannette had been away from work for more than a week, and she missed it.

Hoping that Erin would see the text and respond, she paged through a couple of magazines. Finally she gave up and navigated the challenge of Zach's tiny indoor shower. She dressed in another pair of her recently purchased jeans and a short-sleeved knit top.

Her boots hadn't rubbed blisters on her feet and the white straw hat would be perfect for riding. She felt like a Westerner, although a slightly bored Westerner. Thank goodness Sarah had invited her for a ride. And she should be back before Zach came home.

Then she realized that if she locked the door behind her as she'd planned to, she didn't have a key to get back in. She checked around the outside for a hidden spare and didn't find one. Oh, well. Zach was at the ranch, so she'd find him there and ask to borrow the key.

With that problem solved, she climbed into her rental car and headed slowly and carefully back to the ranch. She drove straight down to the barn, where Sarah was already saddling the smaller of two brown-and-white Paints. Jeannette parked and walked over to help.

"You're right on time!" Sarah called out.

"I've been lookin' forward to it." She approached the larger of the two horses. "Want me to go ahead and saddle this guy?"

"Sure. I picked Spilled Milk for you, so you might as well get to know each other. He's partial to women so you two should do fine together."

"I'm sure we will. You're a handsome boy, Spilled Milk." Jeannette copied Sarah's saddling technique. The process was similar to what she was used to with an English saddle, so she probably could have muddled through on her own. Truthfully she hadn't saddled her own horse in a while, but she'd learned as a kid and the process came back quickly.

A groom had always saddled a horse for Jeannette's mother whenever she rode, and Jeannette had fallen into that habit, too. Saddling Spilled Milk herself did allow her to become acquainted with the horse, just as Sarah had said. A scratch under his mane, a pat on his withers and some murmured words of greeting made a huge difference in how she felt about the upcoming ride. Wherever she moved would definitely be horse country and from now on she'd personally saddle any horse she rode.

After she tightened the cinch, she mounted up to check the length of the stirrups. "These seem a little long," she said to Sarah. "But I'm used to the shorter ones of an English saddle, so you'd better tell me if this is right or not."

"They look fine to me. When you stand up in them, you should have a little daylight between you and the saddle, but not a whole lot. Yeah, that's perfect. Ready?"

"You bet. Can't wait."

Sarah climbed on her horse. "Then we're off. In the beginning the trail's wide enough for us to ride side-by-side, which makes it easier to talk."

Jeannette walked Spilled Milk down a path that led through a meadow filled with the buzzing of insects and a riot of red, yellow and purple wildflowers. Breathing deep, she savored the familiar scent of horse and oiled leather. Tension flowed out as she exhaled, and she vowed to spend more time with horses in the future. They never failed to relax her.

Sarah rode alongside on her dramatically marked brown-and-white Paint. The mare carried herself like royalty, arching both her neck and her tail as she pranced more than walked down the trail.

"Pretty mare."

Sarah patted her horse's neck with obvious affection. "This is Bertha Mae."

"Bertha Mae?" Jeannette laughed. "Lookin' at her I would have guessed a far more exotic name than that."

"That's the name she arrived with, and nobody thought to change it. Now I wouldn't want to." She glanced over at Jeannette. "I don't know if you've heard that my first husband died in a rollover with a horse trailer."

"Regan told me about it. That must have been a terrible time for your family."

"It was. Really terrible. But we all came through it, including Bertha Mae."

"She was the horse in the trailer?"

Sarah nodded. "At first I wanted nothing to do with her. Nobody did, although it wasn't her fault, poor girl."

"No, but it's understandable that you wouldn't want to be around her." The squeak of leather and the buzz of insects created a comforting background that seemed to invite confidences.

"Eventually I started going out to the barn to talk to her," Sarah continued, "which helped me and probably helped her. She had to have been lonesome, although she wasn't as ostracized as I'd thought. Jack had secretly begun to work with her. Aside from being traumatized by the accident, she'd never been ridden."

"That's incredible." Jeannette gazed at the well-mannered horse. "You'd never guess that she'd been through all that."

"It was mostly Jack's doing. Four years ago he rode her in Gabe and Morgan's wedding ceremony, and she's been a wonderful saddle horse ever since. I love taking her out on the trail."

"What a heartwarmin' story. I'm glad you told me."

"I guess it's my way of illustrating how time can work wonders. I'm so encouraged by the healing that seems to have taken place between you, Regan and Drake. Thank you for placing yourself in what has sometimes been an uncomfortable situation."

Jeannette grinned at her. "Aw, 'twarn't nuthin', ma'am."

"Heaven help us, you're learning the lingo."

"Not really. That was straight out of a movie. But I feel more a part of the ranch after last night's party. This ride helps, too. I can't tell you how much I appreciate the invitation."

"Zach mentioned that you were comfortable around

horses, so it seemed a shame not to take you out for a ride. How's that Western saddle treating you?"

Jeannette leaned back against the cantle. "It feels like an easy chair compared to what I'm used to, so I'll need to watch myself and make sure I don't nod off."

"Want to go a little faster?"

"Oh, no! I didn't mean to imply I was bored. Just very relaxed. Trust me, that's a good thing. I tend to be way too tense and driven."

"Then I'm glad I brought you out here before you have to head back to a more frantic pace."

"So am I." She thought of her recent decision to move and that it would logically take her out West. This ride through wildflowers on a warm August day, with the Grand Tetons still topped with last winter's snow, gave her a taste of what summer was like in Jackson Hole.

But the winter months were legendary for the bitter cold and blizzards that kept people indoors for days. She decided to get a woman's perspective on that. "How do you cope with winters here?"

Sarah gave her a curious glance before answering. "We concentrate on the cozy factor."

"Oh, really?" Jeannette laughed. "That sounds kind of fun."

"It is, although when the kids were toddlers I'd be lying if I didn't say there were days I wanted to tear my hair out. But you learn to be a family. When the electricity goes out and you're operating on generator power, you conserve that resource. Instead of watching TV or listening to music, you light candles, play board games, or…find other ways to amuse yourselves and keep warm."

From Sarah's tone, Jeannette knew exactly what she was talking about. "You make it sound romantic."

"It can be, especially with the right man. It helps to be very good friends with whoever shares your living space. Much as I loved Jonathan, my first husband, he had a tendency to get moody in the winter. Pete is the most optimistic and joyful person I know, even without one of those light boxes to counteract the lack of sun. I confess it's easier to be snowbound with Pete."

Jeannette thought about being snowbound with Zach. He'd probably be fine. "I'm afraid I'd be the one who'd go stir-crazy and cause problems," she said.

"You might surprise yourself." Sarah hesitated. "Are you contemplating a winter vacation in Jackson Hole?"

"Maybe." She didn't dare say more. Zach couldn't get wind of her plans to move. That would only add pressure to an already tense situation. If he ever decided to start a new legal practice, it needed to be for his sake and not because she'd dangled the possibility of her moving to Shoshone as an enticement.

"If you do, let me know. You're welcome anytime, and we usually have room except right before Christmas. We fill up with extended family then."

Jeannette gazed at her. "You have no idea how much that offer means to me. A few days ago I thought I'd never be accepted here."

"As I said, time can work wonders. I've been treading a fine line because I have a daughter-in-law who wasn't eager to be your friend."

"Morgan. I know. Thanks to Lily, I think Morgan and I could become friends."

"I think so, too. And then there's Tyler. She's like a daughter-in-law even though technically she's not. But the ice is cracking there, too."

"I'll need a bit more time to win over Cassidy."

"Yes." Sarah chuckled. "That little redhead is a spitfire. She sees everything in terms of black and white, but she'll mellow. If you come back this winter, I predict you'll make friends with Cassidy."

"I'd like that." She noticed that Sarah had made no mention of Zach or what the future might hold for the two of them. Sarah's generous invitation wasn't conditional on whether she continued to see Zach. Sarah was extending her friendship to her regardless of what happened with him.

That made the gesture even more precious. Apparently Sarah had decided that she was worthy of being included in activities at the Last Chance. She might not be family, but she was welcomed as a friend of the family. She was no longer a person to be shunned. That was a personal triumph.

Sarah gazed out at the wide path stretching ahead of them. "Are you *sure* you don't want to go faster? Spilled Milk has a lovely canter."

In her current jubilant mood, a canter across this meadow sounded excellent. "Let's go for it!"

In no time they were covering ground so fast that she had to clap a hand to her head to keep her hat from flying off. At last Sarah held up an arm and they slowed to a trot, and then a walk.

Sarah's cheeks were pink and she looked far younger than her sixty-nine years. Because she was an experienced trail rider, she'd secured her hat with a string under her chin. Jeannette had thought the string was too dorky, but next time she rode like this she'd use one.

Sarah turned Bertha Mae back in the direction they'd come. "Fun, huh?"

"Too much fun. I loved it."

"Think of us while you're back in Virginia. And do

consider coming out sometime this winter. See how you like us when the snow's on the ground."

"Thanks. I will." She looked over at Sarah, and for the first time wondered if her hostess were indeed playing matchmaker. If so, she had an extremely subtle touch. And it was working.

15

At some point during the day Zach remembered that Sarah had invited Jeannette for a ride and there would be a problem with the key to the Airstream. He removed it from his key ring and tucked it in his other pocket. He'd make sure he got it to her one way or another.

As it turned out, he was involved in stacking sections of the new platform in the tractor barn at the time Sarah and Jeannette were scheduled to ride out, so he missed her. But after he finished working on that project, a job that left him hot and sweaty, he walked outside and spotted Jeannette's rental car parked near the barn.

The sight of it there made his pulse leap, which indicated just how far gone he was. He didn't even have to see her. A glimpse of her rental car was enough to make his heart beat faster. He was a sorry mess, and he had less than twenty-four hours to sort things out.

Or maybe he had more than twenty-four hours. He might have twenty-five or -six. He wasn't exactly sure when her plane left. He should have asked, but he hadn't realized how critical every minute would become. Because he wanted to maximize his time with her, he wanted to have a few hours off tomorrow until she had to leave for the airport. He'd need to ask for that today and hope Jack would give it to him.

Wednesday was normally his free day, so if he could switch it to Monday, he'd be all set. Even after a month of having a boss, he still hadn't adjusted to the idea of accounting for his time. Every so often he'd chafe at the concept that he couldn't leave when he chose to do so. He'd spent too many years in charge of his own calendar, and now he was working a specified shift.

Not that he was complaining about that. God, no. He loved ranch work and was grateful for the opportunity Jack was providing. Even if switching his day off wasn't possible, coming in after she left for the airport shouldn't be a big deal. He wasn't exactly a key man around here.

That didn't bother him, either. It was comforting to be a cog in a wheel for a change instead of the whole damned wheel with overhead up the wazoo. He was glad he no longer had an office full of employees who depended on him to bring in the big bucks.

So what if he felt a little prick of irritation when he had to ask for time off? It was a small price to pay for the peace of mind he'd gained by downsizing his life. He'd done the right thing, no matter what Jeannette thought about it. She couldn't see things from his perspective right now, but eventually she might.

As luck would have it, Jack Chance, his boss, happened to pull up in his cherry-red truck. Zach decided that red worked way better than black in this environment. Anyone who had grown up here would know that, but he was from L.A. and had spent his life driving on freeways. He still had much to learn about the cowboy way.

He walked over to the truck as Jack climbed down

from the cab. "If you have a minute, I need to ask you something."

Jack shut the door of the cab. "What's that?"

"I'd like time off tomorrow so I can stay at the campsite until Jeannette leaves for the airport."

"I think that can be arranged. When does she leave?"

Here came the embarrassing part. He should have checked it in advance. When he was in the swing of things as a lawyer, he always stayed up on details. "I'm not sure, but I figure middle of the day. She's flying east, so she'll lose time and won't want to arrive too late."

Jack nodded. "You have no idea what time her flight is, do you?"

"No, I don't."

"Hang on. Let's call somebody who might know." He consulted his phone and punched a button. "Yeah, Drake, do you know what time Jeannette's flight leaves?" He paused. "That might be close enough. What airline did she come in on? Okay, thanks." He disconnected. "He thinks it's sometime between eleven and noon."

"That would make sense."

"I'll look online." Jack brought up a screen on his phone. "Here we go. I'll bet she's leaving on the eleven-fifteen out of Jackson Hole. That's the right airline, and the timing matches Drake's estimate."

"That's probably the one, but I'll confirm it with her."

Jack gazed at him. "Yeah, do that. But you might as well take the whole day off and then work Wednesday instead."

"Okay. Thanks."

"No problem." Jack continued to study him. "How's everything going?"

"We have the new platform stowed."

"I mean with Jeannette, brainiac. Did you suggest that she might want to come back here and start a law firm?"

"I did."

"And what was her reaction?"

Zach didn't want to have this conversation but it couldn't be avoided without refusing to discuss it. After the interest Jack had taken that seemed rude. "She thinks the person opening the law firm should be me."

"Oh, really? And while you play legal eagle, is she gonna put up preserves and crochet afghans?"

Picturing that very un-Jeannette scenario made him laugh. "Hardly." But he hadn't considered what might happen if he did what she wanted and started practicing law in Shoshone. "It doesn't matter. I don't want to get back into law."

"Oh." Jack tipped back his hat. "And what does she think of that?"

"Don't know yet. Either she accepts my decision and decides to open an office here, or she disagrees with me and decides to stay in Virginia as a result." He was proud of the calm way he laid out those two alternatives, even though option number two made his stomach clench.

"Any idea how it'll go?"

"Hell, I don't know. Last night she made it clear that she doesn't want to be with me unless I…how did she describe it? I'm supposed to *use my gift.* She thinks I was put on this earth to be a lawyer. I think that's bull. I'm hoping she backs down from that position, but if not, she'll stay in Virginia because I have no intention of practicing law again."

Jack blew out a breath. "If she stays back East, it will suck for you, but it will also suck for me."

"Why?"

"Well, I wasn't going to bring this up and muddy the waters, but old Barnaby Hanks, who's handled ranch legal issues ever since I can remember, is retiring and moving to Florida."

"So what? He must be transferring his clients to someone."

"Oh, yeah, some guy in Jackson, and I guess I can deal with that, but I'm spoiled. I'm used to having my lawyer right here in town. True, he's been threatening to retire for years and I think we're his only remaining client, so I get why he wants to leave, but I don't have to like it."

"How long have you known about this upcoming retirement?"

Jack tugged his hat back down so it shaded his eyes. "Oh, a while."

"More than a month?"

"Maybe."

"Did you hire me with the idea I might come in handy when this guy retired?"

Jack shrugged. "It's possible that such a thing crossed my mind. And then Jeannette blew into town and you two became chummy, so I got all excited at the prospect of having *two* lawyers on hand. Now it seems I might go from two to zero and I'm stuck with some stranger in Jackson."

"I never said I'd help you with your legal issues, Jack."

"I know you didn't."

"Besides, legally I couldn't without getting a license to practice in Wyoming, and I have no plans to do that."

"Maybe not right this minute you don't, but you're supersmart. You could get licensed in no time flat if you had to." Jack peered at him. "Couldn't you?"

"I don't know. But the question's moot because I don't plan on doing it. Now I have a question for you. You hired me for my potential legal advice but if I don't agree to take the bar exam, am I out of a job?"

"Hell, no. That's not how I operate, Powell. You've only been here a month, but you should know that I hired you as a ranch hand and as long as you do the job, you're welcome to stay. If you choose to get licensed in Wyoming, that would be a bonus, but if you don't want to, that's your choice."

Zach smiled in relief. "Glad to hear it. I wish Jeannette had the same attitude."

"So do I, because at least then she might decide to set up shop here. I also think you'd be a much happier cowboy if she agrees to hang around. But I'll work with what I've got."

"That's a good approach." Zach would do his damnedest to adopt that approach in the next twenty-four hours.

"It's just that Barnaby and I would sit on the front porch of the ranch house and drink coffee or beer, depending on the time of day, and hash out whatever legal question had come up. He did the same with my dad. I have a tough time believing some guy will drive down from Jackson to hang out on the front porch with me."

Zach glanced over at the two-story log ranch house with its long covered porch lined with rockers. "I don't know, Jack. It's a hell of a front porch. I'd invite him down and see what happens."

"Frankly, I'd rather sit with you in one of those rockers. Are you *sure* you won't consider it? You'd have no trouble building a practice here. You could work fewer hours and make more money. Doesn't that tempt you at all?"

"Yes." Zach shoved his hands in his pockets and stared at the rugged profile of the Grand Tetons. "And that's what scares me."

"Scares you? I don't under—"

"We'll have to table this discussion." Zach watched two riders come toward them. "Your mother and Jeannette are back."

Jack turned. "So they are." He lowered his voice. "Maybe Mom softened her up some."

"Softened her up? Is your mother part of this campaign, too?"

"I wouldn't call it a campaign, exactly, but she's also angling for the two-lawyer solution."

"I hope to God she didn't mention that to Jeannette," Zach said in an undertone. He smiled and waved at the riders. "Jeannette might feel like she's being double-teamed."

"Mom wouldn't mention it. I warned her not to. I said the situation was still very tenuous."

"No shit."

Jack laughed. "Don't give up, brainiac." Then he raised his voice. "Welcome back, ladies! Have a good ride?"

"Great ride!" Jeannette's cheeks were flushed a becoming pink and her green eyes sparkled. "What a perfect day for it." She looked completely at home in the Western saddle.

Gazing up at her, Zach wished they'd met earlier. He could have taken her out riding last Wednesday. But if she agreed to move here, he'd work riding into his schedule on a regular basis.

He'd considered buying the little rental cabin that sat just outside the boundaries of the Last Chance. Drake had lived in it when he'd arrived from Virginia and Jeannette had stayed there for a couple of days before moving to the Bunk and Grub. If Zach bought it and Jeannette agreed to live there with him, they'd be close enough to take a couple of horses out on his day off. He'd considered buying his own horse, although that might be a bad idea now that he was working full-time.

"Zach?" Sarah's voice broke into his thoughts. "Would you mind taking Bertha Mae back to the barn for me? I promised Morgan I'd babysit the grandkids and I'd like to freshen up before they arrive."

"Be glad to. I can handle both of them if you like." He stepped forward and took hold of the mare's bridle in one hand and the gelding's in the other as the two women dismounted.

"If nobody minds," Jeannette said, "I'd like to unsaddle Spilled Milk and rub him down myself."

Sarah glanced at her with obvious approval. "I not only don't mind, but I'm glad you want to. It's the sign of a good horsewoman to take care of your own mount. Normally I do, but those grandkids will be here any minute."

"Then you'd better get goin'." Jeannette held out her hand. "Thank you so much for the ride. I loved it."

Sarah beamed as she clasped Jeannette's hand in both of hers. "It was fun, wasn't it? You'll just have to come back when you can stay longer. Believe it or not, we sometimes ride in the winter, too, if the snow's not too deep. And I've also been agitating for a sleigh."

Jack laughed. "And I'm looking into it, Mom. You aren't the only one agitating. Your grandchildren are all about the sleigh. I'm sure you've had nothing to do with that, though."

"Of course not." Sarah winked at Jeannette as she released her hand. "You have a safe flight home. Hope to see you back soon."

"I'd like that."

"So would I. Take care." With another warm smile, Sarah turned and hurried toward the house.

"That sleigh's going to be the death of me," Jack muttered. "I ordered it from a guy down in Cheyenne who specializes in 'em and he's taking for*ever* to make it. First he promised it by Labor Day. Now it's Halloween. It may actually show up next June."

"For one horse or two?" Jeannette asked.

"One. It'll be tricky enough to get one horse used to the thing, let alone two. Besides, the holiday song is about a one-horse open sleigh, so that's what we're going for."

"She'll love it," Zach said.

Jeannette nodded in agreement. "She absolutely will. And the grandkids will go nuts over it. I would have when I was a little girl. Heck, I still love the idea."

Jack looked at her, his expression as warm as his mother's. "Then come out this winter and give it a whirl. I've ordered cozy lap robes and the harnesses will have bells on them."

"Sounds wonderful."

"It will be if that little old sleigh-maker gets the lead out. Listen, Zach, why don't you and Jeannette take care of the horses and head on back to your campsite after that? Stowing the platform in the tractor barn was my main objective for the day, so you might as well knock off a little early."

"Thanks." Zach was appreciative, but he was all too

aware that he wouldn't have been allowed to leave without Jack's permission. He might need another few weeks to get past that and accept that he was paid to work a given number of hours per week. Only the boss could set his own hours, and the boss was no longer Zachary Powell.

He hadn't minded that so much when he hadn't had anything else to do. But having Jeannette here made a difference. He found himself wanting a little more freedom of movement.

Jack held out his hand to Jeannette. "I probably won't see you again before you fly out. I gave Powell the day off tomorrow so you two can spend a little time together before you drive to the airport."

"Thank you." Jeannette shook his hand. "I've enjoyed myself here. I can see why Regan talked about the ranch so much, and I'm glad I finally was able to see it."

"The door's always open."

"I'll remember that. Goodbye, Jack."

"I prefer *until we meet again.*" He smiled and touched the brim of his black Stetson before heading off toward the ranch house.

Jeannette gazed after him with a bemused smile. "He sure is rollin' out the charm."

"Can't blame him for that. You're a beautiful woman."

She chuckled. "Thank you, but I don't think this is about my looks."

"No, he also likes you."

"That's good to hear." She reached for Spilled Milk's bridle. "I'll take charge of this guy, now."

"Okay." Zach turned the gelding over to her and they started back to the barn. "Sarah picked a great horse for you."

"She did. She seemed eager for me to have a good time out there." They walked in silence for a moment. "Isn't Jack the one who suggested to you that I could open a practice in Shoshone?"

"Actually, it was Regan, but it turns out Jack would be very happy if you did that."

"Do the Chances have a good lawyer? I never thought to ask."

"They do, but he's retiring."

"Aha! No wonder Jack and Sarah are bein' so nice to me."

He tethered Bertha Mae to the hitching post and began unsaddling her. "It's not only because you're a lawyer."

"I know. They wouldn't want me around if they didn't like me, so that's gratifyin'. But my profession doesn't hurt my cause."

"Guess not." From the corner of his eye he observed her efficiency as she unsaddled the gelding and set both blanket and saddle on the hitching post as he'd done. She'd be right at home on a working ranch.

She paused to glance over at him. "Did Jack ask you to get back into law? He must have. It'd solve their problem."

"He did."

"And what did you say?" Hope glimmered in her eyes.

He met her gaze. "I told him no."

16

JEANNETTE HADN'T EXPECTED Zach to have a sudden change of heart, but she wished he'd at least say he was willing to give the idea some thought. "I'm sure he was disappointed to hear that."

"I'm sure he was." He shrugged. "But I don't want to hold out false hope to the guy."

Or to her, either. He hadn't said that, but she was a smart woman. She could figure it out.

He broke eye contact. "I'll bring out the brushes so you can start on that while I put away the tack."

"Okay." She watched him heft Bertha Mae's saddle and walk into the barn. Too bad he looked so damned good doing it. She'd have an easier time being upset with him if he didn't look so gorgeous.

His jeans and sweat-stained T-shirt fit as if he'd been sewn into them. With his scuffed boots and his dusty hat, he looked a lot more like a cowboy than a lawyer. If she didn't know better, she'd swear he'd been doing this job all his adult life.

For the first time she wondered if she'd misjudged the situation. Maybe Zach would finish out his days as a ranch hand and be perfectly content. It was his life, after all, and if that was what he wanted, that was what he should get.

He reappeared with a plastic carryall that she found quite familiar. It could have come out of her parents' barn. As a kid she'd loved using the brushes, curry combs and hoof picks, but then she'd had her debut.

After that rite of passage had been completed, her mother had insisted a young lady shouldn't be mucking out stalls and grooming horses. The Trentons had employees to handle those chores. Jeannette had been taught never to lose sight of the fact she was a Trenton.

At the time she hadn't put up a fight. But as she brushed the gelding's brown-and-white coat and pulled a comb through his mane, she realized that her mother had deprived her of something she'd loved, all in the name of gentility. Fortunately the attitude was different on the Last Chance. Women were encouraged, even expected, to help take care of the horses.

After Zach had stowed the tack, he returned and picked up a brush. "When I saw you in the barn that first day, I recognized your love of horses, but I didn't know you had experience taking care of them."

"I learned everything I know before I became a Southern belle and was told working down at the stables wasn't ladylike."

"What were you supposed to do, sit on the porch and drink mint juleps?"

"Pretty much. Come to think of it, how did you get so comfortable with horses?"

"When I was in college, I worked as a camp counselor during the summer. Somehow I was put in charge of the horses we had at the camp, and I loved it. But once I became involved in building a law practice, I forgot about horses." Dust flew as he stroked the brush across the mare's flanks.

She watched the way he worked. He did have an affinity for the job.

"Anyway, when I finally started questioning my life, I remembered how much fun I'd had caring for these guys every summer. I set out to find a ranch that would hire me."

"And ended up at the Last Chance, obviously."

"Luckily, yes. I'd heard wonderful things about the place. Thank God Jack was willing to give an inexperienced cowhand a trial run."

She tore her gaze away from the sight of his muscles flexing beneath the thin T-shirt. "It's easy to see why you love it here."

"Then you must also see why I don't want to give it up for a desk job."

She started to say something and thought better of it. Obviously he believed that opening a law practice in Shoshone would ruin his cherished life as a cowhand. Maybe it would. He might be an all-or-nothing kind of guy who could either be a gung-ho lawyer or a laid-back cowboy, but not both.

Even so, she couldn't shake the notion that this life wasn't a perfect fit for him. When Jack had magnanimously given him the rest of the day off, he'd winced as if he didn't like being reminded of his employee status. The reaction had been subtle, something no one else might have caught. But she was invested in him now and was attuned to his moods.

She couldn't resist prodding him to see if she could get that reaction again. "It was considerate of Jack to give you the rest of the day off and switch your free day, too."

"Yep, it was." Zach tossed the brush in the carrier. "I appreciate it." His response was totally appropriate, but there was a slight edge to his voice as if he had to force himself to say that.

Maybe that meant nothing and he'd get over his resentment of being subject to the impulses of his boss. Jack seemed like an excellent boss and his whims were probably benign. Yet he held the power.

Zach was by nature a leader and an independent thinker who'd spent years being in control of his working hours. If losing that control continued to bother him, even at a subconscious level, his resentment could fester. He might not notice the change as bitterness crept into his soul, but if she hung around, she would.

"About done?"

Startled out of her thoughts, she discovered that she was standing motionless, the brush resting against her horse's flank while she stared into space. "Almost." She began brushing vigorously, so vigorously that Spilled Milk turned his head to gaze at her as if wondering if someone had given her a jump start. "I was daydreaming."

"I hope it was about taking a solar shower when we get back. I'm looking forward to that."

That thought galvanized her even more, but she wasn't sure that shower was in their future. "Didn't we use up the water yesterday?"

"I refilled it before I left this morning. That's my routine. Then it can warm up during the heat of the day and be ready when I get home."

She peered over her horse's rump and discovered Zach watching her with a telltale glow in his eyes. For sure he was thinking about having sex in that shower, and now she was, too. Her body tightened in anticipation as she quickly finished grooming Spilled Milk. "Done."

"Great. I'll take the brush." He came over to get it, walked back and leaned down to drop it in the plastic carrier. His lithe movements seemed particularly sexy today.

But then anything he did might seem sexy right now. She was imagining him naked under the shower in the golden light of late afternoon. That image would probably haunt her in the days ahead, and if she had any sense, she'd let him take that shower alone.

Apparently she had no sense, because she'd already decided to join him there and revel in the experience one more time. After they turned both horses out into the pasture, they climbed into their respective vehicles. He'd suggested that she lead now that she knew where she was going. That way he'd get her dust instead of vice versa.

She accepted his gallantry, although she suspected he had an agenda just like Jack and Sarah. He wanted her to move here to be with him. In the next fifteen hours or so, he'd pull out all the stops and she would be tempted to give in. She already knew that, too.

Giving in would be a mistake, but she needed to be clear in her mind about that before his loving wiped out all her noble intentions. She had the space of this drive to shore up her defenses.

The timing was wrong—not so much for her, but for him. She was ready to make a major change in her life and a small practice in a little town like Shoshone sounded exactly right. Zach was convinced he knew his future path and maybe he did, but she wasn't buying it.

He needed to figure things out on his own, though. In the end, everyone did. She'd get out of his way and let him do that. She didn't know how long it would take, or if he'd ever change his mind about practicing law. Maybe she and Zach had no future.

That thought was horribly painful, but she should face the possibility with a plan. Thank God she did have savings, because that would help. Once she was back in Virginia she'd begin the process of leaving her old life behind.

She'd notify the firm and stay on long enough for an orderly transfer of her caseload. She'd begin packing up everything she planned to take with her. In her spare time, she'd study for the Wyoming bar exam.

Because she needed an alternative if Shoshone didn't work out, she'd research other small towns in Wyoming that might be good places to settle. All of that would take several weeks, weeks in which Zach might have an epiphany. If not, she'd journey on her own to whatever spot seemed the most like Shoshone to begin her new life.

Her convictions firmly in place, she parked near the Airstream and climbed out. Zach pulled his truck in behind her car. She'd barely had time to draw a breath before he was out of the truck.

Setting his hat on the truck's dusty fender, he strode toward her, his gaze purposeful. "Shower time."

She laughed as he pulled her into his arms. "We need to go inside first."

"No, we don't." He took off her straw hat and put it on the hood of her car. "We can strip down right here. I do it all the time." He grinned as he slipped his hands up the back of her shirt and deftly unhooked her bra. "But doing it with you will be way more fun."

Her heartbeat sped up. "What about towels?"

"It's warm. We'll air dry." He pulled her shirt over her head and tossed it next to her hat.

Undressing outside shouldn't be any different from yesterday when she'd walked out of the Airstream naked. Yet somehow it felt more daring, maybe because of the intensity in his gray eyes as he slid her bra straps down her arms.

"I love looking at you."

Her nipples tightened beneath his hungry gaze. "I love lookin' at you, too." She reached for the hem of his T-shirt, tugged the shirt over his head and threw it in the general direction of her car. She had no idea where it landed because she was too busy drinking in the sight of his bronzed chest.

"Come here." He drew her forward, watching as her nipples made contact and quivered against his warm skin. "Your breathing just changed."

"So did yours." Their rapid breaths created a sensuous friction that made her tremble with excitement, yet they were barely touching.

With a groan he pulled her against the solid wall of his chest. "Damn. I want you so much."

"I want you, too." She flattened her hands over the firm muscles of his back and gazed up at him. "We could go inside and save the shower for later."

His fingers flexed against the denim covering her backside. "We can save the shower for later, but we don't have to go inside."

The implication made her slick with desire, but she wanted more than a climax. She wanted to feel him deep within her, thrusting rhythmically until that shared moment of release. "We need to go inside for what I want."

"Maybe not." He backed her against the car and unbuckled her belt. "Tell me what you want."

"This." She cupped him through his jeans. His erection strained against the zipper. "All of this."

He gulped in air. "Okay, then." He abandoned his quest to unfasten her jeans, reached into his pocket and pulled out a condom. "Please watch over that."

"Zach! You just happened to have a—"

"No mystery there." He knelt down and expertly pulled off her boots one at a time. "Shoved it in my pocket before I left this morning. Wanted to be ready for anything." He stood and cupped her face in both hands. "Looks like it was a good decision." His mouth claimed hers in a short but very passionate kiss that left no doubt where this episode was headed.

He didn't waste any time getting there, either. Her jeans and panties joined the rest of the clothes on the hood of her car. Then he unfastened his jeans to reveal how ready he was.

Desire shot through her, hot and demanding. She reached for him, needing to touch that stiff, sleek answer to her lustful prayers. A drop of moisture had gathered at the tip. She wanted—

"No." He caught her wrist. "I might come."

She moaned softly in frustration as his beauty was covered with latex.

His breathing grew more labored. "Then I…I couldn't give you what you want." He swallowed. "Grab hold of my shoulders."

As she did, he bracketed her hips and lifted her up against the fender. Her breath caught as he pressed her against the warm metal. The sensation of that metal on her bare skin was so erotic that her body clenched in response.

"Wrap your legs around me." Urgency sharpened his tone.

She didn't have to be asked twice. She desperately needed the gift he was about to bestow.

He held her steady, took a shaky breath and slid in. The motion required no time and almost no effort. "You're drenched."

She exhaled slowly and fought to keep from coming right that very second. She looked into his eyes, dark as thunderclouds. "It's…no mystery," she said, repeating his words.

"Guess not." He held her gaze. "Just be still for a bit."

She nodded.

He gave her a crooked smile. "Never tried this before." He took another ragged breath. "Don't want to… rush it."

"Me, either."

His glance traveled over her. It lingered on her hair, her lips and her breasts. "You look so good in the sunlight. Like you're glowing."

"Maybe I am."

"I'd believe it." His voice was husky. "Especially there." His gaze continued downward and settled at the juncture of her thighs. "Where the fire is." His cock twitched.

Unable to help herself, she tightened in response.

"Ahhh." He sucked in a breath and tensed. Then he relaxed slightly and looked into her eyes. "What you do to me, Jeannette."

"The same thing you do to me, Zach."

"And do you know how great that is?"

"Yes."

"I've never made love to a woman outside up against a car. Only you could inspire me to do that."

"Only you could talk me into it."

"I know." Holding her gaze, he eased out and pushed

back again. “We’re good together.” He initiated a slow rhythm.

“Uh-huh.” She was in no position to argue. But she was in a perfect position to receive the kind of pleasure that he excelled at giving. Each thrust took her higher until she began to whimper.

He pumped faster. “We…belong together.”

“Mmm.” She’d lost the ability to form words. Nothing mattered but the steady beat of his powerful strokes. They drove her to the edge of sanity and touched off little explosions every time he sank into her quivering channel.

“You’re almost there.” He was panting, now. “I can feel it. I know you, Jeannette. *I know you.*”

“Yes.”

“Come for me.”

“Yes…yes…*yes.*” Sweet surrender. A release so strong her body was wracked with the pulsing rush of it as she gasped and breathlessly chanted his name.

“I’m here. I’m here, love.” With a deep groan, he rocked forward and shuddered against her.

I’m here, love. His words echoed in her mind as she held him and absorbed the aftershocks of his climax. She couldn’t argue with those words, either. She was his love. And he was hers. No matter how it all turned out, that much would still be true.

17

FOR THE PAST MONTH, Zach had looked forward to each morning. Until this one. He and Jeannette hadn't slept much, but they'd had plenty of sex, more than he'd thought possible for one night.

In between the incredible bouts of sex, they'd rested and talked. He had no doubt she was as much in love with him as he was with her. But that didn't seem to matter any more than the great sex. She wouldn't agree to move to Shoshone.

Instead she insisted that he needed more time to adjust to his new way of life. What she really meant was that he needed time to grow bored. She'd never come right out and said that, but he'd picked up on it, anyway.

As daylight approached, he considered whether professing his love openly would change her mind. He decided that it wouldn't, so why put himself in such a vulnerable position? Instead he made love to her once more for what could be the last time.

He tried not to dwell on that as he got up, pulled on his jeans and made coffee. She showered in the tiny bathroom, and he stayed away from that end of the trailer when she left the bathroom to dress in the hallway. Watching her do that would make him want to touch her and coax her back to bed, which wouldn't accomplish anything—except maybe make her miss her flight.

At one point he'd thought about doing that on purpose. She'd probably be upset with him, though, and he'd only delay the inevitable. He couldn't expect Jack to give him a second day off, either.

Somehow he had to get through the next hour or so before she left. He felt the urge to do something for her, so he scrambled eggs and made toast to go with the coffee. "Breakfast is ready!" he called out.

"Oh." She appeared in slacks and a silky-looking blouse, her Virginia lawyer's clothes. She was still in her bare feet and didn't have makeup on yet. "You didn't have to do that."

"And you don't have to eat it. I needed something to occupy my time." He sounded surly, which wasn't how he wanted her to remember him. He managed a smile. "Never mind. I'll put it out for the raccoons."

"No, you won't." She padded into the kitchen. "I'd love some breakfast."

"Then have a seat and I'll bring it to you. I hope you like your eggs scrambled."

"I do."

Spatula in one hand and a plate in the other, he glanced at her. "Would you tell me if you didn't?"

"Yes. Scrambled is how I make them at home."

"Which you hardly ever do, I'll bet." He knew she wasn't a cook.

"Hardly ever, and even then in the microwave."

"Jeannette, if you're eating this breakfast to be nice, then please don't." Okay, he still sounded surly but he couldn't seem to help it.

"I'm eating this breakfast because you fixed it for me, which has nothing to do with being nice. I'm doing it because I—" She ended the sentence abruptly and her cheeks turned pink.

He understood what people meant when they talked about heartache. His chest hurt something fierce. "Because you what?" he asked softly.

Pressing her lips together, she shook her head.

"It won't kill you to say it, you know."

She swallowed. "I don't want to make things worse."

"I don't think they can get much worse."

"Zach..."

"Oh, what the hell. I love you, Jeannette. You know it and I know it. And what's more, you love me, which was what you almost said just now." He heard the anger and frustration in his voice and sighed. "That's not how those words are supposed to be said, either. Sorry about that."

"I...I have to go." She got up from the table and hurried out of the kitchen.

As he listened to her throwing things in her suitcase and banging around in her haste to leave, he stared at the spatula and plate he was holding. How he'd love to hurl the plate at the nearest wall and howl like the wolves that roamed the nearby hills. But he didn't want to leave her with that image of him, either.

So he made sure the burner was turned off and unplugged the coffeepot. He hadn't put on his boots, but it didn't matter. Opening the front door, he walked out on the little stoop and down the steps. Dry pine needles pricked the bottoms of his feet, but he didn't care.

Hands in his pockets, he stared at the Grand Tetons. The timelessness and immensity of those jagged peaks with their whipped-cream topping of snow usually calmed him and gave him perspective. It wasn't working this morning. The peace that he'd found here was gone.

Behind him the trailer door opened. He turned as she came out, purse over her shoulder and pulling her suitcase while she balanced on four-inch heels.

"Let me help." He hurried up the steps and took charge of the suitcase.

"Thank you." She didn't look at him.

He carried the suitcase to her car and heard the click as she used the remote to unlock it. He stowed her case in the backseat and glanced up just as she started to slide behind the wheel. "Whoa, whoa." He rounded the car and grasped her arm. "Come back out of there for a minute. You can't just get in and drive away."

She glanced up at him. "I think it's for the best."

"I promise not to say anything that will make you uncomfortable, but we deserve a proper goodbye."

She was silent for a moment, and then she got out of the car and faced him. "Goodbye, Zach."

"You're acting like you're in front of a firing squad."

"It feels a little like that."

"Well, it's not like that." Stepping forward, he cupped her face in one hand and brushed a strand of hair back from her cheek as he gazed into her emerald-green eyes. "You're an incredible woman, and I'm glad we met."

She took a shaky breath. "So am I."

"Goodbye, Jeannette." Leaning down, he kissed her softly. Then he released her and stepped back.

Her eyes remained closed. With his hands fisted at his sides, he resisted the urge to haul her back into his arms. He wanted to kiss her until she changed her mind and decided to stay, no matter how long that took. The way she looked as she stood there trembling, it wouldn't take long at all.

He let the moment pass. She'd made her wishes clear and he'd only be taking advantage of this difficult moment right before she left. That wouldn't be very noble of him.

She opened her eyes and cleared her throat. "Goodbye, Zach." Then she climbed into the car and started the engine.

He should have thought to move the truck to make it easier for her. But she pulled forward and engineered a creative backing job to successfully avoid banging into it. He was impressed, because if she were as wrecked by this parting as he was, she couldn't be all that steady.

Although going into the Airstream would have been far cooler on his part, he stayed where he was until she made it to the dirt road. She beeped the horn once and he raised a hand in farewell. Then she was gone, her tires kicking up dust as she drove away.

He dreaded going back inside, but the sooner he got that over with, the better. Bracing himself for the emptiness he'd find there, he climbed the steps and walked through the door. He'd expected silence. He'd expected the memories to flood him.

He hadn't expected her scent to greet him the minute he walked in. It was a subtle perfume, a cross between a spice and a floral. He hadn't consciously taken note of it while they'd been together, but it hit him like a sledgehammer now.

Torn between throwing open all the windows to let it out and closing them tight to keep it in, he did neither. Instead he quickly put on socks and boots, pulled on a T-shirt and poured himself a cup of coffee. Then he started toward the door. He'd sit outside and read for a while.

But he turned back when he realized the plan required reading material. Crossing to his bookshelf, he looked through the offerings. He grabbed a camping magazine he hadn't finished. Then, for reasons he didn't want to examine too closely, he also took the study guide for the bar exam.

Unfolding one of his camp chairs, he picked a spot in the shade of a pine tree and settled in. With luck, he'd become absorbed in his reading and get past the crushing impact of Jeannette's departure. First he picked up the magazine.

Jumping from one article to the next, he searched for something that would engage him and help him forget his troubles for a little while. Nothing in the magazine accomplished that. With a sigh, he tossed it down and reached for the study guide. That probably wouldn't work, either.

Hours later, his stomach rumbled, reminding him that he hadn't eaten anything. To his complete astonishment, he'd made it almost halfway through the study guide. He was fascinated by the similarities and the differences between California's bar exam and this one.

More than fascination gripped him, though. He was intellectually excited for the first time in months. He felt a little bit like Rip Van Winkle waking up from a long sleep.

He wanted to finish the study guide and then read through it again to make sure he had a handle on it. But mostly he wanted to take that bar exam, if for no other reason than to see if he could pass it as easily as he expected he could. He didn't have to tell anyone about it, though.

Assuming he got his license to practice law in Wyoming, he could decide at that point whether to do anything with it. Maybe passing the exam would be enough for him. It would be his secret project, and he'd take one step at a time. Ironically, this kind of challenge might be the only one capable of taking his mind off Jeannette.

A PACKING BOX sat on the floor of Jeannette's kitchen along with a pile of brown wrapping paper. She stood in front of her cupboard of dishes. They were lovely and expensive, a complete set of twelve she'd bought soon after being hired at the law firm.

The pattern of tiny flowers and vines curled gracefully around the edge of each plate, saucer and cup. Several years ago she'd thought these dishes were the height of gracious living. Unfortunately, they didn't fit the person she was now. In her new life she imagined a table filled with chunky pottery in bold colors.

She thought of Erin, her former assistant at the law firm. Erin would love these dishes. That decision made, Jeannette started wrapping the dishes and tucking them in the box, although they wouldn't go with her out west. They'd stay where they belonged in Virginia. She'd buy a new set of dishes when she arrived in...wherever she decided to go.

Four weeks had passed since she'd left Wyoming, and she'd heard nothing from Zach. She'd researched other towns as planned, but she'd held off choosing one of those alternatives. Her lease had another month to run, so she was in no big rush to make that decision.

Her hope that Zach would come through might be fading, but it hadn't totally disappeared. He could still call. What a shame if she rented a U-Haul and moved prematurely. So she'd taken her time with packing, which had allowed her to be more thoughtful about what she was taking, and what she was leaving behind. Like these dishes, for example.

The cupboard was nearly empty when her cell phone rang. She picked it up from the charger on the small desk in the kitchen without thinking much about the call. She'd been handling lots of details recently that had required many phone calls. Then she saw the name on the screen and felt light-headed.

She was breathless as she answered and didn't care. "Zach?"

"You *quit* the law firm?"

"Uh, yeah. And by the way, I'm fine. How are you?"

"Ticked off! When were you planning to tell me you quit?"

"Whenever you called." She took a calming breath. "So here you are, and now you know. How are things in Shoshone?"

"They were fine when I left."

"You left? So where are you now?"

"Outside your door."

The phone still to her ear, she raced to her front door, flipped the latch on the lock and swung it open. Sure enough, there he stood wearing his best cowboy clothes and that black Stetson he called his party hat.

He held up the study guide for the Wyoming bar, a duplicate of the one she had on her bookshelf. "And while we're discussing stealth moves, what were you thinking writing a message on the next-to-last page?"

"I didn't want you to see it until you were almost done." Her chest grew tight. He was here, but what did that mean, exactly? "Did you…did you read it?"

"We can discuss that later. Right now I need a place to stay. I figured since I put you up, you might be willing to return the favor."

"Of course."

"Great." He picked up a small duffel she hadn't noticed because she was so busy feasting on the sight of him and making bargains with herself. He'd at least read to the end of the study guide. That might be enough for now. If he'd done that, then he couldn't be totally opposed to taking the exam, and with some encouragement, that could lead to—

"Can I come in through this door, or are you planning to send me around to some other entrance?"

"Oh!" She stepped back so he could walk in. "Sorry. I'm still gettin' used to the fact that you're actually here." She breathed in the scent of him. Oh, yeah. Reading the study guide was plenty. She would work with that.

"Good thing I showed up before you moved and left no forwarding address." He dropped his duffel on the floor along with the study guide.

She closed the door and turned to discover he'd taken off his hat and laid that on top of the duffel. "I wouldn't have moved without—"

"God, Jeannette!" He pulled her into his arms and kissed her with a desperation that made her heart sing. When he lifted his lips from hers, he continued to pepper her face with kisses. "I thought you'd already made partner, and because it's a weekday, I went to your office, but they said you'd quit, and I had to sign my life away to get your address, but Erin came through for me because she remembered who I was."

"Erin's a sweetheart."

"Yes, she is, but *you.*" He pulled back to glare at her. "You are one devious woman. What in hell's going on with you?"

"I'm leaving Virginia."

"And your destination would be?"

"Now that you're here, I'm thinking Shoshone."

He stared at her. "But you said you wouldn't move there until I got my act together."

She wound her arms around his neck. "I know, but if you read through the study guide, you're at least considerin' the possibility of a law career. That's close enough."

"It is? Damn. I could have saved myself a lot of work."

"What does that mean?"

"I just got the word. I passed the bar in Wyoming."

"You did?" She hugged him tight. "That's fantastic!"

"There's more."

"More?" She leaned back to gaze into his face. "Like what?"

"I rented some office space in town."

"Zach! You're really doin' it."

"Guess so." He cupped her bottom as if he had the right to.

She decided he did. "What about your job at the ranch?"

"I'll put in some time on weekends, but Jack would much rather have me as his lawyer than his ranch hand. I'm also thinking I might buy some horse property in the area so I can own a couple of saddle horses. I came here thinking you'd be settled into your partnership and wouldn't be interested in joining my new firm, but I had to at least ask, and now I—"

"I'm so in."

He grinned at her. "You do realize you have to pass the bar exam."

"Been studyin'."

"Oh, really?"

"Ever since I left. I've just been waitin' for you, cowboy."

"You have put me through it, lady."

"For your own good. You never would have come to this decision if I hadn't given you some space to figure it out."

He sighed. "You could be right about that. But writing what you did near the back of the study guide? That was…"

"All I could think to do." She'd been frantic to leave, but at the last minute she'd pulled his study guide from the bookshelf and scribbled *I love you* near the end of the book. "And I meant it."

He tugged her in closer. "You do realize how that incriminates you, right? I now have written proof."

"Are you going to use it against me?"

"You bet. Now you have to marry me."

"I thought you might insist on that."

"Any objections, counselor?"

"Not a one. It's time to make this legal." She smiled up at him. "I love you, Zachary Powell."

"I know you do." He feathered a kiss over her lips. "I have it in writing."

Epilogue

BEN RADCLIFFE HAD been itching for a challenge, and Jack Chance had just brought him one—building a custom saddle that would be a surprise for the woman who received it. That meant Ben wouldn't meet her or the horse who'd wear the saddle until after the job was finished. He'd never attempted such a thing before.

Jack had brought the necessary measurements for the horse and the woman, and he seemed to know roughly what he wanted. The saddle would be a showstopper embellished with silver and turquoise accents. Jack was prepared to pay the price, too. Apparently his extended family was chipping in so they could afford to be extravagant.

"I realize this is somewhat short notice." Jack wandered around the shop and paused to inspect each of the three saddles Ben was currently working on. "My brothers and I had a hell of a time figuring out what would make a good seventieth birthday present for her. She's…special."

"I'm sure she is." Years ago Ben would have felt a pang of envy at hearing some guy praise his mother with such obvious affection. Now he felt nothing at all.

"Anyway, once we decided on a saddle designed specifically for her favorite horse, Bertha Mae, I asked around. Everyone said there was this guy in Sheridan who hadn't been in business that long but he did fine work." Jack glanced at Ben. "I like what I see, and I also like the idea of patronizing someone who's just starting to get recognized."

"I won't kid you. Making a custom saddle for Sarah Chance and her favorite horse will give me bragging rights."

Jack met his gaze. "If you do a good job, I'll spread the word myself."

"I'd appreciate that."

"But we're already well into October. And we want this to be a fancy-ass saddle. Can you do it?"

Ben looked at the Remington calendar tacked on the wall. "You said her birthday's December nineteenth, right?"

"Yeah."

"I can do it."

"Excellent. Also, I need you to deliver it to the ranch, but not too soon, because we'll have to hide it. I hate to say this, but her grandchildren can't keep a secret worth a damn."

"Understood. I should show up around the eighteenth, then."

"That would be perfect, assuming the weather cooperates."

"I have a four-by-four truck and I'm used to driving in snow."

"Normal snow, sure, but a blizzard could muck things up. I suppose, worst-case scenario, you could email a picture and we could show her on a tablet at her birthday dinner, but that's not what I'm going for."

"I'll make it over there."

Jack gave him a long look. "I believe you will. And I hope you can stay for the party so you can see her face when she gets her first glimpse of it."

"I'd like that."

"It's Christmas week, though. If you have to get back, I understand."

"Not really." Then he wished he hadn't said that. In his life Christmas was just another day, but when he admitted that, people tended to feel sorry for him. "I mean, I can shift things around if necessary. It's the beauty of being single."

Jack smiled. "I remember those days." He stepped forward and held out his hand. "Then we have a deal."

"Yes, we do." Ben grasped his hand. "You'll see me on the eighteenth. Will I need a cover story?"

"Oh, yeah." Jack rubbed his chin. "Just pretend you're there to buy a horse. Mom will be so busy with Christmas preparations she won't pay much attention. But I'll have a room made up so you can stay a couple of nights."

"Looking forward to it." Because his own family was a complete disaster, he was fascinated with the idea that some might actually work.

The Chance clan's devotion to their matriarch indicated they might be such a family. Making the saddle for her would be good for business. Helping celebrate her birthday at the Last Chance Ranch would be a nice bonus.

* * * * *

Keep reading for an excerpt of a new title
from the Western Romance series,
A COWBOY'S DUTY by Marin Thomas

Prologue

July
Boot Hill Rodeo, Boot Hill, Arizona

"Ready?"

"I'll never be as ready as you are." Dixie Cash grimaced at her friend Shannon Douglas—one of the top female bull riders in the country.

Shannon was forever on the lookout for a rough stock competition and when Five Star Rodeos had agreed to sponsor women's bull riding in three summer events, Shannon had promised to find five women crazy enough to ride with her—Dixie being one of them.

"Here." Shannon held out a bank draft.

"I feel bad taking your money." Dixie shoved the check into the front pocket of her jeans.

"You're worth every penny."

When Shannon had mentioned the rodeos, Dixie had just been hired as a part-time receptionist for a construction company in Yuma. She'd wanted to help her friend but needed money to launch an internet business for her homemade organic bath soaps. Then Shannon had made Dixie an offer she couldn't refuse—a thousand dollars per rodeo.

"Looks like Veronica Patriot has set her sights on Gavin Tucker."

Dixie's gaze followed Shannon's pointer finger. Figures the blonde buckle bunny would target the handsome bareback rider. "If the cowboy knows what's good for him he'll avoid that tramp like the plague." Dixie had run into Gavin—literally—at the Canyon City Rodeo in June when she'd tripped over his gear bag and knocked him to the ground.

"The bull's more of a spinner than a bucker," Shannon said. "Stay centered." The tan Charbray stood docile in the chute, but once freed all hell would break loose.

"Ladies and gentlemen, turn your attention to gate two. Dixie Cash is about to tangle with Bad Mamajamma." The crowd stomped their boots against the bleachers and whistles filled the air.

"If the Cash name sounds familiar it's because Dixie's got six older brothers who rodeo. Earlier today, Merle Cash took third in the saddle bronc competition."

While Shannon and a rodeo helper fished the bull rope from beneath Bad Mamajamma, Dixie pulled on her riding gloves and adjusted her headgear with its protective mask.

Let's get this over with. Dixie straddled the fifteen-hundred pound nuisance, found her grip then nodded to the gate man. The bull pounced for freedom, the first buck almost unseating Dixie. Anticipating a wild ride, she held her breath through the first of two tight spins, squeezing her thighs against the animal's girth.

Bad Mamajamma decided he'd had enough of Dixie and kicked out with extra force. As if she'd been shot from a cannon, Dixie catapulted through the air. She hit the dirt hard, but instinctively curled her body into a ball and rolled away from the bull's hooves. The bullfighter stepped in front of Bad Mamajamma, affording Dixie an extra second to gain her footing. She ran for the rails and scrambled to safety.

"Well, folks, Dixie Cash gave it her best effort." The announcer discussed Shannon's upcoming ride, but Dixie stopped listening when her boots landed in front of Gavin Tucker.

"Good try," he said.

Try being the operative word. "Thanks." *Brilliant, Dixie. A cowboy with killer looks and nice manners goes out of his way to talk to you and you mumble "thanks"?*

"How long have you been riding bulls?" Gavin asked.

"Started this summer."

A dark eyebrow lifted. "Gutsy gal."

More like crazy. For the life of her, Dixie couldn't find her tongue. Turned out she didn't have to. Veronica Patriot materialized out of nowhere and sashayed her way between Dixie and Gavin. She placed her French-manicured talons on Gavin's chest and thrust her heaving bosom in his face. "Time to celebrate, cowboy."

Dixie despised Veronica. The woman had done a number on her brother Porter—used him to make another cowboy jealous then left him high and dry with a broken heart.

"Sorry, I've got plans." Gavin's soulful brown eyes beseeched Dixie.

"What plans?" Veronica propped her hands on her hips.

Dixie had read her share of silent *help me* messages from her brothers. The look Gavin sent her begged her to rescue him from the clutches of the evil buckle bunny. *What the heck*.

"Gavin and I have a date," Dixie said.

"Pardon?" Veronica frowned.

"That's right." Gavin inched closer to Dixie and the scent of dust and faded cologne went straight to her head. When he rested his arm across her shoulders a little shiver raced down her spine. Gavin couldn't have been more than six feet tall, but her five foot six inches fit perfectly tucked against him.

Veronica's gaze bounced between Gavin and Dixie. "What kind of date?"

"A boy-girl date." Dixie smiled sweetly.

"Honey, a girl like you can't handle a military man."

Dixie had heard that Gavin Tucker had been stationed in Afghanistan before he'd left the army. "What do you think, Gavin? Can I handle you?"

He grinned.

Disgusted, Veronica snorted like a pig and stomped off.

"Thanks." Gavin released Dixie and stepped back.

Wishing he still had his arm around her, she said, "No worries. Veronica can be a pest."

"Are you celebrating later with your lady bull rider friends?"

"Probably."

"I'm heading over to the Spittoon. Maybe I'll see you there."

"Maybe."

Gavin walked off and Dixie couldn't help but think he was exactly the kind of man she'd like to marry someday.

GAVIN STEPPED INSIDE the Spittoon, a bar on the outskirts of Boot Hill, and surveyed the crowd. The place was packed, noisy, and smelled like stale beer, dusty cowboys and easy women. And he hoped Dixie Cash was among the clientele—not that he thought she was a party girl. There was something about the petite, tomboyish cowgirl that drew him. She showed the same courage and spunk as the women he'd worked alongside in the army.

He made his way to the bar, ordered a beer, then found a dark corner away from the crush of bodies. Keeping his back to the wall he searched for the blue-eyed brown-haired girl-next-door. He spotted her at a table next to the dance floor engaged in conversation with her friends. As if she sensed his scrutiny, their eyes connected and Gavin felt the subtle stirrings of arousal.

A former soldier had no business being with a girl like Dixie—that fact in and of itself fed Gavin's desire, and adrenaline pumped through his veins. If there was one thing he was addicted to, it was adrenaline. After six years of living on the edge…living with danger…he was drawn to taking risks. And Dixie Cash was definitely a risk.

"Well, well, well."

Gavin jumped an inch off the floor. *Damn.* How the hell had Veronica Patriot snuck up on him? His temper flared but he counted to ten, as a therapist had once instructed him to do when he felt threatened.

"What happened to your boy-girl date?" The buckle bunny narrowed her eyes.

"Dixie's—"

"Here." Dixie sidled up to Gavin and slipped her arm through his. She stood close enough that her soft breast pressed against his biceps.

"You're not his type." Veronica sneered. "Besides, don't girls like you have curfews?"

"She's right, Gavin. We should leave. It's past my bed-time." Dixie batted her dark lashes and suddenly Gavin's jeans felt a size too small.

Reminding himself that Dixie's flirting was an act to help him out of a tight spot, he said, "Ready when you are."

"Don't you want a real woman, soldier?" Veronica thrust her bosom out, flaunting her attributes.

After a lengthy glare-down, Veronica stepped aside and Gavin led Dixie across the dance floor and out the door. It wasn't until they were almost to his truck that he realized he still held her hand. He stopped and glanced over his shoulder. Veronica had followed them outside.

"She doesn't give up easily, I'll give her that," Dixie said.

"How would you feel about leaving with me in my truck?"

"I don't know. Can I trust you?"

"Sugar, if I harm one hair on your head, your brothers will hunt me down."

"You're right. I'll go for a ride with you."

Ten minutes later… "She's still following us." Gavin glanced between the road and the rearview mirror. Dixie's stomach growled and he threw caution to the wind. "You up for Chinese takeout? We could eat at the motel. If Veronica sees us go into my room together maybe she'll give up."

"I don't believe that woman knows the meaning of surrender, but I won't turn down a free meal."

Veronica trailed them to the restaurant and then the motel where she parked across the lot, facing Gavin's room. Ignoring their stalker, he and Dixie sat on the king-size bed, ate chop suey and watched the old spaghetti Western, *A Fistful of Dynamite.*

Near the end of the movie, Gavin peeked out the window. Veronica's Mustang was gone. The woman had finally left him alone. He checked his watch—half past one in the morning. Time to drive Dixie back to the Spittoon so she could be on her way home. "Coast is clear." He turned from the window.

Dixie lay curled in a ball on the bed, her hands folded neatly beneath her cheek, her chest rising and falling in deep, even breaths. In sleep, she appeared innocent and cuddly and he wanted to lose himself in all her sweet goodness. But Gavin didn't dare crawl onto the bed with Dixie and risk falling asleep. He couldn't take the chance he'd experience the recurring nightmare that had followed him home from Afghanistan. He lowered the volume on the TV and made himself comfortable in the chair. He'd gone many nights without a wink of sleep, but the longer he watched Dixie's slumbering body the more exhausted he became.

The sun streaming through a gap in the curtains woke Gavin at the crack of dawn. He wasn't sitting in the chair—he was lying on the bed. Sometime in the middle of the night he'd crawled under the covers. He rolled away from the light and came face-to-face with a wide-awake Dixie.

He held his breath, waiting for her to make the first move—she did. Her lips brushed his, then came back for more. One kiss turned into two…three…then clothes started flying off.